Prayers for Sale

ALSO BY SANDRA DALLAS

Tallgrass

New Mercies

The Chili Queen

Alice's Tulips

The Diary of Mattie Spenser

The Persian Pickle Club

Buster Midnight's Cafe

Praise for *Prayers for Sale*

"This satisfying novel will immediately draw readers into Hennie and Nit's lives, and the unexpected twists will keep them hooked through to the bittersweet denouement."
—*Publishers Weekly*

"Forgiveness and redemption are the themes of this gentle novel about hardscrabble lives."
—*Kirkus Reviews*

"The idea of selling prayers conjures images of pre-Reformation Catholicism or, at the very least, stops you in your tracks to think a bit. Like the lives narrated, this novel by the author of *Tallgrass* runs the gamut of heartache, hardship, and happiness as Dallas skillfully weaves past into present and surprises everyone at the end. Fans of Lee Smith, Sue Monk Kidd, and Kaye Gibbons will love this book."
—*Booklist* (starred review)

"I found myself engrossed by this Denver author who masterfully brings to life a 1930s Colorado town called Middle Swan (based on Breckenridge) along with its population of miners, fancy ladies, gamblers, and con men."
—*Colorado Springs Independent*

"Dallas is masterful with the historical fiction genre. *Prayers*, like many of her novels, is set in Colorado. This one, set in the fictional Middle Swan, tells the story of a mining town in the Colorado high country. Middle Swan is the home of Hennie Comfort, who came west after the Civil War to marry a miner after her first husband was killed in the war. Putting down a Sandra Dallas read is nearly impossible. This book is filled with secrets revealed as the reader learns about the lives of the characters. The secret revealed in the final pages is top-notch. . . . [F]ans are in for a treat with Dallas's most recent novel."

—*The Daily Camera* (Boulder, Colorado)

"*Prayers for Sale* is a finely crafted tale that celebrates women and their resiliency."

—*Deseret Morning News* (Salt Lake City, Utah)

"*Prayers for Sale* is as bighearted as Hennie herself, who hands out stout winter coats to miners' wives, saying they're hand-me-downs when, in fact, they're brand-new, ordered in secret from the Sears catalogue."   —*The Washington Post*

"Her dexterity is evident on every page, and *Prayers for Sale*—an answered prayer for discerning readers—adds to a distinguished body of intelligent, humane, and affecting work."   —*Richmond Times-Dispatch*

Prayers for Sale

SANDRA DALLAS

St. Martin's Griffin
New York

This is a work of fiction.
All of the characters, organizations, and events portrayed in this novel
are either products of the author's imagination
or are used fictitiously.

www.stmartins.com

Book design by Kathryn Parise

THE LIBRARY OF CONGRESS HAS CATALOGED THE HARDCOVER
EDITION AS FOLLOWS:

Dallas, Sandra.
    Prayers for sale / Sandra Dallas. — 1st ed.
        p.   cm.
    ISBN 978-0-312-38518-7
    1. Female friendship—Fiction.   2. Older women—Fiction.
3. Depressions—1929—Fiction.   4. Colorado—Fiction.   I. Title.

    PS3554.A434P73   2009
    813'.54—dc22

                                        2008035871

ISBN 978-1-250-00058-3 (trade paperback)

Second St. Martin's Griffin Edition: May 2011

10   9   8   7   6   5   4   3   2   1

For Ted Cole

For your grace and courage

Acknowledgments

In 1963, I moved to Breckenridge, in Summit County, Colorado, as a bride. The dredges there had been shut down for years, but despite the town's rebirth as a ski area, Breckenridge still lived under the shadow of the gold boats. The skeleton of one squatted in the Blue River on the west side of town. Two others moldered away in nearby gulches, surrounded by the silent rock piles they'd created. The old people still talked about the screeching that the dredges made and the silence when the boats broke down that woke them from a sound sleep.

When I began research on *Prayers for Sale*, I started with my own file on the town and found there a letter from Helen Rich, a novelist, who lived in a log cabin on French Street with her roommate, the poet Belle Turnbull. "You've really got the bug about doing Breckenridge," she wrote. "I feel quite sure about you and you have the grace to grow . . . As you have found out, the stuff out of which such books are made has to seep into a person." The letter was dated August 11, 1967, and it took another forty years of seeping before I finally wrote about Breckenridge.

The town of Middle Swan in *Prayers for Sale* is based largely on Breckenridge, although there really was a Middle Swan. Prowling through a deserted cabin on the Swan River in Summit County years ago, I found a wooden box addressed to: "*Tom Earley, Middle Swan, Colo.*"

The town may have been only that single cabin, but I loved the name and used it as well as the man, Tom Earley, in *The Diary of Mattie Spenser.*

I owe a great deal to Helen and Belle and their works, especially Helen's *The Willow-Bender* and Belle's *The Tenmile Range,* for, although I listened to the old men on the Blue talking about dredging when I lived up there, I was more interested in lode mining and didn't write down a word of what they said. I've drawn heavily on Helen's notes, now in the Western History Department of the Denver Public Library, and on Mary Ellen Gilliland's books on Summit County, especially *Summit: A Gold Rush History of Summit County, Colorado.* The librarians at Western History were diligent in turning up materials on gold mining. Chuck Bond of Keystone tracked down information on dredging, while Bill Fountain in Breckenridge shared his extensive research on the gold boats, culled from Summit County newspapers. Buff Rutherford filled in the blanks about mining and mountain people, answering obscure questions about history while waiting for church services to begin in Georgetown.

My longtime friend Jim Richards dealt me a fine poker hand, and Todd Berryman provided banking information. Nationally known quilter Teddy Pruit conveyed her love of Southern quilts. Novelist Arnie Grossman, author of *Going Together,* kept *me* going, as he always does.

More than any of my other books, *Prayers for Sale* is a collaborative effort. Danielle Egan-Miller and Joanna MacKenzie, my agents at Browne & Miller Literary Associates, LLC, read what began as a loosely connected collection of short stories, many based on Colorado history, and insisted that I turn the lot into a novel. They worked with me through several drafts to develop the story. Jennifer Enderlin, my superb editor at St. Martin's Press, shepherded the book through the editorial process, from smoothing out rough passages to coordinating promotion with Joan Higgins and Dori Weintraub.

Prayers for Sale wouldn't have had a prayer of a chance without the help of all of you.

Most of all, I want to thank my family—Bob, Dana, Kendal, Lloyd, and Forrest, Mary and Ted, Mike and Sheila—who are my answered prayer.

Chapter 1

The old woman peered past the red geraniums in her deep front window at the figure lingering in the moon-white snow at the gate. In the gloom of the late winter afternoon, Hennie Comfort did not recognize the woman, who stood like a curious bird, her head cocked to one side as she looked at the fence, then the front door, and back at the fence again. Hennie watched, thinking it odd that anyone would wait there, mute as the snow itself. Why would a body stand in the cold when she could come inside by the stove?

Hennie had gone to the window to read her letter in the winter light, because the heavy snow had weighted down the wires, causing the electric to go out. It was too dark inside now to read, although Hennie knew the words wouldn't be any different from what they were when she read the letter at the post office that morning.

For years, Mae had urged her to move out of the high country. This time, she'd made it plain that if Hennie insisted on another winter on the earth's backbone, Mae would come to Middle Swan herself and pack up her mother and take her below, to Fort Madison on the eastern edge of Iowa. Mae was a loving daughter, but she was as stubborn as Hennie. "You can spend your summers in Middle Swan, Mom, but I insist that from now on, you live with us during the winters. What if you slipped on the ice and broke your leg? You could freeze to death before somebody found you."

Mae was right, Hennie admitted to herself. If she fell, the snow would cover her up, and nobody would know where she was until she melted out in the spring. It was foolhardy for a person as old as she was to stay another winter on the Swan River. Besides, it was selfish of her to let Mae worry, and Hennie was always sensible of the feelings of others. But Lordy, she didn't want to live on the Mississippi.

Hennie set the letter on the table and returned to the window to look at the woman, covered now in white flakes. She'd be frozen solid as a fence post if she didn't move soon. So the old woman opened the door and walked into the snow in her stout shoes, her hands tucked into her sleeves. "Hello to you," she called.

The stranger looked up, startled, a little frightened. She was a new-made woman, not much more than a girl, and Hennie had never seen her before. "Oh!" the stranger said, clasping and unclasping her bare hands, which despite the poor light, Hennie could see were red and chapped. "I don't mean to be nosy, but I was wondering how much?"

"How much for what?"

"A prayer." The girl tightened the triangle of plaid wool scarf that covered her head before she thrust her hands into the pockets of her thin coat.

Hennie was confused for a moment, and then realizing what had confounded the girl, she laughed. "That sign's been there so long, I forget about it."

"It says, Prayers for Sale. I'm asking how much do you charge, and is it more if you're in need than if you're wanting just a little favor? Do sinners pay more than the righteous? And what if the Lord doesn't answer? Do you get your money back?" The girl asked all this in a rush, as if she didn't want to forget any of the questions she had pondered as she stood frozen-still in the cold.

"That sign's older than God's old dog."

"How come you to sell prayers?"

"I don't."

"The sign says so. I've seen it three times now. I came back because of it," the girl persisted. "I can pay, if that's what you're thinking. I can pay."

Hennie chuckled. "That sign's a story. I'll tell it to you if you'll come inside."

"I've got a nickel. Is that enough for a prayer?"

"Lordy, are you needing one? No money will buy a prayer, I tell you, but I'll give you one for free, if you're in need of it." Hennie put her arms tight around herself to squeeze out the cold, for she had gone into the storm without her coat.

"I need it. I do."

"Just you come inside then and tell me why."

"I can't. I've got to get home and fix Dick's supper. But I'd be obliged to you if you'd say a prayer—a prayer for Sweet Baby Effie, sweet baby that was, that is. Maybe you could ask that wherever she is, she's not taken with the cold—I never knew it to be so cold—but just any words will do."

"I'll ask it," Hennie said, turning and gesturing toward the house, but the girl wouldn't follow. Instead, she took a step backward.

"I thank you," she said, carefully laying her nickel on the crosspiece of the fence. Then she turned and fled. Rubbing her arms now against the cold, Hennie watched until the little thing disappeared into the storm. Then she picked up the five-cent piece and went inside, placing the coin in a mite box that she kept for Bonnie Harvey to take to church. Hennie herself didn't attend services, hadn't in a long time.

As she sat down in a kitchen chair, Hennie picked up the letter, but instead of holding it up to the window to read again, she pondered the young girl. Something about her was familiar, although Hennie was sure she'd never seen her before. It might have been the way she said her words, which told Hennie she was from the South. Or perhaps it was because the girl was new in Middle Swan and appeared to be not a day older than Hennie herself when she'd arrived long years before.

Hennie looked out the window again, but there was no sign of the girl returning, no sign that she'd even been there, in fact. The old woman wondered why the girl wanted a prayer; she seemed to have a powerful desire for one. Well, Hennie knew the need for prayer in her life, and she would do what she could. So slowly, she knelt on her old knees beside the chair, clasped her hands together, and asked God to keep Sweet Baby Effie warm. Then she mumbled, "Now, Lord, there's a girl, a poor girl, by the looks of her, that's needing your help—and maybe mine, too. I'd like it right well if you could tell me what to do." She paused and added, "And I'd be grateful if you'd find a way short of dying to keep me from moving in with Mae."

⊘⊘⊘⊘⊘

"You've got it pretty good here," Hennie Comfort said, looking around the room with approval. She ducked her head as she went through the door to Nit's cabin, not only because she was a tall woman, even in old age, but because the doorway was that low.

Rooted to the ground, the cabin, built of peeled logs polished by the sun and wind and snow to a rich gold-brown, was ramshackled outside. Within, there was only one room, and that not much bigger than a coal shed, with a door and a window that held four panes of glass. But the place was tidy, cozy even. A rag rug covered the worn linoleum that was ribbed from the uneven floorboards beneath it. The log walls had been freshly chinked and papered with the *Denver Post*, the pages right side up so that you could read them at your leisure. A bed was shoved against one wall. The tops of its tall wooden head- and footboards pressed in on each other, making the mattress sag even more than it would have if the boards had been upright. The bed was Dionysius Tappan's old bed. He'd died in it, wheezing and blowing with the miner's puff, and then the cabin had sat vacant until the young couple moved in.

The pretty girl ought to have a better bed, Hennie thought. But young folks who hadn't been married long wouldn't worry so much about a good bed. They might even feel lucky that they had a place to sleep, what with this being 1936 and a depression not likely to end soon. The girl had spread a quilt over the mattress, a patch quilt in gay colors that would brighten the long winters. A second quilt, a design of eight-pointed stars, newly made with new and old fabrics, was folded over a wooden bench. Hennie was always sensible of the quilts.

A pie safe, the green paint half worn off its tin panels, stood near the cookstove, and a crude split-bottom rocking chair, once painted blue, sat in the far corner. The only other furniture in the room was a small table and two dynamite boxes that served as chairs. The girl's husband—she'd said his name was Dick when the two had met outside Hennie's house a few days earlier—must have picked them up at the gold dredge company. "Pretty good, all right," Hennie said again.

"It's a gem of amber," the girl replied. She clasped and unclasped her hands in delight. "Would you sit?"

"If it wouldn't put you out any," Hennie replied.

"Oh no. I'm starved for company. I get so lonesome. But my hand had an itch to it this morning, so I knew I'd be shaking hands with a stranger. You're my only caller—that is, my first caller. I guess there'll be others . . ." Her voice trailed off.

"I reckon so. Not many know you're here yet. I didn't myself till you stopped at my fence." After meeting the girl in the snow, Hennie had inquired at the Pinto store about the new couple.

"They live in the Tappan place. I don't recollect the name. He works the dredge," Roy Pinto had told her. Then he'd shaken his head. "There's some in Middle Swan that resent him getting hired on. They're out to get him. Besides, he's not stout enough for dredge work." Not many were, Hennie had replied.

Hennie gave the girl her name and said she lived at the end of French Street, in the two-story hewn-log house, just before the road turned to go up to the old We Got 'Em mine. Hardly anybody remembered the We Got 'Em, but Hennie liked to say the name. She remembered when Chauncy Stark had come running down the trail yelling, "We got 'em, gold ore like you never saw." "But you know where I live," Hennie told the girl.

The young thing nodded and said, "I'm Nit Buckley... that is, Nit Spindle. I haven't been married very long, not even two years, and sometimes I forget I'm married. I mean, I'm glad, because I love Dick and all, but it still seems strange to be somebody's missus instead of me."

"Pleased to meet you again, Mrs. Spindle," Hennie said. "I gave the prayer like you asked, gave it more than once." When the girl turned away, embarrassed, mumbling her thanks, Hennie knew she'd have to wait until Nit felt like talking about the prayer, if she ever did. It wouldn't do for Hennie to push the girl just to satisfy an old woman's curiosity. So instead, she drew the clean dishcloth off the top of the pie she was holding and presented the dessert. "This pie's nothing special, but it'll do you if you're hungry." In fact, the pie was a thing of beauty, with a perfect crust, pinched around the edges, the latticework woven, not just

laid on, and it was stained red where the juice had seeped
onto it. "It's a welcome-to-home present," she added quickly,
in case the girl thought she was bringing charity. There'd
been that other young couple on the Upper Swan who'd
lived on a little flour and porcupine meat, too proud to accept help. They wouldn't take relief even from the county.
Those two had nearly starved before somebody took them
down below where they'd come from. "I bottled the raspberries last summer," Hennie continued. "Picked them myself
up by that burned place that's under the saddle on Sunset
Peak, before the bears got to them. The bears are harbonated still, and so are the raspberries. Fresh raspberries, now
that's the best eating there is, might near be."

Nit's eyes widened as she took the pie and set it reverently
on the shelf of the range. "Thanks to you. I'll return the compliment someday," she said. "I'm glad it's not pieplant. I don't
love pieplant. I just don't love it. But I've always been a fool all
my life about raspberries. I never expected to find them here.
I mean now, that is, this time of year."

"I'll take you raspberrying come summer. I know the best
places all around. You can find rhubarb just anywhere. All
you have to do is look for an old cabin. But like you say, you
don't just love it." Hennie took off her heavy wraps and laid
them on the bed, before she seated herself slowly on one of
the boxes. "I ought to know the place for raspberrying. Almost seventy years have I been living in Middle Swan." She
didn't add that this might be the last year. Although Mae
had written that Hennie could spend her summers in
Middle Swan, the old woman was afraid that once she was
settled in Iowa, she'd most likely stay put. Mae would find

reasons for her not to return to the high country. Hennie reminded herself that if she was ever to deal with her life's deepest secret, she'd have to do it soon.

"Seventy years? Why, I didn't know Colorado'd been here that long." Nit flushed and bit her lip, looking anxious for fear she'd given offense.

Hennie only laughed. "It hasn't. But I have. I'm almost as old as these hills—eighty and six." She didn't look it. Oh, her skin was brown from years of living too close to the sun, and her hair was the color of the snow that had fallen for days now. But there was a toughness and sense of purpose to Hennie Comfort that belied her age. And while she'd never been pretty, she had been handsome and still was, with her tall angular body, her large mouth and straight nose set in a long face. She sat upright, her back straight as a pine, not stooped like most mountain women.

Nit stared at Hennie, about to say something but too tongue-tied. She shook her curls and said at last, "We've got coffee, the grounds not used but once."

"I'll take a cup if it wouldn't rob you."

"No, ma'am. It would not." Nit turned quickly and busied herself at the range, putting kindling into the firebox, watching the fire flare up, adjusting the damper, then adding stove wood. After she dipped water from a bucket and poured it into the cast-iron tea kettle, fitting the kettle into the eye over the firebox, the girl lifted down a basket and took out a bundle wrapped in newspaper. She removed the paper to display two fine teacups and saucers, which she polished with a dish towel before setting them on the table.

"Oh my, real English bone china," Hennie said.

"Sometimes I'm afraid to use them. They're delicate as birds' eggs, and I've got nary another. But you're my first caller." She paused. "I guess I already said that."

Hennie wanted to tell the girl that cracked mugs would do for her, but seeing Nit's pride, she said instead, "I thank you for the honor."

"I didn't mean you'd break them." Nit turned back to the stove and spooned the used grounds into the coffeepot, then added a spoonful of fresh. She poured boiling water into the pot and let the coffee steep, the grounds settle. "I hope you don't think I'm putting on airs, Mrs. Comfort. The cups are a wedding present, and I love them so. I'm saving them for good, for callers such as yourself. Have you ever seen anything so pretty?"

A long-ago look came over Hennie Comfort's face. "Somebody gave me china cups as a wedding present, too. I was younger than you." The old woman had packed them in a barrel of flour for the trip to Colorado, and she had them yet, chipped and mended but still good enough to use.

Nit said she was seventeen. Small, with clear pink skin, her bobbed hair the color of the rust that covered Middle Swan's abandoned mining machinery like a patina, and wearing a prim little dress with cap sleeves and a sash, she was just a chunk of a girl.

Hennie told her she'd been fourteen, going on fifteen, when she'd married.

"It's old enough," Nit said.

"That was eighteen and sixty-four. There was a war, and Billy was taken for a soldier and scared he wouldn't come home."

"Did he?"

Hennie Comfort shook her head.

Nit waited for her guest to say more, and when she didn't, the girl brought the pot to the table and poured the coffee. She returned the coffee to the back of the stove to keep warm and sat down on the box across from Hennie. After a minute, she jumped up, saying, "I forgot my manners," and reached for a sugar bowl on the shelf and set it on the table. She took down a pickle jar that served as a spooner and placed it in front of Hennie. "You use the silver spoon. It's real silver," she said.

Hennie didn't care for sweetening in her coffee that late in the day, but rather than hurt the girl's feelings, she picked up the spoon and dipped it into the sugar bowl. "It's as fine a spoon as I ever saw. When I married, I had but two spoons, and they were tin."

Nit flushed. "I shouldn't have bragged. Mostly, we don't have any stuff that costs a lot." The two were quiet for a moment, sipping the coffee. Then the girl asked, "Were your people for the Union?"

"We weren't for anything, not to start with. We didn't want the war in our part of Tennessee. But if you didn't enlist for the Confederacy, you got shot. Billy didn't have a choice. He was only two years older than me, but they told him it was his time."

"Tennessee!" Nit almost shouted. "Ah gee, I'm from Kentucky."

"I thought you might be. Welcome to Middle Swan, Mrs. Spindle." Hennie held up her cup in a toast. She'd been right, after all, about the girl being from the South, and she was glad she'd come to welcome her. Hennie remembered the long days after she herself had arrived, lonely because she had but one friend in the camp, and that one lived high up on the mountain at a mine, too far to visit every day. The other women in Middle Swan didn't call on Hennie. Only later did she learn that they were hookers. Still, she wouldn't have minded.

Nit thanked her for the welcome, and the two sat a minute longer, picking up their cups, sipping, and carefully setting the cups down on the saucers, which had a design of pale pink roses on them. When she finished her coffee, Hennie reached into her pocket and took out a bit of sewing.

"Oh, you quilt!" Nit said. She took the square from the older woman and examined it, running her fingers over the squares and triangles that made up a pattern the younger woman knew—Bear Paw.

"Lordy, I love it! I'd rather quilt than eat on the starvingest day of my life. Law yes! I reckon I do love it!" Hennie told her.

"Why, me, too. I don't know why I do, but I do." Nit jumped up and returned with her own workbasket. "I love to quilt and watch the snow come down. I've been doing it all week since we came here. Imagine snow in May. Why, I had my cotton coming up long before now."

"May, June, July. I've seen it snow in Middle Swan every month of the year. If you like snow, you'll be happy here." Hennie commenced sewing, taking stitches the size of mustard seeds.

Nit removed her own piecing from the basket and set it in her lap. After a bit, Hennie asked to see it, and Nit shyly handed her the square. "I'm not so good," she said. "It's just an old scrap quilt." She didn't have to explain that a scrap quilt was made from fabric leftovers of every pattern and color; there wasn't a woman who didn't know that.

"Nobody starts out a perfect quilter," Hennie said, marking down in her mind to give Nit some of her scraps, for it wasn't likely that the girl, who would have come by train, for few cars could get into Middle Swan in the snow, had thought to pack leavings from dresses and shirts. Hennie, on the other hand, had brought her scraps on the trip west, because she'd come by covered wagon and wanted something to do in the evenings around the campfire. Of course, it had turned out that on the trip, she hadn't had a minute of leisure to pick up her needle, except for mending—and then that time when she'd gashed her arm. Hennie had sent the man whose wagon she rode in for her sewing basket, and while he watched, she'd sewn up the gash herself. The man had fainted.

"Did you make those over there?" Hennie asked, indicating the quilts on the bed and bench. The girl twitched her shoulders, uncomfortable at the attention, and nodded. The quilts were thick, lumpy, probably filled with rags or worn-out quilts for batting, and they were put together with large stitches—not quilts that a fine stitcher like Hennie would make. Instead of edging the quilts with binding, the girl had turned the backsides over the quilt tops and stitched them. And they were pieced from a variety of fabrics—mattress ticking, feed sacks, old towels, domestics that had been dyed with onions, walnuts, and red clay. But the variety of colors was like sunshine on a day when storm clouds hovered over the Tenmile Range, so gay and bold that Hennie wanted to shade her eyes.

"I can see they're from the South," she observed, for she was familiar with quilts. "Some folks tell where a woman's come from by the way she talks, but I tell from her quilts. Women from the East bring those fancy red and green quilts, and there isn't a woman in Kansas who hasn't made a Drunkard's Path. Oh my yes, your quilts are from the South. Happy quilts, I'd call them." Hennie smiled at the girl, thinking it was all right if a woman quilted with her heart instead of her hands.

Nit's face burned, and to hide her embarrassment she took the cups to the stove and poured more coffee. As she set the coffee down on the table, there was the sound of metal scraping far off up the river. The creaking of the dredge boat's bucket line went on day and night. "I can't stand that chatter. It punishes my ears, and I can't sleep," she said.

"You'll get used to it. After a bit, you won't notice it at all. One day, the bucket line'll break, and the noise'll stop, and that's what will wake you," Hennie told her. She didn't add that when the dredge was silent too long, the women in Middle Swan got fidgety, worrying that the dredge had been shut down on purpose because of an accident. The girl would learn soon enough about the dangers of the gold boats. No need to tell her now.

"It's a funny way to mine gold, with a boat."

"It's not mining. It's dredging. A real miner works underground, not on a rackety boat." Hennie's voice was sharp. She was one of the old people in Middle Swan who hated the gold boats. But then, most people did. Even some of the folks who worked on the dredges hated them. But they didn't have any choice. Even with the price of gold at thirty-five dollars an ounce, only a dozen mines were open. The men who toiled underground nowadays owned the workings, and they employed just a handful of others. The laid-off miners found jobs on the huge dredges that squatted in the mountain streams up the gulch of the middle branch of the Swan River and over on the Blue River at Breckenridge. Those were paying jobs, and the dredge men were grateful for the paychecks. Men in Middle Swan fought for those jobs, and Roy Pinto had been right when he said they resented an outsider getting hired on. Nit's husband would have to be careful.

A gold boat was a big, brutal thing, with a high gantry like the gallows frame of a mine. A dredge sat in a pond of its own making and used a bucket line made up of huge iron scoops that were permanently attached to a revolving chain. The buckets went down through the water in the front of the boat, down thirty or forty or fifty feet to bedrock, scooping up dirt and rocks, then rode the chain up a ladder to the top of the gantry. Large rocks were separated out, while sand and gravel were dumped into a kind of sluice box. Then the sand and gravel were washed away, leaving the heavier grains and nuggets of gold behind in the riffles of the box. The waste went out on a conveyor belt and was dropped behind the boat in piles as high as the chimney of a two-story house. The riffles were cleaned every week, and the gold melted out and molded into a brick. Where once a good, clear river had flowed, there were mountains of tailings that dammed the water and forced it to trickle through gray piles of rock.

Dredging was dangerous work. A man could get caught

up in the bucket line and lose a finger or worse. More than
one worker had died when he touched the electric. In winter,
the decks and gangplank froze and a man might lose his
footing—or maybe get pushed—sliding into the icy water.
With his heavy boots and coat, he would sink into the
dredge pond with barely a cry. Even if someone heard him
and rescued him before he drowned, he'd likely come down
with pneumonia, which at ten thousand feet was just a
slower death.

A real miner, now, he worked underground and was as
comfortable as you please, because the mines were warm in
winter, cool in summer. Of course, mines were as dangerous
as the gold boats. Hennie knew that as well as anybody, better than most. A miner got old early from working underground. He could be crushed in a cave-in or blown to
kingdom come with blasting powder, or he could get rock
dust in his lungs and develop the miner's puff. Not for nothing were the drills used in the mines called "widow makers."
Some men couldn't take it underground, where it was as
dark as a dungeon. But unless a blast released a wall of underground water, which was rare, you didn't drown in a mine.
It might be said that dying in a mine was a better way to go,
although it was dying just the same.

A man was proud of his work as a miner, proud of how
he developed a feel for where a gold vein twisted or hid after it looked like it had pinched out. Mining was a calling.
And there was always hope of a big strike—finding rich ore
or even breaking through into a honeycomb. She remembered Lonnie Trucker, who'd done just that years before—
hit the rock wall with a pick, and that pretty little vug like a

honeycomb of gold had opened up. Lonnie mined it out with a trowel, saving the biggest nugget for himself. He carried it around wrapped up in a doll's quilt that Hennie had given him, unfolding the blanket to show off the nugget, just as if it had been his son. Folks called that nugget "Trucker's Baby."

Men weren't proud of their work on the dredges. Dredging was a poor excuse for a job, Hennie thought, no better than working in a big factory. But there was no call to tell that to Nit Spindle. Or to warn her husband to watch out for foolishness. Most likely, he'd learned that already.

Hennie took a few stitches in her quilt square, made a knot, and bit off the thread. "I expect your husband works on the Liberty Dredge," she said. The Liberty was the gold boat on the Swan River above Middle Swan, the boat whose clanking had interrupted them.

"Oh yes, ma'am. Dick's a deckhand."

Hennie asked how he'd gotten hired on.

Nit replied that Dick's cousin once removed worked at the dredge company's office in the East. She chewed at her finger. "Do you think people hate us for that? Maybe Dick took the job away from somebody else."

Instead of answering, Hennie said, "Not everybody wants to work on a dredge."

Nit sighed. "I thought maybe that's why nobody's come calling. But we were so desperate. There aren't any jobs at home, so Dick wrote his cousin. He's always been partial to Dick. I've been afraid that people here didn't like us 'cause Dick took a job that rightly belongs to somebody else. I'm so lonesome."

The old woman reached over and patted the girl's hand. "They'll come along. A mountain woman, now if she wants to visit, she makes an errand. If she comes on an errand, she pretends it's a visit. Don't fret. They're just taking their time thinking up errands."

Hennie remembered again how lonely she'd been that first year and how she'd vowed to call on every new woman in Middle Swan, and over the years, she had. Except for the hookers. She visited them at first, but they looked at her warily, their eyes shifting back and forth. They didn't ask her in, and Hennie knew she made the girls uneasy. She meant well, of course, but one of the prostitutes told her, "Most women like you want to send we girls to a farm. Well, I come from a farm. Why do you think I turned out?" And Hennie had understood, because she knew too many women in Tennessee who had gone to the grave young from farm work.

Hennie's eyes watered then for no reason, the way old women's eyes do, and she reached into her pocket for her handkerchief, but instead she pulled out a smoky blue feather. "I forgot about this. I found it on the trail this morning, lying in the snow. Now what do you suppose a bluebird's doing here this time of year?" She placed the feather on her palm and held out her hand to Nit. "Go on. Take it. You can pin it on the wall. Bluebirds are luck. Up here, they're like bits the Lord cut out from the sky, just like you'd cut quilt pieces, and sent down to us."

"Oh gee!" The girl took the feather and stared at it. Suddenly, she burst into tears.

Now what have you gone and done, old woman? Hennie asked herself. She set down her sewing and got up to put her

arms around the girl, who cried even harder at the tenderness. Hennie patted her on the back, but the crying continued. "There now, dearie. I was lonesome, too, when I first came
here, lonely as the devil at a revival meeting, as they say. But
I came to like it right well. Why, in no time at all, I couldn't
hardly stand to go down below. I can't breathe in that thick
air. You'll find a woman along the Tenmile Range, now it
takes her a time to warm up, but once she does, you'll never
have a better neighbor. And a good neighbor's worth more
than money."

The words only made Nit sob harder. There was nothing
for Hennie to do then but let the girl cry herself out, and after a bit, the tears slowed, then stopped. Nit sniffed and
wiped her eyes with the backs of her hands. "It's not that,"
Nit said. "You see, that feather's the color of my baby's eyes.
I had to leave her behind when we moved here, leave her in
the cold ground." Nit reached into her pocket and withdrew
a handkerchief that was white and neatly folded, and blew
her nose. "She's all alone, my little girl. I buried her under a
marker that says 'Sweet Baby Effie,' but what if nobody re-
members who Effie Spindle is? What if the sign falls away? I
asked you to pray for her that day at your house. I left the
nickel for you. I'd be obliged if you'd pray she won't be forgot."

"I will." Nit's tears brought an aching to Hennie's own
heart, for she understood the girl's sorrow. "You don't have
your people there?"

Nit shook her head. "When we got married, Dick and I
wanted us to go out to ourself. So we moved away from our
homefolks."

"Then God will tend that baby's grave."

The girl stared at Hennie.

"You've got to believe that. Besides, it's just a grave. Your baby lives in your heart now." Hennie seemed to debate something with herself, and the thinking took a long time. Was there any reason to bring up what had happened so many years before? If she let herself talk about it, she wouldn't sleep that night but, instead, would thrash about, reliving that time, because the pain never went away but only lay hidden in her mind. The story took such a toll on her that she rarely told it anymore. But she felt a kinship with the girl, who seemed little more than a baby herself. Besides, Hennie had asked the Lord to let her be the answer to Nit's prayer, and He sometimes answered prayers in the oddest way. The old woman couldn't overlook that. So, sighing, she said deliberately, looking down at the sewing in her hands, "My baby's eyes were that color, too. She's buried in Tennessee. I never went back. Not once."

"In seventy years?"

Hennie shook her head. "I couldn't go back. I have my grievements." One still needed to be attended to, she thought, but didn't tell that to Nit.

"Was she dead-born, too, like Effie?"

"She was eight months and two days when she got taken. Or maybe three days. I never knew for sure."

"Why couldn't you go back, Mrs. Comfort?" The girl leaned forward. Her eyes still glittered with tears, but there was a questioning look in them. "Did you think you'd left her all alone, and you were afraid to see what became of her grave? That's what it's like for me. I feel I just left Effie by herself in the cold. If she'd been born alive and got sick, I could have helped her. I'm real good with the herbs. There's a plant for every disease if you have the sense to find the right one, but Effie never lived long enough to get a disease. She was just born a small, puny little old thing that never took a breath."

Hennie patted the younger woman's hand but did not speak.

"Didn't you ever want to see your girl's resting place once more? I couldn't bear it if I never saw Effie's again. They say you shouldn't name a dead baby, but I did anyway, named her for Mrs. Effie Pickle, who tended me during my labor."

Hennie shook her head. "I just couldn't stand to be there again, knowing my little Sarah was under the ground and never deserved it—God's precious child. I couldn't look at the place where she'd died. Sometimes, it's easier for me to look ahead than back."

Snow, which had stopped when Hennie set out for Nit's cabin, was falling again, big, wet flakes, a sloppy spring snow, not one of the screaming mountain storms of winter, and the light was gone from the room, but neither of the women thought to strike a match for the kerosene lamp. "How did she die?" the girl asked in a whisper.

Hennie went as rigid as a drill bit. "Drowned. Drowned in the creek where there wasn't six inches of water." She sighed deeply, recalling that tiny body, clad in a white dress that Hennie had embroidered with forget-me-nots.

"Oh, Mrs. Comfort! There's been a lot of suffering in it for you." The girl cried softly now.

Nit's quiet sobs went to Hennie's heart, and in a minute,

a tear wet the scrap of quilting in the old woman's lap. Hennie sniffed. She was not a woman who cried much, and she didn't want to add to the girl's misery. "There's some here that know the story. I'm known in Middle Swan for my stories, but not this one. I haven't told it in a long time, not since I stopped going to church. There's not many that remember it."

"Do you need to tell it now? Do you feel the need of it?" The two seemed to have changed roles, and it was the girl now who offered solace to the old woman. Nit stood and took down the dipper hanging beside the stove. She filled it with water from the bucket, and held it out to Hennie. "Would you drink?" she asked.

Nit's concern made Hennie's hands shake, for there was not a great deal of tenderness in a mining camp. She steadied the dipper and drank the water, which was cold. Most likely, it was melted snow, because the cabin didn't have a well, and the stream was a long walk away.

The girl took the dipper and hung it up. "I don't mean to pry."

"You didn't." Hennie picked up her needle and took two or three stitches on the quilt square, but it was too dark to sew, and she knew the stitches were crooked and she'd have to take them out later. She stabbed the needle into the cloth. "I try not to bother folks with my troubles, and this happened so long ago that it's best forgot. But you never really forget a thing like this, just like you'll never forget about your little Effie." She paused, still debating with herself. "It's not a pretty story." The old woman looked at Nit, half hoping the girl would stop her, for she still didn't want to tell the

story. She'd have a bad case of the blue devils tomorrow if
she did.

Instead, Nit leaned forward, her eyes on Hennie's face,
waiting for the woman to continue. Hennie felt a hairpin
loosen in her white hair, which was pulled into a knot at the
back of her neck. Without thinking about it, she scooped up
stray hairs with the loose pin, which she secured in the knot.
After a minute, she folded the sewing, although she did not
put it into her pocket. Then taking a long breath, which was
more of a sigh, she began. "Back then, I wasn't Hennie Comfort. In those days, I was called by the name of Ila Mae
Stubbs."

❀❀❀❀❀

In the golden days before the start of the War Between the
States, Ila Mae was the precious only child of Obadiah
Stubbs, a successful miller, and his wife. They lived in White
Pigeon, Tennessee. The girl was raised with advantages, attending a school for young ladies where she was taught to cipher and write a fine hand, sew a seam with stitches as tiny
as specks of salt. Her framed sampler, with its embroidered
house and willow trees and a verse about serving the Lord,
hung in the place of honor over the mantel in the parlor.

Ila Mae was not a pampered child. Although the Stubbses
had servants—paid servants, because Obadiah Stubbs op-
posed slavery and owned neither man nor woman—Ila Mae
helped at the cook stove and the laundry tubs. She loved the
days spent in the barn and the garden, and truth be told, she
was happier at the flour mill where the men argued about
whether to join the North or the South if Mr. Lincoln were

elected president than she was dressed in satin over corset and hoopskirt, gossiping at the tea table with her mother's friends. Like her father, Ila Mae did not hold with human bondage, and as a girl of strong opinions, she sometimes joined the men's conversations. Even at that age, she was one to speak her mind.

"Teach her to curb her tongue, and she'll make a good match," said Barton Fletcher, foreman of the Stubbs Mill.

"Some like a woman that speaks her mind," Obadiah replied.

"None I know. A husband could teach her."

"A husband that harms a hair on her head will be the worse for it," Obadiah thundered.

Both men were aware that Barton's son, Abram, had a fondness for Ila Mae, but they knew, too, that she would have none of him. Abram Fletcher was a handsome-made man, but he was randy and ill-tempered as a hornet and had too high an opinion of himself. He'd been spoiled by his mother and never made to work by his father. "Rather than marry with him, I'll betroth myself to a hog," Ila Mae told her father when he asked her view of the young man. Obadiah was not upset by his daughter's answer, for he considered Abram to be a fortune hunter.

While Obadiah did not hold with the war, he thought nonetheless that when the fighting broke out, it was his duty to enlist for the South. He was killed at Shiloh. Had Ila Mae been older, she might have been trained to run the mill, for she had a clear head, and her father had no quarrel with a woman who was ambitious. But she was a girl yet, so the mill was entrusted to Barton Fletcher. The mother left business affairs to him, while, dressed in widow's weeds, she sat long days in the parlor, the curtains drawn against the light. Death, when it came only a year after her husband's, was welcome to her.

By then, Barton Fletcher was running the mill with a free hand. Because her father had trusted him and he had eaten at their table, Ila Mae looked to him for guidance. She did not know a man would cheat a girl out of her inheritance, and when he told her to sign a paper, Ila Mae did so. Barton smirked at her then, handed her forty dollars, and claimed that she'd just sold him the mill and the house where she'd lived all her life, and every other thing that had belonged to her mother and father.

She could stay on in the house, Barton told her, if she would marry his son. But Ila Mae would not allow Abram Fletcher to court her. Besides, she thought the world and all of Billy Lloyd and had promised herself to him. Billy wasn't pretty like Abram. He was short and square-built, and at times, when riled, he had a temper. But he was a better man than Abram, kind and quiet-spoken, almost always showing a sunny disposition. Some thought those qualities made him soft and cowardly, and hoping to eliminate him as a rival, Abram used some trifling matter to challenge Billy to a duel. Given the choice of weapons, Billy selected fists, and he beat Abram nearly senseless. Ila Mae worried that Abram would try to even the score, but Billy said that Abram was too afraid of another fisting.

Obadiah had liked Billy, had told Ila Mae he would not mind if the boy joined him in running the mill one day, although he asked the young people to wait until Ila Mae was

sixteen to wed. But homeless now, with both of her parents
dead, Ila Mae found no reason to postpone marriage.

Ila Mae and Billy moved into an old log blockhouse on
land Billy had inherited when his own parents died. The
house was hidden away in the timber just off the Buttermilk
Road, so-called because a farmer had blazed it to haul his
milk into town. Ila Mae loved her new home, with its
thatched roof and a fireplace that Billy himself built out of
mud and rocks. He put in a window, too, because he didn't
want Ila Mae to live in a blindhouse. "It's okay for a mole
like me, but not a girl as pretty as stars." Billy blushed then,
because he was not much for fine words.

Ila Mae reddened, too, for she knew she was not pretty.
Her face was strong, not soft, and brown from working outdoors, and she was as tall as Billy. "You're not a mole," she
said fiercely. "You're as finely built as an oak tree and just as
strong." He picked her up then and carried her to the house
to show her how strong he really was.

Billy was gentle, too, and Ila Mae loved the way he
stroked her as they lay on a bed on the ground under a strip
of cheesecloth hung from the branches of a tree as a mosquito net. They slept outside in the heat of the summer, and
Ila Mae joyed to the touch of Billy's hand on her hot body.
Sometimes, warm with lovemaking, they lay on their backs
looking up at the stars and talked about their future. Although the war had intruded into their young lives, they saw
years stretching out ahead of them filled with children and a
fruitful farm. "Lordy, we'll live good," Billy promised.

They planted a garden, and what they raised was about
what they had. Billy hunted, and Ila Mae cut the meat into

strips and hung it to dry from a rope that they stretched from the tree in front of the house to the fence. They weren't more than a few hundred feet from a creek, but Billy still dug a well for Ila Mae. The two lived outdoors most of the time, except when the weather was bad, Ila Mae cooking over a campfire. Billy made a frame for Ila Mae to lay her quilts on, made it from pieces of seasoned oak so it would last, and she stitched outdoors, too. They were young, not jelled yet, but Lordy, they were full of life. When to no one's surprise, Sarah was born just nine months and three days after the wedding, "I didn't know a person could be so happy," Billy told Ila Mae.

The couple figured that being back in the woods like they were and Billy not very old and with a family to care for, nobody would expect him to go for a soldier. They talked about whether Billy ought to join up. He was willing, for he was more of a Confederate than Ila Mae. Besides, other young men had left their families to fight for the South, he said.

But Ila Mae pointed out that by then, everyone knew the South wouldn't win the war, and what was the good of risking his life for a cause that was lost? Better to stay where he was and help the families of Confederate soldiers, as he had been doing. There wasn't a widow along the Buttermilk Road who didn't know she could ask Billy Lloyd to mend her fence or hunt a lost cow. "You'll be here to rebuild after the peace. The men coming back'll be wounded and sick, and you can help them," Ila Mae told Billy, and he agreed. They were green yet and didn't know they were fools.

White Pigeon had a home guard. It was made up mostly

of old men and the lame—soldiers who'd come back missing a leg or an arm or who'd gone queer in the head from the
noise of the guns and the cannons, and the fear. But there
were local boys in the guard, too, single men who ought to
have joined up themselves. Ila Mae didn't understand why
they weren't made to be soldiers. The guard was supposed to
protect the women whose husbands were fighting the Yankees. But instead, they strutted around, threatening to arrest
anyone they didn't like for not being patriotic. They stole
guns and crops, saying such was for the army, but the home
guard sold it all and kept the money. Folks around White Pigeon knew to stay away from them. Ila Mae knew that, too,
because Abram Fletcher was one of the guards.

One morning, Ila Mae came in from cutting Christmas
greens and found the home guard in her yard. The men had
dragged Billy out of the house without his shoes on and tied
him up in a wagon. He was bruised and had one eye nearly
swollen shut from fighting with the guards. Abram Fletcher
was there. "So you married a feather-legged man, Ila Mae,"
he said.

"That's a black lie! If there's any cowards about, it's you,
Abram Fletcher. You tied up Billy because you're afraid he'll
fist you. How come you haven't joined up? Are you too lazy
or just too scared?"

Abram didn't like that, but with the other men around,
some of the older ones once friends of Ila Mae's father,
Abram didn't dare strike her. Instead, he punched Billy, saying, "Your wife would make a better soldier than you." Billy
kicked at Abram, who dodged and laughed.

Ila Mae knew that if she said more, Billy'd get the worst

of it, maybe get beat up a ways down the road. So she bit her tongue and said, "I'll get Billy's shoes." There was frost on the ground, and she didn't want Billy's feet to freeze.

Ila Mae went into the house and came back with the shoes, but just as she reached the wagon, Abram, who was seated on the bench, larruped up the horses. The wagon lurched, knocking Billy onto his side. The men started up after Abram. Ila Mae threw the shoes at Billy, but only one of them landed in the wagon. She picked up the other from the ground and ran after that wagon as long as she could, but she never caught up to it, and the farther it went, the farther behind she got. Finally, Ila Mae just stopped and waved and called, "I love you, Billy."

"I'll be back. I promise. I'll come home," he yelled, as the wagon went around a bend in the Buttermilk Road. She didn't see Billy after that. She would have followed him all the way into town then, but she couldn't leave Sarah alone in the cabin. So Ila Mae picked up the shoe and went back to the house and fed Sarah, then walked into White Pigeon with the baby, but she was too late. Billy'd already been taken off to the Tennessee volunteers—him wearing one shoe. Ila Mae never saw him again, never knew where he went. He wrote her—one letter anyway. There might have been more, but one was all she received. Billy wrote that if he ever got the chance, he'd come home, and Abram Fletcher and anybody else who tried to make him go back had better watch out.

Two or three months later, folks in the neighborhood spotted a soldier hiding out in the woods. They knew he was a Confederate because he was dressed in gray. Talk was that the soldier was Billy, but Ila Mae knew he wasn't, because by the time Billy was in the army, there weren't any uniforms left. Besides, the man had on two shoes. But most important, if he were Billy, he'd have come to see his family right off.

Whoever he was, he didn't come to the farm. Instead, while Ila Mae was sitting at her quilt frame one afternoon, Abram and some of his fellows rode up. They'd been drinking. She could tell that right off, and she was scared, because they were all young. None of the old men who might have calmed them down were with them.

"Where's your man?" one of the guards called out to Ila Mae.

"He's in the army, least he ought to be," she replied. "That's where you took him, isn't it?"

"We heard he's run off and is somewheres out in the woods, hiding like the yellow scum he is," Abram Fletcher said, leering at her.

"What makes you think that's Billy?" Ila Mae asked.

"Because Billy's not good for much 'cept taking to ground." The men laughed at that, and one took out a jug and handed it about.

"Billy's too much of a man to run!" Ila Mae told them.

"Well, ain't we men, too, and white at that? Not yellow like Billy," Abram said, and the others laughed again.

"You can look all around. He's not here," Ila Mae told them. She continued quilting, taking the worst stitches she'd ever made in her life but keeping on sewing because she didn't want the guards to think she was afraid of them.

One of the home guards dismounted, and he went into the house. Ila Mae heard things falling onto the floor. In a minute, the man came out with the skillet of cornbread she'd left on the hearth to bake. He'd wrapped the hot pan in the Seven Sisters quilt she'd made just after she was married. "I thought Billy'd be hiding under the bed, but he ain't there. Found his dinner, though," the man said, passing around the skillet so that the others could scoop out the cornbread with their hands. Then he flung the skillet into the woods. Abram took the quilt from the guard and tucked it in front of his saddle.

"You going to tell us where he's at?" Abram rode his horse over next to Ila Mae, so close that the animal knocked against the quilt frame. Abram reached down with a big knife and slashed the center of Ila Mae's half-finished quilt. "Martha Merritt sewed a Yankee flag in the middle of her quilt. If she hadn't lit out, we'd have took care of the traitor. You get what I mean?" he asked.

Ila Mae knew what he meant. "I told you, Billy's in the army. He hasn't been back since you took him off to town."

"We'll see about that." Abram climbed off his horse then and grabbed Ila Mae's arm so hard that she thought he'd pulled it out of its socket. "I always did fancy this girl," he told the others.

Despite the pain in her arm, Ila Mae made a fist, ready to defend herself. No man but Billy had ever touched her, and she didn't intend for any other man to try.

"Now, Abram," one of the men said. "We ain't here for that."

"Aw, what are you thinking?" Abram replied. "She's not so lucky. I just thought we'd tie her up so's she'll tell us where Billy's at."

"Maybe we ought to beat her with a whip," the man with
the jug suggested. That was whiskey talk and it scared Ila
Mae.

Abram took down the rope that had been strung for
meat drying, and he tied Ila Mae's hands together. Then he
fastened her hands to the crosspost of the well. After he finished, he leaned down and kissed her hard. Ila Mae spat at
him, and he slapped her across the face, then put his fingers
through the gold hoops in her ears and ripped them out.
"We'll come back later on and see if you've changed your
mind," he said, then whispered, "You be nice now, and I'll
show you a good time." He mounted his horse and rode off
with the others, the earrings in his pocket, Ila Mae's Seven
Sisters quilt still affixed to his saddle.

Although Ila Mae wasn't able to move, she was grateful
that the men were gone. Her ears ached, and her wrists hurt
where the rope was tied too tightly. She cried out, hoping a
neighbor would hear her; with Billy gone, the old farmers
still living in the neighborhood were in the habit of checking in on her. Even if none of the neighbors heard her cries,
somebody would come down the Buttermilk Road and set
her free. Or one of the guards might sober up and be bemeaned by what the men had done and come back to cut
her loose.

At the worst, Abram would return. As the day wore on,
Ila Mae's arms began to swell, and she developed a terrible
thirst. She was tied to the well, but she might have been in
the middle of a desert for all the good that the water did her.

Still, Ila Mae didn't lose heart until she became sensible
of Sarah, who began to cry. Ila Mae ached for the little girl,

hungry and thirsty, although she knew the baby was safe inside the crib Billy had made for her. Ila Mae pulled with all her might, hoping the rope would come loose, pulled until she scraped the skin off her wrists.

It was on toward evening, when Ila Mae heard Sarah calling, "Ma, Ma," for Sarah was a bright thing who even at that young age knew her mother was *Ma.* Ila Mae realized the sound was louder than before. She wrenched herself around toward the house and saw then that the little girl was in the doorway. The man who'd gone into the house had upset the baby's crib, and Sarah crawled through the door and out into the dirt. Ila Mae called to her, "Sarah, come to Mama. Come to Mama, sweet girl."

Sarah heard her mother's voice and laughed and crawled toward the well. But something turned her head, and despite Ila Mae's pleadings, the little girl sat in the dirt and played with sticks. When she grew bored, she looked around and began to crawl again. Ila Mae called her to come, and she did, but with Ila Mae's hands tied over her head, the mother couldn't grab the baby. Ila Mae tried to hold the child with her feet, but Sarah pulled away and started down the hill, cooing and talking. The baby must have tumbled then, because after a time, the little thing began to cry. The crying grew fainter and farther away, until Ila Mae could hear it no longer. She called until her voice gave out, but she never again heard her baby's voice. Ila Mae strained her eyes trying to make out the baby in the moonlight, but she couldn't see her, either. She pulled at the ropes that bound her until they rubbed almost to the bone, but the restraints held. Finally, she gave up and closed her eyes and prayed—prayed that someone would come along and free her or that Sarah would crawl back up the hill to safety. Billy was gone and Sarah was all she had now. What if Billy survived the war, only to come home and find that his little girl had perished? Or maybe he wouldn't come home, and she'd have lost them both. Bitter tears ran down Ila Mae's face, and with her hands tied, she couldn't even wipe them away.

Just at dawn, Ila Mae heard something stir behind the house. A man darted across the yard, and Ila Mae called out. It wasn't much of a sound, because her voice was gone, but the man heard her, and moving from tree to tree, he came close. He was the Confederate, and Ila Mae thought he was there to rob her.

"You got yourself in a pickle," he said.

If God had heard her prayer and sent this man, then maybe Sarah was all right, Ila Mae thought. But they had to hurry. "Quick. They think you're my husband, Billy, hiding out. The home guard tied me up because I wouldn't tell on you, and my baby's crawled off. I can't see her. Please help me, mister," Ila Mae whispered. "Please hurry."

"You won't turn me in if I do? You got to promise me that."

"I won't turn you in. My word's as honest as gold. They made my husband enlist and he'd run off, too, if he could."

The soldier studied Ila Mae a moment before making up his mind. Then he cut the rope. He took her raw wrists to rub the circulation back into them, but Ila Mae wouldn't wait. "I've got to find Sarah. She's my baby, and she's loose out here. Help me."

The two took off down the hill, Ila Mae going one way,

the man another, and it wasn't two or three minutes before she heard him call, "Missus."

There was such sadness in his voice that Ila Mae knew he'd found Sarah. She tried to rush to him, but her feet were as heavy as if they'd been weighted down with sad irons, and she could hardly move. It seemed as if it took her five minutes to go three hundred yards. When she reached the soldier, he was squatting down next to Sarah, who was lying facedown in the creek. The surface of the water had frozen a crust around her face. When she picked up that tiny body, dressed in the white gown that was now ripped and stained with dirt, Ila Mae saw that Sarah's face was wet, and she dried it with her hands, then wrapped the baby in her apron and carried her to the house. She could not cry, because her heart was too broken. Her mind was dull, and her stomach seemed as if she had swallowed a lump of clay. A voice inside her kept saying, "Sarah's dead. Sarah's dead." And Ila Mae felt as if she were dead, too.

The soldier wasn't a Rebel, he told her. He was a Union man who'd been captured and escaped and taken the uniform from a dead Confederate. He was a good man. He built a fire in the hearth and cooked up some bacon for Ila Mae, then heated water so that she could wash Sarah. He told Ila Mae that his little girl was just about Sarah's age. "I ought to never have left her, and your man ought to be here now," he said.

Ila Mae wrapped Sarah in a quilt to warm her, just as if she'd been alive. "Have you had her baptized in the Lord?" the man asked. "I'm a preacher and can do it if it would ease you some." Ila Mae had been waiting until Billy came home before asking a preacher to bless the baby, so she told the Yankee that she'd appreciate it if he'd say the words over the child. Ila Mae drew fresh water from the well, and the man made a wet cross on the dead child's forehead and said a Bible verse from memory. The words comforted her a little. Then Ila Mae dressed the baby in a clean gown, and they laid Sarah in a little grave that the Yankee dug in the burial ground out back where Billy's people rested.

After that, the soldier offered to walk Ila Mae to White Pigeon, but she told him no. She had to stay beside the grave. She couldn't leave Sarah alone. Besides, if the home guard caught the Yankee, he'd be shot. "Take my husband's clothes from the trunk. You'll be safer in them than dressed like a Confederate. Throw your uniform in the fire." She filled a pillowcase with bread and bacon and a sack of cornmeal. "Go west," she told the Yankee. "That's where they're fighting. You'll run into the Union Army. If you see a boy with one shoe, don't shoot him. That's my husband."

"I seen plenty of men barefoot but never one with one shoe. I'll keep a lookout for him."

"I'll say a prayer for you."

"The name's Simon Smith, missus, but the Lord's acquainted with me. I'll keep you and yours in my prayers, too," he replied, and was off.

Ila Mae never knew if he made it.

She wrote Billy to tell him Sarah was dead, although she didn't tell him how it had happened. Time enough for that after he returned home, although he never did. After the war ended, a man came looking for her. He and Billy were pards in the army, he said, and they'd promised each other if one of them got killed, the other would tell the family. The man couldn't write, so he came all the way to Tennessee to find her. Billy was shot less than a week before the war was over. The man said Billy died easy, saying he'd given his life for a noble cause and wasn't sorry, but Ila Mae knew that was what they always told the widows. She never found out where he was buried.

In a day or two, after the soldier was well away, Ila Mae forced herself away from the little grave and walked into White Pigeon and told what Abram and his fellows had done. People believed her and wouldn't speak to him after that. When the fighting was over and the soldiers came home, they ran off Abram, declared he had bemeaned the town and wasn't ever to show his face there again. Not long after that, a soldier came to Ila Mae's cabin and set $500 on her table. He said the men had had a talk with Barton Fletcher and told him that if he didn't want to leave White Pigeon like Abram, he'd have to come up with more than $40 to buy her father's house and mill. The men said she could have a better life with the money, but that meant nothing to Ila Mae. She believed she'd already lived the happiest days of her life.

⬤═❦═⬤

The bucket line, which had stopped while Hennie was telling her story, started up just then, the clanking and screeching breaking the stillness in the room, jarring Hennie loose from the past. She hated the sound of it, but she was relieved to hear the clatter, for it meant no one had been hurt. When there was an accident, the dredge stayed shut down for a long time. "You see, it was just a little thing wrong with the dredge," Hennie said.

With an effort, Hennie put the story of Sarah out of her mind. She glanced at the window and saw that it was black as tar outside and exclaimed, "Law, you've got supper to fix, and here I've been talking. That's what happens when you live by yourself. You lose sight of the time. I'll get on home and fix hotcakes. I can't seem to take them for breakfast, so I have them at night." She wondered if she could swallow the hotcakes after telling her story. Hennie stood and looked around for her coat.

Nit stood, too. She noticed the dark and struck a match and lit the kerosene lamp between them. It sent out a weak circle of light that didn't illuminate much. The corners of the room were still in shadow. The girl's eyes were red, and she wiped them with her fingers, then put her hand on the old woman's arm. "Did Ila Mae—I mean, did you, back when you were Ila Mae—burn the quilt you were working on the way you did that army uniform?"

At first, Hennie didn't understand, but when she did, she smiled, because the question tickled her. Only a true quilter would remember such a thing as a spoiled quilt. "The Murder quilt," she mused. "That's what I call it. I put it away half done, and I've kept it all these years. There might be a use for it yet."

"What use?"

Hennie shook her head. That quilt was one of the things she had to deal with before she left Middle Swan.

"What happened to Abram Fletcher?"

Hennie pulled away from the girl and went to the bed for

her coat. Her back to Nit, Hennie put on the coat and tied a scarf around her head, as she thought what to say about Abram Fletcher.

"Do you hate Abram Fletcher still?" Nit continued. Hennie had put on her mittens and was fumbling with the buttons, so the girl fastened the old woman's coat for her.

"No, I guess I don't hate him anymore. But I never forgave him. What he did lodges in my heart like a wild licorice burr. You don't forget. You never forget. You don't forgive, either. But time passes, and you find peace of a kind. You will, too, Mrs. Spindle. That's why I told you my story. You'll wake up and go an hour without thinking about your baby. And one day, when you think of her, why, you'll remember her sweetness, not her death." Hennie sighed.

"Your story heals me," Nit said.

The old woman thought to tell the girl that there would be other babies, but she wouldn't, for she knew that might not be true. Hennie herself had suffered miscarriages in Middle Swan. Instead, she said, "You know, I believe Sarah's death was as painful for Abram Fletcher as it was for me."

"How can you say that?"

Hennie stared at the light on the table, then looked Nit in the face. "That's a story with no ending. But I've got other stories, happier ones. You come over. I'm there most days, and I'd welcome the company. You come and sew and hear my stories. You know what a storyteller is, don't you? It's a person that has a good memory who hopes other people don't." The old woman chuckled and stood in the cold doorway a minute. "I promise you you'll find peace yourself, Mrs. Spindle. Not tomorrow, but one day."

She studied the girl a moment longer, thinking again how much Nit reminded her of herself at that age. There was indeed a reason the girl had stopped at her gate for a prayer, and maybe the Almighty had Hennie Comfort in mind as the answer. Perhaps it was tied up with letting the old woman stay in Middle Swan a little longer. It surprised her sometimes the way the Lord replied to a prayer, for He didn't always answer the way Hennie would have answered it if the two of them had traded places.

Nit stood in the doorway and watched as Hennie disappeared into the darkness. Then she called after the old woman, "I thank you for your story. And I'm awful proud we got acquainted."

Chapter 2

The roofs of the French Street shacks smoked as the sun melted the snow on them, and the eaves dripped steady streams of water. Hidden in the doorway of her house, Hennie watched Nit make her way up the trail, her feet in their rubber shoes seeking rocks in the mud. The girl stepped so lightly that she could have walked on eggs and not broken them.

The houses, snuggled close to the ground, were winter-worn, the paint rubbed off, the roofs in need of patching where the wind had torn away the tarpaper. Fences were busted down from the heavy snows that the wind had pounded against them. Even now, in the shadowy places, mounds of dirty snow stood three feet high. Where the sun had melted the snow, a few green patches pushed up, but most of the yards were dead yet, and gray from chimney smoke and from the ashes housewives threw on the ice that lay on the paths to the clotheslines and the privies. Snow covered the rusted-out engines and broken machinery that littered Middle Swan yards. It was an ugly scene, but it meant that winter was coming to an end.

Nit slowed next to a raw-board house where a dirty quilt hung behind a broken window to keep out the cold. A large slattery woman wearing an apron over her coat stood in a pair of men's overshoes, hanging sheets on a line, a ragged dog beside her. Nit shaded her eyes with her hand, because the glare of the bright sun on snow brought a hurting to them. She stopped and greeted the woman, who was standing next to a heavy wicker basket, but with the screeching of the dredge in the distance, the woman didn't hear her. Instead of calling out again, Nit stood quietly, waiting for the woman to turn around.

Her back to Nit, the woman slogged through the mud in her yard, carrying a sheet to a bare place on the line. As she lifted it, she slipped, dragging the wet laundry through the mud. "You cussed thing!" she cried, throwing the sheet into the basket, where it scraped its muddy end against the other laundry. "You go to West Hell!" She stamped her heavy shoe in the mud, splashing brown flecks onto her leg. Then as she picked up the laundry basket to take it into the house, she spotted Nit. The girl smiled, but the woman snarled, "You see something you think is funny?"

"No, ma'am. I was just waiting—"

"Waiting for what? Waiting for me to fall down and drown in this muck? Is that what you was waiting for? Don't you say a word to me while I'm mad." The woman glared at

Nit. "You see my butt? Well, kiss me on it." She picked up the laundry basket so that the muddy edge rubbed against her coat. "Jesus God!" she swore. "Come on, Asia," she said to the dog and went into the house.

Nit blushed, but whether from the insult or the woman's sharp tongue wasn't clear. The girl ducked her head to stare down at the street, and Hennie slipped back inside the house, for she didn't want Nit to know she'd witnessed the girl's humiliation.

Nit moved along the trail to the two-story log place with the shake roof and stared for a minute at the sign, the letters not painted on but carved into a board that was silver-gray and splintered with age: PRAYERS FOR SALE. Nit looked at the sign for a full minute, while Hennie waited, not knowing if the girl was in need of another prayer or had just come to visit. As Nit stared at the lettering, Hennie opened the door and stepped outside.

"Just you come in, Mrs. Spindle," Hennie cried, joyed to see the girl. "It's a fine day for a visit, with the sun blazing and the snow drying up ever as fast as rain in July. Why, it won't be any time till the lupine and the Indian paintbrush pop up their heads."

"I hope you don't mind me calling on you," Nit said timidly, glancing back over her shoulder, but there was no sign of the angry woman. "I stopped to say hello to a lady hanging up her laundry"—she jerked her head toward the old house—"and she was as friendly as a mad dog. She's quaint-natured, and she swore something terrible."

"That would be Thelma Franks, who you'd be hard-pressed to neighbor with. Her profanation is scandalous.

There's a piece of gutter in her spine that makes her rage so. She's mad today because a thief stole her two-way stretch girdle off the line last night. She came raging over here and asked if I'd taken it. Now what would I do with her girdle? It would fit around me twice. I think the wind was the thief, for I can't see why anybody would want the old thing. It was almost out of stretch. Or maybe Asia—that's that worthless pup—got it."

"Asia's a funny name for a dog?"

"Her husband called it that name. He said he wished the thing was on the other side of the world." Hennie lowered her voice. "She isn't really Mrs. Franks. She lives with him, but those two won't marry because they fight too much."

"She told me—I like to die when she said it . . ." Nit blushed, as if she wasn't sure whether to repeat the words, but she did. "She told me to kiss her on her butt."

"That's not a thing I'd like to think about."

Nit giggled. "What's West Hell?"

"She said that, did she? I believe she's well acquainted with it. That's a place worse than hell itself. I've heard some say it's Middle Swan in February." The old woman unlatched the gate for Nit, who handed her a dish, Hennie's own raspberry pie plate with Hennie's dishcloth, newly washed and ironed, covering it. Hennie peeked inside and exclaimed, "Snickerdoodles, my favorite. Why, you didn't have to bring me anything."

"Mommy always said never return an empty plate." Nit had a forlorn look on her face and added, "But these are a poor excuse for a cookie. I made them twice, and they fell as flat as stack cakes both times."

Hennie told the girl it was the altitude that affected her cooking and suggested she use more water and less lard. "It takes a while to learn to cook up here. Water this high up boils at a lower temperature than you're used to, so you have to leave things on the stove longer. You'll learn. I did." Hennie didn't add that she'd served Jake unleavened bread and hard beans for weeks, and he didn't say a word until he came home one afternoon and found her crying over her spoiled supper. He told her it wasn't her fault but the altitude's, and to ask another woman in the camp about cooking, so Hennie called on her nearest neighbor, Laura Burke, the madam at the Willows, for help.

"I been asked by wives what they done wrong in the bedroom but never the kitchen," Laura said, and when Hennie laughed, Laura invited her inside for a cup of tea. Laura told the young bride, "Bake your bread with a pinch less of leavening, and if you want beans for Sunday dinner, put them on the stove Friday night."

Hennie was so pleased with the advice that on baking day, she left a loaf of bread wrapped in a tea towel at the back door of the hookhouse. And the next morning, the towel, freshly laundered, was lying on Hennie's doorstep.

"Well, I wish I knew about that before I started," Nit said. "I hate to put cookies like these in Dick's lunch bucket. I have a pride in what I give him."

"He won't mind," Hennie said, knowing she spoke the truth. She'd met Dick Spindle the week before when the young couple was tramping about in the snow, the boy holding tight to his wife's hand, treating her as if she was as delicate as a china doll. Nit's husband wasn't much more than a child himself, the flush of youth still on him. Hennie asked how he liked working on the dredge, and he said fine. But Hennie knew from Roy Pinto at the store that the workers were rough on him, especially the boss, Silas Hemp. He was a real stinker and took especial delight in devilment. Later, Hennie asked the Almighty to find Dick another line of work for him, one for which he was better suited.

Hennie leaned over to smell the cookies. "Your stomach doesn't see what they look like. These'll taste awful good," she said. "I was just about frying some bread for breakfast, but I'd rather have a snickerdoodle." Hennie walked back over the stepping stones to the door. "I was wrecking my mind thinking what to do today, and here you've come along for a nice visit."

Hennie held the door so that Nit could go ahead of her. The house, which was as neat and tidy as if Hennie had just finished spring cleaning, smelled of cloves. The room they entered was large and served as living room with a fireplace constructed from big, smooth stones along one wall, a dining room, and a kitchen. A door in the kitchen opened outside, and a second door led to an inside bathroom, a luxury in Middle Swan. There was another doorway in the back that opened onto a bedroom, where a spool bed was made up a foot high with quilts. A staircase along one wall led to more bedrooms. Hennie's house was a pure mansion compared to Nit's cabin.

"It's the prettiest-looking house," the girl said, looking around again, stopping for a minute to take in the framed sampler over the fireplace mantel.

In Middle Swan, a person who entered a room was supposed to say, "You've got it pretty good here," but the girl didn't know that, so Hennie smiled and replied, "Thanks for the compliment." She shut the door, and the house was so thick and tight that the two women barely heard the rumbling of the dredge.

In the center of the room was a frame with a quilt laid on it, and Nit went over to peer at the quilt top. The design was Bear Paw, and Nit studied it for the square that Hennie had worked on at the Spindle place. The girl had a good eye for fabrics, but Hennie had pieced the blocks from so many different materials that Nit was bewildered. She spread her fingers over the quilt top, touching the corners where the pieces fit together perfectly, rubbing her index finger over the quilting stitches, which were as tiny as if they'd been taken on a sewing machine. A kitchen chair sat askew beside the frame, where the old woman had been working just that morning.

"If you live by yourself, you can set up a frame and work on it till your heart's content. A standing frame's better than one hung from the ceiling, for it's always here, ready for my hands," Hennie explained. "This frame's the one Billy made for me in White Pigeon seventy years ago, and I've never used another. He cut saplings and planed the wood himself, then sanded it down till it was smooth as window glass. Here you can see where he used a hot poker to make the holes because he didn't have an auger." Hennie lovingly swept the back of her hand along a row of holes that were still charred black. The frame itself had been polished to a patina by the woman's hands.

Hennie thought how like her daughter Mae it was to understand what the frame meant to her and to provide a place

for it in the house in Fort Madison when the old woman
moved there. But Lordy, what would Hennie do with the
quilts she made? Mae wasn't partial to quilts. Besides, Hennie wanted to do more with her last days than piece quilts
nobody wanted, looking out at a river that was as slow as a
fishing worm. She'd move to Fort Madison if she had to, but
she wasn't ready to say "deep enough" to life. "Deep enough"
was what the miners said when they quit a mine.

The old woman pulled herself out of her reverie and said
to Nit, "Billy told me he wanted a worthy frame, because
quilting was pious work and pleasing to God. I myself couldn't
have said it better."

"Oh my!" Nit clapped her hands together at the thought.
"It's a lovely quilt," she added, making Hennie wonder if she
should present it to the girl. A person couldn't have too
many quilts in Middle Swan.

But maybe she should wait until she finished a nicer quilt.
This one wasn't much better than a scrap quilt, made up of
fabrics Hennie'd had for a long time. "A quilt's like the family Bible. It's got everybody's mark in it, memories of everybody's lives. There's pieces from my old dress that I wore when
I came to Middle Swan and another from a shirt I found
hanging on a tree in Poverty Gulch, just outside the Terrible
Mine, which hasn't been worked in fifty years. I never knew
how that shirt got there. I let it hang all summer before I decided nobody was coming for it and I took it." She ran her
hand over the quilt top and stopped at a white cotton scrap
with a design of tiny black feathers and tapped her thimbled
ring finger on it. "Mrs. Sabra—she was the dressmaker in
Middle Swan—gave me this one. It's left over from a shirt-

waist she made for Bijou, who worked…" Hennie stopped, for she didn't know how the girl felt about hookers. "For a lady long ago. I guess every scrap has its story. But you're a quilter. You know that."

Nit pointed to a piece that had a luminescent quality, the blue the color of a peacock's feather. "What's this from?"

Hennie laughed. "Why, it's from the Pinto store. I saw that material there fifty years ago, and I had to have a piece of it. I never saw anything that color outside of a book. It was dear-bought. I didn't want anyone else to have it, so I took it all, the whole bolt, cost me five dollars. Then I was so ashamed of myself for being greedy that I gave pieces of it to one and all. You see a piece of that blue in a Middle Swan quilt, and you know it came from me. That blue's been in every one of my quilts, too. Still, I'm mighty saving of it and don't give that material to just anybody these days." She paused and added, hoping to let the girl know that she was esteemed by the old woman, "But you might have a piece, if you like."

"Oh," Nit said, sensible of the honor.

Hennie opened her pie safe and rummaged around in it until she found the blue and tore off a strip. She handed it to the girl, who ran it across the palm of one hand, ironing it with the fingers of her other hand. "I'll save it till I'm good enough to use it. I'm getting better with my quilting, you know. Dick says when I set my mind to a thing, I do it. He's the same way. That's why we get along." Nit studied the fabric. "We went out to ourself the day we got married so's we could make something of us. If we'd stayed with our home-folks, we'd have turned out just like them." Nit thought over what she'd said and added, "I mean, I love them, but they're easy to satisfy." The girl put the blue fabric into her pocket. "Like I say, I'll keep it for a good quilt."

Hennie waved her hand and told Nit to use it now. What was the use of saving it? she asked. Besides, Nit was already a fine quilter, Hennie added. The girl wasn't, but the quickest way to insult a woman was to criticize her quilts. "Would you welcome coffee?" Without waiting for an answer, for Hennie'd never known anyone who wouldn't welcome coffee, she said, "Now, just you sit, and we'll have us some with our cookies. If I take hotcakes for supper, then I got the right to eat snickerdoodles for breakfast." She hurried into the kitchen part of the room and fed chunks of wood into the cookstove, then went to the sink and turned on the faucet, filling the teakettle with water.

"Just think, running water," Nit said. Hennie felt a tenderness toward the girl, for hauling water was hard work. Maybe that young fellow Nit was married to hauled it for her. He surely did seem to dote on his wife. The two reminded her of Billy and herself.

Hennie laughed and explained that she had to wrap the pipe with strips torn from old quilts and keep the water turned on a little in the cold months so that it didn't freeze up, and even then, in January and February and March, the water wasn't reliable. "Still, I live nice," Hennie said, sighing. She chattered as the water boiled and she poured it over the grounds in a brown and white speckled pot. Then she transferred the brew into a silver coffee server that was only a little battered and took down her own good cups and saucers. She placed everything on the table with the pie plate of cookies. Hennie went to her cupboard for a clear-glass spooner shaped like a log cabin and told Nit there was sugar in the bowl beside the condiments caddy in the center of the table.

The two sat and chatted about the weather while the sun crept through the big windows, spreading its warmth across the floor. She did have it nice there, snug as a harbornated bear, Hennie thought with contentment. Few people got to live in such a nice house for going on seventy years. She hoped Nit had such a fine house one day. Maybe she would, since Dick Spindle was a worker. So was Nit. That was something else the two had in common with Hennie and Billy.

The old woman picked up her cup, knocking her thimble against it, and laughed. "You'd think I'd remember to take this off, but Billy gave it to me for a present, and it fits me like a wedding ring. I have a dozen thimbles, but I've used the same one since I came here. I guess I must have pushed about a million stitches through the fabric with it."

"Didn't your other husband ever give you one?"

"Why no," Hennie said, thinking that no, Jake Comfort had not been sensible of her quilting the way Billy was. She didn't often compare the two men, but now she thought how the husbands had complemented each other, one weak in a way the other was strong. If Jake didn't pay attention to the quilts, he was proud of her gardening, how she grew the biggest and longest-lasting roses in Middle Swan and was the first in the spring to pick her lettuce and spinach. Billy took care of her as if she were a little girl, which, come to think of it, she had been when they were married. Jake encouraged her to be self-reliant. Her first husband was as sunny as the day, while dark spells like a winter storm came on her second. But both had loved her fiercely, and she'd loved them right back.

They finished their coffee, and Hennie stood up. So did the girl, picking up her cup and saucer to carry them to the sink. "Leave be. We'll go to quilting," Hennie said. "Grab you a needle, and go to work."

Nit carried a straight-backed chair to the frame, and the two women sat down beside each other at the quilt. The girl took out a needle stuck in a piece of flannel tied to the end of the frame and threaded it. Then she chose a thimble from a cup on the table. "You sure you want me to do this, Mrs. Comfort? My stitches aren't as fine as yours. They are every one too big."

Hennie waved away the objection, although she knew she might take out Nit's work later. Nobody else would notice the girl's big stitches, but Hennie would know that they were there, and she was too proud to let her quilts be anything but near-perfect. Not for anything would she tell her guest not to quilt, however. Why, she wouldn't insult even Mrs. Franks that way, Hennie thought, glad that Mrs. Franks didn't sew.

The two quilted quietly for a few moments, Hennie thinking how nice it was that women gathered over a quilt frame for companionship and gossip, but they could be content with the silence, too. After a few minutes, Hennie got up and opened the door, letting in the sunlight and the fresh air, the sound of the dredge—and a lazy winter fly that buzzed around the room. The winter had been hard on all God's creatures, and Hennie didn't have the heart to swat the insect, although she would be ruthless with his brethren come summer. The fly flew back out the door.

"This is as nice a place as I ever saw," Nit said after a while.

"I'm lucky in my choice of a home, that's for sure."

Nit stopped stitching, her hand over the quilt, thinking. Then she asked, "How was it you came here, to this house? I'd like to know that. How was it, Mrs. Comfort?"

The question brought a warm feeling to Hennie. "My husband built it for me. I said I wanted a house tight enough to keep out the wind in winter, with room for my quilt frame, a bedroom upstairs with a window that opened so that there would be nothing between me and the stars, and front windows big enough so my geraniums could sun theirself all year long. And that's just what I got. From the day I set foot inside, I never wanted to live anyplace else. In God's own time, I expect I'll die here."

She said that last bit before she thought, *No, God's time has passed,* and she would die elsewhere. But Hennie didn't correct herself for she'd told no one yet of her decision to leave Middle Swan. She wasn't ready to hear her friends cluck over her good fortune in having a daughter with a mansion who wanted her mother to live with her. Nor did she want folks knocking on the door, asking could they rent the old place from her, maybe buy it. Jake had built the house for her, and Hennie couldn't bear the thought of anyone else living in the place she loved so.

"It's been a happy house then?"

Hennie considered the question. The house had seen its sorrows, but like Hennie herself, it had endured. And it had let her survive the long winters when the snow drifted above the windowsills and the sun was too weak to come more than a foot through the window glass. During that time, the cold never left her old fingers and toes, and the blue devils came, enough to nearly drive her out of her mind. But then she would go to quilting, cutting and stitching the pieces together like a crazy woman to fight off the dark memories, the murder of her baby and the loss of others not yet fully made, as well as the deaths of old friends, the men mutilated in mine accidents, the women dead in childbirth. A mining camp was a cruel place, Hennie thought, for she had seen the way the mountains took their revenge on those bold enough to tear up the land.

The bright scraps of color that Hennie's fingers fit into patterns never failed to cheer her, lifting her spirits, letting her know that spring would begin and then the precious summer. Summers and quilting, they were gifts from God. There had been grievements and back-sets, but yes, she said, "I've been happy in this house—more often than not."

The girl took two stitches, using her thimble to push the needle back and forth through the fabric sandwich of quilt top, batting, and back. "What've you got here for your batten?" she asked.

Cotton batts, ordered out of the monkey book, Hennie told her.

"Cotton. That's like quilting through butter." Nit sighed with pleasure. "At home, we used old quilts or wore-out dresses, sometimes overalls. My, but you can't get your needle through overalls," she said. Sometimes she gathered milkweed for filler, and once, oilcloth. Of course, those fillings were for plain quilts. With her quilts for good, Nit picked the cotton herself, dug out the seeds, combed it, and laid it on. "Cotton makes a good soft quilt. Warmth was mostly what I cared about. We had to use three or nine quilts on top of us to keep warm in that dogtrot I was raised up in. You remember dogtrots, don't you?" She lifted her eyes to the old woman, who nodded. Two rooms, one on each side of a hall that was open to the outside at both ends so that any dog that took a notion could run through it. Dogtrots were raised three or four feet off the ground, so they were nice and cool in summer, but in winter with the open breezeway and the air coming up from under the floorboards, you couldn't ever keep warm in a dogtrot.

Hennie shook her head at the memory of those old cabins from her girlhood, colder in winter than anything she'd ever known in a Colorado blizzard. "It's a wet cold there. You couldn't hardly get warm if you sat on a cookstove."

"I'd have froze if it wasn't for sleeping in a bed with my four sisters—five red-haired girls in a bed. We were rightly as close as twins. My sisters didn't know what to do with theirself after I married Dick and moved off to the other end of Kentucky," Nit said. "The day I got married was the first time in my life that I ever slept in a bed with just one other person. I was afraid I'd get lost. I miss my sisters, but I have a powerful love for Dick, and like I said, we went out to ourself so we could move up in the world. But I never thought we'd leave Kentucky. Then Dick got the job on the dredge, and you know what the Bible says about a woman cleaving to her husband. So I followed him to Middle Swan." The girl paused and looked at Hennie, who was bent over her stitching, listening and nodding her head. "Now, don't think I'm too forward, Mrs. Comfort, but I'd like to know how was it you came to Middle Swan? Excuse it if I'm too forward."

"Not too forward, not at all. It's likely my favorite story." Hennie stuck the tip of her needle into the fabric and wiggled her fingers to get the kinks out of them. She wondered how it was that the rheumatism crippled them so much that she could barely grasp a rake and had to use both hands to lift a heavy pan off the stove, but it didn't affect her quilting. Don't think too closely, she told herself, just be grateful. When it's raining pudding, hold up your bowl.

The girl, too, lifted her pretty head from her sewing. Her needle hand was poised above the quilt, as she watched Hennie.

"Won't you be tired of hearing me talk?" Hennie asked.

"Oh no, ma'am. You remind me of home. Your talk is pleasing to me."

Hennie told herself she was an old fool to ask the girl the way she had, just to get her to tease for a story. What if Nit decided she was indeed tired of the old woman's ramblings, that she asked only to be polite? But Hennie had a feeling the girl did indeed like her stories, that she would mingle them with her own and tell them long after Hennie was gone. Stories were a living thing. They changed to suit the teller or the times. Hennie liked the idea that a part of her would remain behind in the stories after she moved to Fort Madison.

The old woman picked up her needle. The thread was almost used up, so she took a back stitch, then worked the

thread under the quilt top and snipped off the end. She cut
a new length and licked its end, then with the aid of a mag-
nifying glass that was wired to the end of the quilt frame, she
threaded the needle. "Remember, I was still Ila Mae back
then," she began.

The seasons following the war were harder than the war itself. After the peace came in 1865, Ila Mae worked her fields
alone, not minding the hard labor because it exhausted her
and she could sleep without thinking about Billy and Sarah—
especially Sarah. Billy at least had had a little chance at life,
but not the baby. Ila Mae wasn't able to bring herself to walk
by the place at the creek where the little girl had drowned,
not only because her child had died there but because Ila
Mae was a little afraid she might seek the same fate—
although how a grown-up girl could drown herself in that little bit of water, she didn't know. Still, there were days when
Ila Mae didn't understand why she bothered to live. She'd
lost everyone she loved, and she was tempted to join them.
But she didn't, because she knew that Billy would want her
to keep on living.

The war had been difficult enough, what with men gone
and shortages and the home guard riding in and taking what
it wanted. But things only got worse once the fighting was
over and done with. Men came through the woods then, desperate men who stole Ila Mae's corn and ate it green, took
clothes off the line, or came up to the door, demanding a
handout. Some of the soldiers were starved and anxious to
get on home, and she didn't mind sharing what she had with

them, thinking maybe some woman somewhere had divided her supper with Billy. But other men frightened her. Their eyes glittered, and she saw madness in them. More than one looked at her in such a hungry way that Ila Mae rushed into the house, latched the door, and took down the shotgun. She always carried a knife in the pocket of her apron, and she knew she could use it, especially if Abram or any of his fellows came around. Abram himself had left out after the town turned against him, disappeared someplace, but Ila Mae didn't know but what he might sneak back, so she still carried the knife.

Ila Mae thought she would live on that farm forever, alone, for what choice had she? Where could she go? She didn't know anyplace but Tennessee. Most of the boys she'd grown up with had gone to war and hadn't come back. Two or three of the men in town came around and looked her up and so forth, talking sweet, saying they'd always admired her and that she needed a man to protect her. But Ila Mae knew that she needed protection from them, for it was the $500 that Barton Fletcher had been forced to pay her that they were after. She didn't fancy a fortune hunter who'd expect her to cook and clean, plow and plant and harvest for him, while he loafed in town, spending her money.

So that first winter after the war, she made the harvest by herself and filled her root cellar with vegetables and her pie safe with bags of dried apples and wild cherries. And she chopped enough wood to see her through the winter. Sometimes she gathered for quiltings with the other war widows, but not often, because they all were that close to starvation to spend time on fancywork. Those who made quilts didn't use good fabric but cut up worn blankets and Confederate uniforms and pieced tack quilts. There wasn't time for real quilting.

Ila Mae survived the winter, but with spring came a sadness so great that sometimes she wasn't able to get out of bed in the mornings. She saw the endless years stretching out ahead of her, the days all the same, herself alone. When she heard birdsong, Ila Mae remembered Billy singing as he went about his work, and when she saw dogwood flowers looking as if they were floating in the dark woods, she remembered the blessed morning Sarah was born.

The weight of what she had lost pressed on her heart. She couldn't stand to know she'd never have a boy put his arms around her and tell her she was as pretty as a May morning or hold her hand as they walked across their fields in the moonlight. There'd be no baby to play under the quilt frame, no boys she would teach to read, no daughter whose hair she'd braid with wild daisies.

As the weather grew warm, Ila Mae went often to the place where Sarah was buried. She sat by the little grave as the sun made its way from one half of the sky to the other, not caring that there was planting or hoeing to be done. She paid a man two of her dollars to carve the baby's name on a tombstone and place it at the head of Sarah's grave. She'd have paid for a marker for Billy, too, but she never knew where he was buried.

When she wasn't in the fields or the family cemetery, Ila Mae walked—across the fields, through the woods, along the Buttermilk Road, wherever her feet took her. She was in the biggest kind of grief. Other women had it worse, them with no land and no money, along with no man. But because they were hers, Ila Mae's troubles seemed hardest to bear.

One morning, after she came in from planting violets around Sarah's stone, Ila Mae found a neighbor waiting. He'd been to the post office and brought her a letter that had been sitting there for a week or a month, he didn't really know. Ila Mae never went for the mail, for anyone who would have written to her was dead, so she couldn't imagine who had sent the letter.

"You go over a sight of ground in your perishinations. I feared to leave this in the house where somebody might appropriate it. They steal such as you'll never know," the neighbor had said. "I'll be bound to say, I wish you had a man like Billy to help you, for farming turns a woman old."

So does war, Ila Mae thought, but didn't say so, for she was not the only woman worn out by the past few years. She put the letter aside and drew water from the well and offered the man the dipper. Then they sat under a tree, talking about crops and the weather, little things, the way husbands and wives did. After he left, Ila Mae was more troubled than ever, for it was comfortable being with a man. It was always the little things—the talk of whether rain would come and how pretty the apple blossoms were that year—that brought home to her that she was alone. She remembered how Billy always picked the first apple blossoms and put them into a tin cup for her. They made the house smell like springtime. Billy said apple trees were a double blessing, first for the blossoms and then for the apples.

After the neighbor left, Ila Mae only stared at the letter, not opening it. Her days were so much the same that a piece of mail was an exciting event, and she wanted to savor it, to wonder who'd written the letter and why. She waited all day and until after she ate her supper and put away the dishes. It was dark then, and Ila Mae laughed to think she'd waited so long that there was no daylight to read by.

She went to the little hanging candle cupboard that Billy had presented to her after Sarah was born. It was crude, with a single drawer and, above it, a shelf covered by a slanted flap on which Billy had carved stars and the year of Sarah's birth—1864. Ila Mae kept her money in the drawer, under a rat trap, thinking no one would believe she had hidden the coins beneath such. Under the flap she stored her few candles, safe from mice. She hadn't lit one since Billy went off to war, but why was she saving them? A letter was as special an occasion as she was bound to have. So Ila Mae removed one of the tapers, lit it with an ember from the fireplace, and placed it in a tin holder on the table, where it sent out a pale circle of golden light.

She held the envelope for a moment, frowning at the writing, which was even, the capital letters a series of flourishes that seemed familiar, a little like her own. Using the knife she kept in her apron pocket, she slit the envelope. As she removed the sheet of paper, a tintype fell out. Ila Mae studied the picture of a woman and two men, and then she knew who had sent the missive. She propped the picture against the candlestick and smiled at her friend Martha Merritt. The two had gone to school together, until Martha's father, a Northern sympathizer, moved his family to Pennsylvania, for the home guard had made things too hot for those not in favor of the Confederacy.

Martha's likeness, in a paper frame marked "W. G. Chaimberlain, photographist, Denver," showed a woman much older than Ila Mae's childhood playmate, but she was Martha nonetheless, and she sat between two men. Perhaps one of them was Martha's husband. Hennie put the letter on the table, smoothing the fold lines so that the paper lay flat. Then she began to read out loud, so that she could linger over every word:

Dearest Friend Ila Mae

I hope this finds you in good health. We have got through the war fine. I am sorry to hear from a mutual friend that Billy was killed and also your daughter, and I offer sincere sympathy. I married a Yankee soldier, and we have moved to Colorado Territory to make our fortune in gold mining. Enclosed is a picture of my husband, Charles Grove by name. He is on the right. You can see he is as handsome as a peddler and as good a man as ever lived.

The other is Jacob Comfort, Mr. Grove's pard in the war, and he is the reason I write after so long a silence. I showed Mr. Comfort your likeness, taken when we were girls at school, and told him you are cheerful and not afraid of hard work, can write and cipher (also that you have chestnut brown hair and blue eyes, although you are tall.) Now, here is the truth of it: Colorado Territory has many men and few women; Tennessee has too many widows. Do you not see a common solution to both problems? The widows of Tennessee ought to move to this place?

I said as much to Mr. Comfort, who considered the situation and said if you are willing, he would like to correspond

with you. But, says I, it will take months for letters to go back
and forth, and between them, Ila Mae might decide to marry
with someone else, if she hasn't already. Why do I not write
her and invite her to come to Colorado Territory? Mr. Com-
fort is so taken with the idea that he proposes to pay your way,
and if you don't care for him upon meeting him, the money is
of no consequence, since he will throw himself off a moun-
taintop. He is a good man, Ila Mae, as kind as his name,
clean and industrious, not like many who inhabit the camp—
Middle Swan, by name. I would fancy him myself were I not
already married to Mr. Grove, who is my true love.

I believe it would be a good thing for you to come here to
the Swan River and see for yourself what the opportunities
are. If you do not care for Mr. Comfort, you will find others
who would be pleased to make your acquaintance, men of
good character, not just old bachelors. If one of them does not
suit you, why, there are other opportunities for a woman.
And I, of course, would be pleased to see again my oldest
childhood friend, for I miss those happy days when we sat
and sewed together. They live in memory only, and they will
never return. Please respond at your earliest convenience.
Your affectionate old playmate awaits your reply.

Martha Merritt Grove

P.S. Mr. Comfort says he would send you a separate like-
ness of himself, but he believes it would be a waste of money.
Says he, if you like, he will send you a lock of his hair to poison
the rats with. You see, he has a sense of humor like your own,
not such a bad thing in a marriage, I have discovered.

MMG

March 11, 1866

Ila Mae reread the letter before she set it aside to study the tintype. Martha's husband was indeed a well-made man—tall, for he loomed over Martha, with dark, curly hair and such a pleasing countenance that her friend must have fallen in love at first sight. But Mr. Comfort was the one who interested Ila Mae. He had a plain but open face, his eyes set a little too close together, but they were intense. And he had a firm mouth that suggested resolve. His hair was thin, and Ila Mae chuckled to think that the man had offered to send her a precious lock of it. She was not able to gauge his height, for the three subjects in the tintype were seated, but he appeared to be shorter than Mr. Grove. Ila Mae, who was indeed tall, did not care to look down at her husband. Nor could she tell his complexion, for the tintype was dark, and the cheeks of the subjects had been tinted pink. But she liked the look of Mr. Comfort's hands—stubby but thick, hands made for work. He was not a man to sweep her away, but he appeared to be a solid man. Ila Mae had been swept away by Billy, and that could last her for a lifetime. A solid man would suit her.

The idea of traveling all the way to Colorado with the hope of matrimony struck her as foolish. But it amused her, too, and as she folded the letter and returned it to its envelope, Ila Mae smiled, grateful to Martha for a few minutes of pleasure. She would write tomorrow, refusing her friend's offer.

Ila Mae did not sleep well that night. She awakened several times to remember the letter and the likeness of Mr. Comfort. As she lay in the dark, the possibility of her moving to far-off Colorado seemed remote, and she would tell

Martha so. But when she awakened in the morning after a few hours' sleep, she believed that leaving Tennessee was a wise course. Why should she stay? She had no family, and before too many years passed, she would wear herself out with the heavy farmwork. There was Sarah's grave, but it was a place of death. It was in Ila Mae's heart that Sarah lived. And Billy, too. Billy had told her once that if anything ever happened to her, he wouldn't want to live where he was reminded of her every day. Remembering that, she felt that Billy was telling her it was all right to move on.

Ila Mae thought about Colorado all that day. And the next. She didn't reply to Martha's letter for a week, and when she did, Ila Mae told her friend that she was willing to give Colorado Territory a try.

She wouldn't take Mr. Comfort's money, however. Ila Mae was determined to pay her own way, so that she would not be beholden to anyone. She would look him over and decide for herself—and appraise the other men in the camp, as well. And if none of them suited her, she would find a way to make a living on her own. Surely there was a need for a woman who could cook and launder, sew and quilt and even make bonnets. Did women hunt for gold? Perhaps she, too, would find a gold mine. Before Martha's letter had arrived, Ila Mae believed she would spend the rest of her life as a caretaker of the past. But now she saw a future, one with a husband and maybe children. Besides, a move to Colorado would be an adventure. Ila Mae had not realized until then how predictable, how ordinary her life had become.

As soon as Martha's response to Ila Mae's reply arrived, asking how soon she could leave, Ila Mae sold her farm to a neighbor and made arrangements to go west with a group of gold seekers. Many in the South were heading for the gold fields to make a new start, so finding a wagon train to join was not difficult. Ila Mae agreed to travel with a man taking a sickly wife and two small boys to Colorado, sharing their wagon and victuals in exchange for cooking and tending the children. Because there was little room in the wagon, the man grumbled when Ila Mae insisted she be allowed to take more than her trunk. But she threatened to outfit her own wagon rather than leave behind her tender possessions—the Friendship quilt her friends presented to her just before she left, each one of them working a Churn Dash block and signing it, and the quilt frame and candle cupboard, both made by Billy.

The family she traveled with left her in Denver, where Ila Mae found a freighter leaving for the Swan River. He was a large man, who needed the wagon bench for himself, but he said he would take Ila Mae along if she and her accumulations could find a place among the freight.

Ila Mae arrived in Middle Swan in a chill rain, wrapped in the Friendship quilt and huddled on top of a mountain of provisions. The camp did not impress her. It was raw new, the log buildings thrown up like jackstraws along a mud trail, and not a one of them was painted. Neither flowers nor grass softened the houses, and there were no trees, only stumps where the pines had been cut down for firewood or building material. She wondered if flowers grew in that high, cold place, for she could not imagine living without them.

She had never heard so much noise. Freighters yelled as they flicked their whips at burros blocking the trail, and the

burros protested in their honking bray. The thud of axes
and scraping of saws swept down the mountainsides, along
with the clatter of waste rock as it was dumped into yellow
piles that spilled out of mine openings high above town. The
miners added to the frenzy, yelling instead of speaking. The
sounds of fiddles and singing came from three saloons
housed in the finest buildings in the town. The excitement
was different from the calm, lazy ways of White Pigeon, and
Ila Mae was swept up in it.

As luck would have it, Martha was standing in front of
the assay office, her husband and Mr. Comfort in tow, just as
Ila Mae's freight wagon came to a stop. They had come each
day for a week, hoping to be there when Ila Mae arrived.
When Martha saw her friend, she whooped and rushed to
her, skirts dragging in the mud.

Ila Mae glanced past Martha at the two men, and she saw
right away that Mr. Grove was indeed a handsome-made
man. And Mr. Comfort had a pleasing look. He was not
quite as tall as Ila Mae, but he was shaven and wore clean
clothes. She was suitably impressed—more than Mr. Comfort must be with her, Ila Mae thought, considering her
bedraggled appearance. She was vain enough to wish she
could have washed her face and dried her clothes before
meeting him.

Martha didn't wait for Ila Mae to get out of the wagon
but climbed in beside her and hugged and kissed her. Then
after the men helped them out of the wagon, Martha took
hold of her senses and said, "And this is my dear husband."

Ila Mae smiled and tried to curtsy, but her wet skirts
nearly pulled her down. So did her surprise, for the shorter

of the two men stepped forward and took her hand. In the name of peace, she didn't know how she could have been more confused. Martha had told Ila Mae that her husband was the man on the right in the tintype, but she must have meant *Martha's* right.

"*You're* Mr. Comfort?" she asked the handsome man, who stepped forward and bowed a little, taking her hand. His eyes were merry with amusement, for he understood at once that Ila Mae had expected him to be the short Mr. Grove.

He looked her up and down, taking in her miserable state, and said, "And you are a little wet hen. Welcome to Middle Swan, Hennie."

The name made her smile. It was a new name for her new life. And so she buried Ila Mae, and at that moment, Hennie determined to marry Mr. Comfort if he would have her. She had hoped for a good man, a solid man, but she'd never expected one who would make her laugh. Or would make her tingle with wanting the way she had when she first glimpsed him. Perhaps he would even be a man she could love.

There was no courting, no walking to church. Jake showed Hennie his cabin, and she remarked on the orderliness of it. He told her he wasn't a rich man and wasn't likely to be, because he didn't believe he had the luck for it. But he'd work hard, he promised. She didn't need to worry about that. And he'd do the best he could to take care of her.

Still, Jake Comfort was a complicated man, and in those few days they allowed themselves to know each other, Hennie learned that he had a dark side. He was too fond of whiskey, and he had memories of the war that haunted him, made him jump when he heard a loud noise. He said he didn't sleep well.

"My first husband was a Confederate," Hennie told him.

"Martha said as much. I enlisted for the Union. What are your sentiments?"

"I never wanted the war. I didn't care who won. I just wanted it to end."

Jake nodded, satisfied with the answer. "War's a terrible thing. I don't intend to ever fight again." His eyes glinted, and he turned away, pounding his fists into a jackpine. Hennie had seen soldiers in White Pigeon who struggled with things in their heads, and she stood quietly, waiting, until the darkness lifted from Jake. "I'll not inflict my war on you," he said.

"Mr. Comfort, I would not want a husband who closed himself off to me."

"War's not something to be shared."

"War's griefs are."

"I said I'll keep my demons to myself," Jake told her harshly, and Hennie said no more. She knew when a subject was closed.

A day later, he warned Hennie, "A mining camp's a hard place for a woman."

"I've come from a hard place for a woman," Hennie responded. "At least, in a mining camp there's hope." She loved that about Middle Swan—the hope as well as the excitement, the belief that with the strike of a pick, a person might find a fortune. What she liked best about a mining camp was that it had no past.

"I come with encumberments," Hennie told Jake, for she

had picked up what the wagonmaster called a stray on the trail west. Jake would be taking on more than just a wife. But Jake replied that he would take Hennie even if she'd come with a wagonload of children, chickens, and dogs.

Less than a week after they met, Jake took her into a grove of aspen trees and got down on one knee, taking her hand. "Hennie, it would please me more than a diamond ring if you would marry me."

Hennie was so happy she didn't know anything. They were wed that afternoon, Martha and her husband standing up with them. Hennie's wasn't always an easy marriage, and she wondered more than once if she should have insisted the time they talked about war that Jake share his memories with her, because they haunted him until the day he died. Hennie believed she might have helped him if she'd understood his terrors. Still, it was a fine marriage, as good a marriage as ever was, and Hennie never regretted coming to Colorado. She'd been given a second chance at life, and she thanked Jake for it—and Billy, too, because Hennie always believed that Billy had showed her the way.

❦

Nit clapped her hands together and said she'd never heard anything so romantic, even on the radio. "Your stories comfort me," she said. She finished off her thread and cut it with Hennie's scissors, then looked through the window at the sun high in the sky and remarked, "I better get gone." She paused a moment before she stood up, her brow furrowed in concentration. "I wanted to ask you something else." Nit bent her head over the quilt, and Hennie couldn't see the girl's face, only her shining red hair. "How come you to have that sign about selling prayers if you don't sell them?"

Hennie chuckled. "That's another story, but it's a short one, and I'll tell it. Jake and I had been married three or four years when I told him I was so happy that I had nothing else to pray for. 'Why,' says I, 'I've got prayers to sell.' He was so tickled by what I said that he made the sign for me and nailed it to the fence. It was a joke, but every now and then somebody like you comes along asking for prayers, and like I told you, no money will buy them, but I'm happy to say them for free. I've never lost anything by giving it away." Hennie secured her needle in the quilt, then stood and helped Nit with her coat, walking her to the door. "I've got an abundance of prayers."

"Do you say them in church?" Nit asked.

Hennie studied her a minute. "I say them wherever I am. I'm not well acquainted with the church in Middle Swan anymore. I have not stepped foot inside for some time."

The old woman thought Nit was going to ask the reason for that, because the girl looked at her, pausing in the doorway and staring intently at Hennie. But Nit seemed to have a sense about things, and instead, she asked, "Do they work? I mean to say, does the Lord answer your prayers?"

Hennie shrugged. "The Lord takes His time, more than He ought to if you ask me, but He answers most of them."

The old woman watched as the girl went through the gate and disappeared down the trail. "You answer my prayers for other folks, but You're not always so quick on mine," Hennie muttered, looking heavenward. The Almighty hadn't kept Billy or Jake safe. And there was Sarah's death that troubled her yet. Now she had the quandary about moving away from Middle Swan, and of course, there was that other business that had gone on so long and left the pricker on her heart. She'd have to deal with that before she left Middle Swan, for it had to be settled. She didn't want it to vex her in Fort Madison. No, not all of Hennie's prayers had been answered.

Chapter 3

Hennie Comfort smiled to herself at the orderliness of
the Pinto All-Cash General Store & Mining Supply.
That Roy Pinto was as persnickety as a woman. Everything
was in its place behind the U-shaped counter, and the places
hadn't changed since Theodore Roosevelt was president.
The first time.

Hennie herself couldn't abide disorder; she knew the instant she stepped foot in Jake Comfort's cabin seventy years
before and saw the covers pulled tight across the bed and
the plate and cup and frying pan washed and stacked neatly
on the table that the two of them would get along. Of course,
she'd have married Jake if he'd been a messy old batch, but it
was extra nice that he was as tidy as she was.

So Hennie looked with some satisfaction on the rows of tin
cans lined up on the shelves of the grocery side of the store,

the pictures of the tomatoes and peaches and the little cows on the milk cans all facing forward. Bags of sugar and flour were stacked on the nearby shelves. Another shelf held the tin bins of spices and sultanas. The lettering identified them as sultanas yet, but most everybody called them raisins now, and they no longer had to be stoned. The black tins were once painted with scenes of castles and mountains, but the containers had been used for so long that the pictures were nearly scratched off. Hennie remembered when they were new, back when Roy's father operated the general store.

She ran her eye past the shelves of foodstuffs and along the back of the room where the picks and gold pans and other prospecting supplies were kept, then continued along the hardware side, past the saws, the hammers, and the axes, the stacks of overalls and jumpers, work shirts, heavy caps, and gloves, to the housewares section, with its heavy white crockery and blue-and-white speckled pie tins, string mops and player piano rolls. Skillets and black iron kettles and red-handled egg beaters hung from the ceiling.

Hennie stopped as she always did to study the bolts of cloth, stacked by color, like a rainbow. She could tell without asking that Roy Pinto hadn't ordered in any new blues. Then she glanced past the signs advertising Royal Gelatin dessert and Chase and Sanborn coffee, Ipana toothpaste and Tender Leaf tea, to the boxes of doughnuts and sacks of light bread lying on the counter next to the big glass candy containers. Their rounded glass ends stuck out toward the room to display the candy; the openings faced behind the counter. The lids were on springs so that tiny hands couldn't slip into the jar and snag the strings of rock candy, clear and faceted as quartz, or the licorice babies, hard as drill bits.

Hennie turned to the oil stove that glowed red in the middle of the room. Chairs were gathered around it, but they were empty. The miners of the Warm Stove Mine and Hot Air Smelter had gone home to dinner. They'd been there earlier. Hennie could tell from the dirty coffee mugs, the wet floor around the spittoon, and the apple peelings, still yellow, in the kindling box. The leather bellies liked to spit and jaw and eat the wrinkled apples that Roy Pinto kept in a barrel in front of the counter.

There were fewer of the leather bellies now. Most of the folks she'd known in her early days on the Swan were gone, and come winter, she would be among them. But she would savor every day left to her, and she told Mae that she wouldn't leave until the end of the year; to Hennie that meant the very last day of the year, December 31.

The moving couldn't be helped, the old woman thought with a sigh, because Mae wasn't the only one who worried about her. There were the members of the Tenmile Quilters, who visited her house in winter storms, pretending they'd come on errands, when they really were there checking to see whether Hennie was all right, if she'd fallen or suffered a stroke. Although she wasn't ready just yet to cross over, Hennie didn't worry about dying. Even the thought of going to sleep in the cold while the snow covered her like a pure white quilt didn't scare her. But she didn't want to be worrisome to others, and her spending her last days in Middle Swan, she had to admit, would be harder on her friends than on her. She'd never let herself be a burden before, and she wouldn't start now. But oh, she didn't want to go, to live out her days in her daughter's upstairs.

Mae had written that Hennie would have a big, sunny room to herself. There was a place in it for the quilt frame, and Hennie could look out on the hills and the river as she stitched. But the old woman didn't care about small hills and big rivers. She liked her mountains close up and harsh, and streams that rampaged with snowmelt in the spring. And as for quilting, while it was a part of her life, it was not the sum of it, and the old woman did not care to spend every waking hour with a needle and thread. But Hennie had no alternative to living with Mae. She'd asked the Lord for help, but He'd been busy elsewhere and hadn't even given her a hint He remembered her.

Hennie glanced around the Pinto store, wondering how many more times she would see the familiar scene before she left. And although Mae had agreed Hennie could live in Middle Swan in the summers, the old woman wondered if she would ever really return.

Lost in thought as she was, Hennie believed she was alone in the store—except for Roy, of course. He was making a din in the back room, where he kept the pipes and rolls of tin and sheets of corrugated iron. He liked to tinker with them. Then she became sensible of two women standing at the end of the counter near Roy's fetching stick. The gold dredge had been hollering and screaming so when she entered the store that neither of the women had heard her. Hennie peered at them a moment and recognized the girl Nit Spindle, looking as raw new as she had those two times

they had called on each other. The woman with her was
Greta Garbo. Hennie wondered if Nit had any idea she was
talking to Greta Garbo.

"We just moved here, and you're the first girl I've seen that
isn't older than God," Nit said, hugging her coat around her
body, which was as thin as thread. It was warm enough inside
the store, but being from Kentucky, the girl wasn't used to the
cold. She'd have to get a heavier coat if she was to stay the
next winter. "I could die of lonesomeness, might near. A body
doesn't know how to get acquainted in a mining town."

"I'll bet," Greta said, raising an eyebrow and scuffing her
boot along the worn area in the wooden floor. Thousands of
pairs of shoes had created a wear pattern like an outline
along the front of the U-shaped counter.

"There must be a plenty of men, but not many girls in
Middle Swan."

"That's about right." Greta was wearing a little red straw
hat, and she used the flat of her hand to push the veil into
place. Now, why would a woman, even one as fool stupid as
Greta Garbo, wear a hat like that in such weather? Hennie
wondered.

When Nit smiled, Hennie thought again how young the
girl was, especially for one who had married and lost her
firstborn. Hennie knew how she felt, of course, and glanced
toward the ceiling, sending up a reminder to the Lord that
she was willing to be His way of helping Nit. But He'd better hurry up, because she didn't have all that much time.

"I hope you won't think me bold, but I wish you would
come by my house for coffee. I've had but one caller. You'd
be my second," Nit said. "You'll come, won't you?"

Greta put her hand on her hip and sized up Nit. "Are you kidding me, honey, or are you just plain dumb?"

It was time to put a stop to things, for the girl was neither jesting nor stupid but just naïve. So Hennie shuffled into the room in her rubber shoes, and both girls turned to look at her.

"Mrs. Comfort," Nit said, looking pleased at seeing the old woman. She turned to Greta. "Mrs. Comfort's the one I told you about, the one who called on me. I got out my new china teacups and saucers. They're real nice, aren't they, Mrs. Comfort?"

"Nicest I ever saw," Hennie answered.

Before Hennie could say more, Roy Pinto, a sawed-off runt of a man although a decent enough fellow without a little man's cockiness, emerged from the back. "Here now, what's this?" he asked Greta Garbo.

"I come in for my cigarettes. You got my Luckies?" she asked.

"Yeah." He reached under the counter for a package of Lucky Strikes and handed it to Greta and took her money. Greta opened the pack and shook out a Lucky, tapping it on the counter, then fitting it into a black holder decorated with rhinestones. She looked at Roy expectantly, but he frowned and said, "Don't expect me to give you a light, girl. I don't like a woman that smokes. It don't look right. No sir."

Greta sniffed and reached into her purse for a kitchen match, which she struck on top of the stove, and lit the Lucky. She drew the smoke deep into her lungs, then blew it out through her nose. Ignoring Roy Pinto and Hennie, Greta tilted her head at Nit and said, "So long, kid. I'm sure glad

to meet you." She didn't sound as if she were, but Nit didn't
appear to catch the tone.

"I'm proud to make your acquaintance," Nit told her.
"Remember to stop by. It's a log cabin on Nugget Street.
They call it the Tappan place."

Hennie thought that Greta started to say something
smart but stopped herself and replied, "I don't guess I could,
but thank you just the same." She raised her chin a little, and
without a word to the other two, she left the store.

"She knows better than to bother the customers," Roy
Pinto said. "She's downright spiteful. I think it's because she
hasn't had her coffee yet. None of the girls are any good until they've had their coffee."

"Well, who is?" Hennie asked.

"Oh, she didn't bother me. I bothered her." Nit thought
that over. "I mean, I introduced myself to her. Maybe she
didn't like it that I was so forward, but I meant no misrespect.
Or it might be she thought she wouldn't be welcome to smoke
at my place"—Nit glanced at Roy accusingly—"but I don't
mind a person that smokes. She didn't tell me her name."

Hennie and Roy Pinto exchanged glances and Roy
shrugged. "It's Greta. Greta Garbo," he said at last.

"You're fooling me! Ah gee, not the real Greta Garbo?
You're sawing off a whopper! Greta Garbo doesn't live in
Middle Swan."

"I don't suppose," Roy snickered.

"Well, imagine having the same name. Isn't that something?" Nit smiled so brightly at the other two that Hennie
had to smile back. Roy didn't.

"Before that, she took the brag name of Queen Marie. I

don't know why they're all the time changing their names," Roy said sourly. He sucked the end of his mustache into his mouth.

Nit looked confused and turned to Hennie.

"You couldn't leave well enough alone, could you?" Hennie asked Roy, annoyance in her voice. "Now see what you've done?"

Roy studied Nit a moment. "Greta works at the Willows. She's one of Sweetie Purvis's girls."

"I don't know the Willows," Nit told him, even more confused than before.

"There's no sense being dumb about a thing," Roy said roughly, his teeth working the mustache. He'd been looking at Hennie, and now he turned to Nit. "The Willows is a hookhouse. I misdoubt you don't know what the hookhouse is." He rubbed the stubble on his face with his hand.

Hennie interrupted. "It's been my experience you're not so good at explaining things. I came for a nickel's worth of yeast cakes. Roy, you go get me that yeast."

"Have it your way, old lady." As he went along behind the counter to the refrigerator, he said over his shoulder, "I wouldn't want to miss out on a five-cent sale. No sir."

Hennie turned to Nit. "Just you come." Hennie took the girl's arm and led her to one of the chairs beside the stove, then sat down herself, heavily, as if her bones hurt. But everybody's bones hurt in the cold weather when there was no sign the snow would stop. Oh, there had been that false spring, but it hadn't lasted long, and now it was snowing again.

The old woman took off her woolen scarf and folded it, setting it in her lap, then unbuttoned her old coat. As she did so, she wondered when she'd accumulated the coat, maybe fifty years before. Well, it was made of good stuff. It would last another fifty, even if she wouldn't. For a minute, Hennie ruminated about the coat. Jake had bought it for her when the ore assayed high, and promised to buy her a fur coat later on, but the ore was only a pocket, and he'd had to go to work for wages. Every time she saw a rabbit or a fox and thought about the poor thing dead in a cold steel trap, she was glad she'd never gotten the fur. She wasn't soft, but she never saw the sense of a living thing dying such a cruel death just for some woman's vanity. Still, she thought, a fur coat when the wind blew down off the Tenmile Range would feel mighty good. Maybe they made fur coats out of foxes that died of old age.

"The hookhouse," Nit said after she was settled. "You don't mean..." When she looked up at Hennie, the girl was flushed, but whether it was from the heat of the stove or embarrassment, Hennie couldn't tell. "You don't mean a whorehouse?" She pushed her elbows into her sides and looked at her hands.

"I think you understand," Hennie said. She reached into the barrel and took out an apple, but it was mushy-feeling, so she got up and peered into the barrel until she found one with only a few dotty places. She polished it on her scarf and held it out to the girl. "There's nothing to be upset about. I expect there's been a hookhouse in Middle Swan since eighteen and fifty-nine, when the first prospectors came here. It's a fact that when men outnumber good women, if you want to call them that, the other kind comes in. Not that hookers aren't good in their way. I never minded them."

Hennie herself was flustered, and Roy Pinto, watching from behind the counter with the yeast in his stubby hand, appeared to be enjoying the old woman's discomfort. "You tell her good, Hennie."

"Somebody had to tell me. I was as green as a willow shoot when I came to this camp—and Middle Swan wasn't any more than a camp back then—not that it's much more now. When I saw Cockeyed Lil strutting up and down the street in her red stockings, I told Jake I wanted a pair just like them. He had to tell me why I didn't." Hennie blushed a little, remembering that later on, Jake gave her a pair of red stockings to wear for him. "You remember Lil, don't you, Roy?"

The merchant shook his thick head and said that was before his time.

"Lil was a beauty, except for that cast in her eye. She wore yellow, yards and yards of it. Yellow dresses, yellow hats. And she rode a horse astride. Nowadays, women think nothing of that, but back then, riding a horse astride like a man was a scandal. And then there were those stockings. I haven't thought about them in a long time. I'd like a pair right now." Hennie pushed her foot forward and lifted her long skirt a little, showing a flesh-colored cotton stocking.

"And I'd like to drive a Cord Phaeton automobile," Roy told her.

Nit was nibbling at the apple like a little mouse, her head down. "That Greta Garbo must have thought I was a real dope trying to get acquainted with her like I did," she said softly.

"Naw. She was just suspicious. She's not used to talking

with ladies such as yourself," Roy Pinto said with rough kindness. "Don't give it no thought."

"A hookhouse," Nit whispered.

"Well, you have to say it keeps the boys out of the saloons and pool halls." Roy guffawed.

Hennie waved him off, and Roy set the yeast on the counter and walked heavily to the back room, stopping to align a can of peas that was turned sideways. Hennie reached into the barrel for an apple for herself, rubbing at the loose skin before she bit into it. The apple was soft, but they were mostly all soft this far from apple season. She thought for a moment how nice it would be to have an apple tree in her yard, but apple trees didn't grow at ten thousand feet. They grew in Fort Madison, however. She'd remember that when she got to feeling discouraged about the move.

Nit set her apple in her lap. It had little rows of bites around it, like she'd made a bracelet for the apple. "I know about sorry girls. We had them at home, but I never met one before. I reckon they're shameful."

Hennie caught a scent of vanilla and thought the girl had put it behind her ears. She was a clean little thing, and tidy, too. She must be a good wife to Dick Spindle. "Some are, some aren't, just like folks in general," Hennie said. "There's girls that will cozy up to a miner and pick him clean, tough as a boiled owl they are. Even a pack rat will leave you something, but those hookers take the least little thing. Others are just as nice as you please. Most of them are regular women who chose that kind of work—or had it chose for them."

Nit seemed to study Hennie as if she wondered whether

the old woman was trying to put one over on her. "I guess I never thought about it."

"I could tell you about them." The older woman settled into her chair, glad for an audience, for she'd been cooped up at home in the storm for so long that it was a wonder her voice hadn't rusted. Besides, it was cozy by the stove, like sitting on a log in the sun of a summer morning, and she was in no hurry to leave. But she wished she had her piecing. Storytelling was always nicer when she had her quilting to occupy her fingers. She reached into her pocket in hopes she'd put a patch and a needle there and forgotten about them, but she hadn't. Coffee would be nice, too, but there was no sign of the coffeepot that Roy kept on top of the stove. Well, a body couldn't expect him to give out free apples and coffee both, when she'd spent only a nickel on yeast.

Of course, Roy Senior would have made coffee for her. He'd have given her anything in the store if she'd married him, but Hennie was always too particular about men. She wouldn't wed a man, even one as decent as Roy Senior, just for a frame house and a lifetime supply of canned beans. She'd rather be alone with her quilting and her prayers than married to a man she didn't love with all her heart and soul. Besides, being married to Roy Senior would have made her Roy Junior's stepmother—and Monalisa Pinto's mother-in-law. Hennie rolled her eyes at that thought.

The girl leaned forward a little and watched Hennie with glittering eyes, making Hennie wonder why women always seemed to be so crazy to hear about hookers, even when they disapproved of them. Well, Hennie wouldn't disappoint her. Besides, she knew some good stories about the girls, and enough of them to keep her at the stove until lunchtime. She wouldn't have so many more opportunities to tell her stories. "I don't suppose you ever heard of Silver Heels?" she asked.

Nit shook her head, and Hennie settled into her chair. "Silver Heels worked in a dance hall thirty miles over the mountain in Buckskin Joe. She had the face of an angel, and she wore silver slippers to show off her feet, which were as tiny as a Chinaman's wife's. That's why the miners called her by the name of Silver Heels. Some of those girls that worked in the saloons and dance halls were hard-boiled as rocks, but Silver Heels was just a little bit whorish, not enough to hurt."

Silver Heels had worked in Buckskin Joe a year or two when the smallpox came, and the men began dying like fish in mine runoff, Hennie continued. The girls left town so they wouldn't catch it, but Silver Heels stayed to nurse the miners. She cooked for them and washed their faces with cold creek water when they were out of their minds with fever, and she wrote letters to their folks back home after the boys died, claiming she was a minister's wife, and saying they'd died in the bosom of the Lord.

"Oh my," Nit said, but Hennie held up a finger to show she wasn't finished with the story.

"Silver Heels herself caught the pox, and the boys feared for her life, but she came out of it. Her pretty face was gone, however, all poxed up and ruined. So she left out. No one knew where she went. A few years later, a woman wearing a heavy veil showed up at the burial ground to put flowers on the graves of the miners who'd died in the epidemic. You couldn't say for sure who she was, because her face was covered, but the Buckskin miners knew. They said she was Silver Heels, and they named a mountain for that hooker," Hennie finished.

"But you said she was a dance hall girl, not a sorry girl," Nit said.

"One and the same," Hennie told her, getting up to add a few sticks to the fire to take off the chill. She left the stove door open, because a blaze, even one in an old gasoline drum that had been turned into a stove, cheered her. Hennie sat down, moving around a little to get comfortable and thinking Roy Pinto ought to get some decent chairs instead of Monalisa's worn-out kitchen chairs. Then she chuckled to herself as she realized Roy didn't want to make it too comfortable for the leather bellies. Settling down, she said, "Most of the hookhouses in Middle Swan are on the other side of the river, and when a girl turns out, it's said she's gone 'over the Swan.' Now, I'll tell you about them."

⚜⚜⚜

Hennie knew about prostitution before she moved to Middle Swan, of course. As a girl before the war, she'd been warned to stay away from Mrs. Buckle's house in White Pigeon. The house was a frame shanty with the paint worn off, set back in a grove of dark trees. A boy once dared Hennie to run up and knock on Mrs. Buckle's door, and she'd done it, for you had to take a dare. Hennie'd expected Mrs. Buckle to throw a rock at her or, worse, snatch her up and drag her inside for some evil purpose. But nothing happened. Later, when she understood what the house was about, Hennie realized it had been morning when she knocked, and everybody was asleep.

Besides, there was nothing to fear, since Mrs. Buckle and the girls were careful not to offend the women and children of White Pigeon. When they went to town, they spent their time in the dance hall and saloon. Hennie had seen Abram Fletcher come out of a bar with a prostitute, both of them drunk. Watching him with the girl made Hennie feel dirty, for Abram was trying to court her then.

After the war ended, more than one widow of her acquaintance began entertaining, trading an evening for a small coin or a sack of flour, or even a handful of potatoes. Hennie was disdainful and asked, "What will your little ones think?"

"I expect they like to eat," came the reply, and Hennie felt put in her place.

She realized then that morality was for folks with full bellies, and she came to realize that if things had been different, if Sarah had lived and they had been destitute, Hennie herself might have "entertained." She'd have done anything to keep that precious baby from starving. So when she moved to Middle Swan and learned that some of her neighbors were soiled doves, as they were called then, Hennie wasn't shocked, wasn't even surprised.

Women in mining camps weren't much better off than the war widows. If a woman in Middle Swan lost her husband to death or he had taken off, she couldn't do much besides set up a boardinghouse—providing she had a house. Or she might take in washing, rubbing clothes on rocks instead of a scrub board and rinsing them in creek water cold enough to make your hands too numb to feel the cloth. Hennie figured entertaining might be a better line of work than washing clothes.

For the most part, the hookers had a hard life, although some had happy endings. A few got married. Others moved in with men, and when it looked like it was going to stick, folks started calling the girl by the man's name. There were half a dozen women in Middle Swan who lived as man and wife but never had the words said over them.

One, in fact, who worked at Sweetie Purvis's place, had been a nurse, and when the influenza came in 1918, she went over to the pesthouse and cared for the sick. She took up with one of her patients, a man who'd been using her for a year, and called herself by his name. She had a son about six months later; Hennie didn't have the nerve to ask who the father was. The "husband" turned into the most biddy-pecked man on the Tenmile Range, as stuck in that marriage as if he'd taken the wedding vows.

After she'd been in Middle Swan for a while, Hennie found it natural that the fancy women were part of the fabric of the town. They were a little like a scrap of bright damask in the middle of a crazy quilt, a little flashier than some of the other fabrics, but still nicely fitted in.

Most hookers didn't fare so well. The girls died from liquor or laudanum, and sometimes, they got beat up. They committed suicide, and a few were murdered. Some girls just wasted away from sadness. Most likely, that was what happened to Minnie Lincoln, who worked at the Briar Rose. A few weeks after Hennie arrived in Middle Swan, Minnie had a baby.

Hennie had seen the girl walking around the camp, her belly swelling more and more every day. The two stopped to talk sometimes, for the hooker knew nothing about babies.

"You've got to drink milk, lots of milk," Hennie cautioned her.

"Milk? Where'm I going to find a cow? All we's got in Middle Swan is oxen. I ain't going to milk a steer."

Perhaps Minnie had meant to make Hennie blush, but Hennie only laughed. She paid a farmer in the valley who kept dairy cows to deliver milk to the hookhouse once a week and tell Minnie it was from an admirer, for Hennie didn't want Minnie to think she was interfering. But the girl knew, and she sought out Hennie for advice about caring for the baby once it arrived.

"I guess I got to have me a house to leave the little feller while I'm working. Babies are undesires at a hookhouse," Minnie said.

"You can't leave a baby by itself! All kinds of things could happen. What if it choked or the house caught fire?" Hennie replied. "You'll have to hire someone to watch it."

"And how am I going to pay for that? You think men will give me tips when I tell them I got a baby needs tending?"

Hennie was silent, a little ashamed, for she'd never considered how small an amount of money a prostitute made. She wondered how she could help Minnie, but she was stumped. She wouldn't mind tending the baby nights while the woman worked, but she hadn't been married long and didn't know if Jake wouldn't want a baby staying with them.

Minnie gave birth to a boy, and in a month, she was back at work. One night, she got drunker than $700, ran off to

Buckbush with a miner, and forgot about the baby for a day. "Lordy, he was screaming like a steam engine when I got home. I get so forgetful when I drink. What am I going to do with him?" Minnie asked.

Hennie shook her head, thinking Minnie didn't understand how precious a tiny life was, how easily it could be snuffed out. "You could find another line of work," she suggested.

"Doing what? You think if I was fit for anything else I'd be hooking? Maybe I ought to give him out," Minnie said. "I didn't know babies were so much bother."

She looked at Hennie hopefully, and Hennie took her meaning, but she didn't respond. If she wasn't sure Jake would let her tend Minnie's baby at night, she surely did not know what he would think of raising Minnie's boy as their own. Billy, on the other hand, would have taken in every unwanted baby in White Pigeon. When Sarah was an infant, Billy would pick her up and hold her as if she were a piece of glass, afraid he would scratch her with his rough hands, saying what a miracle she was. "I hope the Lord gives us a hundred," he'd told Hennie when he first held his daughter. Hennie, still hurting from childbirth, had looked up, startled, and Billy had laughed and insisted he was only joking. But she wasn't so sure. Hennie hadn't yet talked about babies with Jake, about the babies they might have, but she'd come to know him as a kind man, and she hoped he felt the way Billy did.

So that evening, she made Jake an extra-fine dinner, using some of her precious sugar to bake a cake. Then she fixed her husband a toddy and sat down beside him in front of the fire.

"How many children do you want?" she blurted out, chiding herself for not having thought out her words ahead of time.

Jake looked at her curiously. "I figured it wasn't our choice. We'd just take what came."

Hennie nodded. "A boy. Do you want a boy first?"

"Or a girl. If we don't get a boy, maybe we'll have a girl. One or the other." He smiled at his little joke.

"But you'd want a boy, wouldn't you?"

A foolish grin came over Jake's face, and he reached for Hennie. "What's this about? Are you in that way?"

"Oh no," Hennie said quickly. She tried to calm herself by getting up and poking at the fire, watching the sparks flare up as she broke the burning log in half. "What if we were to have a boy now, one that's already made?"

Jake didn't answer, and she turned around. "What if?"

"A foundling," he said. "Whose?"

"Minnie Lincoln's."

"A hookhouse baby?" he asked, his voice rising.

"You can't blame the little feller. Minnie can't take care of him, and what's to become of him?" she said in a rush.

"I didn't know you were acquainted with her."

"She's been asking me about babies, and I've told her as much as I know, but she's a poor mother. If somebody doesn't take the little feller, Minnie's liable to forget all about him. There's no other woman in camp to take him but me!"

Jake shook his head. "I don't know, Hennie."

Hennie sat down on Jake's lap then and put her arms around his neck. "He's the sweetest little boy you ever saw. Why, he even looks enough like you to be your own. I mean..." Hennie stopped, not daring to look at Jake. She stared past him at the chinking between two logs on the far wall while she pondered the thought that had come into her mind. It was possible, she told herself. After all, Jake was manly, and who knew what he'd done before she arrived in Middle Swan. "I didn't mean..."

"I know what you didn't mean."

"Is it—"

"Not likely," Jake broke in.

"But if it is—"

"I said 'not likely.' I never asked you to tell me your secrets. I won't give out what I did before I met you." Without another word, he stood and went out the door. Hennie undressed then and got in bed and when Jake returned, the smell of liquor on him, Hennie pretended to be asleep.

They didn't discuss the baby the next day or the day after that. And then it was too late. The little feller crossed over. Nobody blamed Minnie, because babies had a hard time up there where the air was thin, and maybe his lungs hadn't developed. Even with the best care, many babies didn't make it on the Swan. So it was no surprise that Minnie's boy died.

The prospectors came to Hennie then and asked to buy a bit of quilting to wrap the baby in. She told them any money wouldn't buy it, and gave it to them. They wrapped the baby in the little quilt and laid him out in a piece of long tom and buried him in a prospect hole.

Someone said a prayer, and the men covered up the makeshift coffin with dirt. When it was done, a man she didn't know thanked Hennie for attending the burying. "I should have looked after him," he said in a ragged voice. "I was his father."

Minnie quit Middle Swan after that, moving over to Buckbush, where she changed her name to Minnie Grant. She told Hennie she'd come around sometime and look her up and likewise, but she never did. A few months later, she taken out, disappeared just like that, and nobody ever heard of her again.

Minnie Lincoln was a regular working girl, and her leaving wasn't remarked on, for there were always others to take her place. But Bijou, who arrived on the Swan in the 1870s, was different. She was special. The miners called her the Blond Venus.

Hennie thought that Bijou was something out of a picture book—hair so blond it was almost white, and long enough that she could sit on it. She had eyes as blue as a columbine, and her face was delicate like a columbine, too. Most hookers were standoffish, but Bijou was as sweet as her looks. She took a walk every afternoon, and Hennie would go out into her garden just to see her pass by and say hello.

Hennie loved Bijou and felt beholden to her. When Mae had the diphtheria, Bijou brought her a spray of white roses tied in a gold ribbon. (Hennie made herself a crazy quilt later on, just so she could use that bit of ribbon.) The married women in Middle Swan stayed away from the Comfort cabin, fearful they'd carry home the sickness, but Bijou offered to sit with Mae, so that Hennie could get some rest. Hennie thanked her kindly but told her no, because Mae was better by then, but that didn't make Hennie feel less beholden.

Bijou did other kindnesses. Once, she stopped with a bouquet of wildflowers after Hennie lost a half-made baby she was carrying, one of several miscarriages she suffered during her marriage to Jake. Hennie was only a few weeks along, and she always wondered how Bijou knew she was pregnant.

Half the single men in Middle Swan and some of the married ones, too, were in love with Bijou, but she didn't give her heart to anyone, not until she met Harold Halleck, a mining engineer from Denver. He came to Middle Swan because his family owned the Honeymaid Mine up at the top of Plug Hat Hill. The Halleck Mining Company was started by Harold's father, who'd died, so Harold ran it for his mother and sisters.

He fell for Bijou right off. It didn't seem to matter one bit that she was a prostitute. Bijou was smitten, too. She worshipped Harold, thought he was the pope of Rome, and she wanted to be his wife. Harold wanted that, too, and in their way, the couple considered themselves betrothed.

There was no way those two could marry, however. Bijou was famous, not only in the county but as far away as Denver. Harold couldn't marry her and bring the Blond Venus home to his people. They would have bemeaned her and made her life a misery. And Harold had pledged his father on the old man's deathbed that he'd never sell the mining company, that he'd run it and support his mother and sisters. "It isn't in the stars for them," Hennie told Jake. He hadn't known she was friends with Bijou, either, but he wasn't surprised. He'd learned by then that Hennie didn't hold with convention, that she would take up with anybody she wanted to. He guessed it didn't matter who his wife be-friended.

One afternoon, Hennie was outside tending her yellow roses with Mae, when Bijou stopped a minute to tell her the little girl was the prettiest flower in the garden. "I hope I have one just like her," she said.

Hennie knew right then that Bijou was carrying a child. Hennie said, "Just you sit," not thinking for a minute she was inviting a hooker into her home but only that Bijou was a woman expecting a baby who shouldn't be standing in the hot sun. Hennie gave her a drink of water from the dipper, and Bijou held it like it was a crystal goblet and thanked her so prettily that Hennie blurted out, "To say Mr. Halleck's people are better than you, I couldn't." Hennie was horrified at those words, because it wasn't her business. And when she thought about it later, she wasn't sure that Bijou was aware that everybody in Middle Swan knew about her and Mr. Halleck. And some of them even prayed for her.

But Bijou acted like Hennie's words tickled her to death. She handed Hennie the dipper and said there wasn't a wine in the world that tasted as sweet as mountain water. She glanced over at Hennie's PRAYERS FOR SALE sign and said, "I'd like to pay you to say a little prayer for me."

"I've done it already, and I'll do it again, but no money will I take."

"I thank you kindly."

Bijou stopped working on Venus Row and got a place of her own. Of course, Harold could have put her up in style, but that wouldn't have set right with Bijou. She wanted to be a wife or nothing. The two of them talked and talked about getting married, but they just never could work it out. They didn't believe God His Self could make it come out for them.

One day, the lovers quarreled, and Bijou told Harold that he was released. He left for Denver and didn't come back. Hennie knew what happened, because she'd come across Bijou in the woods, crying.

"How could he leave, you having a baby and all?" Hennie asked.

"I haven't informed him."

"He has eyes, doesn't he?"

"Men don't have eyes for that."

Hennie didn't argue, because Bijou knew more about men than she did. "What will you do?" she asked. Because she couldn't seem to make another baby herself and her arms ached to hold a little one, Hennie wondered if Bijou wanted to give out the baby. Maybe this time, Jake wouldn't mind taking in someone else's child. He had a kind heart, and Hennie knew his disappointment each time they lost a chance for a baby of their own. He ought to have children. What did it matter if he wouldn't be their natural father?

"I'll keep it. I couldn't give it away, if that's what you're thinking. I just couldn't. But what's to become of us?"

"There are a dozen men in Middle Swan, some as rich as a bishop, who'd marry you this afternoon."

"But I don't love them."

That was an odd thing for a hooker to say, because most of them dreamed of catching a man with money, and love was a luxury they couldn't afford. But Bijou was different, and Hennie knew she wouldn't marry anyone but Harold.

"I wish I was better at praying," Hennie said. She went to

the stream and made a cup of her hands, carrying back cold water to Bijou, who wet her fingers and patted her face.

"I'm grateful to you, Mrs. Comfort," Bijou said, and Hennie knew she wasn't talking about the water. "I'd be pleased if you'd keep on praying, but I don't think Mr. Halleck will come back."

Bijou waited another two weeks, until she was sure Harold really had quit her. Then she took an overdose of laudanum and killed herself. The girls in the hookhouses on Venus Row said it was the noblest thing she ever did, but Hennie didn't see it that way. She thought it was a waste of a precious life—two lives.

Hennie herself washed and dressed the body and laid it out in a coffin, which an admirer had purchased. She embroidered a silk pillow, for she thought Bijou ought to have a fine place to rest her head for eternity. Then the men who'd known Bijou dug the grave, as was the tradition in Middle Swan. Bijou's family—the girls in the hookhouse—provided jugs of hard liquor to keep them going. The grave was the deepest one in the End of Day burial ground, and the men were the drunkest Middle Swan had ever seen.

It was maybe a week after Bijou died that Harold Halleck came back to Middle Swan, strutting down the street in a good suit, carrying a walking cane and a big box, strolling right by Hennie's house. She rushed outside and ran after him all the way down the trail to Bijou's house. But before Hennie could reach him, he knocked on the door and asked for Bijou. "That whore killed herself over some man that weren't worth a nickel," said the woman who answered, because the house had already been rented.

Hennie reached Harold then, and she touched his arm. "Mr. Halleck," she said.

He turned to her, confused. "Bijou's dead?"

Hennie led him back to the trail, for the woman at the door was curious, and what Hennie had to say was private. She didn't want Bijou to be the subject of more gossip.

"I brought her roses—and a ring. I have a diamond wedding ring in my pocket. I was going to propose marriage," Harold said, shaking his head in bewilderment. He took a ring out of his pocket and looked at it.

"It's too late," Hennie said softly. "She thought you quit her. She didn't see any other way for her and the baby."

"A baby?" Mr. Halleck looked at Hennie sharply. "I didn't know about a baby."

"I know," Hennie said.

Tears came to his eyes, and he wiped them with a silk handkerchief. "I would have taken care of them, both of them. You see, my sister just married a mining man in Denver, and I turned the company over to him. That's why I've been gone so long. I didn't write, because I wanted to surprise Bijou. I was going to tell her we could move to San Francisco and get a fresh start where nobody would know a thing about her."

Harold held on to Hennie's arm to steady himself. Then he asked Hennie to show him Bijou's grave, and the two of them walked together to the burial ground. He scratched in the dirt and buried the ring. Then he opened the box of flowers, and one by one, he tore the petals off the roses, scattering them over the grave. Hennie thought the bright red mutilated flowers floating down onto the dirt looked like blood. She felt like an intruder on Harold's grief then, so she left the man alone with his sorrow. "I'll have tea waiting for you—or a toddy," she said. "You stop by the two-story log place when you leave." Harold didn't answer.

With a last look at the grave, covered now with the torn roses, Hennie started toward the gate. She had almost reached it when she heard the gunshot and rushed back to the grave. Harold lay dead on top of the rose petals.

Hennie wrote to the Halleck family, asking that Harold be buried next to Bijou. But she received no reply. The Hallecks shipped the body to Denver and buried it in the family plot, under a monument with the words "Love and Honor" on it.

❦❦❦

The door of the Pinto store opened, and a man, low and square, like a timberline-stunted tree, came in. Hennie wondered why mountain men always seemed to be runted— rooted to the ground as if they were built for long winters and heavy snows. He took off his plaid cap and tucked it under his arm, bowing a little to Hennie and asking, "How's yourself?"

"I am deteriorating at a normal rate," she told him.

"That's about to be expected," he replied.

"And you, Davy?" Hennie asked

"Same." He stuffed his mittens into his pocket and held his hands over the stove, rubbing together fingers that were gnarled with arthritis and grimy with dirt. One thumbnail was black.

Roy came out from the back room then, wiping his hands

on his overalls and smelling of Tenmile Moon. He nodded at Davy.

"Look, Pinto, how many gallons of gasoline do I need to get to Denver?" Davy asked.

"About a hundred and fifty, if you're driving that old Packard touring sedan of yours in this weather. That machine ought to be up on blocks like everybody else's this time of year. You'll never make it," Roy told him. "Besides, that heater wouldn't warm a gnat."

"We'll see. She says she has to go to Denver to have her teeth made. Then she wants me to take her to eat at the Neisner Brothers' luncheonette." He pronounced the word "luncheon-eddie." "I tell you, sir, I got no choice." Davy reached his grimy hand inside his shirt, and Hennie wondered if he had fleas, for he couldn't stop scratching.

"Take the train."

"She won't ride a train. If I don't take her, she'll hurt me on my bum, and I won't hardly ever sit down no more."

"You ain't got the backbone of a fishworm," Roy told him. "You'll run off the road going over the top. It's snowed pretty bad up there last night. Just when you think it might be spring, another storm blows in. Always happens."

"I know it." Davy put his hat back on his head and pulled the earflaps down. His face was as gray as the storm outside. "You coming on out to fill 'er up, or you want me to go down the Swan to get my gasoline?"

"Have it your way." Roy took a dirty woolen jacket from a hook behind the counter and went outside to the Skelly gasoline pump in front of the store.

As he left, Davy turned to Hennie. "Tap 'er light."

"And yourself, Davy," Hennie replied.

The two women stared through the open doorway as the gasoline went up and down in the big glass pump. Davy took out a cigarette and lit a match, turning his back to the wind and cupping his hand around the flame, but the wind blew it out. He struck another match, but the wind took it, too. Davy shoved the cigarette under an earflap of his cap.

Nit craned her neck to see the woman through the Packard's windshield. "You think all her teeth's fallen out?"

"They got pulled a long time ago, and she had a set made back then," Hennie told the girl. "But she dropped them down the privy, and now she won't wear them."

"Hello, yes. I wouldn't, either," Nit said.

Shivering in the cold blowing through the door, the two watched as the man paid Roy and drove off. Roy came back into the store, rubbing his nose, which was red, with pores as big as matchheads. "Judas Priest. That hammer-headed bastard is going to take an automobile over the hump in this weather. I never saw a man so stubborn. Damn fool." Roy started to say more, but became sensible that Nit was listening. "Begging your pardon, ma'am," he said, but Nit giggled. So he gave her a sly look and went on to the back room, muttering, "Horny-toed bastard."

Roy had just closed the door when the firehouse siren went off, and the girl jumped.

"Just the noon whistle," Hennie said. "I best be getting home before the soup burns up." She put her arms inside her sleeves and pulled the coat around her.

"I've been thinking," Nit said. She studied her apple, which was mostly brown spots now. So she opened the door

of the stove and threw the apple into the coals, where it siz-
zled. "Middle Swan's about as different a place as there is
from Kentucky. But I think the people aren't so different,
women anyway."

"How's that?" Hennie asked.

"They're strong. I think you have to be strong to live
there or here. Like you," Nit said.

Hennie thought that over. "Like you, too, Mrs. Spindle.
Maybe you don't know it, but you are. You'll see."

"Do you think so?" Nit asked, pleased. "I'd like to be
strong. Do you really think I am?"

Before Hennie could answer, the door opened, letting in
the moan of the dredge and a stern-looking woman with a
plate covered by a napkin.

"How's yourself?" she asked Hennie.

"Good as ever," Hennie replied. "And you?"

"Same."

The woman looked Nit up and down but didn't speak.
"I've got his dinner," she said to Hennie and continued on
into the back room and shut the door.

"Don't mind her. She keeps her nose so high in the air, she's
liable to drown in a good rainstorm," Hennie said. "Monalisa
Pinto thinks she's the second coming of Jesus Christ."

"It's a good thing that Greta Garbo wasn't here when she
came in. Mrs. Pinto would have knocked her dead with the
look she gave me," Nit said. A horrified expression came over
her face. "Maybe she thinks I'm one of those sorry girls."

"No. You can set your mind at rest." Hennie rose and
buttoned her coat. She picked up the yeast and left five pen-
nies on the counter. Nit stood as well, and the two walked

out of the store together, Hennie closing the door and test-
ing it to make sure that it was shut tight.

"Mrs. Pinto is what they call her, but she's not. You remember me telling you about that hooker from the Willows,
the one who was a nurse and got hitched up with a man?"
Hennie chuckled and started down the street, leaving the
girl standing in front of the store with her little pink hand
over her mouth.

Chapter 4

The Liberty Dredge gave an enormous shudder, then with a groan of agony, the gold boat shut down, and the silence awakened Hennie Comfort. Or perhaps she awoke because of the sound of birds chattering. With all the hollering the dredge made, Hennie hadn't heard the dawn call of birds in a long time. She pulled herself into consciousness, sensing that something was different. Then she heard the scream of a camp robber and sprang out of bed—that is, as much as an eighty-six-year-old woman with rheumatism in her knees could spring. She found her carpet slippers and shuffled on rubbery ankles to the window she'd left open the night before and peered out.

Summer had come, not the false summer that promised so much, then disappointed, but the real summer. Yesterday was winter still, but today it was summer, a perfect June day.

Even if she had not been able to see it with her own eyes, Hennie could smell it—the scent of the earth, the perfume from the sun on the jack pines. Hennie had thought the night before that she might sleep late, maybe even make herself a cup of coffee and return with it to the bed to enjoy the sleep-warmth of the quilts. But that was before she knew that summer would arrive. The deadly sin of slothfulness was for winter. Summer hours were too precious to waste, especially when this summer might be Hennie's last on the Swan.

There were two seasons in Middle Swan, the leather bellies of the Warm Stove Mine and Hot Air Smelter, the old-timers who spent their days around the wood-burning stove in the Pinto store, liked to say—this winter and last winter. In fact, the high country had three seasons. Winter lasted seven months, nudging aside spring. Then one day, winter gave way to the short, intense summer, so perfect in its sunshine and clear mountain air that foreigners, as the people from out-of-state were called, flocked to Middle Swan to camp out in the old prospector shacks and log cabins that they'd bought for back taxes. They left in September, with the coming of the color, although the weeks of fall, when the aspen leaves came into their wire-gold tint, were every bit as beautiful to Hennie as the warm months.

Hennie didn't stop to think on the seasons now. She dressed quickly and hurried into the kitchen, where a few fire coals glowed in her cookstove, and added kindling, then stove wood, until the surface of the range was hot enough to fry an egg. She dropped a spoonful of bacon grease into the heavy black skillet heating on the stove, let it sizzle, then slipped in an egg. While the egg fried, Hennie sliced a piece of bread and fitted it onto a fork, then removed a stove lid and held the bread over the fire to toast. When the bread was toasted and buttered and jammed, she slid the egg onto a heavy white plate and took the breakfast outside so that she could eat on a stump that was placed just right to catch the first rays of sun as it peeked over the mountains.

As she ate, listening to the sounds of the dredge, which had started up again, Hennie surveyed the yard. The lettuce seeds she'd planted under the snow had sprouted and broken through the earth to form long green rows, and the tips of pieplant had pushed up through the dirt, their green leaves tightly furled and their bright red stalks barely showing. Spears of grass were greening in the yard, and she spied the leaves of the wild daisies that grew alongside the house. The delphinium behind the daisies had survived the winter—last summer, she'd washed them with soapy water to kill the aphids, but she hadn't been sure the tall flowers would make it.

Yellow was almost ready to peek through the buds of the yellow roses, the roses that folks called "women's gold." Her rosebushes were the descendents of starts Hennie had brought across the prairie when she'd come from Tennessee. She'd wrapped them in a dishcloth that she dampened each morning of the journey with precious water, and they survived and thrived.

The buds on the lilac were swollen, not dried and brown as they were so many summers when the cold kept the bloom off the bushes. Soon, when Hennie lifted her bedroom window, the only window in the house that was made to open, she would smell the lilacs as she went to sleep. Hennie thought of how Jake had loved the garden. Most men, now they didn't care much about flowers. Jake was different. He'd stop on his walk home from a shift and pick a bouquet of Indian paintbrush or wild daises for her. Once she'd opened his lunch bucket to wash it out and discovered a perfect pink rose inside.

She'd had a good life, Hennie reflected, but there were things left for her to do before she went below. The girl Nit needed help if she was to become a mountain woman. Hennie had a lifetime of stories she wanted to tell one more time. Then there was that other matter that pricked the back of her mind, just this side of consciousness. It ought to be resolved before she moved on. With her days on the Swan growing shorter, she had to come to terms with it after all these years. But the old woman wouldn't think about that now that the summer air warmed her bones.

In a week or two, Hennie would feel safe planting her geranium starts outdoors. A month before, she had taken cuttings from the plants in the windows and stuck them into jars of water to root. The geraniums would go into the ground beside the white daisies and blue delphinium, and they would all bloom for the Fourth of July—"the liberty garden," Mae called it. Hennie smiled now, remembering how Mae would wake as the first charge of dynamite went off on the nation's birthday and rush out to make certain the flowers were perfect. Hennie and Mae and Jake had loved the Fourth of July more than Christmas—the parade, the picnic, and the hard-rock drilling contest that Jake won three years in a row. Even Jake's benders didn't dampen their enthusiasm for the holiday.

How could anybody be disheated on such a fine day? Even Thelma Franks wouldn't spoil it, Hennie told herself as her neighbor came out of her house, leaving her door open, and walked to the trail, its mud of a few days before dried now to a powder. Hennie set down her plate and rose to greet her neighbor. "It's a fine day," she called.

"It'll be hot as hell's kitchen before it's over," Thelma said. "How's yourself?"

"Good as the day," Hennie said. When Thelma looked glum at Hennie's fine state, for the neighbor liked to look on the bad side of things, Hennie searched for some ailment that would please the woman. "Except I'm having dark shadows before my eyes."

"Same," Thelma said, with what sounded like relief. "I hurt my foot, too, and I'll be crippled all day long."

Hennie was in no mood to hear complaints. "It's time for spring cleaning."

"Done a'ready."

Last year or the year before, Hennie wondered, eyeing the dirty quilt Thelma had hung in her doorway in November to keep out the winter's cold. Inside, Hennie knew, Thelma's house would smell of sour blankets and damp wood. She changed the subject, saying brightly, "I guess it's time for the summer people." The outsiders in their bright clothes and white shoes, their big cars loaded with new blankets and towels, and jars and boxes of groceries from the Piggly Wiggly and the A&P in Denver, always cheered Hennie.

"They're no better than motor gypsies. They think themselves grand and mighty, but they're lucky, that's all. I'd be lucky, too, if Bert hadn't made me spend my life on the devil's backbone."

Hennie remembered when Thelma Franks had arrived in Middle Swan, almost as young then as Nit was now. Bert Franks hadn't been made for luck, and right off, he'd hurt his leg in a mine accident. Now he operated a still in a shack behind the house and made kill-devil so foul that the federal agents never bothered to shut him down, figuring, Hennie supposed, that anybody who drank the bootleg would repent and give up the stuff. Most of the time, Bert sat in a chair, reading poetry. Thelma had her grievements.

"They make me tired," Thelma said of the summer people. "I got to get to the Pinto store for my tonic. My arthritis flares up when the seasons change. I'd buy a prayer off of you if I thought it would help." Thelma nodded at the ancient sign nailed to Hennie's fence that read PRAYERS FOR SALE.

"Free to neighbors."

"You're an odd one. You say prayers for one and all, but you haven't set foot inside the church for years. And you once a Christian woman! You've got your ways." Thelma turned away and started toward the store, stepping into the only puddle of mud in the trail. "Jesus God," she said, but there wasn't much feeling in the swearing, and Hennie knew her neighbor was glad for summer, too.

Hennie scraped the remains of her breakfast onto a rock for the squirrels and went back inside. There was work to do, the summer clothes gotten out and the winter ones washed and put away, the drawers and cupboards cleaned, the quilts aired. She glanced at the sky and judged the sun would be bright for a while yet. She needed a cloudy day to hang the quilts on the line, for the sun along the crest of the earth was so strong it would fade them before it slipped behind the Tenmile Range. She thought to wash the cupboards, but the day was such a gift that she could not bear to spend it indoors. Perhaps she'd walk up the trail to timberline, pack a lunch. She might even invite her young neighbor to go along. The girl would be almost crazy by now from being cooped up in her shack in the dying days of winter. If she were home in Tennessee, the child would have been barefoot for a month or two.

Hennie went inside and tidied the house, cleaning the ashes from the fireplace and carrying them outside to spread on the flower beds. She swept the floor, and when it was still too early to call on the girl, she cleaned the pie safe, washing the shelves and sides and rinsing them with clear water with a sprig of dried lavender in it. She hoped the lavender bushes hadn't died over the winter. Nobody else could make lavender grow in the high country the way Hennie did, but nonetheless, the cold killed even her lavender some years. Then she cleaned the ashes from the firebox of her cookstove and spread them, too, in her garden. But the sunshine called her, and she went outside and raked and swept the yard of pine needles that had fallen during the winter. She'd wait for another day to grub out the sage.

When enough time had passed, Hennie returned to the kitchen and cut up yesterday's potatoes for a salad, mixing them with oil and a little vinegar and a crumbled slice of bacon. Then she made jam sandwiches, using the last of the currant jam she'd cooked from the fruit picked last summer along the railroad tracks. She placed the potato salad and sandwiches in a large lard bucket, along with pickles, a jar of chowchow, and a hunk of yellow cheese. She added two tin cups, for the water high up would be clear and sweet and cold from the melting snow. Then she wrapped a bit of quilting in a napkin and set it on top. When she was finished, she slipped a sweater around her shoulders. Who knew when the weather might turn again? Hennie had worn the sweater so long that she'd forgotten it had once belonged to Jake. She'd taken to putting it on after he died, when the warm wool on her shoulders reminded her of the way Jake held her before he went off to work in the mornings. Like most miners' wives, she never bid her husband good-bye of a morning without thinking, *Will he come home in one piece?* She wondered if Jake thought the same, but she never asked. Talking about such a thing would have been bad luck. Perhaps he knew all along what would happen to him.

As Hennie shut the door, she saw Thelma again and thought it would be a kindness to invite that neighbor to come along on the picnic. Lord knew, Thelma might welcome a bit of Hennie's dinner, plain as it was. The time Hennie had taken supper at the Franks's house, she'd found the meat so tough, she couldn't cut the gravy with a knife. But with all her complaining, Thelma would spoil the day for the girl. Besides, Hennie hadn't prepared enough picnic for three. So with only a fleeting moment of guilt, she headed down the trail for the Tappan place.

❧⟡❧

The girl had pulled the old blue rocking chair out of the house and was sitting outdoors, her eyes closed, her face held up to the sun. Already, her pale skin had turned a darker shade of pink. She heard the old woman's steps and opened her eyes, then jumped up when she saw Hennie. "You must think I'm the laziest thing on earth. I tried to clean the house, but I just piddled with it, and it's a mess. I couldn't stay inside on such a day. I couldn't at all," Nit Spindle said.

Hennie knew that Nit's description of the house wasn't true, for the girl's home was always as neat as her own. Most likely, Nit had finished her work and was wondering how to spend her day. "It'd be a sin," Hennie replied, setting her lard bucket on a stump. When the girl pointed to the rocker, Hennie sat.

"Mommy gave me this chair when me and Dick moved away, so's I wouldn't forget her. But I would never forget my family. It was made by my great-grandpaw, made while he hid out in a cave from the Yankees. He painted the chair blue, for he didn't want to forget the color of the sky." Nit looked up at the mountain sky and shook her head, while Hennie thought that she had indeed picked the right person for the last telling of her tales. The girl had an ear as good as Hennie's for stories. "I never saw a sky this color, so bright it hurts my eyes," Nit added.

"You best protect your skin against it, dearie. Redhead's skin's the worst to burn," Hennie warned. "Up here where the air's thin, you'll fry like a hotcake. Put you on a sunbonnet."

"I haven't one."

"Then wear you your feller's old hat."

The girl nodded, but instead of going inside for the hat, she sat down on a rock beside Hennie. Young girls today didn't like a white face like they used to. They wanted to be suntanned, and the girl, Hennie thought, was just the slightest bit vain about her looks. You couldn't force a person to take your advice. But one bad burn from the sun shining through the thin air and the girl would learn.

"I was going to sun my quilts," Nit said.

"Same, but I'll wait for a cloudy day. The sun's too bright this close to timberline. It'll fade them."

Nit thought that over and nodded, and Hennie wondered why a woman would take such good care of a quilt and not herself. It was the way of most quilters, however. They prized their work more than they did themselves.

The old woman rocked back and forth in the sun, drowsing a little. Then she remembered why she'd come and roused herself. "I've got dinner in the bucket, and I ask would you like to go up above where the gold boat's working and have us a picnic. The food's slim pickin's, just leftovers, but it'll suit if you're hungry."

Nit clasped her hands together in delight. "I baked a chess pie this morning. We'll take it along." When Hennie looked confused, the girl explained, "Brown sugar and eggs mostly."

"Kentucky pie! That's what we called it. Why, I haven't thought about Kentucky pie since I came to Colorado. It suits me fine. But what will your man think when he comes home to supper, and there's no hereafter?" The boy, slim like he was, could use some fattening up, the old woman decided.

Nit frowned in thought. "We'll take half of it," she said, giggling at the compromise.

"Why, that'll make a party." Hennie glanced up at the

sun, which was edging up to the midpoint in the sky now. "Just us hurry. If it rains, it'll come in the afternoon. Take your rubber shoes. The trail's not dry yet." The girl went inside and returned, bareheaded, with a pie tin, a dishcloth tied around it with string. She placed it carefully on top of Hennie's picnic, then put the lard bucket over her own arm. Touched by the girl's thoughtfulness, Hennie pretended not to notice that Nit had picked up her burden.

Just as they started, the girl slapped her arm and muttered, "Drat skeeter!"

"We'll find us some tansy leaves to rub on us. They keep the accustomed pests away just fine."

"For sure?" asked Nit. When Hennie nodded, the girl said she knew all about plants and their uses, learned from an old lady at home who kept a medicine house, a tiny cabin whose shelves were loaded with crocks and tins of dried plants and herbs, and jars of concoctions. "I know plants for any kind of hurting a person's got," Nit said. Hennie told her they'd look for plants high up. She knew a thing or two about medicinal herbs herself.

The two walked through the old town and out past the gold dredge, which squatted in a pond of its own making, silent as snow the whole morning. Dick stood on the deck, and the two women waved to him, Nit turning back a time or two to catch a glimpse of her husband. "I sure worry about him," Nit said. "When the dredge was shut down, that Silas Hemp made Dick go over the side for something. Then the boat started up, and Dick almost fell off."

"Mr. Hemp's a mean one," Hennie agreed. She remembered when the man had tried to mine one of Jake's old

claims, saying it was abandoned. But it wasn't, and Hennie
had forced him out. To get even, he'd left dynamite lying in
the drift, and if she hadn't had a notion to look for a meanness, the stuff might have killed somebody. But Hennie
didn't tell Nit about the dynamite, for she didn't want to in-
crease the girl's worries.

The two women continued along to where the road trick-
led off into a narrow trail, edged here and there with crusts
of snow. As it grew steeper, Hennie slowed her pace, although not for herself. Despite her age, she could still climb
a mountain as well as any man. But the girl wasn't used to
the altitude yet, and Hennie didn't want to tire her.

"Here's where I get rose hips for jam," Hennie said, stopping next to a patch of wild roses so that the girl could rest.
She pointed to currant bushes that were just leafing out under the fallen timbers of an old mill, but said she'd show Nit
a better patch, the one beside the railroad tracks. "There's
paintbrush there and the pink flowers we call summer's half-
over." Hennie almost hated to see them bloom, for it meant
that Middle Swan was on the down side of summer and winter was coming.

"Anemones?" the girl asked. "What about anemones?"

"There's only one yard in Middle Swan where anemones
grow, and it belongs to a fellow in prison for selling whiskey
mixed with wood alcohol. Nobody lives there now. Might be
we could dig up some, although they never grew for me."
She paused. "They were Mae's favorites—my daughter," she
added in case Nit had forgotten. "She loves an anemone best
of all. I told her an anemone is proof God loves women,
although I can't say it makes up for childbirth." The two

chuckled, and Hennie added, "Anemones and quilting. Yes, I'd say there's a god, and maybe even that God's a woman."

Hennie looked at the girl to see if the blaspheming had shocked her, but the girl only laughed and asked, "Does Mae quilt?"

Hennie smiled, switching the lard bucket from one arm to the other, for she had picked it up at the stop. Mae never took to quilting, she said. "That one couldn't sit still long enough to thread a needle. Sewing was a grievement to her." Hennie slowed a little, for the altitude got to her now. She hadn't climbed this high since the fall. Or perhaps it was age that slowed her. Hennie didn't want to think so.

"Maybe she isn't really your daughter." Nit couldn't help but laugh at her own wit.

Hennie was silent for a long time then, mulling something over, which made the girl fidgety. At last, Hennie said, "No, she isn't, not my natural-born daughter leastways. But in every other way, she is the best daughter a woman ever had. Every day I thank the Lord for Mae, because Jake and I weren't blessed with children of our own." There was no reason to tell the girl about the half-made babies she'd lost when they were three or five months along, no need to remind Nit of her own sorrow or make her fear another pregnancy. Women weren't supposed to count those babies, but Hennie mourned the little lives that had never been lived.

"Ah gee, Mrs. Comfort. I didn't mean to ask a question of a personal nature."

The girl looked so dejected that Hennie said, "It tires me to talk when there's climbing to do, and this mountain's as steep as a horse's face, but I promise I'll tell you about her

when we get to the toppen part." She bent over and picked a
red berry the size of the nail on her little finger. "Here's you
your first strawberry. Go ahead and eat it. There's no use to
save it. Why, it'd take most of a day to pick enough for a pie,
if you could find them." Hennie carried the bucket again,
and the two walked on in silence, both winded, until they
reached timberline. The pines were stunted there, and some
were bare of branches on one side, where the wind had taken
them. The trees grew in patches, as if they'd failed in their
struggle to march up to the top of the mountain, which was
bald and covered with snow.

"You can see the whole world up here," Nit said, as they
broke into the clearing. "I'll bring Dick. We can make a
camp. Why, we love sleeping outside in a summer night."

"No such a thing," Hennie warned, explaining that lightning storms sent huge balls of electricity rolling across the
open field. Three summers before, she said, two foreigners
sleeping in a tent hadn't had the sense to go below when the
rain came, and they'd been struck by lightning.

"There's so much I've got to learn here. At home, I was
thought right smart, but I don't know a thing about these
mountains."

"You'll learn. You've already got a start," Hennie replied.

"Then I thank you for it," Nit said. "Because of you, I'm
coming on to feeling a kinship to this place."

The old woman led Nit to a favorite spot of flat stones,
recalling that she and Mae had come there when the girl was
small. Drifts of snow remained under the trees and the tun-
dra was spongy, but the spot Hennie chose was dry, and the
women sat down. Hennie reached into the bucket and took

out two tin plates, two tin forks. "I brought these forks with me to Colorado. When we went visiting for supper in that long-ago time, we took our forks with us, because nobody had them to spare. One woman there was who even gave her forks names—Big Andy and Little Bets."

Hennie handed the girl a sandwich, which Nit opened, exclaiming over the jam. She'd brought jam jars with her, she said, but they'd been broken, and she was hungry for a taste of preserves. They finished Hennie's lunch, eating every-thing, for the climb had sharpened their appetites. Then Nit removed the dish towel from her pie plate and offered a huge piece of sugar pie to Hennie, who held it in her hand and sampled it, telling the girl she'd never tasted better. "I remember now. I made Kentucky pie for Mae, brought it to this very place for a picnic. I'd forgotten about that." She added for politeness's sake, "It wasn't as good as this one."

The girl beamed. "Dick says it hurts his teeth, but he still eats it, mostly between slices of bread for a sandwich."

"A man'll do that." She paused. "You've got a good man, Mrs. Spindle."

"I couldn't ask for better. Still, I've found out a husband isn't everything to me. There's lots of things I can't talk to Dick about. I mean, he'll listen. Dick's good about that. But he doesn't understand the way a woman does. Have you no-ticed that about a husband?"

Hennie nodded. She'd noticed.

"I wished he'd asked me if I wanted to come to Middle Swan. I'd have told him yes, because a wife's supposed to, like the Bible says. She's supposed to follow where he goes. But he

could have asked instead of telling me. He could have had a consideration for my feelings." She added quickly, "I don't want you to think I'm finding fault."

"There isn't a wife who doesn't feel like you," Hennie told her. "That's why the Lord made friends. They can be a burden, but most times, I'm gladder for my friends than I am for almost anything, maybe even quilting. I'm proud to say I have as many friends as I do quilts."

"I'm obliged to say my friends are better made than my quilts," Nit said. She grew still a moment. "I wish I could make more friends here. It seems like I'm not worth much without friends and..." Her voice trailed off, but Hennie knew the girl had meant to add, "a baby."

The two were silent then, until they finished the pie, every crumb, and returned the dishes to the bucket. Then Hennie said, "We'll go down in just a breath or two, but I'd like to sit a minute." She opened the napkin and removed colorful shapes of fabric and laid them out on a rock, fitting them together to form a meandering line.

"Quiled Rattlesnake." Nit seemed delighted to recognize the pattern.

Hennie frowned a minute as she picked up two pieces and pinned them together. *Coiled* Rattlesnake, she thought, for a quilt pattern could have a dozen names. She took out her needle and began stitching the pieces together. The girl reached into her own pocket and removed a quilt square that she'd begun. Hennie leaned over to look at the piecing. The girl offered the square, and Hennie studied it, turning it around and then exclaiming, "Why, it's a coffee cup. Isn't that the smartest thing? You could lay abed in the morning and drink your coffee under that quilt. I'd like to see that top finished."

She leaned toward the girl. "When it's done, we'll have it put in at my place, since there's already a frame set up; you remember it. I reckon you've got no room for a frame in that house of yours, unless you hang it from the ceiling. I never liked to quilt on a frame suspended." Hennie handed back the piecing. "That'll make a right pretty quilt. My, you're a clever girl."

Nit flushed under her pink sunburn, for like any woman, she was vain about her sewing, even if it was nowhere as good as Hennie's. To hide her embarrassment and because she was as curious a woman as Hennie, she asked, "How come that girl Mae wasn't your natural-born child? You said you'd tell me." When Hennie didn't answer right away, Nit mumbled, "Forgive it. Dick says I'm bad for asking questions."

Hennie patted the girl's hand and said the story wasn't a secret. "You want to hear it?" she asked.

Nit grinned. "I expect that's why I asked." She took a few stitches in her quilt square, then lay back against the rock and placed the square over her face to keep out the sun.

Hennie pinned another scrap to her piecing, because she always talked better when her hands were busy, and waited until the girl was settled in before she began. "Mae wasn't mine, and she wasn't adopted exactly. I found her."

Nit sat up quickly, letting the quilt square fall off her face. "You what?"

"That's right," Hennie said, picking up the bit of quilting

and handing it to Nit. "I found her." She added, "You remember me telling you that when I met Jake Comfort I had
encumberments? Well, that was Mae."

⊗⊙⊘

The little girl was sitting in a clump of trees someplace in
Kansas Territory when Ila Mae's wagon train crossed in
1866. She might have been hiding, Ila Mae thought, and she
would have passed right by her, just as the others did, if it
weren't for the girl's dress, which was homespun, dyed in the
oddest shade of blue. Ila Mae thought someone had abandoned a quilt or a shirt, and she started for the fabric. Then
the child held out her arms, which were sunburned and
scratched from the bushes, and Ila Mae realized that she was
looking at a girl. Ila Mae gasped, not only at finding a lost
child but because the tiny thing looked just the way she'd
imagined Sarah would have looked if she'd lived to be two—
or maybe three. Who could tell the age of the poor little
thing?

Ila Mae knew the girl was not from her own wagon train,
but just in case, she scooped her up and went to each family
and asked. No one claimed the child. There were but three
women in the train besides Ila Mae—a mother with eleven
children, a woman who drove her own ox team and had the
care of a wagon by herself, and the sick mother whose little
ones Ila Mae tended. None of them cared to take the girl,
and of course, the men wouldn't have her.

One said the child must have wandered off from a farm
and ought to be let be, but there were no farms in the area;
the train hadn't passed one in days. Another man told Ila Mae

the girl might have been on an earlier train and someone would come for her, so give her a biscuit and leave her behind. The others agreed that as how she had found her, Ila Mae was the one to take the responsibility. Ila Mae would no more have left that girl behind than stayed there herself, for her heart was tender, still bruised by the death of her own child.

Later, at their nooning, Ila Mae gave a man one of her dollars to ride on to the wagon train ahead and inquire if a girl was missing. He returned to say all the children were accounted for. But he'd learned that a few days earlier, a wagon had lagged behind the others and been attacked by Indians. Before the men in the train could reach the family, the Indians had killed and scalped the mother and father, and taken the children. The men found the bodies of an older boy and a newborn baby, but there was no sign of the rest of the children—two of them or was it three? No one remembered. Mostly likely, Ila Mae's little girl belonged to that family and had wandered away when the Indians weren't watching her, because the damn savages killed their hostages instead of letting them go. Ila Mae shuddered to think the girl's yellow curls might have hung from a tepee pole.

So she kept the little child, whom she called Mae, after herself, and she cared for her all the way to Denver, the girl walking beside Ila Mae much of the time. She intended to leave the baby there, but Denver had no facilities for lost children. And although she made the rounds of the wagons camped about the city, she found no one to identify the child. Besides, the poor little orphan clung to her so, that Ila Mae had no choice but to take Mae along with her to Middle Swan.

When she arrived at the camp, riding on top of that freight wagon in the rain, the baby sleeping on her lap under the Friendship quilt that covered them both, she warned Jake Comfort that he might have to take on two females instead of one. Jake only grinned, replying that he was well satisfied with the bargain. All he could offer Ila Mae in return, he said, was himself and a yellow dog.

That first year Hennie lived in Middle Swan, she wrote letters to the postmasters at Mingo in eastern Colorado and Topeka in Kansas, inquiring whether anyone was searching for a lost girl. The man on her wagon train who'd brought her news of the Indian attack hadn't asked the family's name or where they'd come from, so Hennie wasn't able to track down Mae's relatives. She asked the *Rocky Mountain News* in Denver to print an article about the foundling, but the only response to it came from a woman who wrote to Hennie, asking her to make sure Mae wasn't a boy, for her own twelve-year-old son had run off.

After a time, there was nothing more that Hennie could do, and she was glad. By then, Mae was as much a part of Jake's and Hennie's lives as if she'd been their own, and truth be told, Hennie didn't want to find the girl's people. As the years passed with no other children joining their family, Jake and Hennie came to believe Mae was the Lord's blessing.

So Mae lived in Middle Swan as the Comforts' daughter, but when she was grown, she left out, and the girl's leaving had pained Hennie. That was Hennie's own fault, however. She and Jake didn't want Mae to live out her life in a mining camp, so they sent her down below to attend school. Hennie knew the day Mae enrolled at the University of Denver and

saw what the world was like beyond the Tenmile Range that the girl would never return to the high country. That had been Hennie's intention all along. For Hennie, leaving war-numbed Tennessee for Middle Swan had been a step upward, and now, leaving Middle Swan was a chance at a better life for Mae. Hennie didn't want her daughter to have to bear the hardships that Hennie had endured—the brutal way of the mines, the harsh winters, the pneumonia and influenza that claimed women and babies not strong enough for the mountains. Oh, Hennie loved the mountains, but she knew Mae's life would be easier away from them.

Mae married a man who started a fountain pen company in Fort Madison, Iowa, and the two moved to the banks of the Mississippi. Hennie visited, but she was a person who'd lived in the mountains too long, and her blood had grown thin. She'd as soon walk in a barrel of molasses as visit there in the summer. And in winter, that Mississippi River cold went clear through her. So the mother and daughter kept in touch through letters, as well as Mae's occasional visits to the Swan. They were as close all their lives as if Mae had been Hennie's own flesh and blood. It was Hennie's love for Mae that had sent her out into the world, and now it was Mae's love for Hennie that insisted the old woman move to Iowa.

❧

Hennie stopped talking when the sound of thunder rolled across the mountain, and she looked up to see clouds hovering over the mountain peaks.

"It's a-coming on to rain," Nit said, standing up and dropping her patchwork in a cluster of pine needles.

Hennie picked up Nit's sewing and dusted it off, handing it to the girl. "Just you come. We've got to get below before one of those electric storms hits." She felt the hair on her arms stand up and shoved her own sewing into the lard bucket and grabbed its bail handle. "We'll take our backtrack."

The girl clutched her patching and followed the old woman as she scurried below timberline. Reaching the trees, they heard another clap of thunder as loud as a dynamite charge, and Hennie felt an itching in her scalp and the back of her neck.

"That noise pesters my ears," Nit said, putting the palms of her hands over her ears. "I guess it's not summer, after all."

The rain began to fall then—chill silver mountain rain, not the gentle spring rain Hennie knew as a girl in Tennessee, the kind that she'd let wash over herself in gladness while the mud squished up between her toes. Mountain rain was as cold as melted snow.

"We can't stand under these trees," the old woman said. She continued down the trail, until she reached the faint impression of a turnoff and led the way through the pines, past drifts of snow that wouldn't melt until summer was almost over, to a deserted shack. She removed two blocks placed so that porcupines wouldn't gnaw the door, and pushed her way into the cabin. The shack smelled like a bunch of stewed owls, so Hennie left the door open, but that let in the cold. The girl shivered so that Hennie picked kindling off a pile and placed it in the fireplace, then found a baking soda can with matches in it and lit a fire. She took off Jake's old sweater and placed it around the girl's shoulders. "The rain won't last but a few minutes," she told Nit.

"This storm uneasies me. I wished there was a feather bed. We could lie down on a feather bed and never get struck by lightning," Nit said, snuggling into the sweater. "Lightning never hits a feather bed. It's a fact." When the girl had warmed, she looked around the cabin, which had a built-in bunk in the corner and two rough chairs. She pulled one of them to the fire and sat down, reaching for a half-rusted Log Cabin syrup tin on the floor and showing it to Hennie. "This looks just like my little house. Do you think he'll mind if I take it, the man who owns this place, I mean?"

"Take it. Nobody's lived here since Joe Sarsfield. He's been dead a long time. Some folks called him Vinegar Joe, on account of he was so sour. He was a sooty-looking man, a complainer, and as hard as a pine knot. He didn't have to live up here so close to timberline, leaving Maudie snowed in for the winter. Wouldn't give her hardly enough money to buy food, either." Hennie's face twisted in pain at the memory.

"His wife?" Nit asked, placing the syrup can in the lard bucket.

"Yes."

"That sounds like another story," Nit said.

"It is, or more of one I've already told you. Most of my stories fit together one way or the other," Hennie said. She sat down in a chair beside Nit, took off her rubber shoes, and propped her feet on a box in front of the fire.

⚜

Maudie Sarsfield was the workingest woman on the Tenmile. She quilted for others for a half-dollar a spool. She spent a week using up all the thread on the spool, because she took six or eight stitches in an inch, but she liked doing the stitching. "Quilting keeps me from going queer," she told Hennie. Maudie stitched her initials on quilts when she was finished. Not one in ten women she quilted for ever noticed the *M.S.*, but Maudie took pleasure in it. She knew it was a bit of foolishness, but that was her way of being remembered. After all, a woman didn't leave much behind in the world to show she'd been there. Even the children she bore and raised got their father's name. But her quilts, now that was something she could pass on. Joe wouldn't value her quilts after she crossed over and would likely tear them up for rags or horse blankets. But if her initials were hidden in some other woman's quilts, why something of her would go on living.

Of course, Maudie kept all that to herself, because if Joe knew how much quilting pleased her, he wouldn't have allowed her to do it. Joe Sarsfield was mean enough to insult Jesus Christ.

He was cruel to his wife in other ways. He could get out in the winter, go into town if he wanted. But Maudie was frail and couldn't walk through the snowdrifts. She didn't see a well day in her life living up here at the top of the Swan. The women knew that, and they made the trip up the mountain every whipstitch to visit with her and give her a little human comfort. One or two hinted that Maudie ought to leave Joe, but she knew he'd hunt her down and kill her, and there were some who believed he'd have that right. More than once, he threatened to put her in the asylum. Maudie never told these things to the women who were her friends, but they had a way of knowing.

Hennie understood things weren't good between Joe and Maudie, but she hadn't understood just how bad they were, not until that day she'd stopped by the cabin and found Maudie not an hour away from giving birth. "Where's Joe? Did he go for the doctor?" she asked.

"He left two days ago. I expect he's on a high lonesome somewhere." Maudie twisted in agony on the bunk. "He didn't know the baby was coming or he'd have been here. I know he would have. The baby's early," she added, pleading in her voice so that Hennie would not say a word of criticism about Joe.

Hennie wondered why a wife would protect her husband that way, but Maudie must have her reasons, she decided, and only sniffed. "They're all early up here. It's too late to go for the doctor. You're too far along to be left alone. I guess it's up to you and me to deliver this baby—mostly you." She chuckled to ease herself and to make the woman in the bed smile. "Being early means a small baby and an easy delivery."

The labor didn't last long, but Maudie was sickly, and it was all she could do to push out the baby, a mewly thing, tiny but healthy. Hennie wrapped the baby in a bit of towel and was just finishing cleaning up the bed when Joe stalked in, drunk, cursing his wife because supper wasn't on the table.

Hennie swallowed down her anger and told him, "Maudie needs her rest. She's just given you a daughter."

"A daughter!" Joe took a swig from the bottle in his hand. "I'd rather have a sow than a daughter for all she's worth. I told her a son. I wanted a son. All this time, and nothing but a girl!" he said, raging as if he'd swallowed a kerosene lamp. "I guess she's not woman enough to give me a son, just a hard-boiled brat of a girl."

Hennie glanced over at Maudie then, grateful that the woman had gone to sleep and was spared her husband's anger.

"Now she's done with it, she can get up and fix my supper."

"I'll do it," Hennie said, mad enough to wring the man's stringy neck. Hennie knew he wouldn't cook his own food, and if she didn't do it, Joe would pull his wife out of her sickbed as soon as Hennie left. She wondered then about the bruises she'd seen on Maudie's arms and legs. Most likely, the man had taken a stick to his wife.

When Joe had eaten and finished his bottle, Hennie told him, "Don't bother Maudie now. She needs her rest."

"Don't you be telling me what for. The Bible says women's to be silent around their men."

"What do you know about the Bible?"

"I know that much."

Hennie wanted to remind Joe of some other things the Bible said, but she'd have been wasting her breath. Besides, Maudie would suffer if Hennie got the best of Joe. So instead, she told him she'd bring his dinner the next day.

That night, however, a terrible storm swept across the mountain range. It raged for days, leaving Hennie snowbound at home. As soon as the trail was passable, she put on her snowshoes and went to Maudie. The woman was sitting in a rocker in front of a dead fire, staring straight ahead, when Hennie pushed open the door.

"Where's your baby?" Hennie asked.

Maudie didn't answer for a long time. "Gone under."

"Oh, Maudie." Hennie knelt beside the woman, taking her hands. "I'll help with the laying out. I brought along my piecing, a doll quilt for Mae. It's almost done. We'll wrap her in that."

"Joe's got rid of her." Maudie said it just like that—"Joe's got rid of her"—as if he'd just stood at the door and thrown the baby into the trash heap.

Hennie shuddered as she wondered whether the little child was alive when Joe took her from her mother. That would have been murder, a terrible thing to accuse someone of doing, and Hennie didn't ask. She feared what Joe would do to Maudie if he found out she'd told. And Hennie was afraid of what Joe might do to her for knowing. Or what she'd do to him.

Hennie didn't tell anyone her suspicions, but she gave it out to the women along the Swan how things stood with Maudie, and they made sure she was provided for. There were some that gave their prayers. Hennie would have bought prayers off *them* for Maudie, but they weren't for sale. They were freely given. This one gave her a sack of onions, saying they'd rot if Maudie didn't take them, and that one brought her scraps for her piecing, telling Maudie it would be a blessing to take them because she was so sick of the double-pink, she couldn't stand to take another stitch in it. Even women such as Hennie who joyed to quilt took their tops to her to be quilted. Instead of paying her money, which Joe would have taken, they brought her groceries from the Pinto store.

Women had a way of sharing, and Maudie knew that it

would be an unkindness to turn them down, for she was well aware they acted out of love. Accepting the work was her way of thanking the women for their generosity. When Maudie opened the door and saw one of her friends standing there, happiness spread across the disheartened woman's face.

She loved visiting with the women, but Mae was her especial joy. Hennie believed Maudie must have seen her own baby's face in Mae. The woman begged Hennie to bring Mae with her when she called, and on the few times Maudie made it down to Middle Swan, she stopped at the Comfort house, asking if Mae was about. Hennie, who'd told her Mae's story, thought Maudie felt a kinship with the little lost child, for the woman was as lost a person as Hennie ever saw.

Hennie called on Maudie for the last time to find the woman in the cabin, lying in the bunk, Joe sitting in front of the fire. Hennie had brought along a pie, which she set on the table before she went to her friend. Maudie roused herself and turned, her hand covering the side of her face. But her hand wasn't large enough to hide the burn.

"The fool woman burned herself. She screamed her eyes out till I thought I'd have to fist her. What the hell you waiting on? Bring me that pie. I ain't had a decent thing to eat for two days. I need a drink, too. You got any about you?"

Hennie turned on him. "You get the doctor!"

"Get him yourself."

"Git! Now!" Hennie snarled. "Or I'll tell every man in Middle Swan what you did to your wife." Hennie was mad enough to gouge his eyes out.

For a minute, she thought he might get up and try to kill her, and she didn't care, because she was angry enough to fight a panther. But she knew Joe was a coward. He whined and fussed, muttering he hadn't done a thing, but after a time, he put on his coat and left. Hennie wondered if he'd really bring the doctor, but maybe it didn't matter, for she knew Maudie was dying. There was no need for a doctor, but it was in Hennie's mind that Maudie would die easier if her husband wasn't around.

After Joe left, Hennie went to the sick woman and folded back the quilt. Maudie lay there naked, her whole side burned, as if she'd fallen into the fire—or been shoved, Hennie thought. Maudie would have ripped off her fiery clothes, then lain down on the bed and suffered for hours. As she put her arm under Maudie's pillow, Hennie felt an angel crown under the woman's head and knew that little mass of feathers wadded up in the pillow meant the woman didn't have but a little while left on this earth. "Maudie?" Hennie said, touching her friend's hand.

The woman opened her eyes and muttered, "Hennie?" She tried to raise her head but couldn't. So she squeezed Hennie's hand instead.

"Joe's gone for the doctor."

"No use. I'm done for, and I'm glad. I don't want to live anymore. I prayed you'd come. There's something I got to give you," Maudie said, taking her time with the words. Hennie thought Maudie meant a few coins or a trinket, something she didn't want her husband to have, and Hennie said not to trouble herself.

But Maudie was agitated and wouldn't be still until Hennie brought her sewing basket to her. "It's in the bottom, under a bit of paper," Maudie whispered.

Hennie took the contents out of the basket, noticing the basting threads that had been carefully saved to be reused, the old-fashioned brass pins, and a wooden thimble that the woman must have carved herself. At the bottom of the basket was part of an envelope that had been glued down. Hennie pried it up then stopped, as she stared at what Maudie had saved. It was a piece of Mae's dress, the one she was wearing when Hennie found her. Homespun it was and dyed blue. Only the scrap was new, never even washed.

"How did you get this?" Hennie asked after a time, although she knew the answer. "Mae is... Mae is..." She couldn't speak the words.

"My baby," Maudie said for her.

"You should have claimed her. Why didn't you?"

"Joe would have killed her, too," Maudie whispered. It took the dying woman a long time to tell the story, for her life was draining out of her.

She and Joe and Orleana, for that was Mae's name, crossed the plains in a wagon by themselves. One night, the girl wandered off, and when he discovered her missing in the morning, Joe wouldn't let Maudie search for her. He said that leaving her like that would teach the worthless thing. Maudie refused to leave without her child, so Joe tied her to the wagon, telling her she could go along or get dragged to death.

"He never wanted Orleana," Maudie said slowly, explaining she'd prayed that someone kind would find her little girl

and keep her. She thought the child might even be better off
with the Indians than with her own father. "But you found
her," Maudie said, her burned lips trying to form a smile.

Maudie was right there in Denver when Hennie made
the rounds of the immigrant trains with Mae, asking if anyone had lost a child. The woman hid in her wagon so that
the little girl wouldn't recognize her own mother, but she
heard Hennie say she was headed for Middle Swan. Maudie
waited five years, until enough time had passed that Mae
wouldn't remember her, and by then, Maudie had aged con-
siderably, too. Then she convinced Joe there was easy gold to
be found on the Swan River, and they moved to the Tenmile.

"You saved my girl's life," Maudie said. "He'd have killed
her, just like he did this baby. He said there wasn't any reason for girls to live, and their crying made him crazy. Joe
knew I loved the babies, loved them as much as I hated him.
He wouldn't let something I loved live." She explained that
she'd seen Joe smother the infant before he took her outside
and buried her.

Maudie said that just before she died, when there was
nothing else Joe could do to her. Hennie sat beside the
woman, listening to the scuffling noise made by pack rats
moving around in their secret place in the wall. She wanted
to ask the date Mae was born, but by then, the woman was
past knowing anything. When Joe returned, the doctor with
him, Hennie told them it was too late. Maudie had crossed
over.

"Who's going to take care of my old dog?" Joe asked.

At that, Hennie slapped him hard, as hard as she could.
Joe made a fist, but the doctor grabbed his arm and told Joe

if he so much as touched Hennie's little finger, he'd have to
account to the entire camp.

∽ॐ✸

Hennie stared into the remains of the fire for a moment,
then went to the door, pushing it open as far as it would go,
and looked out at the trees that were dripping rain. The
heavy scent of pine came into the cabin. The rain had
slowed and the sun was shining through the trees. "Devil
rain," the girl said, nodding toward the door. When Hennie
didn't understand, Nit explained, "Rain and sun at the same
time."

"Devil rain," Hennie repeated. "I guess that means the
storm's done with. Just us go now."

"I'm glad you told me about Mae. It makes me think
some babies had it worse than my sweet Effie. Your story
heals me." The girl stood and returned the sweater to Hennie. The two went outside and gathered firewood, setting it
on top of the stack in the cabin, for it was the custom to replace any wood that was used up in a place of refuge. Then
using a stick, Hennie raked the embers in the fireplace and
watched them die, careful not to leave as much as a fire coal.

"What happened to Joe?" Nit asked, as they shut the door,
and Hennie returned the two blocks of wood to their place.

"He died," Hennie said with a mirthless chuckle. "I didn't
let on about Mae being his daughter, for fear he'd claim her
out of meanness. There are some that think even a father
like Joe has a right to his child. But I told about Joe killing
the baby. I said it was Maudie's deathbed confession, and folks
know I'm not a liar, so they had to believe me."

There was talk in Middle Swan about putting Joe on trial and hanging him or sending him off to prison. Some of the men were for making meat of Joe right then. Others thought Joe ought to have to live with himself, and when the Reverend Shadd arrived in Middle Swan later on and heard the story, he agreed, saying Joe would have died a thousand deaths if each day he'd had to face what he'd done—not that Hennie cared in the least what the Reverend Shadd said. "Joe saved everybody the trouble of deciding his punishment when he got drunk and wandered outside the cabin and froze to death," Hennie finished.

Water dripped off a jack pine down Nit's neck, and she stopped to rub herself dry. "Did you ever tell Jake and Mae who her folks were?"

"Yes. They had the right to know. I wondered how Jake'd take it, because Joe'd done him a meanness—high-graded a claim Jake was working. But when I told Jake, he said, 'Vinegar Joe's daughter? Great day, Hennie, you saved our girl from a terrible fate.' Jake never loved Mae less for knowing who she was."

Later, when Mae was older, Hennie told her, too. "I owed it to Maudie. She needed something more than quilts to be remembered by. Mae named her middle daughter Maudie. Funny thing was, Mae always looked more like me than Maudie or Joe. How do you explain that?"

The girl didn't answer. She followed Hennie down the path onto the main trail, scattering the pine needles that had gathered in ridges after the rain.

"If you're a praying woman, you might say a prayer for Maudie," Hennie told Nit. As the two reached the path beside the dredge, Hennie herself said a prayer—or maybe it was an order: "Lord, you make sure Maudie has a little happiness. And you tell her Mae's doing fine, and she'll be taking care of me soon." Hennie frowned and added, "Not that I need to be taken care of."

Chapter 5

The Coffee Cup quilt was put in and ready for the Ten-mile Quilters. Hennie had basted the top to the batting and the back, then stretched the quilt sandwich tightly in the old frame, whose side rails were set to allow a comfortable reach for the quilters working from both directions. She was glad to see a quilt in the frame, for it had been empty since she'd finished her Bear Paw, and the room looked out of sorts without a quilt in progress.

Hennie had promised the girl Nit Spindle that she'd arrange a quilting after Nit finished her own top. With many hands, the quilt would be completed in hours, but even more important, the girl would have a chance to get to know her neighbors. "There isn't a better friend than a mountain woman," Hennie had told Nit. Still, in the high country, where the blood ran thin, women were standoffish. They didn't take to strangers. A person could live on the Swan for ten or twenty years before she was considered "one of us." By making Nit a member of the Tenmilers, Hennie would force the others to accept the girl.

There was another thing on the old woman's mind, too, for she had invited a second woman, one even newer in Middle Swan than Nit, to attend the quilting.

So when her Bear Paw was done, Hennie had taken it out and bound it off, leaving the frame empty while she completed the blocks for her Coiled Rattlesnake and bound them together with sashing. Then, because she didn't want to put that quilt into the frame until the Coffee Cup was done, she'd turned to carpet rags to occupy her hands. She'd torn strips and rolled balls for weeks, it seemed, and her fingers itched to quilt again.

The house had been scrubbed and flowers picked and set in jars around the room so that the place smelled of Chinese lilacs and yellow roses. The windows in the big room weren't made to open, but no matter. Even in the heat of late June, the house, with its thick walls, was cool. Hennie opened wide the front and side doors to let in the fresh air and turned on all the lights. The big house, with its deep-set windows and log walls, was always a little dark. As she surveyed the room a last time, Hennie's eyes stopped on the silver frame, worn through from so many polishings that it was mostly pot metal now, and picked it up. "The girl needs help," she told the long-ago picture of Jake, setting it down quickly as she heard footsteps on the path. "If this isn't the way I'm to be the Lord's instrument, then the two of you best figure out how I am—and before snow sets in. And I could use your help for myself, too, Jake. You know I've got something to settle before I go below."

Nit was the first to arrive. She set a plate of fried chicken and a basket of half-moon pies on the kitchen table, saying, "I brought a little something or other," and clasped her hands together to keep them still. "You think those ladies will laugh at my quilt?" she asked, putting a hand to her cheek to stop a nervous twitch. "Quilts are different at home. We pay no mind to the quilting, just take big old stitches to get done. And I never attached binding before. Maybe they'll think it's a fool thing to use coffee cups for a design. I don't know why I ever did." The girl smoothed her hair, which had been freshly washed and set in pin curls, then brushed until it shone. She wore a pretty dress with a little round collar. The girl had dressed in her best to make a good impression.

"They'll like it fine," Hennie soothed her, thinking that while the girl might never be a first-rate quilter, she had improved in the weeks that she'd lived in Middle Swan. She was better than some, including Bonnie Harvey, who didn't know how to quilt any more than a dog did. There was hope for Nit. "We get so tired of trading the same old patterns that they'll be joyed to find a new one."

"You think so?" Nit asked, as if she didn't quite believe it.

"Maybe not Monalisa Pinto, but she's airified. She never likes anything. Put no dependence on what she says. You could understand a goose as good as you could understand her."

"She's right smart of hardness," observed Nit, recalling the

snub the woman had given her the day Nit first saw her at
the Pinto store. Monalisa hadn't softened to her since.

Hennie was almost sorry they'd invited the storekeeper's
"wife" to become a member of the Tenmile Quilters and it
was Hennie's own fault. She'd felt sorry for the woman, who
had worked at the Willows before she took up with Roy Pinto.
Hennie thought that asking Monalisa to become a Tenmiler
would help the woman's reputation, and it had, although
Monalisa never was grateful. Folks put Monalisa's days as a
hooker out of mind, but the woman herself couldn't seem to
stop looking for slights, which Hennie supposed was why she
acted so high-and-mighty, quibbling over little things and
pointing out faults in others. "Sometimes, we call her 'Mrs.
Pickaround.' Not to her face, of course." Hennie was a little
ashamed of herself for the remark, for she was not a long-
tongued woman. She added quickly, "But she quilts first-rate.
A woman isn't all bad if she turns out good quilts."

She stopped to contemplate a moment before she continued. "A quilt circle's like a crazy quilt. You got all kinds in it.
Some members are the big pieces of velvet or brocade,
show-offish, while others are bitty scraps of used goods, hoping you don't notice them. But without each and every one,
the quilt would fall apart. There's big and small, old and new,
fancy and plain in a quilt circle. Some you like better than
the others. We have our differences, and Monalisa is a trial,
but it's a surprise how we all come together over the quilt
frame, even Monalisa. We're as thick as a lettuce bed."

Nit asked about the other quilters, and Hennie obliged
her, hoping the gossip would put the girl at ease. Carla

Swenson was a retired teacher from the high school. Her sweetheart had been killed in a mine accident when Carla was a young woman, and she'd never married. Gus Bowes, Carla's intended, and his brother worked the old Yankee-Dives mine, using a rope ladder to carry up the ore on their backs. The brother went to town for dynamite, and when he came back, he found Gus dead at the bottom of the mine shaft. Carla never gave her heart to another. Hennie remembered that awful time and how she'd visited her friend day after day to restore her spirits, advising her to keep her mind on the happiness that she'd had with Gus, not the loss. "Don't you believe a short time together is better than no time at all?" Hennie asked. Then Hennie told her the story about Billy.

Bonnie Harvey was Carla's sister, and she had enough children for the two of them—nine. "Her husband's a miner. She's a Baptist." Hennie pronounced the word "Babtis." Carla was dark-headed, as thin as a needle, but Bonnie was plump and blond and looked like a star that fell from heaven.

Edna Gum was a highborn lady, and her husband was vice president of the Swan River Dredge Company, but she was plain as a shoe, and you wouldn't guess in a million years that she was rich, Hennie said. "She's mannerable, but she never puts on airs. Edna's got silver things, but she acts like they're nothing better than the tin the rest of us use. And she doesn't dressify like Monalisa Pinto."

Another new woman had been invited, Hennie added, a woman newer even than Nit in Middle Swan. She had arrived in town only a week or two earlier, and Hennie had met her when she went calling with a Gold-and-Silver Cake.

When Hennie examined the newcomer's quilts, she decided there was nothing to be done but to invite her to the quilting. "You never saw anything so finely made. Her name's Zepha Massie, and she's a shy thing, but that doesn't matter over a quilt frame. There's something about stitching together that draws a woman out." Hennie lowered her voice, although there was no one else to hear her. "I hope you'll be especial kind to her, because she doesn't know a soul."

Nit nodded importantly and said, "I'll do the best I can."

Hennie explained that three of the Tenmilers had moved below the year before, because they couldn't take the altitude anymore, and if the club wanted to finish a quilt in a day, it had to find new members. Since Hennie was the only founding member of the Tenmile Quilters left in Middle Swan, she could invite anyone she liked to join. Zepha's quilting skill wasn't the only reason Hennie had asked her to come, of course. Zepha wasn't young; she looked like she'd never been young, but she wasn't as old as the Tenmilers, and Nit needed a friend close to her own age. Much as she loved Nit, Hennie knew she was more like a mother to the girl than a friend Nit could gossip and giggle with. "Mrs. Massie didn't say where she'd come from, and I didn't ask. Sometimes it's best not to," Hennie said.

"You think she's done a wrong thing?"

"No, I didn't get that from her. But you never know why a person comes here. It's been that way since ever in a mining town. There's always those that want to get away from the past and start fresh, especially now, with times so hard. You don't know what a person's had to do to keep body and soul together. Mountain folks have their secrets, and it's best not to pry. They don't want you to know, and sometimes you're better off not knowing."

"Have you got secrets, Mrs. Comfort?" Nit laughed at the idea.

"I've told most of mine or forgotten them," Hennie said. She added quickly, "I don't reckon I've got any secrets you'd want to hear, at any rate." Of course, there was one secret she'd kept, a story left untold. Hennie couldn't tell it until it had an ending, and she hadn't decided yet what the ending would be.

Nit didn't ponder Hennie's reply, because they heard footsteps on the flat stones that led from the street to Hennie's door, and two ladies entered the house, their arms filled with sewing baskets and plates of food covered with dish towels.

"Why, make you acquainted with Bonnie Harvey and Edna Gum," Hennie cried, glad that the two had arrived before Monalisa Pinto.

Edna, a portly-looking woman, set a pound cake on the table and exclaimed, "Are those half-moon pies? I haven't had half-moon pies since I moved to Colorado. I'll bet you brought them. I'm just so glad you came, Mrs. Spindle. Are they peach?" she asked Nit, who nodded and twisted her hands nervously. Hennie smiled, for the women were as friendly as she had hoped.

Bonnie put down a big bowl of salad and went to the quilt frame. "What's this design?" she asked, frowning. She walked around the quilt and answered her own question. "It's coffee cups. I was looking at it upside down. Coffee cups. Isn't that fine!"

"And every one's a different fabric," Edna added. "I'll have to ask you for your pattern, Hennie."

Hennie swallowed a smile, because Edna knew full well that Hennie hadn't made the quilt top. Hennie liked the old patterns. Besides, some of the Coffee Cup blocks were askew, and the corners didn't come together properly. Hennie would never put in such a quilt for her friends to see. In that nice way Edna had, she was trying to make the girl feel at home.

When Hennie pointed out that Nit had made the top, the girl stammered, "It's just an everyday quilt."

"That's the best kind. They ought to all be everyday quilts. If you don't use them, what good is a quilt?" Bonnie asked. "I never saw the sense of making a quilt that gets stuck away in a drawer."

"I hoed corn to get the money to buy the goods for the sashing," Nit told her, as Carla Swenson entered the house, ducking her head as she came in, because she was taller even than Hennie. She set two loaves of bread, still warm from the oven, and a jar of pickled beans on the table.

Right behind her was Monalisa Pinto, clutching a little jar of relish. Monalisa was the only one in the room wearing a hat. "How's yourself?" she asked Hennie.

"As good as if I was half my age, except my arthritis troubles me some."

"Same," Monalisa said.

They didn't hear the new quilter, Zepha Massie, a pale, gaunt woman who walked across the stones as quietly as a cat and was standing in the doorway, looking in. She'd have stayed there a long time if her little girl hadn't begun to chatter.

"Just you come in," Hennie said, taking Zepha's thin hand, noticing that although her dress was patched, Zepha, too, was wearing a hat. It was a worn straw one, the back edge a little ragged, as if it had been nibbled by a mouse, but nonetheless, it was a hat, and it was set at a fashionable angle on the woman's yellow curls. "Make you acquainted with your new neighbors."

"You brought a child," Monalisa said, her lips, which were as thin as crackers, turning down a little.

Carla interrupted, "The dear little thing. I'm sure glad to meet you."

"She's just a little cotton-top feller, not bigger than a cricket, much. Well, I've been awful little all my life, too," Nit said, stooping to look the child in the eye, but the tiny girl grasped her mother's hand and wouldn't return Nit's gaze. "She can sit under the quilt frame. Someday maybe I'll have a little girl to sit under the frame," Nit added wistfully.

"I did that when I can first remember. Isn't that right, Bonnie?" Carla said.

"We sat there when we were just being raised up. Then the women asked us to thread their needles. I thought it was because we were getting responsible. I didn't know those ladies couldn't see well enough to thread them theirself. Now we're just like them." Bonnie laughed. She asked Zepha, "What's your little girl's name?"

"Queenie. I named her myself."

"Well, who else would?" Monalisa muttered, stretching the sides of her rayon dress, because her slip peeked out below. "Named her for the Queen of England, did you?"

"I named her for a real nice lady," Zepha said. She handed

Hennie a flour sack and explained, "I brought you a bag of ashcakes."

"My favorite. We'll eat royal," Hennie said. Now that all the women were there, Hennie assigned them places on either side of the quilt frame, putting Nit and Zepha side by side and as far away from Monalisa as possible. The women exclaimed over the quilt top, even Monalisa, for none of them would be so rude as to criticize another woman's quilt to her face.

Zepha took out a worn thimble, a china one that had been broken and glued back together, and picked up a needle and thread. She pulled it through the fabric and began to take stitches the size of sand grains. Hennie complimented her, and Zepha said shyly, "I'm pretty well acquainted with quilting. I like it better than anything in the world nearly."

Nit asked if Zepha's husband worked on the dredge, and Zepha, not looking up from her sewing, shook her head. "We came here because we heard there was work for a fellow that could fix things. Blue—that's my man—if there's ever a good fixer that ever lived, it's Blue. You got anything that needs done, you ask him." She seemed exhausted from talking and let out her breath, looking down at Queenie, who was sucking her fist.

"Where'd you come from?" Monalisa asked, stopping her stitching to peer through her rimless glasses at Zepha.

The others glanced sharply at the storekeeper's wife, for such a question was a violation of good manners. "My, my needle goes through this quilt nice. I'm glad you didn't make an overalls quilt," Carla said quickly. "You can't hardly get a needle through an overalls quilt, even for tacking."

"A Mormon blanket. That's what you call an overalls quilt," explained Bonnie.

"Why, I didn't know that," Hennie said.

But Monalisa wouldn't let them change the subject. "I ask where you came from."

"Kansas," Zepha told her, staring at Monalisa with eyes the palest shade of blue Hennie had ever seen. "We come from Kansas. Don't let anybody tell you different."

"You don't sound like Kansas. I hope you're not from Texas. I don't trust a man that's from Texas," Monalisa persisted.

"I believe my husband was born in Texas," Edna said quietly. She ran her hand through her permanent wave, catching Hennie's eye and letting her right eyelid dip just a little. Mr. Gum was no more from Texas than Jesus Christ. Edna loved to bait Monalisa.

"That gambler was from Texas, you know, the one with the palomino horse. What was his name, Hennie?" Bonnie asked, changing the subject. Hennie was pleased, for she had an excuse to tell a tale. "I was just a little towhead then, but I remember him," Bonnie added.

Hennie finished stitching around the Coffee Cup square in front of her and leaned back in her chair. Jake had bought her the chairs one Christmas when he'd leased the Madonna Mine and had found a pocket of high-grade—sturdy oak straight chairs that would last a hundred years, he'd said. Only Jake hadn't lasted that long. "I was a grown woman, getting my first gray hair back then," Hennie replied. "His name was called Mutt Elmore." She smiled at the memory.

The women were quiet, watching Hennie, until Nit, who

could hardly keep herself still, asked, "Gee, are you going to tell us about him?"

Hennie pulled herself out of her reverie. She was getting old, she thought, because she didn't often allow her mind to wander and let an opportunity to tell a story slip by. My, she would miss telling stories, for in Fort Madison, no one seemed to care about what had happened in the Colorado high country. "I guess I could. It's not much of a tale. Are you sure you want to hear it?"

"Hello, yes!" Nit burst out, then reddened as the others turned to her.

Hennie paused to cut a piece of thread and lick the end, then after two or three tries, she thrust it through the eye of her needle. The women smiled at each other, for they knew Hennie liked to take her time beginning a story.

"I heard some of your Hollywood people gamble," Monalisa barged in. Edna sent her a sharp look, and Monalisa looked down at her quilting. She'd finished a Coffee Cup, too. "I'm almost ready to roll," Monalisa said.

"Hold your horses. I'm not," Bonnie told her.

"Tell us about the gambler, Hennie," Edna said, before Monalisa could interfere again with comments about film stars. She liked to talk about movie stars as much as Bonnie did religion.

"All right," Hennie agreed quickly, so that no one else would interrupt. "His name was Mutt Elmore, but you already know that."

In those long-ago days, the miners spent their leisure time hanging around the saloons, for they slept in shifts in the boardinghouses and had no place else to go when they weren't underground, Hennie explained to Nit. "For a nickel, a man could buy hisself a glass of beer and get a free meal thrown in. Of course, there were plenty who got drunk—and gambled. Mutt Elmore was one of the gamblers."

Hennie had held her needle in the air since she began the story, and now she stopped talking to catch up with the other quilters. "Ready to roll?" she asked.

"Not yet," Bonnie said. For a woman who took such big stitches, Bonnie ought to have been faster. "I'm rougher than a cow's tongue when it comes to quilting," Bonnie admitted.

"You're better than some," Hennie told her, for not for the world would she say a critical word about her friend's stitching.

Then the old woman continued, "One day, when Mutt was as drunk as a boiled duck, he rode that horse—Starlight, its name was—through the door into the saloon. It wasn't a regular door, but a pair of those swinging kind you see in the picture shows, wide enough for Starlight," she explained to Nit. Tables and cards and glasses went flying, but Mutt didn't care. "He rode right up to the bar and ordered hisself a beer, sat there in the saddle and drank it, while the horse did its business on the floor."

"How disgusting," Monalisa said. "I think we're all ready to roll now."

The women stood up and loosened the quilt in the frame and rolled it over one of the side rails to expose an unquilted section, which they fastened in place. Then they sat down again, all but Monalisa, who went to a little side mirror to study herself. Although on the hard side, she was nonetheless a pretty woman. Monalisa reached into her pocketbook for a tube of lipstick and rubbed it over her lips,

then touched her finger at a dab of color that extended beyond her mouth. She wiped her finger on a handkerchief, for
even Monalisa would not want to stain someone's quilt.

Hennie waited until Monalisa sat down before she continued. "That's not the whole story," she said, rolling her thread
over her finger to make a knot, then pulling the knot through
the quilt top to hide it in the batting. "Mutt thought that riding into the Gold Pan on Starlight was so funny that he got
to doing it every time he came into town. The barkeep took
a pure fit at the Gold Pan smelling like a stable and him having to clean up after that horse, and he told Mutt if he didn't
quit that, he wouldn't be welcome anymore. But Mutt kept
right on riding into the Gold Pan, and if the bartender
wouldn't sell him a beer, Mutt would sit there on that horse
all night anyway. At first, the other fellows thought it was
pretty funny, but after a bit, they got mighty tired of Mutt
and Starlight."

"What did they do?" Nit asked. She was so absorbed in
the story that she had stopped quilting. So had Zepha, who
sat motionless, listening to Hennie.

Hennie glanced at the quilt in front of her and saw that
she had lagged behind again. She held her tongue while she
worked her needle in and out of the fabric, then noticed that
a corner of one of Nit's squares had been stitched too close
to the edge, and raveling showed through. Hennie secured
the piece. She took a few more stitches, pulled the thread
through, then paused with her needle in the air. "They sawed
out all around the floor in front of the bar. The next time
Mutt rode through the door, the floor gave way under him,
and him and the horse both fell through."

"Served them right," Monalisa said, while the others laughed.

"Maybe not the horse," Hennie told her. The saloon was built right over the Swan River. Hennie didn't know if Starlight hit his head going down or just what happened, but the horse drowned as dead as four o'clock.

Zepha clucked her tongue and exchanged a glance with Nit. The two younger women looked tickled with the story.

"They just left Starlight there. But then he got to smelling, and they had the darnedest time getting him out, had to take out most of the floor. Now that's the dyin' truth," Hennie said.

"What happened to the man?" Zepha asked in a low voice, glancing around her, as if she wasn't sure she should have spoken.

Hennie thought a minute. "Why, I don't know. He just disappeared, I guess. He was around for a time. Then he wasn't. Do you know where he went, Carla?"

The other woman shook her head. Back then, men just went and came, she said.

"They still do," Edna added, resting a fleshy arm on the quilt and peering out the door. "Lookit there, it's raining a bit, sun and rain at the same time."

"Devil rain," Hennie said.

Monalisa looked up sharply. "I haven't heard of such a thing."

Hennie caught Nit's eye, for Nit had been the one to tell her about devil rain. "Why, I can't hardly know why you haven't," she said.

"You think there's more rain coming?" Zepha asked. "I ask it because I heard the bread wagon pass over."

Hennie looked at her blankly, and Nit, who knew the expression, explained that the bread wagon was thunder. Nit exchanged a glance with Zepha as if the two of them shared a secret.

"You can't ever tell in these mountains," Hennie said. "It's best always to expect rain, maybe snow."

"Oh!" Zepha exclaimed. "This place is the strangest I've ever been. To think you have to use a blanket in the middle of summer! I hope it doesn't get much colder come winter." The women, even Nit, exchanged glances with each other, but none wanted to apprise Zepha of winter along the Tenmile Range. Hennie marked it in her mind to look through her trunk for a coat that her daughter, Mae, had worn as a baby. It ought to fit Queenie. And if she couldn't find it, she'd order one from the catalogue and say it had been Mae's.

Edna, who'd finished her portion of the quilting, pushed back her chair, stood and stretched her back like a cat.

Hennie looked over the quilt and asked, "Everybody ready to roll again?" The women got up and adjusted the quilt, worked the kinks out of their backs, and went to quilting once more. Bonnie glanced over at the food but didn't say anything. It was Hennie's call as to when they ate.

"Maybe Mutt got run out of town. He hadn't the brains of a sapsucker and used one of those little things you fix to your sleeve to hold a card. What do you call it?" Hennie asked.

"A hold-out," Bonnie said.

"How do you know about hold-outs?" her sister asked.

"I know plenty about gambling. You forget I lived next door to Missouri Rice."

"Some of us here knew that name mighty well once," Hennie said. She felt a tug on the hem of her skirt and glanced down to see the little girl, Queenie, looking up at her. She was chewing on a piece of her mother's cornbread, and the floor was covered with crumbs. "I think I've got a doll of Mae's someplace that ought to be played with," Hennie told Zepha.

The woman said not to bother. She reached into the pocket of her apron and brought out a rag doll with an embroidered face and a patchwork dress. As Zepha handed it to her daughter, Carla caught her arm and said, "Look at the tiny dress. It's got a piece of that old-fashioned paisley." She pointed to a scrap of material that was pink and white and purple.

"Pickle," Zepha said. "The lady that made me a present of it called it Persian pickle."

"Persian pear was the name my grandmother put to it. That scrap's as pretty as your special blue, Hennie," Edna said, referring to the peacock blue cotton that Hennie had bought years before and still used in her quilts. "Why look, there it is right here in this top," Edna added, pointing to a coffee cup that had been pieced out of the blue. The women looked up at Nit, who blushed, because Hennie was partial to the women she gave scraps to.

"Who's Missouri Rice?" Nit asked, changing the subject. She looked at Hennie as if she sensed another story.

"Tell her," Bonnie said, adding, "It's a better story than Mutt Elmore's."

The others watched Hennie expectantly, and Edna said she hadn't heard about Missouri Rice, either.

Hennie glanced around the frame. Some of the quilters were ready to eat, she knew, but Missouri Rice was a good tale, and Hennie'd never let down a person who wanted a story. Besides, she herself would rather talk than eat. "I'll tell you. Then we'll have our dinner." Bonnie and Carla knew about Missouri Rice, because they were in on it, she said. Edna wasn't living in Middle Swan then, and Monalisa, "I don't recollect as to whether you were around then, either, were you?" Hennie glanced at Monalisa, who didn't reply. Hennie knew full well that Monalisa had been in town, but she was working at the Willows then and hardly a member of the Tenmilers. What's more, Missouri Rice might have been one of those who'd snubbed Monalisa. There was nobody so down and out that she couldn't look down on someone else.

"I don't recall," Monalisa replied.

Hennie nodded, not wanting to put too fine a point on it, and began her story. "Missouri Rice was a Middle Swan lady that married Otto Rice, and he wasn't worth shooting. I wouldn't have took up with him if he was strung with pure gold. He was as handsome as a hog—and a gambler to boot." She took three stitches and rested her needle.

⧌⧍

Otto Rice was also a con man. He played three-card monte and the shell game. In the shell game, he'd put a pea under one of three walnut shells, then quickly move them around. He'd get some sucker to put up money, thinking he could spot the shell with the pea under it, but of course, Otto had already palmed the pea. Jake Comfort was as smart a man as ever was to spot the switch. There wasn't anybody could fool him. So he put up a dollar on a game Otto was running, thinking to catch Otto when he slipped the pea into his hand, but right in the middle of moving around the shells, Otto said, "Damn mouse," and before he could catch himself, Jake looked away. Jake told Hennie he didn't mind losing the dollar to see a man who could cheat a fellow that good.

Not everybody admired the way Otto cheated, however, and after a time, suckers fell off for Otto's tricks. He turned to poker and other card games, and he stuck with them because he was took up with the gambling fever. When he thought he could get away with it, he cheated. Otto would sit in the Gold Pan all day looking for somebody to play cards with. He was partial to poker, but when he couldn't get up a game, he'd bet on anything—how far a mouse would run across a floor before the cat got it, when the first snowstorm would come in the fall, how long before one of the girls at the Willows would find herself a husband. He'd even bet on whether the sun would come up in the west in the morning.

Unlike most sporting men, Otto was married, and he loved his wife and kids more than just about anything except for gambling. When he was flush, he shared the winnings with them, always buying presents. He ordered silk dresses from Denver for his wife, Missouri, and enough toys for the kids, a boy and a girl, that they'd think it was Christmas. And then he'd go and gamble them away. If Missouri went out to quilting, she never knew when she got home, but whether her best dress was missing.

Otto went through a little bit of money that Missouri had inherited. He gambled away her jewelry, even her gold wedding ring. He took her dresses, the girl's doll, the boy's wagon. The only thing that was left to them was their house, which was one of the nicest in Middle Swan. Otto promised Missouri, promised on the children's heads, that he'd never risk their home, that he'd stop gambling before he did, but you'd as easy keep a squirrel on the ground as keep that man from cards. Many's the time Missouri went to Hennie, crying that she knew it was only a matter of time before Otto gambled away her home.

And that was just what he did. One afternoon, a stranger wandered into the Gold Pan, asking for a whiskey. Otto sized him up—the man looked young and was duded up—and invited him to sit down at the poker table. The man, who introduced himself as Jim Book, protested, saying what he knew about cards wouldn't fill a shot glass.

Otto insisted he was just putting together a friendly game, low stakes, so the man wasn't risking much. Jim bragged that he was as smart as a bee sting, and he guessed he might try a hand at that. He sat down with Otto and two or three other men, one of them Jake Comfort.

Jim won the first few times, because Otto was setting him up. The man turned gleeful, acting biggity at his luck, laughing and pounding the table and ordering whiskey for the other players. The loungers at the Gold Pan gathered around to watch, because it was always a treat to see a goose being plucked, although most of the men had lost to Otto at one time or another and didn't have any reason to want him to win. They'd just as soon both men lost.

The more Jim won, the more reckless he became, insisting on bigger and bigger stakes. He lost every now and again, but that didn't dampen his enthusiasm.

The stakes got higher—and higher—and Otto thought he'd take the sucker for a bundle. After all, he'd had a streak of luck that week, and he figured it hadn't ended. He'd take Jim Book's money, then maybe he'd treat Missouri and the kids to a trip to Glenwood Springs, where they'd take the baths. He'd buy Missouri a new wedding ring, too, one with diamonds, get the kids a hobby horse. At least, that was what he told Jake later on. Jake wasn't so sure, because no matter how good his intentions were, Otto always used his winnings to stake another game.

For a time, it looked as if Otto was right, for Jim began to lose big. The other men at the table said it was the man's own fault. He was a greenhorn and didn't have the chicken sense to know he was being plucked. Otto not only could use the hold-out and a sucker reflector, but he could make the pass and change a card, palm a card and bottom-deal. If there was a way to cheat, Otto had perfected it. Finally, Otto moved in to finish off the man, but suddenly, Jim won that hand, then another, and before he knew it, Otto was close to losing everything he'd won all week.

"Better drop out," Jake warned, but Otto couldn't be told, and he nodded at Jim to deal.

Otto picked up his cards and tried not to grin. He placed a bet, and Jim raised him. Jake and the others dropped out, so it was just Jim and Otto playing then. Otto asked for one card, and when he looked at it, he couldn't keep the grin off his face. Jim kept his hand. Otto increased the bet, and then Jim pushed his entire winnings, $500, into the center of the table. "Is your hand that good?" he taunted.

Otto swallowed hard, peeking at his cards from time to time. "I don't have five hundred dollars, but I've got a house. There's none finer in Middle Swan," he blurted out.

"What do I need a house for? I don't live here."

"That house is worth twelve hundred dollars, maybe more. I'll put it up against your five hundred."

The men around the table looked at one another. "Missouri'll kill you dead," Jake warned him, but instead of causing Otto to think, the remark only egged him on.

"You keep out of this, Jake," Otto said. "It's my house, and I'll do what I please. With the hand I've got, you'd go against Hennie if you was me."

"Well, I'm not going against a woman," Jim said. "She'll say she owns half the house, and some judge will side with her, and then where will I be?"

"She don't own any of it. That house is mine, was mine before I married her. I can sell it or burn it down if I want to, and she's got no say."

"He has kids," Jake told the stranger.

Jim shrugged. "That's not my concern." He thought a minute. "You say it's worth twelve hundred dollars. I guess maybe I could sell it for five hundred dollars then."

"I'll buy it," someone called. The rest of the men told him to hush, but instead, the man said, "Well, I will."

Finally Jim agreed, and Otto scribbled a deed to his house on a piece of paper, and when he finished, Jim said, "Call."

Otto grinned at Jim and put down his hand. "Flush," he said, leaning back in his chair until it was balanced on two legs.

He laughed out loud at Jim, and somebody slapped Otto on the back and said, "You did it, you durn fool." The others looked toward the bar, because the winner of a big pot always bought a round of drinks. Only Jake sat where he was, waiting.

Otto was ready to scoop up the pot when, without a word, the stranger put his hand on Otto's arm, then silently set down his cards, spreading them out like a fan. "Full house," he said.

There never had been a man as hard-put as Otto Rice at that moment. He stared at those cards with awe, just like they were the Ark of the Covenant, and slowly leaned forward, letting the chair crash down onto its front legs. "Why, you can't take my house," he said at last.

"He already did," Jake told him.

"How'm I going to tell Missouri? I'd rather eat a fried raccoon than tell Missouri I lost the house." Otto looked hard at Jim. "You're a professional and mean as a striped snake, ain't you? You came in here to beat me out of everything I own. You left me broke as a convict."

Jim only smiled and said, "And you were planning on fleecing a greenhorn? You small-town gamblers make me tired."

Otto swore and whined and begged, but in the end, there was nothing to it but for him to sign over the deed to Jim. Somebody offered him a drink, but Otto shook his head. Otto's face when he walked out of that bar was as black as a hat, and he swore he'd never touch a card again.

"The next time you come again, we'll remind you of that," the barkeep told him.

"You won't have to. I'm not going to follow drinking no more, neither," Otto vowed, and Otto never took another shot of liquor as long as he lived. He never picked up a card again, either.

Missouri bemeaned Otto for a few days, until her fury was spent, and then Jake and Hennie went to the house, where Missouri was all packed up, and gave her the deed, made out in her name.

Hennie and the Tenmilers had worked it all out one day, after Missouri had gone to the Comfort house, bitterer than quinine, saying she didn't have enough to feed the kids. "He's took everything else. I know the house is next," she'd cried.

The women had talked it over and decided there was nothing to it but to get that house away from Otto. Jake had known Jim Book when Book was a professional gambler, before he gave it up and became a preacher down in Denver. So he asked Jim to win that house off of Otto. "You keep the money. Just give us the deed," Jake told him, and after the game was over, the preacher brought the deed right there to the Comfort house, and Jake transferred it to Missouri. Even if he'd wanted to, Otto couldn't have gambled away their home again, because his wife owned it free and clear.

❦

"Time to eat," Hennie said. The women secured their needles in the quilt and stood up, moving to Hennie's kitchen and the big dinner plates. Stacked like they were, the plates were a series of red rims with white showing through where they had been nicked and chipped over the years. But they were real English china, and the women were proud to eat off them. While Hennie took Nit's chicken from the warming oven and dished up her own pot roast from the back of the range, the others removed the dish towels from the platters and plates they'd brought with them and complimented one another on the offerings.

"Sugar bread," Zepha whispered to Queenie, pointing to Edna's pound cake. Bonnie commented on Nit's chicken, and Edna told Zepha she'd hadn't had ashcakes since she didn't know when and had been hungering for them. Carla insisted Bonnie grew the best salad lettuce in Middle Swan; Hennie said she didn't know how Carla could bake such fat loaves of bread at ten thousand feet. They all asked for half-moon pies. Someone even complimented Monalisa on her relish. The women took their chairs from the quilt frame and carried them to Hennie's big table and sat to dinner, quiet while they ate. "It's the best eating I ever did eat," Nit said, as she fed the last of her sugar cake to Queenie, who was sitting on her mother's lap, and the others agreed.

After they were finished with the dinner, they returned to the frame for a final hour of quilting. Drowsy with the big meal, the women were quiet now, gossiping a little, commenting on their stitching. Someone asked Hennie for another story, but she said, "My tongue's been going like a clapper in a cowbell, and I best rest it. But first, I got something to say."

Hennie paused until the others looked up from their stitching and stared at her.

She took a deep breath and blurted out, "This'll be my last year on the Swan. I'm moving below to live with my daughter." Hennie hadn't intended to announce her plans that way, but she'd have to let her friends know sooner or later, and that afternoon seemed as good a time as any. She'd tell them all at once, so there would be less gossip about it.

The women were quiet for a moment.

"You're leaving out?" Bonnie asked, stunned.

Hennie nodded.

"It won't be Middle Swan without you here," Edna said. "You're as much a part of this place as the gold yet in the ground."

"And the rocks on the dredge pile, too," Hennie replied. "But it can't be helped. After all, the Lord would be taking me soon enough anyway. The only difference is I'll be leaving on my own two feet instead of being carried out."

The women were silent then, until Hennie said, "Leaving's not my idea. Mae's been pestering me and wouldn't give me any rest until I agreed to live with her. She keeps asking what if I fell or had heart failure. It's for the best." Hennie felt her eyes water but didn't wipe them for fear of calling attention to the tears.

"Well, I think it's a fine idea," Monalisa interrupted. "Why would you want to spend another winter snowed in with days so dark you can't see your hand unless the electric's on. You made the right choice, Hennie."

The others were quick to agree, interrupting one another to tell Hennie how lucky she was to have a daughter with a fine house with enough space for Hennie to have her own room. They said she wouldn't have to clean out stove ashes ever again, and that living in a town like Fort Madison, she wouldn't have to worry about the milk at the store being sour—everyone glanced at Monalisa when Bonnie made that remark. Carla said Hennie could just sit all day and quilt, which gave the old woman a sense of dread. Quilting was pure pleasure in snatched moments, but Hennie would grow bored with it if she had nothing else to do.

The women chattered so, that Hennie wanted to cover her ears, for she knew they didn't mean a word of what they said. They were as sorry as she was to hear of her leaving.

At last, Hennie interrupted them. "I'm not moving away tomorrow. I'll wait till the end of the year, and I told Mae I'll be back in the summers."

"Of course you will," Bonnie said fiercely.

"That's why I'm keeping my house just like it is. I won't sell it, or rent it, either."

"Of course you won't," Carla said. She looked down at the quilt and announced they were ready to roll.

The women stood and adjusted the quilt so that the final unfinished section was set in. They sat down again, quiet now, waiting to see if Hennie wanted to speak about the move. The old woman told them, "Let's not have any more talk of it. It makes me tired," and the women nodded in agreement.

They stitched quietly, and when the quilt was almost done, Nit asked Hennie what had happened to Missouri Rice.

"I feared one of you would wonder about that. Sometimes you ought not to know the end of a story," Hennie replied.

"You said he didn't gamble anymore," Zepha reminded Hennie.

The old woman gave a sad smile. "No, he didn't gamble, and he didn't drink. He got a job in the Big Minnie Mill and was as good a worker as ever was." She glanced down at her hands, at the thin gold wedding band that was as much a part of her finger as the age spots. Then she looked up at Nit and Zepha. "The problem was Missouri. Maybe she'd put up with too much from Otto for too long. Whatever it was, in the end, she didn't care any more for Otto than the hog cares for Sunday. One day, Otto came home and found Missouri'd sold the house and she and the kids had run off with a miner from the Pelican Kate."

Hennie took a backstitch in the quilt and cut her thread. "That's the end of the story," she said, looking around the table at the other women, who were putting away their needles and thimbles. "And the end of the quilt," she added. Hennie sighed and muttered to herself, "And just about the end of me as a Tenmile quilter."

Chapter 6

The girl looked peaked, her face white, and her breath came in gasps as she stumbled up the trail behind Hennie. The two were headed for the burn on the saddle on Sunset Peak. The old woman slowed to allow Nit to catch up with her. Each of the women carried two buckets. Nit's pails were empty. One of Hennie's contained their dinner, the other a canteen with water enough for the trip up the peak. They would refill it from one of the streams that fed into the Swan before they went downhill. Nothing refreshed a body more than mountain water.

Hennie thought of the number of times that she had climbed that trail and stopped beside a stream, dipping her hand into the wet and wondering if the water Sarah had drowned in felt as icy cold to the baby as the snowmelt did to Hennie's hand. It seemed odd to her, losing Sarah in the manner she had, that she always found the mountain streams comforting. She'd made the hike along that very trail after she'd lost the first of Jake's babies, and had stopped to put her toes into the stream and felt cleansed.

Hennie showed up at Nit's cabin that morning, telling the girl she'd like to borrow a little of her time if she could spare it, because it was as fine a day for raspberrying as there ever was. "We can't let the sun go down on it," she said. The day was only a little past noon of the year, just the right time for picking berries. Besides, Hennie felt protective of the girl, who had been doing poorly. A walk in the mountain air would bring color to her cheeks.

You'd think she was your own daughter, the way you carry on about her, Hennie told herself. But they were kindred spirits, too, the two of them having lost their babies, and the girl still freshly grieving for hers. Only another mother who knew the agony herself could understand that particular pain, and Hennie hoped that her sharing the girl's burden would help. Besides, Hennie thought, there was a reason the girl needed her more than ever now.

Nit had been glad to go, for she'd gotten up backwards that morning, she said, smiling her gladness at an excuse to be away from the house. "If I work at it like I have this morning, I'll not get nothing done anyway." She put aside her scrub board and laundry tubs, and the two women set out, walking at a leisurely pace down Main Street, because it was not a day for hurrying. They greeted Zepha Massie, the woman Nit had met at Hennie's quilting party, and invited her along, but she was greatly agitated. Her face was flushed, her pale blue eyes red, and she admitted, "I almost cried my eyes out this morning. I broke my needle stitching my husband's shirt."

"Don't you have but one needle?" Nit asked. Before Zepha could reply, Nit added, "Well, don't you worry. I've got a needle right here in my pocket you can have." Hennie had reminded Nit to take along her quilting, so the girl's gesture, while small, was generous, for it meant Nit wouldn't be able to sew at their nooning.

"That won't do any good. Breaking a needle when you're sewing on something that belongs to your man means he'll have himself a new love before what you're stitching wears out. Everybody knows that. I'll tell you the truth: If Blue threw me over, I'd die, me with two little ones and a dog."

"There's no need to fuss," Hennie told her soothingly. "You can cut up the shirt to make you a quilt."

Zepha mulled that over, but Hennie's words didn't satisfy her. "What if all the bad luck goes right into the quilt? What then? Tell me that."

"It won't. I know it for a fact," Hennie insisted. "Barbara Annie Moon who lived over to Breckenridge broke her needle when she was stitching her husband's pants, so she cut 'em up and made herself a britches quilt. Her husband was just as besotted over Barbara Annie after they wore out that quilt as he ever was."

Zepha pondered Hennie's words before she nodded. "I could try it. I could be real careful and use that quilt just for good, so it'll last until Blue's too old for devilment." She nodded to herself. "I thank you, Mrs. Comfort. It's a relief off my mind. You won't tell him, will you? If Blue finds out, he'll worry himself sick."

"Not a word."

After Zepha hurried off, the girl and the old woman paused to look at the bric-a-brac in Ye Olde Shop, mostly leavings from folks who had moved away or stuff that Maggie Fox, who ran the shop, had picked up around the mines. "Eli Nash had the first bathtub in town, and Ye Olde Maggie tried to buy it to sell to some tourist as an antique," Hennie said, shaking her head. Maggie never sold much, for most of her merchandise could be found at the dump, but the shop attracted its share of summer tourists, and that was Maggie's goal, Hennie said, because the woman did like to chatter. Nit's eyes lit up when she spotted a white platter in the window, just below the word CURIOSITIES, which was stenciled in black on the glass. The platter was feather-edged with blue, and there was only a tiny chip in it, but the tag said fifty cents, nothing short of robbery.

"Just wait. By the end of summer, she'll sell the whole store for a nickel," Hennie replied. "It's a right pretty plate. I wonder where she accumulated it from."

A few steps away, they encountered Monalisa Pinto by the Skelly pump at the Pinto store and stopped a minute to exchange pleasantries with her. Now that Nit was a member of the Tenmile Quilters, Monalisa had softened toward her. "The store's just got in a bolt of cloth in robin's egg blue with kittens on it. You young girls always like kittens," she said. Nit gave Monalisa a pretty smile at that, although when the woman went on her way, Nit told Hennie that she wouldn't let a cat into the house. "Cats get in your bed when you're asleep and suck your breath," she said.

Just then, the Reverend Shadd passed them on his way to

the store and raised his hat. "Good morning, Mrs. Comfort, and Mrs. Spindle, is it?"

Nit appeared pleased that the man knew her name, for she was shy and scurried out of church on Sunday mornings instead of shaking hands with the minister. "It is. Good morning," she replied, waiting for Hennie to greet the man.

But the old woman turned her back on the minister and was watching a man as aged as she was, taller and with a head of hair that shone like polished silver, come out of the barbershop. He hailed her, and she cried, "Tom Earley, I thought you were dead. Are you back in town? When was it you were planning to come around and see me and have a toddy and so forth?"

He didn't answer her question but, instead, he grinned at Hennie, the smile lines around his eyes crinkling. "Slow down and tell me how's the madam?"

"Couldn't be better now that I've seen you. And you, Tom, you look stout as a mule. How's your health?"

"Same."

"Make you acquainted with Nit Spindle. She's new to Middle Swan. Her husband, Dick, works the Liberty Dredge. Nit, this here is Tom Earley. Tom and his brother Moses came to Middle Swan not long after I did."

"And if I'd seen her before Jake Comfort grabbed her, I'd have married her myself—prettiest girl I ever saw."

"Oh, go on with you." Hennie blushed, then said fondly, "You always had a way with you." It hit her then that if she moved below, she might never see Tom Earley again, and that caused a pounding in her heart, for he was nearly her oldest friend. To still the thumping, she put a hand on her chest and turned to Nit, saying, "Mr. Earley was one of the hardest-working prospectors on the Swan."

"Not that it did me any good. All the gold dust I panned would fit into Hennie's thimble."

"That's right." Then Hennie explained, "But later on, he set up a plant to manufacture mining machinery, and that factory's worth more than any gold mine ever discovered on the Tenmile. Mr. Earley lives in Chicago."

Nit studied the man then. He was dressed in a fine white shirt and a good khaki suit, not flashy but much finer than the overalls and rough twill pants of the prospectors and dredge workers. He didn't wear a ruby stick pin or a gold ring or any other jewelry, but nonetheless, he looked as rich as a Pikes Peak nugget.

"Tom's had a cabin here for almost seventy years, and he can't stay away from these mountains. They do that to you," Hennie said.

"Can't stay away from you, Hennie. Are you still selling prayers?"

"Are you in need of one?"

"It might restoreth my soul."

"You sound like a stump-knocker."

"I read the Bible more now that I'm getting old."

"Old? Oh no. Not you, Tom."

The two bantered for a few minutes, until Hennie insisted, "You come to supper tomorrow evening. I'll bake a raspberry pie as good as you'll never know."

And Tom agreed. "Yep, old gal. I'll bring a loaf of bread."

"He's a good hand to make bread," Hennie told Nit. Then she turned to her old friend. "Us be going now. Tap 'er light, Tom."

"And yourself, Hennie."

As the two old friends paused in their good-byes, Nit wandered over to a deserted store with CANDY, NUTS & LADIES UNDERWEAR in dull gold lettering on the window. The shop's door was secured by a rusty lock, and stuck inside in the window frame was a handwritten note: "Back in 15 min," the words so faded that they were barely legible. Nit peeked into the display window, which was littered with dead flies. The corset on the headless, armless model in the window was dusty and yellow with age, and a slip that once had been pinned to the dummy had crumpled into a pile and was sun-faded.

When Nit turned around to ask about the store, she found Tom Earley gone and Hennie talking to the oldest couple the girl had ever seen in Middle Swan. The man had a face as wrinkled as that of a dried-apple doll, while the woman was as fat as mud, and the parchment skin of her face was powdered with flour. She was bent over, the upper part of her body almost parallel with the ground, and she carried a green birdcage with a yellow canary inside, which she held up for Nit to inspect. "We're taking Henry for his walk," she explained in a voice that was surprising for its youth and merriment. "I catched him gone this morning, but he was only up on the stove."

"It'd kill her if she lost him," the old man added in a voice scratched by mine dust.

"It'd kill me if I lost you, old feller," the woman said, taking the man's hand and squeezing it, and they exchanged adoring looks. The couple moved on slowly then, the woman swaying from side to side as she walked, for her legs were angled from rickets, and his were as wobbly as dishrags. They held the birdcage between them and swung it a little as they made their way down the street.

"They're as old as these mountains. I'll tell you about them sometime," Hennie said. The two women reached the edge of town and started up the trail that led to Sunset Peak. Hennie said again that it was a fine day for raspberrying. The sky was bright enough to hurt your eyes, and a breeze carried the scent of pines on it. Camp robbers and squirrels chattered along the trail, drowning out the screeching of the dredge, which grew fainter as the women climbed higher. The raspberry bushes would be full by now, Hennie guessed. The two would pick all they could carry, with plenty for pies and enough left over to fill half a dozen bottles. Before she left home, Hennie had taken down the jars and rubbers from her shelves and brought out the kettle, so that they could preserve the berries. The two would do the canning at Hennie's house, for the girl didn't have her own bottles. Or maybe they'd make jam. Nit liked her sweetness, and God knew, raspberry jam on a winter's morning took away the blue devils. It was like tasting summer.

When they stopped, the girl leaned against a rock, panting, saying she didn't know what was wrong with her, maybe the altitude. She thought she'd have adjusted by now, she said, "But I feel just like a baked apple."

"It's terrible hot, all right, Mrs. Spindle. Besides, up here, we're a thousand foot higher than Middle Swan. This climb would wind a mule," Hennie told her, although she herself showed no signs of slowing. She reached over and slapped the girl's arm, then held out her hand to show a dead mosquito squashed on the palm. "Drat thing! Did it bite you?"

The girl nodded, scratching her arm until there was a faint ooze of blood.

Hennie told Nit to stay where she was while the old woman walked a few hundred yards down a faint trail and returned with a handful of leaves. "I thought I'd find some by that old cabin. Rub you with tansy, and you won't get you nary another mosquito bite." She held out half of the leaves to Nit and rubbed the rest across her own face and arms. Nit watched the old woman, then wiped her skin with the leaves. "I forgot you told me tansy kept skeeters away. At home, we used tansy tea for the chicken pox." Nit put a leaf into her pocket.

Hennie made a face, for tansy tea sounded bitter. "We'll go ahead, if you're ready. It's not far," she said.

Now that the girl was rested, the old woman started on, leading the way past a mine, whose head frame, weathered to the color of a slag heap, towered over young pines. Deserted cabins, their doors sagged open, were lined up near the mine. Through the door of one, the women could make out a white metal bed, its head- and footboards fanciful swirls of iron. "The Confederate Belle," Hennie said. "It shut down before the century, but it'll take a hundred years before the trees grow up again. They cut them every bit down for mine timbers and stove wood."

Up ahead was a glory hole, its opening surrounded by the golden remnants of discarded ore. The range was potted with the old prospect holes, their waste dumps trailing down the mountainsides like spilled cornmeal. When they reached the hole, which was circled by yellow mine waste, the girl walked over to it and peered down, inching forward. Hennie reached out and grabbed Nit's dress. "Best not. Who knows how far down these shafts go?"

"They ought to fill them up then."

Hennie shrugged and wondered who would do that. The prospectors who'd found the outcroppings and dug the holes searching for gold had moved on long ago or had passed over, most likely. Nobody owned the dead holes. "The bootleggers use them," Hennie said. "In Prohibition time, we had dozens of stills in these mountains. Men here made more money from brewing tanglefoot than they did from mining. The bootleggers charged twenty dollars a gallon and the bars, five cents a shot. We've got stills yet that are running full out, because there's some say homemade is better than anything you can buy legal. You ever see any such activity as that, you head in the opposite direction."

"I know about those things," Nit said, and Hennie bit her tongue at her overbearing way. Of course the girl did. There must be ten times as much moonshining in the Appalachian Mountains where Nit had come from than in all of Colorado.

Hennie held out the canteen. "God himself brewed this—mountain water. Drink," she insisted, explaining that nothing wore out a body faster than lack of water in that dry altitude. The girl did as she was told. Hennie finished the water and detoured to a stream to refill the canteen. They were almost to the burn now, and Hennie led the way through the pines, Nit following, until they broke into the clearing just a little below timberline, and Hennie pointed to the bushes weighted down by crimson berries.

Nit rushed forward and began pulling raspberries off the branches, shoving them into her mouth. In a minute, she remembered her manners and held out a handful to Hennie. "Would you have some?"

But Hennie was already picking berries and putting them into one of the pails. A red smear on her cheek told that she had sampled her share.

"I never saw such bushes," Nit said, as she began filling her own pail. "We can pick them all summer long."

"Not so long as you'd think. There's the bears. Then if we get an early snow, the bushes freeze, and a petrificated berry isn't worth eating."

Nit made a face in agreement, then examined the berries in her hand to make sure she hadn't picked a bad one.

The two worked quickly in the hot sun, Nit stopping every so often to eat a handful of raspberries. By the time Nit had filled one bucket, Hennie was almost finished with her second one. The old woman hurried to top off the bucket, then rose and stretched her back and asked, "Would you eat? I made us butter-and-sugar sandwiches, and there's pickles and hard-boiled eggs. I thought berries would do for the hereafter, but I guess we've already ate our fill."

The two women carried the pails to a spot shaded by a cliff and sat down on boulders left behind eons ago by a glacier. Nit scratched the lichen on a rocky outcrop with her fingertip, holding the gray flakes to her eye to study them. Then she picked up an orange rock that was imprinted with the black outline of a leaf, its veins making a delicate tracery, like lace. "I had me a scrap of material like that once," Nit said.

"It's a fossil," Hennie told her. "That's a real leaf that got laid on the rock back when these mountains were young. You take it with you for a curiosity." Hennie laid out the dinner on napkins and placed the rock in the bottom of the empty pail.

"Would you have it?" Nit asked.

"Lordy, I've got me too many rocks to count, ore samples that Jake brought home, mostly. I never could bear to throw them out. You'll find near' every house in Middle Swan has its collection of ore." Hennie handed Nit a sandwich, and the two leaned back against the rock wall and ate their dinner, handing the canteen of water back and forth. Hennie wondered if she ought to get rid of her ore samples, along with the other useless mining debris she'd accumulated over the years—drill bits, miner's candlesticks, Jake's leather hat that he wore underground, his pick and shovel, his lunch bucket. That was all junk that Mae would have to throw away someday when Hennie was gone. But it would hurt Hennie's heart to get rid of the things now. She'd leave them locked up in her house when she left Middle Swan.

"I never saw so many of those flowers. What do you call them?" Nit asked, pointing to a clump of blue and white blossoms.

"Columbine. In spring, there's more of them up here than you can stir with a stick. They're almost past blooming now." She wondered if Fort Madison had columbine. Most likely it did, although not mountain fields full of them.

"I guess they're the prettiest flowers I ever saw, pretty as their name."

"Jake found this place—just this time of year. He was out one morning with his pick and shovel and was so tickled at all the raspberries he saw that he ran back to Middle Swan and taken Mae and me up here, said he'd hit paydirt." Hennie smiled to herself. "But I knew before we started out that it was a bit of foolishness, because you don't take a lard bucket with you to carry ore. I always said this berry patch was one of Jake's best strikes."

She chuckled at the memory. She and Jake and Mae would go there on a Sunday, after church—back when Hennie attended services—and pick the raspberries. Once, when Mae had stayed at home, Hennie and Jake had gone raspberrying by themselves and fooled around up there, not realizing until they were finished that their skin was stained red from where they'd lain on raspberries that had spilled out of the bucket. Hennie glowed at the recollection that her marriage had been good in that way. She hoped the girl's marriage was just as fine, then told herself what the young couple did together was none of her business. Still, that business could be a good thing for a young girl, could help the girl bear her troubles.

Nit opened her sandwich and licked the sugar sprinkled over the butter, then stuck the two pieces of bread back together and bit off almost a quarter of the sandwich. Hennie watched the girl, amused. Hennie herself took tiny bites, chewing carefully. As a girl, she'd been taught fine manners— always wiped her mouth with a napkin instead of her sleeve, chewed with her mouth closed, didn't talk while she ate. Once, Hennie might have been accused of putting on airs in that rough camp, where miners drank their coffee from

saucers and stirred their meat and potatoes and root vegetables together before leaning over their plates and using
spoons to shovel the mixture into their mouths. But Hennie
was gracious, never commented on anyone's poor table manners or adopted affectations like Monalisa Pinto, who stuck
out her little finger when she drank her coffee. Over the
years, more than one woman had watched Hennie eat and
copied her, and it might be said that table manners in
Middle Swan were a good deal better than they would have
been without Hennie Comfort's influence.

Nit ate the soft middle of her sandwich, then looked at
the crusts, debating whether to eat them. "What you told
Zepha, about breaking the spell if she tears up the shirt for
a quilt, is that true?"

Hennie chuckled. "Now, dearie, you wouldn't want to
make a liar of me, would you?" She added, "Did you ever hear
such nonsense? Imagine, a woman thinking a man would leave
her over a broken needle."

"I don't know," Nit said doubtfully. "I swan there's truth
in what old women say. At home, there's a granny-lady told
me if I shook a new quilt out the front door, I'd marry the
first man who came through that doorway, and was that so?
Hello yes!" She chewed on a bit of crust and swallowed, then
took another bite, because the bread was good. "Of course, I
waited until I saw Dick turn in at the gate to shake the quilt,
because he was the only boy I ever wanted to marry with."
The two women laughed.

"He's a good fellow, your man," Hennie said. She didn't
know Dick well, but she liked him. The way he treated Nit
put her in mind of Billy.

"Dick didn't blame me for losing the baby. I guess I'm lucky in that way," Nit said, as Hennie covered the girl's freckled hand with her own gnarled one. They were silent a moment, until Nit said, "You never told me much about Mr. Comfort."

"Didn't I?" Hennie looked off toward the Tenmile Range. "I guess there's not so much to say. He was as good a man as ever was. And I loved him, yes. He loved me right back. I don't suppose there was a better marriage in Colorado than what we had. Most of the time. The only thing I regret is he died too soon." Hennie shook her head to rid herself of the sorrow in her heart, then looked out over the Tenmile Range a minute before she began her story.

❧

It was nineteen and one that Jake Comfort was killed in a cave-in at the Silver Night, the mine that he and Humpy Moore leased. That mine was silvanite ore—"silver night," they called it. Jake set the charges, and Hennie always wondered if he hadn't counted them when they went off. Of course, it could have been something else, because the mine was a bailing-wire job. The timbering looked as if it'd been done by a one-arm cooper, and the pockety ore wasn't stable. But most likely, it was the counting. The charges blew, and Jake worked his way into the back of the drift, and maybe he hit that last charge with his pick. Hennie heard it, heard the first ones go off, too, counted them and said to herself, "That's not Jake, because he always sets one more charge." Then a while later, she heard the last one.

She wasn't worried, however, because Jake was always

careful. She didn't know a thing was wrong until Humpy and some of the miners working over at the Big Dog carried Jake down the trail to the house and put him in bed, right there in the room off the kitchen. Hennie always kept that bed turned down, just in case. Jake died there. He never woke up.

She didn't have a chance to tell him good-bye, but then, in a mining town, couples said their farewells every morning— just in case. A woman counted herself lucky when her man stepped through the door of an evening. And Hennie had. Each night when Jake came home, she'd given a prayer of thanks.

Hennie always wondered if Jake had been drinking at the Silver Night that day, because he was bad to drink, and she knew well enough that when liquor was in, sense was out. Humpy told her Jake was stone sober, but he'd have denied the drinking even if Jake had been roaring drunk. Jake's drinking was a grievement to Hennie, and she always felt she'd failed Jake, for wasn't it a wife's duty to look after her husband? But Hennie knew in her heart that nagging wouldn't have done anything. Only Jake could have made himself keep away from the liquor. It was the war that made him that way, she thought. Yes, she blamed the war. Jake had seen too much of killing. He'd been at Shiloh and Gettysburg, but he wouldn't ever talk about what happened there. Might be it would have helped him if he had, might have stopped him getting liquored up. He'd wake in the night crying, "Blood, blood!" and Hennie would hold him until he went back to sleep. Sometimes, he'd grab on to her and beg, "Don't leave me. Don't ever leave me."

"Why, what in the world makes you think I would?" she asked once, but he didn't reply, and she didn't ask again.

Jake never went on a bender around Hennie and Mae. Instead, he'd slip out to the Gold Pan or the Prospector and drink for three or four days, and he'd be good for nothing for a week. Then he'd dry out and promise he'd never touch a drop again, and he wouldn't, not for a month or two, sometimes six months, once a full year.

Jake signed the pledge once. Somewhere, Hennie had a little album just like the ones schoolgirls kept for their friends to sign their names and write sentiments. Jake's was a brown leather book with "Temperance Pledge Autograph Album" stamped on it in gold. He had signed it, and so had half a dozen others. The pledge might have done the rest some good, but it hadn't helped Jake. That was because he'd signed it for Hennie's sake. Hennie hadn't asked him to, because she never held with such promises. She knew that Jake didn't want to stop drinking, and signing his name in a book was just a fool thing.

Hennie stared off at the blue mountains of the far range, their peaks crusted with fringes of snow that would never melt. Then she looked down at her bucket and picked out an aspen leaf and a gray feather that were mixed with the raspberries. "My, I don't know why I go on like that about Jake drinking. There isn't a man in Middle Swan who doesn't take a toddy now and then, and I myself put my tongue to it on occasion. Without the liquor, Jake Comfort was just almost a perfect man. In my mind, I never saw Billy getting old, but the day I married Jake, I knew he was a man for my old age—not that we ever got there together." Hennie didn't add that until her husband died, she'd believed that God had given her Jake for her lifetime, to make up for the deaths of Billy and Sarah and the half-formed babies He'd taken. She'd learned then that you couldn't count on bargains you made with the Almighty.

Hennie was glad Jake had lived long enough to see Mae married, she said. "And he left me better fixed than most widows. He had a pretty good education, although I don't know how much schooling he got. Enough to know to put aside the money he made from selling claims. He was a good saver. He wasn't stingy, but he was savin'. He said all the Comforts were savin'. I've tried to be myself."

So she'd never had to accept charity or take in boarders or do laundry after Jake crossed over, she continued. She wasn't rich like Tom Earley, "But I have plenty of what I have, and it's enough for me to live to be a hundred and two." Hennie chuckled and leaned forward. "Now some would like to know what I've just told you about my money, because there's been wonderment about it. So I hope you will keep the information intact and not notify them."

Nit made a cross over her heart and promised. "I wouldn't gossip about you for nothing, Mrs. Comfort. I've never said nary a word of what you told me of a personal nature, even to Dick."

"I had that feeling about you," Hennie said. She moved her knees a little to get out the stiffness, which meant she was about to stand up.

The girl knew that, too, and as she was enjoying sitting in

the shade of the cliff and was not ready to finish the berrying just then, she asked, "Why didn't you marry again? I expect there's twice as many men here as girls, maybe more. Why didn't you, Mrs. Comfort?"

"Lots more," Hennie agreed, amused. She thought about the question for a time before she answered it. Why hadn't she married a third time? She'd wondered herself often enough and never found a good answer. There were plenty of men who'd have had her, and she was fond of several, but the truth was, she'd never felt just right about any of the ones who'd come courting. She'd had two men she'd loved more than a cat loves sweet milk, and she wasn't willing to settle for less. But she didn't tell that to the girl. "Oh, who'd want me, except for some old batch after Jake's money?"

Nit reached into her pail and tossed aside a green raspberry before she took half a dozen ripe berries that she lined up in her hand and fed one by one into her mouth, as if she were nibbling on a necklace of red pearls. "What about that Mr. Earley? He said he'd have married you if you hadn't already got married to Mr. Comfort."

Hennie laughed. "Go on with you. That's just a way of talking." The old woman felt her face grow red but told herself that was just the hot sun.

"Does he have a wife already?" she asked, not looking at Hennie, for she was surely prying.

"No, he never married."

"You think maybe he's a sissy?"

"Lordy, no." Hennie didn't elaborate, but she knew Tom liked women. He was never a wild hog, but he'd had a way with the girls. She'd seen him come out of the Willows often enough when he was young. She was walking past the hook-house once and watched Tom turn out at the gate and, bold as brass, she asked him what he was doing there. Instead of being embarrassed, he laughed and replied that if Hennie didn't know, she had no business living in a mining town.

"Mr. Earley seems to like you fine. He wouldn't be after your money, because he's already rich," Nit insisted. "And if you married him, you could live in a big house with somebody to do the washing and have your own automobile, a Packard maybe, and a diamond ring."

"So, you think I'm a gold digger, do you?" Hennie chuckled. When Nit protested, Hennie waved her off. "If you marry for money, every bit of it has wings and will fly away. I've seen that happen. Of course, that's not to say Tom Earley wouldn't be a fine catch even if he didn't have a brownie to his name." There'd been others who had wondered at Hennie and Tom not marrying, and sometimes, she had herself. "The truth is I'm not so sure it would have worked out between us, and it would have spoiled a good friendship. At my age, friendship means more than a diamond ring. Besides, I'm too old to be interfered with."

The girl stared at Hennie, not accepting the answer, for at her age, a diamond ring meant a great deal. When Nit refused to look away, Hennie sighed. "I guess you can keep a secret, although if I tell you this one, I'm afraid you'll think it looks unreasonable. I admit I don't know the truth of it. But I've studied about it, and I believe Tom Earley loved one woman in his life and still does. I know when you're young, it sounds like foolishness to think a body would spend his whole life mooning over a person he'll never have, but I believe Tom Earley never got out of heart with her, whoever she was. Like I say, this is not a story to be repeated, for it's only what I think, and maybe that makes me a fibber."

Nit nodded, accepting Hennie's conditions, then handed the old woman a handful of raspberries before settling in against a rock.

"There's not much to say here," Hennie warned her. "I think Tom Earley knew this woman before he came to Middle Swan, and he couldn't marry her. I guess it's enough for him to live with his whole life. Some men are like that. There's not but one woman for them, even if she's disappeared and gone."

"Did she die?"

Hennie shook her head. "I believe she was already married and wouldn't leave her husband. Or couldn't. I think it was something like that."

"Oh." Nit frowned, thinking that over, for she was young and not wed long and unused to the complications of love.

"I'll tell you what I think," Hennie said.

❧

Tom and his brother, Moses, and Moses's wife, Jessie, came to Middle Swan from Mingo, out east in Colorado Territory, looking for gold, arriving not long after Hennie did. In the few weeks the Earleys lived in Middle Swan, Hennie and Jessie became friends. Jessie taught Hennie about herbs, because she was a doctor of sorts who specialized in women's ailments. Not until Jessie moved away did Hennie realize the woman was an abortionist, but Hennie never thought less of her for that.

Jessie and Moses were wild and fun-loving, but there was an air of melancholy about Tom. When Hennie asked Jessie about it, the woman replied she thought Tom was sweet on the wife of a homesteader in Mingo. "I don't know what happened with those two, but I expect it was something, because Tom just gave up his homestead, the crops in the ground, and came out here with us," Jessie said. "She was a woman of refinement."

Hennie thought that was so, because Tom once told her he missed talking about books and politics, the way he had with a lady in Mingo. Tom stopped often at the Comfort house, where he and Jake discussed mining, but Tom seemed to like better the times when Jake was away and he could speak of poetry and literature, while Hennie sat with her quilt squares. Once, after he'd observed Jake squeeze Hennie's hand and kiss the top of her head and she'd returned the affection with a smile, Tom told Hennie that he knew he'd never find someone who loved him as much as she did her husband. "I thought I did once," he said, and stopped.

"And what?" Hennie asked, for she was curious. But Tom didn't answer.

Another time, he asked Hennie, "Why does a woman stay with a man who betrayed her?"

"Why do you ask?"

Tom caught himself and replied, "Oh, it's something I read in a book."

Tom and Moses didn't find pay dirt in Middle Swan (although Moses returned a few years later and discovered the Yellowcat). So being restless, they packed up and went to

Montana. But Montana was a bust, too, and Tom left his brother and moved on to the Comstock, where he found a little piece of ground that hadn't been claimed and struck silver. One of the big mine owners threatened to sue him, saying the vein apexed on his property, and that meant he owned Tom's claim. Instead of fighting, Tom sold out and used the money to start his own mining equipment manufacturing company in Illinois. He made more money mining the miners than he would have if he'd struck gold.

Tom Earley always kept a soft spot for Colorado, however, and after Moses died, he bought the Yellowcat. Hennie thought that was so he had an excuse to return to Middle Swan in the summers. He came back at other times, too, when he was needed, such as when Jake died. An hour after receiving Hennie's telegram, Tom was on a train for Middle Swan, arriving the day after the burying. He stayed to make sure Hennie was provided for, going to the banker and checking into the state of Jake's affairs. Hennie knew, because the banker told her so. Tom had asked to be informed if Hennie ever ran out of money.

Tom never forgot Hennie at Christmas, sending her crates of oranges from California and grapefruit from Florida, and he always brought her gewgaws from his travels—carved figurines, china plates, beads. Once he sent her a rug from Persia. If she'd ever stated a longing for a diamond ring, she was sure Tom would have bought her one.

The mountains and old friends meant more to Tom Earley than his money, although it always seemed to Hennie that people with money were the only ones who discounted it. He liked best wandering the hills with a pick, looking for blossom rock, just like any prospector, or sitting in Hennie's front room with a toddy. Hennie knew she was one of the reasons Tom came back to the Tenmile Range every summer, and she was happy for it, for her heart filled with gladness when she saw him. Besides, the two of them had long had a dependence on each other.

Tom never said anything to Hennie about the homesteader's wife, but once when he was spending the summer in Middle Swan, he received a telegram and told Hennie he'd be leaving for a time. She'd never seen such raw sorrow on a person's face before and asked what was wrong.

"Two old friends of mine were killed in a motor car accident," he replied, which Hennie thought was odd, because there hadn't been a single automobile in Middle Swan, and she didn't know they were dangerous. He couldn't say more without choking up, and handed her the telegram, but she didn't recognize the names. She did know the name of the man who'd sent it, Benjamin Bondurant, because he was famous in Colorado history.

When Tom returned to Middle Swan a week later, he was a different man. He'd always been a friendly fellow, but he stayed by himself in his cabin that summer and wouldn't talk to anybody, stayed long past time for him to go home to Chicago. When Tom came back the following summer, his hair, which had been as black as the inside of a mine, was as white as a January blizzard. Once, when he had had too much to drink, he said, "I always figured he'd die, and she'd come to me."

"Who, Tom?" Hennie asked

He didn't reply, only muttered, "Life's uncertain, death's sure."

❧

A cloud moved in front of the sun, and Hennie looked up quickly. She didn't want to be caught in a summer storm high up. But the cloud was a solitary wisp, and in a minute, it floated by, and the sun shone down as hot as ever. Hennie looked to the west, where the storms came from, but there was no sign of weather.

"That's as sad a story as I ever heard," Nit said.

"Well, maybe it's not a real story. Maybe it's just me meddling in Tom's business, and like I say, I'd be obliged if you wouldn't repeat it." She plucked a columbine and set it on top of Nit's raspberries.

"Oh no, not to save my life. I won't ever name it to anybody," Nit promised. She gathered the napkins that had held the lunch and set them beside the pails and started to get to her feet. "It sounds to me like there's not so many happy endings in Middle Swan."

"A mining town's hard on a woman. She ages early. There's many a one died in childbirth or from overwork. Or got left behind when her husband was killed, or he taken out on her. Love dies pretty quick in hard times." Hennie thought that over and added, "Sometimes it dies quick in easy times, too. I'll tell you one more story. Then we'll pick us our berries for the last pail and hit the trail." The sun was warm on Hennie's bones, and she was not anxious to leave. "Can you stand another story?"

"I can. I wouldn't like it half so well in Middle Swan if it wasn't for you and your stories." Nit sat down again, on the other side of Hennie this time, where there was still a bit of shade. The girl had learned now that the sun at ten thousand feet burned her in minutes and added freckles to her skin. She reached for the canteen and took a swallow. They'd have to fill it again for the trip down the mountain. "I'll miss your stories when you leave," she said. "They shouldn't be forgot."

"Then maybe you'll pass them on when I'm gone."

The girl stared at Hennie for a moment before she said importantly, "I will. I surely will."

Hennie nodded, satisfied, and said the story she was going to tell, which was about Martha Merritt and Charlie Grove, was one of her best ones.

Nit furrowed her brow, as if the names were familiar but she couldn't place them.

Martha was her friend from White Pigeon, Hennie explained, the one who'd written her the letter that brought Hennie to Middle Swan.

"I recollect now," Nit said. "She sent you the picture of her and her husband and Mr. Comfort, and you mixed up the men. You didn't know until you got here that Mr. Comfort was the handsome one."

"That's right." Hennie was pleased that Nit remembered and knew that the girl had a good mind for the stories. She would indeed pass them on. "I can see Martha running till today, lifting her skirts and hurrying off down the trail to meet Charlie when he came home late of a day after shift. She wasn't any bigger than a minute and had hair like wire gold, and she was always merry as a marriage bell."

❦

Martha loved Charlie Grove every bit as much as Hennie loved Jake Comfort, although there were some who didn't see how Charlie'd caught such a pretty girl, him being so ordinary. But she was foolish over him.

Martha and Charlie had four boys and buried two, which was middling odds in a mining town. They didn't have much money, because Charlie worked for wages, but that didn't bother Martha, although as a girl before the war, she'd had beautiful clothes, a dogcart, and a servant who fanned away the summer heat. Still, she said she was richer in Middle Swan than she'd ever been in White Pigeon, and that was as true as God's stars. Charlie wasn't happy about the poor way they lived, however, with Martha working like a Turk, the way mining town women did. So when he wasn't in the mine, he was out with a pick and shovel, searching like a fury for precious metal.

When silver was discovered in Leadville, Charlie decided Middle Swan was a bust, and he moved his family over the Mosquito Range to the Carbonate Camp, which was what Leadville was called. That was in 1877. He said he was sure Leadville was where he'd make his strike, and it was. Charlie went out prospecting one hot day, and at noon, he sat down under a lodgepole pine to eat his dinner. Being tired, he decided that shady spot was as good as any to look for silver. So he stuck his pick into an outcrop beside him, and he found pay dirt. He named the claim the Jack Pine, and it was one of the richest mines in Leadville. Charlie filed his claim and announced, "Now my wife can be a lady again!"

It wasn't more than a couple of months before the Jack Pine was bringing in money faster than Charlie could spend it. He invested in other mines, and they turned out to be even bigger producers than the Jack Pine. At the same time, he bought a fancy house in Leadville, and when he decided it was not fine enough for Martha, he built her a mansion in Denver.

Hennie visited there and was surprised to find her old friend was downright unhappy. Martha was embarrassed by the gilt and the marble in the house, and the peacocks that Charlie bought to parade around the yard. She had a house full of servants who had to be looked after, but no children to tend, because Charlie had sent the boys east to school, and that's where they stayed. Martha had to endure endless callers—people asking for money, ministers inviting her to join their churches. "I guess mine and Charlie's souls are worth more now that we're rich," she told Hennie.

Charlie bought Martha a necklace, with diamonds the size of corn kernels. "Have you ever seen a thing so ugly? I won't wear it." Martha held out the awful piece of jewelry to Hennie, who wouldn't have worn it, either. Nor did Martha like the dresses that Charlie picked out for her—gowns made of thick plush, cut with tight sleeves and drapes and trimmed with beads and braid and fur. "I might as well be wrapped up like a mummy," said Martha, who couldn't put them on without the help of a maid. And she disliked riding in the blue carriage with a driver and a footman dressed in blue livery to match. She and Charlie quarreled about other things, such as

Martha inviting the servants to sit in the parlor and listen to musicales that the couple gave for other new millionaires.

Martha hated the way the money changed Charlie. He put on airs and began talking about becoming senator or maybe governor, and he threw away money on his political pals. He avoided his old friends from Middle Swan. And instead of sitting around the fire in the evening with Martha reading aloud to him, the way they'd pleasured themselves in Middle Swan, he went off to his clubs—or elsewhere, for Charlie had turned into a loose horse. He'd stay out all night and come home smelling of liquor and perfume. They had words, cruel ones, about that.

Charlie had his complaints, too. Martha didn't appreciate what he'd done for her, and instead of being grateful, she'd turned into a sharp-tongued woman. "To tell you where it started, I couldn't," Martha told Hennie, who had hurried to Denver from Middle Swan, when she heard Charlie was past caring for Martha. "But I'll tell you where it ended."

One day, a woman showed up at the mansion and claimed she was in a family way. "Charlie's its father," she said, showing as proof a note that Charlie had written to her, saying, "I can't stay away from you." So Martha called it deep enough. When Charlie arrived home late that evening, Martha had his bags packed and told him she wouldn't go it anymore.

"Charlie Grove is the biggest kind of fool," Hennie said, when Martha told her, "but I ought to thump you, too, for what you had between you was uncommon good. You ought to work it out."

"The time's gone by when we can talk things over," Martha replied.

Charlie married the girl. Martha stayed in that mansion with nobody else, the rooms closed up and sheetcovers over the furniture, living on popcorn, baked sweet potatoes, and molasses candy.

Then the silver crash came. In 1893, the government stopped backing the price of silver, and the crash led to the worst depression the West had ever seen, with silver mines shutting down, and thousands of miners going on the tramp. The mine owners were in bad shape, too, and since Charlie'd never put his money into anything but silver, he lost his fortune—his mines, the houses, the horses. Martha lost everything, as well, because instead of taking a cash settlement when she divorced Charlie, Martha had agreed to let Charlie pay her a sum of money every month. She'd wanted that connection with him, Hennie believed. Then Charlie's new wife left him. And it turned out there never was any baby.

Her boys were grown by then, and they wanted Martha to move east so that they could look after her. But instead, she went back to Middle Swan and lived in the house where she and Charlie had been so happy. The boys sent her a little money, and she made do. By then, Charlie had disappeared. Nobody saw him for ten or twenty years, and when his name came up, which wasn't often, everyone assumed he'd crossed over.

Time passed on. It ran on, and one day, Hennie was out in her yard after a summer storm, sweeping away the pine needles, and there came Charlie Grove over the hill, a pick and a gold pan strapped to the back of his burro, looking just like he had forty years before, poor as fool's gold. Hennie said, "Charlie Grove, you get in here and have you a toddy and so forth." He'd hardly lifted the glass and said, "Here's to you," when Hennie got her idea. She told Charlie to wash himself good while she went to Roy Pinto's to buy something for them to eat, for he smelled worse than beaver bait. Hennie went to the store, all right, but she also stopped at Martha's house and invited her to take supper.

There never were any two people as surprised and happy as Charlie and Martha when she walked through the door. Charlie took to courting her all over again, just as he had when they were young, and it didn't take much doing, because Martha had loved him all along. Why, it wasn't any time at all before they got married again and Charlie moved back into the old cabin.

"Finally at last, that's the end of my stories for today," Hennie said. "Now, best us finish picking and be on our way." She started to get up, but suddenly, she stopped. "Why, Mrs. Spindle, we forgot all about our quilting. I must be in my final days, because quilting's the last thing I'd ever forget." She laughed at herself as she reached into her pocket and took out a half-done quilt square and some loose pieces. "Look you, it's Pine Tree. Now isn't that the finest coincidence?" she asked, shoving the quilting back into her pocket.

Nit helped Hennie to her feet, and the two took the empty bucket and went to gathering berries. In a few minutes, the last bucket was full. Hennie covered each pail with a napkin, and the two women started down the trail. Picking raspberries at Mae's house in Fort Madison would be easier, Hennie thought, for Mae had the bushes right in her back yard, but the berries wouldn't be as sweet as those gathered at ten thousand feet on a midsummer's day.

The descent was easier than the climb, of course, but after a time, Hennie called a halt, for she didn't want to wear out the girl. Nit went to the stream and filled the canteen, then the two rested for a few minutes. "I've been thinking, Mrs. Comfort," the girl said. "Whatever happened to Martha and Charlie Grove?"

"I thought you'd get around to that." The old woman chuckled. "It wasn't all sunshine, for old age never is, but those two have had more fun than a little. The second time around, they didn't want anything but each other. It's a good marriage, yes. But then you can judge that for yourself." Hennie waited until the words sank in and Nit sent her a questioning look. "That's right. Judge for yourself. You saw Martha and Charlie Grove this morning. They were walking down the street with the birdcage."

Chapter 7

A look of pleasure came over Hennie Comfort's face as she opened the door to find Tom Earley standing on her threshold. He leaned over and kissed her old cheek, which was still egg-smooth despite the sun and wind and blizzards of more than two thirds of a century living on the earth's backbone.

Tom entered the house and looked around, nodding at the young couple sitting on the broad sofa and telling Hennie, as he had a hundred times before, that she had it real nice there. Real nice, he added, and he was right. The log walls shone amber in the late-day light, and the big furniture with its comfortable pillows made from old quilts was welcoming. Tom handed her two loaves of bread, then took from his pocket something wrapped in tissue paper and tied

with a gold ribbon. "Go ahead, open it," he said with a trace
of excitement in his voice.

Hennie untied the ribbon and folded back the tissue.
Her eyes glowed when she saw the tortoiseshell side combs
edged with silver and dotted with turquoise. "Oh my," she
said, sighing. "These must have been made by the wild Indians." She combed up stray white hairs on the side of her
head with one and fastened the comb to her hair, then repeated the grooming on the other side with the second
comb. "Now, don't I look just as fancy as the Queen of England?"

"And prettier," Tom said, as Hennie went to a mirror and
admired herself, thinking she didn't look so bad at that.
"The silver matches your hair," Tom said.

"Yours, too." Hennie continued looking at her reflection
until she became sensible that Tom was still standing. "Now
where are my manners? You taken off your coat and hang it
on the hook. Would you have a hoot, Tom?"

He removed the wool jacket, which he had worn because,
although it was summer yet in Middle Swan, the nights were
always cool, and there could be frost before long. Hennie
had laid a fire in the stone fireplace, ready to light if the evening turned cold. "I don't want my stomach to rust," he
replied. "I'll take a drink as long as there's one in the house."

Hennie set the bread on the table, then went to the sink
and poured a goodly amount of whiskey into a tumbler that
was standing on the drainboard. She had added a dash of water to the boy's drink and the girl's was almost all water, but
Hennie and Tom took their whiskey neat. "Did I tell you

this is Tenmile Moon, made right here on the Swan?" she asked the boy, as she handed Tom his glass. "Tastiest stuff there is. And it won't give you a Tenmile head. That's what we call a hangover at ten thousand feet."

"Or a blue Monday, either," Tom added.

The leather bellies didn't call it "blue Monday" because of washday. Blue Monday was when you were still hungover from drinking whiskey on Saturday night, Hennie explained. She stood back and lifted her glass. "Here's to your health." She took in her three guests with the toast.

"And the same right back to you." Tom lifted his tumbler and downed the whiskey in one gulp.

Hennie motioned for Tom to sit down in Jake's old chair, a heavy oak piece with wide arms, a chair as rooted to the floor as a stump to the land. Tom leaned his cane against the arm and sat down awkwardly, holding out his right leg, for it was stiff. He propped it on a stool. "You already met Nit Spindle yesterday morning on the street. Now, make you acquainted with her husband, Dick Spindle," Hennie said.

Dick was a tall, thin fellow with sandy hair and wind-burned face, not much older than his young wife, and he stood and leaned toward Tom, holding out his hand. With Tom seated, the two men shook, while Hennie picked up Tom's glass and asked if he wanted another shot.

"I will reply in the affirmative," he said.

Hennie took the tumbler back to the sink and refilled it, handing it to her friend, who only sipped the whiskey now. "Mr. Spindle works on the Liberty Dredge," she told Tom.

"Is that right?"

Dick nodded.

"You like the dredge, do you?"

The young fellow glanced at his wife before he shrugged. "I've never seen nothing that could beat it for confusion. I'm grateful for the job, but I can't say as I like it. Working that deck's rough, and the noise of the rocks falling on those big piles pesters my ears. I'd give out, but there's no jobs wherever. I'm lucky I've not been Hoovered from this one."

As if to punctuate the boy's remarks, the dredge up the Swan gave a loud screech, followed by the grinding of metal. Although the noise was muffled by the log walls, Nit put her hands over her ears. "I couldn't stand to listen to that up close all day long. It uneasies me," she said. "It's not right, Dick working there. He's all but fallen off the boat a dozen times. I don't rest easy when he's working."

Dick colored with embarrassment, and Tom said quickly, "I never liked a dredge. It seems unnatural, tearing up the land that way. Where was green grass, there's nothing but rocks. It won't sprout a pea." He took a sip from the glass and relaxed back into the chair.

"A mine dump won't sprout a pea, either," Hennie reminded him.

Tom thought that over. "But mining doesn't dig up a mountain river."

Hennie guffawed at that. "You taken a look at what mine runoff does to a mountain stream? I wouldn't drink it if it was five parts whiskey."

Tom agreed then that she was right. He asked the boy, "You work for Silas Hemp, do you?"

Dick nodded and looked at the glass in his hand, turning it around a little.

"Worst man on the Swan. You watch out for him," Tom said. "He ran an ore car over a man's legs once, and the poor fellow almost lost them. Silas said it was an accident, but the two had been feuding, so nobody believed him."

"He's more torment to me than forty head of stray ducks. I guess he doesn't like it that somebody else hired me, instead of him doing it, although I know he'd have turned me down." The boy set the drink on a table and studied his hands, with their cracked nails and dirt embedded so deeply in the skin that no amount of scrubbing would get it out. There were scars on his arms, barely healed, and one hand showed the remains of a rope burn.

"Tell him what Mr. Hemp did. Tell him, Dick," Nit said. She turned to Hennie and added, "They done him devilment. I was scared green over it."

Dick took a sip of his drink and shook his head, as if it wasn't manly to talk about such a thing, but Tom prodded him, so the boy said, "You know that big hose they got connected to the pump?" When Tom nodded, Dick continued. "I was holding it when Mr. Hemp turned the valve full on. I had to hang on like sixty just to keep ahold of that thing. I couldn't drop it to turn down the valve or that hose would have whipped me to death. The fellow that used to have that job got his leg broke near off when he set down the hose when it's full on. I'm lucky I didn't hurt myself pretty bad. Mr. Hemp and the others, they just laughed to beat anything." The boy reddened again, uneasy at the way he'd been tricked.

"It's the meanest kind of action," Hennie said.

"Mr. Hemp talks big about dredging, but he doesn't

know nothing practical about it. He's went to school too long," Dick said.

"He has at that. He's overeducated and doesn't have a lick of common sense. I don't know why Will Gum keeps him on," Tom told them. "His looks don't help him, either."

"He's poorly shaped, all right. It's too bad his legs aren't split up because his shoulders would make a better butt than what he's got. Excuse me." Dick looked around, stricken at what he'd said, until Hennie and Tom laughed.

"Silas Hemp cut Dick's wages," Nit whispered, twisting her macaroni necklace around her neck. She had made it herself from different shapes colored by dyes from flowers she'd picked. Hennie told her once that it looked right pretty on her, which was why the girl wore it that evening.

Tom slammed his hand down on the arm of his chair. "You'd get blood out of a beet before you'd get money out of Silas Hemp." He nodded to emphasize the truth of his words. There came a silence after that, and finally Tom asked the boy had he been a farmer.

"Oh, I can farm all right, but I'd rather work in the coal mines. Now that's a job for a man. I'm hoping maybe I could get hired on at a gold mine, 'cause I like it underground better than on top, but there's scarce few mine jobs here."

"Scarce few," Tom said, rubbing his bad leg. "You'd rather work in a mine, then?"

Dick nodded. "I'm not complaining, you understand. And I'm sorry for coming in here with my troubles, what with Mrs. Comfort's being so nice to Nit and all. With the baby on the way, I guess I'm luckier than most."

Nit blushed and put her palms together between her

knees as she looked down at the floor. She glanced at Hennie sideways, then looked back at the carpet, which Hennie had made from rags put together hit-or-miss. "It's of a personal nature. You shouldn't tell it, Dick," she muttered.

"Why, of course he should. Isn't that fine! That's as good a surprise as any I ever got," Hennie told the girl, although she had known for weeks that Nit was pregnant, probably knew it before the girl herself did. Hennie'd even asked the Lord to let her stay in Middle Swan long enough to see the baby safely born.

Tom reached over and slapped Dick on the knee, then raised his glass to Nit. "Here's luck, Mrs. Spindle." Hennie and Dick toasted the girl, too, then Hennie asked Nit how she was feeling.

"Pretty fine, just a little trouble breathing every now and again."

"Just like me," Tom said, and they all laughed. "There's nobody can breathe right up here on the top of the world," he added.

Dick told them they expected the baby after the turn of the year, and Hennie, who thought no, the baby was due sooner than that, warned, "Babies come early in these high mountains. You best be prepared for it." She began quizzing the girl about what she had on hand for an infant, deciding Nit would require help. Hennie'd found a cradle at the dump once and hauled it home, knowing someone would need it one day. It was stored in a shed out back, and with a little fixing, it would do fine for the baby. She wondered if Blue Massie, Zepha's husband, could repair the hickory that was bent like embroidery hoops in the front and back of the cradle but was splintered now.

Hennie and Nit would make quilts and flannel sheets for the bed, and there were receiving blankets to be stitched, layettes to be knit. Oh, they'd have a time, Hennie thought, and smiled to herself at the pleasure of the work ahead for a baby. It would relieve Nit's loneliness—and her own, Hennie realized, for being with the girl kept away her own blue devils. Making baby clothes would keep her from thinking too much about leaving. Weeks before, when she'd realized the girl was expecting, Hennie had gone through her rag bag and pulled out scraps that were just right for a baby's quilt. Now, she'd give thought to the pattern.

Nit and Hennie chatted about babies. The girl was excited, and this was a time for talking joy. Hennie would wait until later to find out if Nit was scared, what with losing her first child before the tiny thing had even taken a breath. If the girl was worried, Hennie would do her best to comfort her. The old woman was glad she'd never told the girl about her own babies who hadn't been brought to term.

But now, she listened to Nit chatter, all the while keeping an ear on Dick and Tom's talk about dredging, about Dick's work on the gold boat. She thought it was a wonder he hadn't been hurt bad on the dredge; most likely, it was just a matter of time before something happened. The old woman hoped Nit's husband wouldn't lose his footing when the boat iced up, maybe slide off the gangway on one of those days when the temperature fell to ten or twenty degrees below zero. His winter clothes would drag him through the broken ice to the bottom of the pond, and that was the worst way to die. It would be bad if something happened to him, especially with his wife carrying a baby. What would the poor thing do if Dick got maimed—or killed? Hennie didn't feel good about the boy working on the dredge, not a bit good. She'd asked once if Dick could get transferred to the dredge shop, where the gold boats were repaired, but Dick said that he'd already asked. Silas Hemp had told him the only job the boy would ever have was on the boat.

"I hope it's a boy. Dick wants him a boy," Nit was saying when Hennie turned back to the girl's conversation.

Suddenly, Hennie jumped up. "Lordy! That tom turkey's about to burn up. Here I am talking and not thinking. I'll get it to the table."

The girl stood, too, saying she would help. And since Middle Swan people weren't much for coddling women, even those who were pregnant—and Hennie herself had taken the girl on a hard climb just the day before—the old woman set the girl to mashing potatoes with the heavy wooden smasher. The girl worked the mallet up and down, just like the stamps that crushed the ore in a stamp mill. The old woman herself lifted the turkey from the oven and transferred it to a platter, letting it sit while she made a heavy gravy with flour and canned milk. Then she set out the food, the beans and potatoes, the creamed spinach and Tom's bread along the center of the table, the turkey at the head, where she asked Tom to sit so that he could carve. "There's nobody carves a bird like Tom Earley," she told the young couple.

They said no formal blessing, for Hennie was not one to pray in front of an audience, but set to as soon as the food was passed, talking little, because eating a meal such as Hennie had prepared was serious business. A time or two, Hennie looked up to find Tom watching her, and the thought crossed her mind that maybe the two of them should have married, after all. She'd loved him best of all the men she'd ever known, except for Billy and Jake, of course. But back when she and Tom might have had a life together, she'd made it clear she would not leave the mountains to live in a city; she'd have dried out like a marsh marigold plucked from its damp. And what she'd told the girl was true: She didn't want to spoil the friendship. Besides, Tom had never asked her.

She touched one of the side combs and smiled at him, and he smiled back, making Hennie think what a wonderful thing it was to have a friend for seventy years. "You want you another toddy, Tom?" Hennie asked. The old man said he wouldn't mind and made to get up from the table, but Hennie, mindful of her friend's bad leg, told him to stay, and she fetched the bottle. She poured whiskey into his glass, then offered the bottle to Dick, who added a slug to his tumbler. Nit shook her head, and finally Hennie poured herself a nip.

Tom tasted the liquor and smacked his lips, which was what Middle Swan folks did to compliment the whiskey. "I guess there's not so much bootlegging on the Swan anymore," he said, ready for conversation now that he was almost finished eating.

"Oh, there's some, but it's not like it used to be," Hennie replied, turning her mind to the subject of illicit whiskey. She looked at Dick and said, "Most folks in Middle Swan weren't in favor of going dry. There was the Order of the

Bent Elbow that fought Prohibition, but the temperance
ladies were too strong." Still, Prohibition didn't have any
more effect on Middle Swan than on the place where Dick
and Nit had came from. Fact was, she said, some of the bootleg was better during repeal than the legal stuff had been
before Prohibition. And it was cheaper, too—pure Tenmile
Moon, made from Colorado beet sugar and the sweetest water in the world, cooked at eighty degrees for ten days and
strained twice.

You could buy a drink in any candy store in town, Tom
added. Confectioners operated speakeasies because they could
buy all the sugar they wanted without the federal agents getting suspicious. "Some of them did turn out a little candy, although you wouldn't want to eat it." Tom laughed. Most of
the soft drink parlors were just fronts for bars, too, he added.

"There were eighteen saloons in Middle Swan that got
shut down in nineteen and sixteen when Colorado went dry,
and by nineteen and seventeen, sixteen soda parlors had
opened up in those saloons. Imagine that," Hennie said. "Remember that ditty, Tom?"

Hush little saloon, don't you cry
You'll be a drugstore by and by.

The drugstore, the barbershop, the hardware, the cigar
shop, Hennie added. All of them were blind piggers, too.
And the St. Philomena Catholic church. "When all the
other Catholics taken out, Doyle Hannigan—'the deacon,'
we called him—stayed on and turned the church into a
speakeasy. He advertised services all day long. He wasn't

even a member. His wife was Catholic. He was just a common moonshiner."

Even Roy Pinto at the mercantile sold Blue John, although he was never thirsty enough to try it, Tom said. "Do you recollect, Hennie, that he kept the bottles in the boxes with the ladies' corsets?"

"I never bought drink off him or a corset, either one," Hennie said. She didn't add that she hadn't worn a corset in forty years.

Tom chuckled. "I figured he cooked up his brew in those pipes he kept in the back room."

"He did, for a fact," said Hennie. "He stored it in the bed of that old truck of his. And he kept rattlesnakes in the back of the truck, too, to keep folks from stealing his hooch."

"Pick your poison," Tom said, "rattlers or rotgut."

There was one old fellow who made his whiskey in an iron kettle and held a horse blanket over it to collect the steam, Hennie went on. When the blanket got too wet and heavy to hold, he wrung out the whiskey and bottled it. "Of course, you could get liquor legal for medicinal purposes," she added. "Middle Swan had the distinction of being the sickest incorporated town in Colorado."

Hennie remembered about dessert then, and she went to the drainboard and cut her raspberry pie into quarters, set them on clean plates, admired them for a moment, and carried them to the table. It was a good pie, maybe the best one she'd ever made, the berries peeking out of the thick lattice of the top crust. Tom, Dick, and Nit made over it so much that Hennie turned the color of the raspberries. Tom asked where she'd accumulated the fruit.

"We picked it yesterday, right after we saw you, up on the burn on Sunset Peak, past that old plater ground," she replied. Hennie turned to Nit. "The word's 'placer,' but 'plater' is what the old-timers call it. Placering was the first way we got out the gold along the Swan. Tom was one of the prospectors back then. He and Moses and Charlie Grove worked a claim on the Swan. Charlie was the unhandiest man I ever saw with a gold pan."

"We sure left that river a mess," Tom told them. He was right about that. The Swan was lined with "sandbars" of yellow waste, the residue of gold panning that had taken place years before along the river. Nothing, not a weed nor a wildflower, grew in the waste, and the water turned a toxic orange as it ran through the tailings. "We fouled our nest, you might say. We hadn't planned on staying, none of us, and we didn't care what we did to the land. When one place was used up, there was always another waiting," Tom told the girl. He looked at Hennie and said, "But some stayed, and the Swan's a better place for it."

Hennie attacked her pie, and the others followed suit, pausing now and again to grunt their approval. "I saw Charlie Grove today. I think he still pans a little gold," she said.

"It gets in the blood," Tom told her, eating the last of the pie and picking up the crumbs of the crust with his fingers.

When they were finished, Tom told Dick, "Light the fire, and let's us have a smoke." He stood awkwardly. Gripping his cane, he limped a little as he made his way back to the easy chair. Nit began to clear the table, but Hennie told her to leave be. The old woman was enjoying the company too much to waste time washing dishes.

As Tom passed the quilting frame shoved against the wall, he stopped to admire Hennie's quilt, the Coiled Rattlesnake, which was made up of pieces that were every color of the rainbow. "I believe I remember you had a dress of that," he said, pointing a gnarled finger at an indigo shade sprigged with black.

"You remember it because you bought the goods for me," Hennie said, bringing cups and saucers and a coffeepot to the table. "I'd admired it at the Pinto store but said it was too dear," Hennie told Nit. "That was just after Jake was killed. Next thing I knew, a length of that cloth was sitting right here in this room."

"I've never been here when there wasn't a quilt in the making," Tom said. "Every quilt must have its story."

"Yes, and some aren't worth the telling. This Coiled Rattlesnake is one of them."

"I reckon you'll breathe your last right there at that frame, Hennie," Tom said, laughing.

Nit glanced up at Hennie then, and the old woman sighed. "I guess you haven't heard about it, Tom. I'm leaving the Tenmile Range when the new year comes. I'll be moving to Fort Madison to live with Mae."

Tom stared at Hennie, stunned. "For good?"

"Mae says I can come back summers, so I'm keeping the house. But I can't say I'll ever be back. Most likely, she'll find some reason to keep me there. I know she'll try. Still, I got the rest of the summer and fall before I go below." Hennie shrugged. "I always thought I'd die here, be wrapped up in a quilt and planted. Not a crazy quilt; crazy quilts are a confusion. Maybe my flower quilt. Yes," she added, "it doesn't have flowers in it, but I call it the flower quilt because there's blue like columbine and turkey-red the color of paintbrush, yellow for butter-and-eggs, and magenta just like summer's-half-over. I wouldn't mine spending glory wrapped up in all that color." Hennie stopped, knowing she was chatting from nervousness. "We'll talk about the moving later on. I don't want to spoil a nice evening."

Tom studied her a long time. Then he nodded and said, "Well, you can wrap me up in your old measles-and-mumps quilt." He explained to the young couple that the measles-and-mumps quilt was the one Hennie put over Mae when she was sick. "You could play checkers on the squares. I reckon it wouldn't be such a bad thing to play checkers for eternity."

"That's not a quilt for burying. We'll stuff you into a gunnysack and throw you down a glory hole," Hennie said, with a fond look at her friend.

"It's my remains, and I say one of your quilts. You can't begrudge an old friend that," he told her, his eyes twinkling. He stared into the floor for a moment. "I know Fort Madison because I had a friend who came from there long ago. It's not so far from Chicago. Might be I'd turn up on your doorstep."

"I'd like that," Hennie said, almost choking from happiness. She hadn't considered that her old friends might visit her in Iowa. "It'll be a relief to do something besides quilt."

"Oh, you don't always quilt," Tom told her. He turned to the young couple. "You may think she's a sewing fool, but she's a wild one. Why, she was known as a moonshiner."

Nit and Dick turned to her, surprised. Hennie could not

tell if the look on their faces was awe or respect or condem-
nation. "Now, Tom. You know I never did that," she said.

"You as good as did. Mick Kochevar said he'd have gone
to prison without you."

Tom smiled as he removed a package of ready-mades
from his pocket and passed it around. The women declined,
but Dick took two, placing the second one behind his ear.
He picked a kitchen match from the blue glass slipper on
the table beside him and struck it, holding the flame out to
Tom before he lighted his own cigarette. He threw the match
into the fire, which Dick had set a match to when they got
up from the table. Now, the flames were settling down to an
even burn, taking the night's chill out of the air.

Hennie poured the coffee, and the others busied themselves passing around the spooner, cream pitcher, and sugar,
doctoring their coffee, tasting it, and adding just a speck
more sweetening. When they were satisfied, they turned to
Hennie, who then took to her chair, a lady's chair from long
ago, constructed without arms so that a hoopskirt could fit
over the sides. She preferred her wide rocker, now so old that
the varnish was worn off the armrests and a wire replaced a
rung that had been broken, but Dick was sitting in it. So she
settled into the lady's chair, like a hen into a nest, and began
the story.

The miners along the Tenmile brewed Purple Jesus, White
Mule, Sneaky Pete, and half a dozen others, but the best
they ever made was Tenmile Moon. Most of the stills along
the Swan were family affairs, and the moonshiners hardly

ever got caught. In fact, every time a moonshiner took the train down to Denver for his trial, he bought himself a round-trip ticket. That didn't mean the government didn't send revenue agents to arrest the bootleggers. But the federal men used passes, which the conductors recognized. They got the agents to talk about who they were after, then wired the details to the station.

Hennie was at the depot one morning when the wire came that the agents were after a man on Galena Street who brewed liquor with the help of his kids. "That's Mick Kochevar," Hennie told the station agent. Mick's legs had been blown off in a mining accident, and his children pulled him around in a little wagon to make deliveries. The Kochevars were borrasca-poor, and those kids would starve if Mick were arrested.

Hennie left the station on a tear, almost running down Horace Wilson, who was getting out of a big truck. "Horace, come along. It's a matter of life and death," she told him, and the two hightailed it to the Kochevar place, where they and the little ones disassembled the still and loaded it into the truck. Horace drove away, and the kids cleared off like running cows. Hennie herself was about to leave when the two federal men showed up, acting friendly.

"How you doing?" one asked.

"I am well and good for nothing," Mick replied.

The agents explained they were traveling men and had heard Mick sold Tenmile Moon.

"You don't know nothing about it," Mick replied. "I ain't any no-account-for-nothing that makes rotgut."

"That's the truth," Hennie said.

"Look out, lady. The rest of us knows a thing or two," the agent told her.

Hennie retorted, "He doesn't make whiskey, because he's a member of the Holiness in good standing, too." Hennie didn't know where that came from, nor did Mick, who jerked up his head, because he was no more a member of the Holiness than Hennie was.

"You show us that shed you got there, and I'll show you holiness," the agent told him.

"I sure would like to if you'd give me a pair of legs," Mick replied.

Until then, the federal agents hadn't noticed that Mick was maimed, but that didn't stop them from yanking the wagon with Mick in it over to the shed, nearly bouncing Mick out onto the ground. "You hurt my foot," Mick cried.

"You ain't got a foot," replied the agent, mean enough to fight a steam sawmill. He told Mick to open the shed, and when the bootlegger couldn't reach the lock, the agent yanked Mick's arm and said roughly, "Do it this way, cripple." He didn't care for Mick's feelings any more than a big groundhog.

"Do it yourself, then," Hennie said, taking the key and throwing it onto the ground.

The agent grunted, then picked up the key and unlocked the door, and the minute it swung open, the smell of mash came rushing out, strong as lye. "Say, this is interesting," one of the men said. The agents recognized the smell, of course, but although they searched high and low, they couldn't find a kettle or a copper pipe or a drop of spilled Tenmile Moon.

"Those hammer-headed neighbor kids has been breaking

in and drinking again," Mick explained when the agents grilled him about the stench. "If I had me some legs, I'd run 'em off. But I'm as slow as cream rising. All's I can do is sit here and do nothing. It's a terrible affliction I have." Oh, he was the darnedest liar!

So the agents gave up and went back to the station, Mick calling after them, "By the jumping, cross-eyed Judas Priest, I don't want to never see you again, coming in here and accusing me of sinful ways, you cussed devils."

***

"That's the best story," Nit said, clapping her hands, and the others agreed.

"Mr. Spindle, would you put a little more wood on the fire?" Hennie asked, and Dick took a log from a huge iron kettle that served as a wood box and added it to the flames. He pushed at the wood with a poker, and when the log had settled in, the boy sat down, reaching for a cigarette from Tom's package and lighting it. The boy nodded his thanks as he lifted his cup to his lips, and discovered it was empty. He looked at the stove, hoping Hennie would offer to brew more, but she took no notice of him.

Instead, she said, "Hold on. Wait a minute. That's not the end of it. There's one more detail. The mail was late that day. That's because Horace Wilson's truck was the U.S. mail truck." She sat back and smiled.

Nit and Dick laughed, and even Tom grinned, although he'd heard Hennie tell the story half a dozen times before.

"Did he go back to making hooch?" Dick asked.

That was the sad part of it, Tom put in. "Mick took him-

self off to a Holiness meeting just for the heck of it, and
Lord, if he didn't join up and stop his whiskey-making. 'The
Lord sees it all, marks it all down, and he knows I'm a sinner,' Mick told me when I went down there to buy a bottle
of hooch. He said we were living in the end of time, and the
devil was after him. A good many folks grieved when Mick
saved his soul." He turned to Hennie. "I never did tell who
turned Mick into a Bible-thumper."

The old woman made to get up from her chair then, for
she intended to make more coffee, but Nit put out her hand,
which was smooth and plump like a baby's. "I have a story
for you," she said, looking at Hennie.

Hennie smiled at the girl, as Tom settled back into his
chair. "Well, let's hear it," Hennie said.

Nit looked at her husband, who nodded once to give his
approval, and the girl leaned forward, her hands on her
knees. She took a deep breath and began. "Back home there
was a moonshiner named Oweny Buckley, and he was cussed
mean, wasn't he, Dick?"

"Amen to that. He was the meanest man I ever met,"
Dick agreed. "You'd get the heebie-jeebies just being around
him. I never just rightly knew how he could get three re-
spectable women to marry him."

Tom and Hennie didn't react, so Nit explained, "At the
same time. He was awful bad to them, wouldn't let them
have hardly a thing at all and made them wait on him like he
was the governor. He kept one at the north end of the
county, one at the sound end, and the third in the middle."

"Did they know about the others?" Hennie asked.

Nit shook her head. "We lived in the south end, and none

of us knew about the other two wives until Oweny was taken in by the federal agents for making whiskey." His south wife, Alice, went to the jail to bring him his dinner, and she found the north one sitting right there beside him on the bunk, Nit said. Those two wives went at it, tearing out each other's hair and cussing worse than anything the girl had ever heard. They might have killed each other if the third one hadn't come along. The three wives bawled and fretted so much that the sheriff came in along with the dry clothes man who'd arrested Oweny for making moonshine. When he found out what the fuss was about, the federal man told Oweny he'd broke another U.S. government law. He said if Oweny didn't shed himself of two of his three wives and settle down with just one, he'd go to jail for polygamy, along with moonshining.

Nit ran out of breath and was red in the face. She leaned over a little further, and her husband patted her on the back. "Oweny said the women sure weren't worth his spending extra time in the penitentiary, so he believed he'd settle down with just one."

Tom slapped his knee. "That's a good one. Which wife did he choose?"

Nit giggled and covered her mouth with her hand.

"You want me to tell it?" Dick asked her.

"No, it's my story, Dick." Nit waited until her husband nodded before she went on. "Oweny saw it was no use and said he wouldn't choose one over the others. He told those three wives to talk it over, and they could decide which one got him." She paused for dramatic effect, just the way Hennie always did. "So they all talked it over, and they all turned him down."

Tom and Hennie laughed so hard that both of them

rocked back and forth in their chairs. When he finally got his breath, Tom asked what had become of the man.

Nit hunched her shoulders and looked sideways at Dick. "That's how come us to leave home. Without a wife, Oweny wanted to live with Dick and me. He's my old pap."

Hennie's eyes bugged out, and Tom's mouth dropped. "That's as good as any story Hennie ever told," he said, and Hennie nodded in agreement.

They were all four of them silent for a while, drowsy with the fire and the dinner and the storytelling. Maybe too much storytelling, Hennie thought. Old folks liked stories about the past, but she wasn't sure a young fellow like Dick cared so much about her mountain tales. The girl did, however. Hennie was sure of it.

At last, Dick stood up. "We better get off to bed. The bed won't come to us."

Hennie rose from her chair, protesting that they were welcome to stay. But it was late, and Dick had the early-morning shift on the dredge. So, he shook hands with Tom, and he and Nit removed their jackets from the hooks. Hennie walked them to the door.

"I'll thank you till you're better paid," Dick said.

"Your friendship's payment enough," Hennie replied, watching the two until they disappeared in the darkness. She closed the door and went back to Tom.

"I'll be shoving off in a minute, too," he said, making no effort to stand. Hennie sat down in Dick's chair and slowly rocked back and forth, waiting for Tom to speak.

"Do you want to move to Iowa?" he asked.

"No, of course I don't want to move. This is my home,"

she said, stopping the rocker. Then her voice softened. "You know, when I arrived here, I never intended to spend my life in Middle Swan. I thought Jake and I would live here a few years and push on." She tipped the rocker forward and chuckled. "I used to want to visit the Holy Land and London, even China. I'd read about those places when I was in school in Tennessee, but somewhere along the road I came over, I forgot about seeing the rest of the world. Now, I'm too old. All I'll ever see is Iowa." Hennie smiled. "And I've seen it before."

"Fort Madison's a nice enough place. I've been there," Tom told her. "And you'll have your daughter and your grandchildren."

"Oh, I know. It's as fine a place as you could ever live. The trouble is what am I going to do there? Mae has a room all ready for me, with a view of the Mississippi River. But I don't want a river that's slower than I am."

"Oh, it has to be better than Middle Swan in January. And you'll be back summers."

"Will I, Tom?" Hennie rocked back and forth a little. "I don't wonder but what I'll wear myself out sitting and not be up to coming back."

"You put too fine a point on it, Hennie. You'll never wear down." He reached over and took her hand, and the two sat silently, watching the fire. "I believe you'd adjust, just as you did when you came here."

"I was seventy years younger."

Tom laughed. "Do you really want to go to China?" He maneuvered himself to his feet.

"I do. China, Persia, the Holy Land, anyplace but Iowa." She laughed, too, at such a notion.

Hennie followed Tom to the door, where he kissed her cheek, lingering a little before he started down the walk. At the gate, he turned, and Hennie called, "Tap 'er light, Tommy."

"Same. Good night, old friend." He touched the first two fingers of his right hand to his lips, then turned and walked along the trail, his steps surprisingly sure for a man of his years. Hennie watched until he was out of sight, then stood longer under the sickle moon, smelling the scent of the pines on the breeze, listening to the gurgle of the Swan River and the screeching of the dredge, which seemed comfortable now, because it was familiar. And she thought that it was an evening to be remembered long after she was gone from the Swan.

Chapter 8

Hennie Comfort was surprised to see the young girl at the funeral service, for she had not expected Nit Spindle to attend. After all, Nit didn't know Frank Slater, although he had worked side by side on the gold boat with the girl's husband. Maybe the girl came because it could have been Dick instead of Frank lying in that coffin. Hennie sighed, hoping the girl didn't think too hard about that possibility but, instead, just thanked the Lord that her husband was safe. After all, Hennie was certain the Almighty had intervened, granting Nit's prayers and her own to look after the boy. The old woman only hoped that God would continue to keep an eye on Dick.

Hennie had heard the dredge go silent two days before, just as if somebody had pulled the switch on the electric and turned off the gold boat. She listened, expecting the dredge to start up again, but after a long time, when it didn't, she went outside and stood on her doorstep. One by one, the doors up and down the street opened, and women stepped out. The women always seemed to know. They sensed the difference between the dredge breaking down and an accident.

"Sure is quiet," one of them said, and they smiled at one another and nodded, as though the boat was giving them a reprieve from the noise. But they were anxious. Hennie could tell from the way they wrapped their hands in their aprons.

"Must be the bucket line. The damn thing is always busting down," Thelma Franks said, walking over to Hennie's fence.

"Must be."

"It's too quiet. Jesus God, I don't like the dredge down in the middle of the day like this. Something isn't right." She didn't say "accident," on account of it was bad luck to say the word.

"Maybe the bucket line," Hennie said, but the two women feared it wasn't.

"Damn dredge," Thelma muttered again. Her man didn't work on the dredge, but that didn't make any difference. Middle Swan was a mining town, and when something went wrong, it was everybody's sorrow.

Hennie hoped it wasn't the Spindle boy who was hurt. Silas Hemp still had a disliking for him, and it was only a matter of time before the boy was hurt or maimed or worse. With a baby on the way and no other jobs available, Dick couldn't quit the dredge.

As the women stood shivering in the cold wind, rubbing

their hands over their arms to keep warm, they heard men running down the road from the dredge, running past the row of open doors. "Who is it?" one of the women called.

The man in the lead ignored her as he turned off on the trail that led to the doctor's office.

"Who is it?" she asked the second man, demanding now.

"Frank Slater," he yelled.

"Is he going to make it?"

The man stopped and ran his tongue across his lips. He shook his head and started up again.

Hennie saw the women relax a little as they passed the name along. Their own men were safe. Hennie, too, was relieved that Dick Spindle was all right. But one of their kind would be needing them. "I'll bake a cake," a woman called. Another said she already had a meatloaf in the oven. Hennie volunteered an apple pie that was cooling on the drainboard. Even Thelma muttered that her bread was about to come out of the oven.

As the women turned to their tasks, another man came running up from the dredge. "Mr. Spindle!" Hennie called, and the boy stopped beside her gate.

He leaned over, taking deep breaths as he held on to her fence post. "Best you say a prayer for Frank Slater and them," he told her. "It was a poor way to die, worse than most."

Hennie waited until the boy caught his breath, for she knew he had the need to tell someone what he'd seen.

Dick exhaled and said, "Frank's an oiler—was. He got crushed betwixt the belt and the pulley of the winch." Dick closed his eyes as if to shut out the scene, and swallowed. "The winchman shut down so's Frank could do his work.

Then Frank signaled to start up again. I don't know what happened. Maybe he reached in the machinery, thinking he could oil a spot he forgot, or might be he caught his sleeve. I was standing right next to the winchman, and he knew something was wrong. So I went in the winch room, and there was Frank caught up in the machinery. His head was crushed, and his hand was almost tore off." Suddenly, the boy broke into sobs.

"I'm sorry, Mr. Spindle. It's a terrible thing for a person to see."

"Mrs. Comfort, it could have been me. Frank was having a hard time, him being stove up from drinking too much last night, and I offered to take his work for him. He was going to let me do it, too, but he saw Mr. Hemp watching him and knew we'd get Hoovered if we switched. Mrs. Comfort, I could have been caught in the machinery, and then what would Nit do?"

Dick wiped his eyes with his sleeve, and Hennie put her hand on his arm. "But you weren't the one, Dick. You can't worry about a thing that didn't happen."

"Next time it could be me. There's always a next time on a dredge."

Hennie nodded, for she was not one to deny the truth. This accident wasn't Silas Hemp's fault, but the next one might be. "You be extra careful," she said.

"I'd be obliged if you'd say a prayer for me." Hennie nodded, although she already prayed daily for the boy's safety, and Dick started off down the street. "I got to catch up with the boys."

Hennie went in the opposite direction, toward the Spindle

house. The girl would be worried about the silence, and
Hennie wanted to tell her that Dick was all right. Halfway
down the trail, she ran into Nit. The girl puffed a little from
hurrying. In just two months since the dinner with Tom Earley, Nit had filled out, and her dresses strained across her
stomach. She tired easily, so Hennie had stepped in to help
ready the cabin for the baby. The two women knitted sweaters
and booties, and cut and sewed sheets for the cradle. Hennie
had taken over Nit's jam- and jelly-making, too, for standing over the hot woodstove made Nit go limp. She wasn't
mollycoddling the girl, Hennie told herself, only obliging
her a little.

"Dick?" the girl asked.

"Sound as a dollar. He's just gone to fetch the doctor."
Not that there was any reason for it, Hennie thought. She'd
seen the bodies of men carried off the dredge—the arms
and legs twisted, the faces mangled—and she told Nit, "Best
to go on home and see to supper."

Nit stared at the old woman a long time before she said,
"I know what goes on with the gold boat. I heard a man tell
Dick that a person that gets caught in the dredge dies worse
than the soldiers he saw in France in the war. Mrs. Comfort,
Dick's got to get off that boat."

❦

So at first, the old woman was sorry the girl had come to the
funeral, worried sick about her husband the way she was. Besides, the poor thing still mourned the death of her infant
daughter, and funerals had a way of making a person feel the
loss all over again. With a new baby inside her, the young

woman did not need to be reminded that death came unexpectedly. There were some who said a funeral could mark a babe in the womb, too. Hennie was not amongst them, although who was she to speak for the Lord? So it might not hurt for the girl to be cautious. Lord, I'd be obliged if you'd take especial care of that one, she prayed, adding, I'm willing to do my part, but I haven't got much time. Indeed, there was a fall chill in the air, and Hennie knew it wouldn't be long until the first snow.

After pondering the funeral situation, Hennie changed her mind and decided that it was a good thing Nit was attending the service, which was held outside at the End of Day Cemetery. Being there marked Nit as one of them. Oh, she'd be a foreigner for years yet—some in Middle Swan were still outsiders after twenty years of living there. But Nit showing up to honor Frank would be noticed and appreciated. Even Monalisa Pinto would give her the least little bit of credit for it.

There was another reason that she was glad the girl had attended the burying, Hennie decided after giving it even more thought. A mining camp was a harsh place, and Hennie never held with being ignorant about a thing. The girl should know that death was the cost of tearing gold out of its resting place at bedrock. The earth took its retribution. Hennie wouldn't be around much longer to explain such things to the girl, and Nit would have to learn them on her own. Pray God, nothing ever happened to Nit's husband, but the girl ought to be prepared a bit, just in case. There was no circumventing providence in a mining town.

Hennie turned her attention back to the Reverend Shadd,

who had just finished his preachment. He told the mourners that God's ways were mysterious to men. The man was right about that, Hennie admitted. She never understood why the Lord took men in the prime of life. There was her first husband, Billy, killed just as that long-ago war between the North and the South ended, a man who didn't live to see twenty years of age. And then her second husband, Jake Comfort, dead in a mine accident at sixty. He was as healthy as a man half his age, and Hennie had expected to live out her life with him, but here she was, a widow for more than thirty years.

Frank Slater was far younger than Jake had been, on the shy side of forty, with three children—and two or three others that'd died of pneumonia or influenza when they were brand-new. Terrible illnesses took little ones in that altitude, Hennie thought as she glanced at Nit. The remaining Slater children stood bewildered now, the least of them clinging to the mother. The oldest child, a boy, stood at the mother's side, trying at the age of twelve to look like a man. And well he might, for who else was to take care of the widow?

The boy would quit school now to go to work, unless his mother found a job, but that wasn't likely. There was little employment for women in Middle Swan, unless it was at the Willows, and even then, a mother with three children was ill-set to work nights at the hookhouse. Unless she was willing to entertain at home, Mrs. Slater would have a hard time of it. But she'd never turn out, Hennie knew, for Mrs. Slater was a righteous woman. Besides, she looked like a Middle Swan housewife, and a prowling husband might just as well stay at home as visit a hookhouse to spend the evening with the likes of a woman who was an image of his wife.

Hennie glanced at the coffin, which was closed, telling everybody gathered at the burial ground that Frank had died a hideous death. The coffin was shut only when the body was blown to bits or the face so disfigured that the undertaker couldn't do his work.

"Dust to dust," the Reverend Shadd said, stooping to pick up a handful of dirt. The minister was old, older even than Hennie, and she wondered why he didn't quit, go outside and live what remained of his life, but she didn't waste her sympathy on him. The aged reverend grabbed the arm of a mourner to steady himself as he stood up. He opened the fingers of his hand and let the dirt sift through them onto the coffin—a fine pine box with silver handles that the dredge company had paid for. Hennie could hear the sound of the dirt and pebbles as they hit what the miners called "the wooden suit." She'd never liked that "dust to dust" saying. It made life sound useless, as if everything a person accomplished during his lifetime was gone with the wind after he died.

She didn't much care for funeral services, either. Nor had Jake, and Hennie had shocked the town by refusing to hold one after her husband died. Instead, six of Jake's friends sat in the house beside the box where Jake lay, sat up with the body through the night. And the next day, men gathered from all over the county to pay their respects, for Jake had no enemies. Men at such an occasion could get drunk in a thought, but Hennie provided drinking whiskey so that they could get drunk the proper way, telling stories, laughing, and

singing. Folks heard them all the way up the Jackass Trail to
the Yellowcat Mine.

A few of the women in town were scandalized by Hennie's method of burying her husband without a service, but
they didn't dare say a thing to Hennie, for Hennie Comfort
had lived in Middle Swan longer than any of them and, like
her husband, was much beloved. They complained to the
Reverend Shadd, however, but he said it was Hennie's right
and that God was more concerned about how a man lived
his life than about the way he was put into the ground. Hennie didn't care in the least what the minister said in her de-
fense.

When the Reverend Shadd finished the words of the service, Roy Pinto and the choir from the church sang "In the
Beautiful Isle of Somewhere." Then as the Woodmen of the
World escorted Mrs. Slater and the children to a Packard
touring car, a brass band struck up "Going Home." At that
instant, not satisfied that it had taken the life of a good man,
the dredge screamed in pain—or as a warning to the living,
Hennie thought. She wondered why the company couldn't
shut down the dang boat for the day to honor Frank and let
the dredge workers attend the service, but she wasn't surprised the thing was operating. Dredge companies had no
souls. The other mourners, so used to the wailing and groan-
ing of the gold boat, paid it no mind, but went about their
business, tending to the graves of their own loved ones, before gathering at the Woodmen Hall for coffee and cake.

The service had been held under aspen trees that had
turned the color of the old gold coins that people in Middle
Swan used when Hennie arrived there in the 1860s. The

mass of leaves was so bright that it brought a hurting to
Hennie's eyes. She all but closed her lids until the leaves
were blurs of gold against the big blue humps of mountains.
Hennie thought she would make a quilt of those shapes one
day, using the last of the precious blue she had bought for
herself so long ago. She'd hoarded the fabric, but now she
ought to cut it up and be done with it. She had pieced so
long—some eighty years—that she saw things in quilt
shapes. Maybe she'd make the quilt after she moved to Fort
Madison, to remind her of the high country, not that she'd
need any reminders. Those mountains, like Billy, Sarah, and
Jake, would live on in her heart.

"His time was nigh," Monalisa Pinto said in her pinch-
nosed way, as she came abreast of Hennie. The wind had
started up, and Monalisa repositioned her long, lethal hat-
pin, anchoring her hat to her head. "How's your health, Hennie?"

"I woke up with my joints stiff. Yourself?"

"Same."

Bonnie Harvey interrupted. "The dredge isn't God. It
wasn't God that took Frank, Monalisa. It was the fool gold
boat, cussed thing!"

"At least he didn't get his head cut right off by the hop-
per like that fellow a few years back. And remember the
deckhand who leaned too far over and got hit by the bucket
line and drowned? And oh, you can't forget the shoreman
who fell off the plank when the boat bucked. You recollect
that, Hennie? Nobody saw him go in. They didn't know he
was missing until the winchman spotted that big red three-
cornered thing floating on the pond."

"I disremember," Hennie said, giving Monalisa a hard look.

Monalisa ignored her. "It was his liver," she finished. "Floating right there in the pond, big as a brisket."

"Oh!" Nit exclaimed, putting her hand to her mouth as if she was going to be sick.

"Now see what you've gone and done?" Hennie told Monalisa, disgusted. "And her about to have a baby."

"Well, she ought to know about such," Monalisa said.

"Where you going, sweetheart?" Bonnie butted in, speaking to her sister, Carla, to Hennie's relief, for someone had to quiet Monalisa. Carla Swenson didn't answer. Instead she wandered off toward the grave of her intended, a man who had died in a mine forty years earlier, only days before the two were to be married. Bonnie sighed. "She loves that man more than if she'd wed him. Maybe if they'd been married a while, she wouldn't still mourn him so. People feel sorry for spinsters and widows, but there's more than one married woman that envies them."

"Are you amongst them?" Monalisa inquired.

"No, I've done right good, as you know well enough, but there are plenty here with shabby marriages."

Hennie nodded, not saying anything, because there was no need to name the women.

"I expect this will be your last funeral up here," Monalisa said.

"I hope so—except for my own," Hennie replied, for she intended to be buried beside Jake, no matter where she died. And she knew that Mae would do that for her. The old woman turned to Nit, who'd moved off to one side, clearly ill at ease. "Why, it's neighborly of you to come, Mrs. Spindle. Mrs. Slater will be pleased you were here," Hennie told the girl, although she knew that Frank Slater's widow was too distressed to remember a soul who attended the service.

"I hope it's all right," the girl said uncertainly. She clasped and unclasped her little hands in front of her coat, which was strained across her growing stomach. "I mean, I didn't know him any more than a duck..." Her voice trailed off. Then she took a deep breath and added, "But Dick did. And I'm thinking if something was ever to happen to Dick, I'd sure be proud to see folks at his planting."

"Planting," Monalisa repeated, a trace of disdain in her voice.

"I think that's a real nice way to put it, much better than 'dust to dust,'" Bonnie interjected. "You did the right thing, Mrs. Spindle. We all feel that way. I'd rather be surprised at who's there than at who's not." She added after a minute, "My, there've been a lot of 'plantings.'"

The women were silent then, each remembering the funerals of loved ones who rested in that place. The End of Day Cemetery was a large one, spread over a mountain meadow, new and old graves mixed together, Christian and Jew and those of no beliefs at all, good men and bad, pure women and some from the hookhouses.

In one spot rested the dozen miners who had been killed in a cave-in at the Pennsylvania Mine, their graves covered with wild daisies. The women of Middle Swan dug those daisies and planted them around their houses, for the daisies

from that cold spot of death were the toughest in the high
country. The graves were marked by fanciful shapes—
obelisks engraved with the deceased's unit and rank in the
Civil War, memorials cast in the shapes of angels and tree
trunks, stones carved with lambs, bearing words of remem-
brance: "Bessie and Ruth, infant daughters of Geo. and Mary
Storey" and "Lamb of God, But Died on Earth to Bloom in
Heaven" and "Sacred to the Memory of Verna Griffin." Hennie looked about for her favorite marker:

> Beneath this stone our baby lies
> He never cries or hollers
> He lived by 1 and 20 days
> And cost us 40 dollars

Hennie never failed to wonder who had put the verse
there, whether it was a bereaved family with a sense of humor or some joker. She thought to show it to Nit, but no, the
girl might not think it was funny.

The women broke up then. "I said I'd cut the cake at the
Woodmen's," Monalisa told them. "Then I have to go home
and fix supper. Cooking's a botherment. I despise to do it."

"My husband's went to Denver, and I'm a woman of
leisure. No cooking is good enough for womenfolks when
the men are gone," Bonnie said, turning to fetch her sister.
"Come along, Carla. We'll go to the hall, and after that, we'll
pop some corn and take it to the Roxy. Maybe there's a picture show with dancing in it. I always like dancing, but the
mister, he won't watch it."

"I'm not going to the Woodmen's, but you'd be welcome," Hennie told Nit, who only shook her head and replied she didn't feel up to socializing. Hennie nodded in understanding and said she was going to stand a minute at Jake's grave. "You can come along, if you'd like."

"I don't mind. I've got nothing to do."

As the other women left, Hennie led Nit past the plots, some outlined with iron fences that were bent from the intense winters. Here and there a wooden fence lay on the ground or a wooden marker leaned crookedly, the name scoured off by the wind and snow. Hennie hoped the girl wouldn't look too closely at the names and dates carved into the stones. So many of them told of babies, two or three or four of them in the same family, who'd died at birth or lived only a few months. And beside them might lay the mother, dead in childbirth.

She stopped at Jake's plot, which had been swept clean of pine needles, showing that after all these years, Hennie still visited it frequently. There was no iron rail or pickets, either, for Jake wouldn't have wanted to be fenced in. Jake was the only one who'd been laid to rest in the plot, because the two of them had buried the remains of the babies high up in the meadows near the sky, close to heaven.

Jake's grave was marked by a large boulder with "Jacob Comfort" chiseled into it, nothing more. "I had some of his friends haul it down from near timberline. They put a rope around it, and down the mountain it came. I wouldn't have Jake marked with a dredge rock," she explained, running her hands over her husband's name. Hennie had stood on that very spot not long before, telling Jake she was worried about the pregnancy of her young friend, but the old woman didn't tell that to Nit. The girl might think she was simple.

"It's peaceful here," Nit said at last. And it was, even with the racket of the dredge in the distance and the sounds of cars returning to town. The wind came up, and aspen leaves showered the two women. The girl leaned down and picked up one of them, placing it in the palm of one hand and smoothing it with the fingers of the other. "It's such a pretty shape. It would work right well for a quilting pattern."

"I never thought of that. Aren't you the clever one!" Hennie exclaimed.

Then the old woman stared at the stone with Jake's name on it, stood there so long that the girl wandered off, reading the names on the tombstones out loud. " 'Lilla Marz, a wife of Ben Marz' and 'Luther B. Smart.' I wonder if Luther be'd smart or not," she said and giggled to herself. Nit continued, reading the names in a plot surrounded by an iron fence: " 'John Hallen, lived 17 days,' 'Johnny Hallen, lived one year, three days,' 'Jody Hallen, lived two years seventy-two days,' 'Baby Jo, lived one hour.' " Nit stopped and frowned. "Do you think the Hallens ever named their babies anything but *John*?" Hennie muttered an answer, and Nit kept on reading the tombstones. " 'Our Baby Vandevier Boylan, Age 2 Years,' 'Sweet & Precious to the Memory of Merry Belle Grace.' Isn't that the prettiest name, Merry Belle Grace? I bet she had a happy life with a name like that."

"Not so happy," Hennie said, ending her commune with Jake, telling him he ought to put in a word with the Lord about Nit, and while he was at it, would Jake ask for help for her in shaking the blue devils she had about moving. "George Grace fell off a cliff in a snowstorm, and a Denver lawyer cheated Merry Belle out of everything her husband left her. She'd gone to him to ask for help with George's estate. George's money was in shares of the Rosalie silver mine in Leadville. The lawyer said Merry Belle was lucky she'd come to him that day, because he knew of a report on the mine that was due to be issued in less than a week, telling that the Rosalie's ore vein had pinched out."

Hennie shook her head at the memory. The attorney said if Merry Belle turned the shares over to him right then, he'd move them for her for $1,500. In a week, they'd be worthless. So she sold George's interest to the attorney. When the report came out, it told that the Rosalie had hit a rich new vein. The lawyer sold the shares later on for $10,000, an amount that would have taken care of Merry Belle for the rest of her life.

"What did she do?" Nit asked.

"*She* didn't do anything. But *I* did. I got in touch with a friend of mine, Ma Sarpy. I'd done her a kindness once, and she'd always said she was beholden to me. Besides, this was just the kind of job she liked."

Nit frowned. "Who?"

"It's not a name that's known much anymore, but once, there was a goodly number familiar with it, some to their sorrow. I'll tell you about her," Hennie said, pleased at a chance to sit and tell a story. There were so many stories yet to tell the girl. She looked around the cemetery until she spotted a stone bench beside a grave. "Sit yourself."

The girl, too, seemed glad for the chance to get off her

feet, for her ankles were swollen, and she was peaked and drawn. It sapped a woman to be pregnant at that altitude. "Do you still think the baby's due at the turn of the year?" Hennie asked.

"I'm not just sure. I haven't had my complaint since before I came here, maybe a month or two before that, but I didn't pay it attention, since I'd had the baby not so long before," the girl replied. "I feel good," she added quickly, "just a little tired."

"Why, I am myself," Hennie said.

"And you're not even—" The girl stopped, not sure she should complete the joke.

"Pregnant," Hennie finished for her and laughed.

Nit smiled, then grew serious. "I tell you, Mrs. Comfort, I get the all-over fidges sometimes. What if something's to happen to Dick on the dredge, like Mrs. Pinto was telling, and I'm left alone to have the baby? And if I lost a baby again, why I can't know what I'd do with myself. I might drown myself in that dredge pond." She stopped and watched as a whirlwind of aspen leaves swirled around them. "I can't tell Dick how scared I am. It would bemean him, because he works hard. But it festers at me, and he knows that."

"Of course it does, at a time like this. You go to a funeral, and you can't help thinking about your own self."

"I worry about it all the time." Dick hated the dredge; he'd rather be underground, Nit continued. Dick liked Middle Swan just fine, better than home, even, and so did she. Why, they could go to the movies any night of the week, and on Saturday nights sometimes, Dick took her to dinner at the Grubstake Cafe. Imagine just sitting down and having somebody bring you your food and you don't have to lift a finger—or help with the dishes, either, she said. "And when I don't want to cook, I just go out and buy something off the hot tamale man that has a cart in front of the Gold Pan. I've got to be good friends with Zepha—and you, of course. Oh, you're the reason I've come to like Middle Swan so much. If Dick had real mine work, everything would be fine." The boat groaned, and Nit looked off in its direction. "I guess there's nothing to be done about it."

Hennie nodded, wishing there were, but she'd searched her mind and couldn't come up with anything. She swept the aspen leaves and pine needles off the bench, and the two women sat down, looking off at the blue sweep of the Ten-mile Range. Nit unbuttoned her coat and rested her hands against the curve of her large belly, staring at the mountain-side, where a clump of yellow aspen was surrounded by a fringe of green leaves that had not yet turned color. She pulled down the hem of her dress, an ordinary dress with an eak in it that she'd added to fit her pregnancy, waiting for Hennie to begin.

"I'll tell you that story now," Hennie said, hoping to take the girl's mind off her worries. "I wish I had my piecing, but it didn't seem right to bring it to a funeral." She closed her eyes and raised her face to the sun again, clearing her throat and collecting her thoughts.

⤜⧽⧽⊙⧼⧼⤛

Emma went by that name of *Ma* Sarpy, although Hennie didn't know where it came from, because Emma wasn't so old when she started working the other side of the law, maybe thirty or thirty-five. Perhaps Ma came from her name, Emma. It didn't matter. Ma Sarpy was a good name, because it threw people off, made them think she was an old woman. Sarpy was her first husband's name. Her second husband was Ned Partner, who was once a famous outlaw. After the two of them retired, they went by the name of Keeler and lived an ordinary life down in Georgetown. The two of them were never caught. Nobody would turn them in, because the folks they cheated wouldn't admit to it. And others who knew what they did—Hennie was one—admired them.

Ned and Emma were con artists. They swindled people out of their money, but they never went after anybody who didn't deserve it. They skinned men by turning their own greed on them, so that they couldn't go to the authorities. Oh, they had no pretensions of being Robin Hood, and they earned a nice living for theirselves in that way, and what they did wasn't legal, but it kind of made folks chuckle. Emma would have gone after the lawyer who fleeced Merry Belle even if Hennie hadn't asked her to, because there was a darkness inside her. Hennie thought that something had happened to her once, because she had a black hatred for men who took advantage of women.

The con was an obvious one, almost too easy to appeal to Emma, who liked to put together more complex schemes. All she did was what the attorney had done. In fleecing Merry Belle, the lawyer had cheated a poor confused widow, so that was just what Emma pretended to be

Emma, Ned, and Hennie—Emma insisted if the con were to be done properly, Hennie would have to be a part of it, for no one would suspicion a fleecing if two women were involved—showed up at the lawyer's office one morning. They told him that they were from Leadville, staying in Denver with Emma's sister, and had picked his name from the directory. By streaking her hair white with powder and rubbing black under her eyes, Emma made herself look sixty. Ned, still a boyish-looking man a few years younger than Emma, put on the clothes of a dandy and pretended to be her son, while Hennie played the role of a spinster daughter.

The lawyer almost rubbed his hands together in anticipation when the three stepped into his office, Emma telling him that they needed legal advice, for her husband had died unexpectedly, leaving them with property in Denver.

"Why, I don't know a thing about property. My son here"—Emma pointed at Ned—"says he wants to buy it, but he don't have the money, and I can't give it to him, for there is his sister..." Emma touched a handkerchief to her eyes. "She must be provided for."

Hennie gave a tight-lipped smile, while Ned sent her a sullen look.

"What did your husband own?" the lawyer asked.

"Real estate," Ned broke in. "I have the description." He handed the lawyer a piece of paper.

The man studied it. "Oh, Broadway. That's not a very good address, I'm sorry to say." He looked at Emma with a sorrowful countenance.

Emma glanced at Ned, who looked away, then at the lawyer. "I don't even know where it is, but my husband said it was valuable."

"Oh, it might be worth something one day—if you could live a hundred years." He gave a bark of a laugh. "I expect your husband bought it for the future. But now..." He shrugged, then leaned forward and lowered his voice. "I have it on the best authority that a rendering plant will be built close by, and that will drive down the value of your property even further, for who would want to build a house or an office block there? We must sell that address as quickly as we can. I'll check into the matter."

"Father was never any good at investments," Hennie said resentfully. "I myself told him not to buy the land."

"How much can we get?" Emma twisted the handkerchief between her fingers.

The lawyer put out his hands, palms up. "I will let you know."

"I need fifteen thousand dollars," Emma blurted out.

"Oh, my dear lady, I shouldn't think the lots are worth even a fraction of that. I have in mind perhaps three thousand dollars. Word may already be out about that plant," the attorney replied.

Crestfallen, Emma stood and thanked the attorney, and the three left. Emma assumed, and rightly so, that the lawyer would be too lazy to check the ownership of the property. He would wait to see if they returned before beginning any work on the estate. No need to put himself out if Emma was simply shopping for a lawyer. In fact, Emma surmised, the man would be surprised if she came back at all.

It was Ned, not Emma, who returned. The following day, he walked into the lawyer's office, looked around to make sure the two of them were alone, and closed the door.

"Ah," the lawyer said. "I have done some checking—"

"Don't play me," Ned cut him off curtly. "I don't care if

Mother and Sister believe a rendering plant will be built near Father's land, but I myself am not such a fool. I know there is talk of a fine hotel going up in the next block, and that makes our property very valuable indeed, worth twice the fifteen thousand dollars Mother wants."

The lawyer observed Ned for a moment, then said, "I should have known you were a very smart young man."

"Yes," Ned agreed. "But not smart enough to pull this off myself, because I don't have the money."

"What do you propose?"

"I don't care about my sister. Or Mother, either. They have held me back in my profession, and Mother expects me to take responsibility for both of them. I won't have it."

Ned looked at the attorney, who nodded and said, "Continue."

"You will put up the money to purchase the property, which Mother can be persuaded to sell to you for thirteen thousand dollars, and we'll buy it together. You'll be repaid your investment when we sell, and I'll give you twenty-five percent of everything over the thirteen thousand dollars. As I say, I believe we can get twice that amount on the market. It's a splendid idea."

The attorney snorted. "My dear fellow. If I were to put up the money, I would buy the property myself."

Ned shook his head. "No you could not, because Mother depends on me for advice, and I will tell her not to sell to you."

The attorney thought that over, pointing out that $13,000 was a great deal of money. He would not consider risking such an amount for less than fifty percent of the profit. The

two of them haggled, Ned offering thirty-five, then forty percent, but finally, he agreed to give the attorney half.

"Now that we have settled that, there is the matter of
trust. How do I know I can trust you?" the attorney asked,
adding, "A man who would cheat his own mother."

"That from a lawyer who would cheat his client?" Ned responded. "You don't know that you can trust me, nor I you. So
we'll put it in writing. You can draw up the paper, and I'll sign
it. Mother will be selling the property to both of us. She'll
never see the document, because her eyes are poor. I shall
have to read it for her, and then I shall tell her to sign it."

The lawyer mulled over the proposition for several minutes, asking Ned a number of questions that Ned answered
to the man's satisfaction. At last, the attorney rose and held
out his hand. "I believe we have an agreement. I shall work
up the papers and have them ready for you tomorrow."

"Cash," Ned said. "I tell you she won't accept anything
else. Father never trusted banks, and Mother doesn't, either.
That's why she came to you and not to a banker."

"That is a great deal of money." The lawyer frowned, running his tongue over his upper lip, but at last, he agreed. As
Ned was leaving, the man stopped him, "What about your
sister? Won't she read the documents?"

Ned sneered. "Her eyes are worse than Mother's, and she
is too vain to wear spectacles. You can put your mind to ease
about her."

The following day, as Ned, Emma, and Hennie walked
into the lawyer's office, the attorney greeted them with a
smile, saying in his liar's voice, "I believe I have good news
for you, very good news indeed."

"Oh," Emma said, slipping into a chair. Ned stood beside her with his hand on her shoulder. Hennie went to the window and stared at a building across the street, trying to settle her nerves, for she was not used to swindling others.

"I have found a buyer who is willing to pay you thirteen thousand dollars for your property, and he has left an offer for that amount. The man is from out of town and unfamiliar with the city. But you must sign the papers this instant, before he discovers the bad news."

"We told you we want fifteen thousand dollars, and we won't settle for less," Hennie said suddenly, her back still to the lawyer.

"Oh, you are greedy. It's a stroke of luck to get this much," Ned told Hennie. Then he turned to Emma. "Mother, don't let's haggle."

"I don't know," Emma said uncertainly.

"It is against my advice," Hennie said, "but I suppose you won't take it any more than Father did."

Emma suddenly looked cagey. "I won't take a note. I've heard of men who cheat widows out of their property with bad notes."

"I anticipated that, dear lady. I have the cash in my safe." He smiled unctuously. "The papers are here for you to look over and sign. Take your time, but I must tell you the sooner we complete the business, the better off you will be. The offer could be withdrawn at any moment."

"My eyesight isn't good," Emma said, turning to Ned. "You had better read the documents."

Ned picked up the paper, in which the widow agreed to sell her property to a partnership made up of Ned and the attorney, not to an out-of-town buyer. After Ned read it, he told Emma, "It's in order, Mother. Sign on the last page."

Before she could do so, Hennie grabbed the document. "It is best I read it, too."

The attorney's face froze as he looked at Ned. But Ned only smiled and mouthed, ". . . as a bat." Nonetheless, the man rubbed his hands together until Hennie handed the contract to Emma and said, "Yes, it appears to be in order, although I don't like it. I don't like it at all."

"Brother is right. We can't be greedy," Emma said, dipping a pen into the inkwell on the desk and writing her name on the paper. As she did so, the lawyer handed a second contract to Ned. "This simply confirms that your son, as your advisor, agrees with your decision," the attorney told Emma.

The document did no such thing, of course. It was a partnership contract in which Ned agreed to pay the attorney a ten percent fee for locating a buyer in addition to splitting the profits fifty-fifty. Ned looked sharply at the lawyer, who merely shrugged. The two had made no such agreement about a fee, but the lawyer knew that Ned had no choice but to sign, what with Emma and Hennie in the room. If the son resisted, he would show his hand in cheating his mother. Ned gave the lawyer a surly look and wrote his name. Then he said, "Sister, do you want to read it?"

Hennie gave him a dismissive wave of her hand. "If you want us cheated out of two thousand dollars, I will have to go along with it."

With the papers in hand, the attorney went to his safe and withdrew an envelope containing the cash, which Ned counted twice, for he did not trust the lawyer and figured the man might try to shortchange them.

Satisfied, Ned gave Emma the money, which she tucked into the front of her bodice. Then she rose and held out her hand. "My dear man, however can I thank you?"

"Your gratitude is thanks enough," he said. "I shall file the papers for your estate and be in touch with you."

With a very large bill, no doubt, Hennie thought.

The con took three days and was as easy as picking up a nickel off a sidewalk. Merry Belle recovered her money, and Ned and Emma made a nice profit for theirselves. They offered to share it with Hennie, but she was uneasy about accepting ill-gotten gains.

When the attorney discovered he had been tricked, he was mad enough to chew splinters. Hennie found out about it, for the Denver address that Emma had given to the lawyer belonged to a friend of Hennie's, a woman who was in on the swindle, although there wasn't the least reason for the lawyer to suspect that. When he discovered he'd been fleeced, that Emma hadn't owned the property at all, he hightailed it to the house, where the three were supposed to be. Hennie's friend, who acted sympathetic about the lawyer's plight, convinced the man that Emma had picked her name out of a directory, just as she had his, and she advised him to go right to the police. But of course, he couldn't do that, for he'd have to reveal that he had tried to cheat a widow out of her inheritance.

<hr/>

"He got what was coming to him. God doesn't put up with people that do meanness on and on and on," Hennie said as she reached over and picked a purple flower, handing it to Nit. "Wild aster, in case you don't know it," she said. She pointed to a white flower like a daisy, with feathery leaves that grew wild across the plots. "And that's chamomile. It makes a real good tea."

"I know chamomile, but I wouldn't gather it where there's dead bodies. Who knows what graveyard chamomile would do to you? I got mine up yonder, in that high meadow."

Hennie was amused that Nit refused to use a cemetery flower, but she wouldn't for the world let the girl know that.

"How did you like the life on the bad side of the law?" Nit asked slyly.

"Oh, I didn't at all. Any minute, I expected to be exposed, but I had to do it for Merry Belle. It's a terrible thing when luck dies. I don't expect she could have lived without that money." Hennie thought a minute as she stretched out her legs. "Emma asked if I'd work with her again, but I couldn't do it. I don't have the soul of a sharper."

The two women laughed, then Hennie asked, "Have you got your wood in for winter? You can't go anywhere in autumn without seeing men sawing their winter's wood. At least, I won't have to do that anymore, for I've got enough to last me till I leave out." Hennie told the girl, "You'll need a mountain of wood."

"Dick's been at it. He says when he's done, he'll build me a chicken coop, and we'll send off for chickens. I sure would like eggs come winter, and they're too precious at the store."

"You can't have chickens in Middle Swan. They'll freeze on the roost—unless you keep them in the house."

The girl frowned at the words and gave an embarrassed

laugh. "Oh, hello, I never thought of that." She stretched her legs, too, and held her face to the sun, in no hurry to leave. "I saw smoke from our chimney go down to the ground. That means fall weather in three days," Nit said. "Chestnut weather, that's what we called fall time at home."

Hennie sighed. "It's the prettiest time of year, autumn is, but the coming of the leaves means snow's not far behind. I've always hated to see winter's dark days come on, this year more than ever, because it means my time on the Swan is almost over." The old woman didn't want to think about that, so she asked, "What does Doc say about the baby?"

Nit looked at the old woman curiously. "He doesn't know about it. I'll send for him when the pains start."

"Some go to see him earlier to make sure everything's all right. It might ease your mind if you did."

"Well, I don't know why. I wouldn't go to a doctor at all if there was a granny woman around, but there's not. I never trusted doctors much. It seems to me they wouldn't know common sense if they met it in the road."

The old woman stood then, for the sun had moved, and there was a chill under the pine trees. The wind had come up, too, and it rattled the dry leaves on the bony aspen branches. "You go on back. I believe I'll walk a little," she told Nit.

The two women went through the arch with END OF DAY CEMETERY in cut-out iron letters, and stopped to say goodbye. The girl shivered, wrapping her thin coat about her belly, which was shaped like a rain barrel, and said, "That wind searches me." She asked if Hennie wanted her to go along for company, for the path Hennie was about to turn onto was rocky.

"No, I've walked these mountains since they were new," Hennie replied, looking up at the hills, which were yellow now in the harsh light. "Tap 'er light," she said by way of farewell.

"Don't trot yourself to death," the girl warned.

The old woman would have liked the company, but she knew the girl was cold. Besides, sometimes she needed to be alone, especially now, because thoughts of death had intruded all afternoon—Billy's, Jake's, Sarah's. Her own days, she feared, were close to spent, and her death would be hastened with the move below, for she was like a turkey that can't be enclosed. She had to range free to live.

Hennie watched the girl until she was out of sight, then stooped down and picked a spray of purple asters, which she tucked into the buttonhole of her coat. "Jake," she said out loud, as she started up the path, "I got to settle things for that one before I go. You take it up with the Lord."

Walking with sure footsteps, Hennie followed the path past the willows and the stumps of trees that had been cut long ago for the mines, whose headframes rose above the pines. There seemed to be more gallows frames than trees along the trail. She was thirsty, but the trickle of water left in the spoiled river the dredge had worked ran red where it leached the iron out of the rocks. Hennie made her way across the piles of glacial rocks to where the dredge squatted in its pond and stood there, watching the ugly thing scoop away an embankment across from her. She stared at the bucket line, thinking, until she was jolted by the long screech of the shift whistle.

Then a voice called from the gangplank, "Hey, old woman."

Hennie turned to see Dick Spindle waving to her. "Wait there. I'll be right quick." He disappeared for a moment, then came running down the gangplank, past the men leaving for the day, dodging a man who had stuck out his elbow just as Dick went by. "This here's for you," he said, handing her a fine walking stick. "I found it this morning, and I couldn't hardly leave it there. I knew I'd find somebody to give it to. I'm awful bad to keep things."

Hennie examined the stick and pronounced it the best she'd ever seen, and it was, sturdy, just the right height, windpolished to a shine, even a knot on top for a knob. "It would tickle me to use it," she said, by way of compliment.

"I'll walk along the drop side of this foxpath if you like. I'm off shift."

"I'd be pleasured." Hennie was amused that Dick had picked the outside of the path along the mountain edge. Her own footing was surer than the man's, she figured, but she wouldn't for anything tell him so, for he had been mannerable. "I just left your wife," she said.

"Nit's partial to you. I don't believe she'd have made it up here in the mountains if you hadn't tended to her."

Such talk embarrassed Hennie, and she changed the subject. "You liking the gold boat any better?"

"No, ma'am. It makes hell look like a lightnin' bug. Nit, she tries to be in good heart, but I know she worries. Sometimes I figure I'm on borrowed time, what with Frank getting killed instead of me. I believe Mr. Hemp wishes it had been me. That's all I got to say about it."

Hennie didn't push the young man. Instead, she said, "Mrs. Spindle told me you like it fine in Middle Swan."

"That's about right. I got no hankering to go back to Kentucky, nor Nit, either. I told her when the dredge shuts down for the winter, we can go on home, see that little grave, but she doesn't care for nothing that way now. She's got a brave heart, and she's thinking about the new baby. I sure hope ... If something happened to me ..." His voice trailed off. In a minute, he said, "I don't know what she'll do when you leave out. Nit says you've been a friend and a mother to her."

"There are others—"

"Not like you," Dick said.

The two of them walked the rest of the way in silence. At the place of parting, Hennie put her hand on Dick's arm. "I don't want you to be in discomfit, Mr. Spindle. Women here are as tough as these mountains," she said, "and your wife's a mountain woman now. She can handle anything that comes down her trail."

Chapter 9

Hennie Comfort felt Mondayish as she watched the snow come down outside her window, a real blizzard. The flakes were thick and soft and endless, and fell straight from the sky, as if they were being dumped from a giant bushel basket. She sat beside her quilt frame and stared through the green leaves of geraniums that all but filled the frost-etched window, to the snow beyond. Her stitches were loopy and uneven and would have to come out. She might as well quilt with noodle as a needle, she thought. Hennie's mind was troubled, and she couldn't understand why. The stove wood was stacked in a box in the kitchen, the brass coal shuttle was full, and the pot of chili that simmered on the back of the range would last until the storm was over. Besides, she had the memory of the night before to keep her warm. She had invited the young couple to supper again, along with Tom Earley.

He'd remained in the high country long after he usually went below. "I like this place above all others, although I won't like it at all if you aren't here. I don't know what I'll do if you don't return next summer," he told her the week before, over supper at the Grubstake. "But of course, you'll return," he added with a little too much feeling.

She reached for her old friend's hand and held it a long time. It wasn't necessary to tell Tom how much his friendship had meant to her over the long years, any more than it was for Tom to tell her how much he cared about her. Neither one of them was ready to say good-bye to the friend of a lifetime; nor did either want to say farewell to Middle Swan.

"Of course I'll be back. I'm not ready to say deep enough to the Tenmile," Hennie said, knowing even as the words left her mouth that they might not be true. "Most likely, I'll live to be a hundred. I believe I have enough money to do that. And if I don't, there's Mae, not that I care to be beholden."

"Oh, you don't have to worry about money." Tom dismissed the idea with a wave of his hand, and Hennie understood that he must have made provision for her in his will if he crossed over before she did. Although she'd found out after Jake died that Tom had arranged with the banker to help her if she ever needed it, she didn't know he'd extended that responsibility after his death.

"You're staying in the high country mighty late this year," Hennie said.

"I'm waiting you out. I'll go down when you do," Tom replied. "Are you ready to go to Iowa?"

"I'll never be ready, but I've sorted through my things and set aside what I want to go with me. I've got most everything I want to take boxed up, except for my clothes and my quilt frame. I'll leave the rest behind." She paused and added, "I wish I could leave my worries behind, too."

Tom didn't say anything but waited for her to continue. He'd always been a good listener.

"I'm still worried about Mrs. Spindle," she continued. "Most likely, she'll have the baby before I leave, so I'll know whether the two of them are all right. But I'd feel better if I knew Dick didn't have to go to the dredge of a morning." Hennie shook her head at the thought.

"There's nothing you can do about it."

"That's just it. I wish I could." She smiled then and held up her glass and said, "That's enough gloomy talk. Luck. To them, and to us, too."

❦

She'd invited Tom to take supper with her last night, then asked the young couple to join them, for she knew that Tom enjoyed Nit and Dick as much as she did. It was a fine evening, one of the most satisfying she could remember. The girl, big as a woodshed now, was feeling fit, and her husband stroked her hand more than once, so proud of his young wife as he looked at her belly. He treated her as if she was as precious as a chunk of wire gold, and she was.

The four of them sat with their toddies in front of the big stone fireplace, watching the flames jump up and listening to the wood pop and send up showers of sparks, as they toasted one another with "mud" and "luck" and "regards."

Outside, the air was heavy, and they knew that snow was coming. They wondered if it would be a big storm or just a dusting that would melt like fog in the next day's sun. Snow already covered the peaks of the Tenmile; it would be there until July, but there hadn't been a real blizzard in Middle Swan yet, although it was the last day of November.

Hennie brought out a heavy winter coat of Mae's and told the girl if she didn't take it, the moths would eat it. Then she presented Dick with a pair of Jake's gloves, leather with fur inside, saying they'd do until the dredge shut down for the winter. He wouldn't want to freeze his fingers. "I found them when I was packing, and I don't have a use for them," she explained.

Hennie had a way about her and offered the gifts in a manner that made the couple feel that they were doing her a favor by taking them. Neither looked at the gifts too closely, or they might have noticed they'd never been worn and that the coat was the latest style. Tom had told Hennie once that if she added up all the coats of Mae's she had ordered from the catalogue to give to needy women over the years, Mae would have had a coat for every day of the month.

The four had seconds of Hennie's scripture cake. Then they helped themselves to the bottle of Tenmile Moon that sat in the middle of the table, Hennie telling Dick that she'd give him what remained of her liquor when she left out, since she couldn't take it on the train.

When they were all feeling mellow, Tom said, "I've got myself a problem." He leaned back in his chair, Jake's solid chair, and Hennie thought that it suited him.

The young folks, comfortable from the food and drink, turned to Tom, waiting for him to continue.

"I had to fire Vern Haslett, the man that's in charge of the Yellowcat." Tom paused and explained to Nit and Dick, "If you don't know, that's my mine up on the Jackass Trail. It's not much of a producer, but I have sentimental feelings about it, since my brother Moses discovered it in the old days. I bought it some years back. There's gold in it yet, and I make wages from it, with enough left to buy a dinner or two at the Grubstake—that is, if Hennie doesn't order the porterhouse."

"Why'd you fire him, Tom?" Hennie asked.

"I caught him high-grading!"

"No! The sappy-headed fool! I'd have told him myself where he could get off. What was his excuse?"

"He said he had a brood to take care of, but I didn't swallow it. He raised a shabby family, and they'd left him long ago. Besides, I paid him good wages. So I told him, 'Get your bindle, and get going.'"

"What's high-grading?" Nit asked.

Tom explained that a miner high-graded when he stole good ore from the mine he was working. Most high-graders took it out in their pockets or their lunch buckets. Tom knew of one fellow who put a chunk of ore on his head, under his hat. Some even sprinkled gold dust in their hair, then washed it out at home.

"Why, that's stealing!" Dick said. "A fellow that'd steal from the man who pays him isn't fit to live with hogs!"

"That's why I told him it was time to tramp," Tom said. "He swore a blue streak at that."

"I hate cussing more'n anything that ever came down my road," Nit told them. "I never saw the sense in blessing out a person."

Except for the crackling of the wood, there was silence in the big room then, until Tom glanced at Hennie, the corners of his mouth turned up a little, and continued slowly. "Now I've got to find a man to replace Vern, a fellow who likes it underground and one I know I can trust. If I don't get somebody pretty quick, I'll just have to shut down the Yellowcat."

Hennie put her hand in front of her mouth to hide a smile. She knew now where the conversation was going, and she looked at Tom with shining eyes, because he'd found a way to answer one of her prayers. "What a botherment," Hennie said at last. "That means you'll put the two other men you've got there out of work if you can't find a manager. Won't one of them take over for you?"

"They're just muckers. Those two are all right if somebody tells them what to do, but I don't believe they'd get much work done on their own. For all I know, they'd sneak off to the picture show at the Roxy in the middle of shift."

"Where are you going to find a good man?" Hennie asked, wondering if lightning would have to strike Dick before he picked up on the conversation. She furrowed her brow and pursed her lips as if she were thinking hard.

Tom shook his head and sipped his whiskey. "That's the trouble, isn't it? Seems like young men don't care about gold mining today. So many young fellows don't have a sense of the underground, not like the old miners did. I believe it might be a thing you're born with. Fellows the age of Dick here would rather work the gold boat." Tom paused, for what he said was not entirely true. But Hennie didn't contradict him, and in a minute, Tom asked, "You don't know of a good man I can hire, do you, Hennie?"

The old woman looked pensive as she glanced at Dick from under her eyelids. She hoped she wouldn't have to hit the boy over the head with a chunk of wood to get his attention. "I'm wrecking my brain."

"I know who can do it," Nit interrupted suddenly, and they all turned to her. "Dick can. He worked underground at home, and he's as honest as the day is long. He knows everything there is about mining. Tell them, Dick."

Both Hennie and Tom looked surprised.

So did Dick. "Aw," he said, blushing.

"Why, I recollect you said something about that once," Tom said.

"I worked in a coal mine back home. I know fellows here look down on that. They act like they're top dog because they mine gold," Dick replied hesitantly. "But I've been inside a gold mine, and I don't see that it's much different. I'm a fast learner. I believe I might could do it."

Tom scratched his head, looking as if he had to be convinced. "Those old boys I've got working there now could teach you, I suppose. But they'd sure as heck try to put one over on you now and then."

"I might look green as a gourd, but I know a thing or two."

Tom nodded. "I'd hate to hire a fellow who'd quit me to work the gold boat when it started up next spring. I wouldn't want to do that."

"Oh no, sir," Dick said. "I wouldn't. I recollect I told you I don't like dredging at all, and I mean it. The dredge pays good enough, and I'm glad to have the job, but if you ask me, a boat's a sorry way to mine gold. It ought to be dug out of the ground with a pick and a shovel, like coal."

"He'd rather work underground than on top of it. He says that all the time," Nit added.

Tom turned to Hennie then for her opinion. "I believe he could do it. Dick's a worker," she said. Then she added, "Here's another thing: He's neat with his work. His wood-pile's the tidiest in Middle Swan, and I've seen the way he keeps his tools in the house, lined up nice and as clean as my silverware. I believe a man who takes care of his equipment like that will be careful. That surely does matter in a mine." She didn't need to remind Tom that Jake most likely had died from carelessness. "And he's awful good to do things for folks. He found that walking stick over there." She pointed to the fine stick that Dick had presented to her the day the two of them had walked together from the dredge.

"I won't allow liquor in the Yellowcat. That's a fireable of-fense. No warning. If I find whiskey on you underground, I'll treat you just like Vern Haslett and tell you it's time to tramp," Tom warned.

"No, sir, I don't drink on the job." They were all silent then, watching Dick, and in a minute, he said, "I believe I'd like that job if you was of a mind to offer it. But I'd have to give a week's notice at the gold boat. It wouldn't be right not to."

"I expect those boys can operate the Yellowcat for a week without causing a cave-in," Tom replied.

Hennie's guests stayed long into the evening, Tom explaining the work to Dick, and Hennie and Nit talking about the baby. Snow had begun to fall by the time the young folks went home, lingering for a time at the door, for it was an evening none of them wanted to end. The couple held hands as they disappeared into the darkness. Tom stayed a minute more.

"Did Vern Haslett really high-grade?" Hennie asked.

"He's been doing it for years. I always considered it a cost of doing business. But I got to thinking after our supper at the Grubstake last week that maybe I didn't have to put up with it anymore." Tom chuckled at that, and the two of them stood in the doorway a little longer, watching the snow come down, Hennie hoping maybe it would never stop and she'd be snowed in for the winter. With luck, the snow would keep on falling until summer, and Mae had promised Hennie she could live in Middle Swan in summer. But although a storm might take its time, the snow always did stop.

"That was a fine thing you just did. You're a good man, Tom Earley," Hennie said.

"Not always so good, but I try," he replied.

"It would be nice if the baby came before Mr. Spindle starts at the Yellowcat, but that would mean this week," Hennie said, as Tom reached for his jacket on the hook beside the door. He told her Nit ought to wait because he'd seen the doctor at the depot that morning, leaving for a few days in Denver.

"Nit says the tyke's not due just yet, but I don't know."

"I helped deliver a baby once."

Hennie gave him an astonished look.

"I can't ever do that again," he added quickly.

Hennie snorted. " 'Can't' is the awfulest word I ever heard. I never like to hear a person say 'can't.' "

"Well, if Mrs. Spindle depends on me, she might just as well give up on it."

"That's the problem. I guess you don't know she lost a baby not so long before she came here. It was born dead. She's scared, and I won't rest easy until I know she's had one that lives."

Tom didn't reply. He'd never been married, so he didn't know how such a thing would eat at a girl, Hennie thought, then wondered if maybe he did. But she dropped the subject. It was one for women.

Tom leaned over and kissed her on the cheek.

"Tap 'er light, Tommy."

"And yourself, Hennie."

Now, as she sat and stared at the snow, Hennie wondered if it was that secret she hadn't yet resolved that ate at her. She had to bring the thing to an ending before she left out, and she still didn't know how to do it. Then it hit her that it was Nit Spindle and not the old secret or the storm or even thoughts about moving to Fort Madison that gave her the all-overs. She couldn't shake the idea that the girl needed her. The old woman had notions, although she could be wrong about them, which made it seem sometimes that she was nothing more than a busybody. Perhaps this was just one of those wrong times, and calling on the girl would only upset the poor thing. Hennie didn't want to go out, not into the damp and cold, when instead, she could stay warm and dry near the coal stove. The stove was an ugly thing, and it smelled, but she was glad for it.

There had been those first winters in Middle Swan, when she built the blaze in the fireplace as high as she dared, but still, she wore her coat and overshoes inside the cabin. Some days, Hennie had Mae play in the bed, under a dozen quilts, so the little girl wouldn't freeze her fingers and toes. Jake said she and Mae could go below during the worst of the winter, find a little house in Denver, where it was warmer, but he was too precious to leave alone. Only later did she realize that the winters had been easier for him, being underground where the temperature was moderate. Women and children, living day and night in the freezing cold of the high mountains, had the worst of it. They were cold all the time.

"What to do, Jake?" she asked her husband's photograph, which sat in a silver frame on the mantel. The two of them had had their pictures taken one afternoon on a trip outside some fifty years before. In the picture, Jake looked as handsome as a barber in a fine coat and bowler hat that the photographer supplied so that Jake wouldn't be captured for eternity in his old jacket and cap. For her sitting, Hennie wore her own cape, which swirled around her like a tent, and a silly bonnet that the photographer insisted she put on. Then someone painted the bonnet's flowers and ribbons blue and touched her cheeks with so much red that she thought she looked like a hooker.

Hennie picked up the picture of Jake and stared at it. In the photograph, her husband didn't look the way she pictured him now. Nor did she think of him as he was at the time of his death. In Hennie's mind, Jake continued to age, so that now, he was still a few years older than she was, gray-haired, a little stooped, but every bit as handsome as the first day she saw him, as fine looking as Tom Earley was now.

"I guess you'd be telling me to see about the girl," Hennie said, returning the photograph to the mantel. She bowed her head for a minute, sending up a prayer for Nit's safety, hoping the Lord would inform her she could stay put. But He didn't. Instead, He seemed to tell her to put on her wraps and go out into the storm, for after all, she'd asked Him to let her be of service to the girl.

It wouldn't do to let Nit know that Hennie was worried about her. So the old woman would tell the girl she couldn't stand to be cooped up in the storm like a harbonated bear. And she'd take Nit the last bit of scripture cake from supper, pretend she'd come on a visit. They would eat the cake with their coffee, for the girl would surely offer to make a pot, especially on such a blustery day. Hennie put on her rubber shoes and her old coat and tied a scarf around her head. She looked around the cozy house again, and with a sigh, she opened the door and went out into the cold.

The wind had come up, sliding down from the high peaks, gathering force, until it reached Middle Swan as an angry gale, shaking the ice on the trees, for a fog the night before had frozen on the limbs. Bits of ice stung Hennie's cheeks. It was a mean storm for so early in the year. Here and there, the wind caught up dried aspen leaves and hurled them at the old woman. Despite the ice and the force of the wind, however, Hennie's steps were sure. She had walked through snow in this place for most of her life. Still, she was glad for the stout stick that Dick had given her, and she carefully poled her way along the trail until she reached the Tappan place and knocked at the door with the knob of the stick.

The girl was slow to answer, and when Hennie finally heard a stirring, she wished she hadn't come, for she feared that Nit had been napping. "You nosy old fool, you should have stayed home and made fudge," she muttered to herself.

But Nit was glad to see her. "Just you come in. I don't like to be alone in this fallen weather," she said, opening the door only enough to allow Hennie to enter, for the girl didn't want to let in the cold.

Nit was wrapped in a quilt and had been sitting in her little blue rocker, pasting pictures in a magazine. The magazine lay open on the floor; a pile of clippings, and a dish containing flour-and-water paste, sat beside the magazine.

"I been putting in pictures of movie stars. Look here. That's a nice one of Ginger Rogers. My, I'd like to dance like that, but Dick would sooner fall in the dredge pond than learn to dance. And here's Hedy Lamarr. And Marion Street, too; she's a starlet," Nit said. "I tried to quilt, but my fingers are so froze my stitches look like they were quilted with an icicle. I got to catch up with my quilts, 'cause I put an old one aside for the birthing and tore up another to wrap the canning jars so's they wouldn't freeze. I covered the potatoes with a piece of quilt, too."

"If you've got anything left of that old quilt, you can make you a dog bed, too, if you had a dog. Quilts just keep getting used till there's no more left of them."

"Quilts are like lives. They're made up of a lot of little pieces," Nit said.

"There's a difference. You can take out the pieces in a quilt. There's not anything you can do to change what you've done in life." Hennie thought a minute, wishing that weren't so. Then she became sensible that Nit hadn't answered and looked at the girl sharply. Nit's face was pale, and she shivered under the quilt. The girl sighed and sat down, and Hennie said, "I can't stand to be alone on a day like this, so I thought I'd come and sit a spell, if you're up to it. There's cake."

"Oh, I'll make the coffee." The girl made no move to stand up.

"You sit, Mrs. Spindle. I'll fix it myself," Hennie said, wishing again that she hadn't bothered the girl. But they had to go through the motions of visiting. It would be poor manners on both their parts not to do so.

"You think it will storm all day?" the girl asked.

"Likely," Hennie replied. Likely today and tomorrow and all week, she thought, busying herself filling the kettle with water and setting it into the eye of the stove over the firebox. She measured coffee into the pot, and took down heavy old cups, instead of Nit's prized china with the roses on it. Hennie's hands were so stiff with cold that she feared she might drop the good cups. When she was finished, she turned to the girl, who had wrapped the quilt tightly about herself. "I could help you to your bed, where you'd be warm. You could have your coffee and cake in the bed. Now isn't that a cozy thought?" When Nit didn't reply, Hennie asked, "Dearie, are you all right?"

Nit looked at Hennie for a long time before she replied. "I don't know, Mrs. Comfort. I was awake all night, with the baby turning over and around. Now, I feel kind of mulish."

"You think the baby's coming?" Hennie asked, alarmed.

"My water's not broke." Nit added, "You can't have a baby if your water's not broke."

Hennie turned back to the stove, where the water had begun to boil. "Where's you the chamomile you dried? I'll fix you tea instead. It'll sit better on your stomach than coffee."

Nit's thin arm made its way out from under the quilt, and she pointed at a pickle jar on top of the pie safe. Except for her belly, the girl was as skinny yet as a plucked porcupine. Hennie unscrewed the lid and told the girl what nice flowers she'd picked and dried, that they would make a good tea. She chose three or four of the largest ones and put them into Nit's cup and poured in the hot water, filling the coffeepot at the same time, for Hennie reckoned she'd be there for a while. If the baby was coming, then Nit would need her, and if it wasn't, the girl still would want someone to give her comfort.

"I brought my piecing," Hennie said, after she'd taken the girl her cup and set her own on the table. She realized she was still wearing her coat, and removed it and sat down, although the house was cold. The Tappan place was always cold, much too cold for a baby, Hennie thought. "Look you. It's a burro. I saw the pattern in a magazine—they said it was for a donkey, but that's the same thing as a burro—and I thought it would be real nice for a baby up here in the gold country. You used to see those burros every day. See them or hear them. My, they were rackety." Hennie was glad she had her quilt pieces with her, for stitching would keep her from fidgeting. "You want I should get your quilting for you, Mrs. Spindle?"

The girl shook her head. "I guess there's something wrong with me when I don't want to do my piecing, isn't there? Maybe I'm just idlesome."

"It's the cold. It stiffens your hands," Hennie said. "Sometimes when I quilt with cold fingers, I have to take out the stitches later on."

The two sat quietly awhile, Hennie planning in her head what she'd do if the girl went into labor. She'd have to find Doc, or she could run to the Pinto place, which wasn't far away, and ask Monalisa to go. Then Hennie remembered Tom saying he'd seen the doctor at the depot and that the man would be away for several days. Hennie closed her eyes and asked the Almighty to let that baby wait until Doc returned. She wondered if the girl was a praying sort. They'd never talked about religion, and because Hennie hadn't gone to church in such a long time, she didn't know if the Spindles attended regularly. The girl understood the church was something Hennie didn't care to talk about.

As the girl picked up her cup, her hand slipped, and she sloshed tea on the quilt that was wrapped around her. "Now look what I've done, and it will stain." Her voice broke, for she was near tears.

"No such a thing," Hennie said soothingly. "I'll get you to your bed, and after that, I'll just scrub out that spill before it sets up." She took the cup from Nit and held the girl's arm as Nit walked heavily across the room. Hennie turned down the covers and fluffed the pillows, before she helped the girl into the bed. Then when Nit was tucked in, Hennie dipped a cloth into the water bucket and scrubbed out the tea stain. She spread the quilt on a chair beside the cookstove to dry, rubbing her hand over the wet spot to smooth it out. "Good as new," she said over her shoulder.

Nit didn't reply, and Hennie returned to the bed. "You sure you're all right, Mrs. Spindle?"

"Just bone-tired of being pregnant," the girl said. "I feel like I'm the little feller's house." She patted her belly.

And a house full of worry, Hennie thought. She dragged the blue rocking chair to the bed and sat down, wondering what she could do to take the girl's mind off her condition.

"Are you thinking you might tell me a story to pass the time?" the girl asked. "I'd like that awful well."

Maybe a tale would calm Nit, the old woman thought, and Hennie, of course, had plenty of them yet to be passed on. "What do you want me to tell about?"

The girl thought a minute. "Gold mining. If Dick's going to be a gold miner, I want to know about mining. Do you have any stories about mining?"

"Aplenty of them. Just wait until I get my piecing," Hennie said, going to the table and picking up the squares and triangles for a burro, then taking her seat in the rocker beside the bed. "There's different kinds of mining," she began, when she was settled again and had set one square of cheddar yellow against another. Her hands were too cold and stiff yet to put a needle to the pieces.

There was placer mining, the first mining that was done on the Swan, placering, or plater mining, as the leather bellies called it. That was as good a way as any of describing it, because the prospector used a big gold pan the size of a platter to swirl the water around. The motion let the specks of gold settle to the bottom, where they could be gathered up. There was so much free gold in those first days that a miner just picked it out of the stream. Panning was good when a man worked by himself. If he had a partner or two, he shoveled the dirt from the river into a sluice box, ran water through it, and let the gold catch on the riffles. Those were little wooden ridges put crosswise in the box, with a piece of old carpet under them to catch the gold dust.

On the hillside just past where the dredge operated, hydraulic mining had taken place. Workers had turned big hoses on the mountainsides and washed everything away. The bare hillside they left behind were every bit as ugly as the rock piles that followed the dredges.

And then there was dredging.

But the best kind of mining was lode mining, following a gold vein as it twisted and turned underground. Lode mining took talent and was the way God intended for men to mine gold. That was what Hennie thought, and that was the way Monte Poor mined his strike.

There wasn't much to set Monte Poor apart from the other prospectors. They were all the same breed of dog. Monte Poor dressed like his name, in old pants and plow shoes, a coat that was more holes than it was coat, a battered hat, and he toted a sack of victuals and an outfit of pick and shovel, gold pan and whatnot. In the old days, a person could look out the window and see a dozen of those boys, dressed in off-casts, plodding down the street after their burros, every one of them thinking he was going to strike it rich. They would find enough gold to go on a high lonesome every now and again and to last them through the winter.

The boys used the gold dust till there was no more left. Then they caught burros and struck out again in the spring, going way up yonder, coming back only long enough to try to talk old man Pinto into grubstaking them. Sometimes the leather bellies were never seen again, and if folks thought about them, which wasn't likely, they didn't know if the prospectors taken themselves to another camp or had gone over the range, so to speak.

Monte Poor must have prowled the hills for twenty years, when he went rushing down the mountain to the assay office.

"You found something, Monte?" one of the boys sitting on the bench in front of the Pinto store asked and snickered. By then Monte had grown queer from being by hisself so much. He'd got unfriendly, too, and didn't trust anyone. It was a common failing among prospectors.

Monte gave the man a steely-eyed look and muttered, "Kill your own snakes."

"Yep, he's found a fortune. Old Monte's going to be the ablest man on the Tenmile," a loafer laughed.

"Only a ten-foot vein of solid gold will beat what I got. A million dollars wouldn't buy that strike off me today," Monte growled.

"You reckon he found it with a stick?" another asked. Monte was a dowser, one of the prospectors who used a forked stick to find gold, just like a farmer witching for water. The boys on the bench laughed at that.

Monte had the last laugh, however. He'd discovered the

Brass Monkey, the richest mine on the Tenmile, and before the year was out, Monte Poor was strutting around town wearing a frock coat, fine leather boots, and a stickpin with a diamond the size of a sultana.

But it didn't take him long to be sorry he'd ever found the Brass Monkey. After all, it was discovering gold, not spending it, that mattered to the prospectors. Everybody tried to cheat him out of his money—politicians, do-gooders, church people. Women tried to trick him into marrying them. One even said Monte was the father of her baby, and Monte had to hire a lawyer to fight her. In the end, Monte paid her off just to get rid of her. But maybe he was the father. Who was to say?

Monte sold the Brass Monkey for more money than any leather belly in Middle Swan had seen before or since, and moved down to Denver, where he bought himself a mansion. But the man had lived by himself so long that he couldn't stand the servants creeping around behind him. And he wasn't comfortable in a place that was clean. So he moved out of the house to a hotel. He joined a club and spent his time sitting in an armchair, smoking cigars, growling at anybody who came close.

He went back to Middle Swan every so often, stood in the street, and looked off at the mountain peaks. Hennie saw him in front of her house one morning, breaking his dowsing stick into kindling and looking at her PRAYERS FOR SALE sign.

"Mrs. Comfort, I'd be obliged if you'd sell me a prayer," he told Hennie, who had gone outside to greet him.

"You know my prayers are free, Monte."

"Then I'd think kindly of it if you'd ask whoever's in charge up there to take away my money, burn down my house, and let me go back up there in the hills again with my burro."

Monte died not long after that. There was a scramble for his money, relatives showing up claiming they were his long-lost brother or son or wife. But he'd had a good lawyer draw up a will. He left his fortune to build a home where old prospectors could live out their days.

❧❦❧

"The Poor poorhouse," Nit said, with a sly smile.

Hennie slapped her knee. "Why, I never thought of that," she said with a little too much enthusiasm, for of course she had thought of that. In fact, the home was known as the Poor Poorhouse.

Hennie stood then and walked to the window, pushing aside the curtain to look out at the storm. The snow was coming down as thick as a blanket, and the wind swirled it so that Hennie couldn't see the cabin across the road. It was a bad day to have a baby, she thought. Then she turned around. "I forgot all about the cake, Mrs. Spindle. Would you have a piece?"

The girl stared at Hennie for a moment, before she said softly, "I couldn't eat even a tiddy-bit right now."

"You still feeling mulish?"

"I am."

"It'll pass. I never knew why the Lord made babies and gold so hard to come by."

The girl gave her a whisper of a smile. "I guess I'll never find a gold mine then, 'cause I wouldn't go through this again for anything but a baby."

Hennie chuckled as she went to her chair and picked up her sewing.

"Oh!" the girl called out suddenly, and Hennie looked up to see Nit's eyes bulging. The girl was sitting up in the bed, her knees drawn close to her.

"Mrs. Spindle, are you all right?"

"Oh, hello no! My water's just broke," the girl said. "I been getting the pains regular since you got here, and I think I'll soon start with the delivery."

"Lordy! Why didn't you say so?"

"I wasn't sure till now, and I didn't want you to think I was a flippy-whippet. Besides, I had the pains last night, and they just went away."

"That's the way of it up here—false labor. You let me help you get on your nightdress. Then I'll clean up the bed and go get help," she said, wondering just who that help would be.

As Hennie moved toward the bed, the girl grimaced. "I don't think we got much time."

"That's good. There's no cause for a long labor."

Hennie was halfway to the bed when there was a knock on the door. She stood still an instant, not knowing whether to answer it or go to the girl. Before she could make up her mind, the door flew open, and Zepha Massie stepped inside. She was wearing another of "Mae's old coats."

"I'm sorry to bother you, Nit, but I had me a presentment so strong I couldn't stay still. I knew you needed somebody, so Blue says to me, 'Woman, I'll watch Queenie. You go and tend to Mrs. Spindle.' I don't want to go where I'm not wanted, but the feeling's so strong. One time in Kansas,

I knew this woman's in trouble on the road..." Zepha saw Hennie then and looked confused. "Maybe I'm wrong. If Mrs. Comfort's here, you don't likely need anybody else."

"No, Mrs. Massie, you come right in. Mrs. Spindle's water's just broke. She's going to have this baby, and the doctor's gone to Denver, the durn fool. Do you have any idea how to birth a baby?"

"I got some knowings about it."

Hennie nodded. She, too, had some knowings, so the two women could do a passable job of delivering the baby—she hoped. Then she remembered Monalisa. "Mrs. Pinto. She used to be a nurse. She's got handier hands than I do. I can't move so quick, so I'd be obliged if you'd fetch her. She lives in the brown house with green shutters on the street that goes to the icehouse. Do you know it?"

"It's not but a hop and a jump." Zepha turned, and moving low to the ground, she left the house so quickly that she failed to secure the door. Hennie went to shut it, watching as Zepha, running like a turkey, disappeared in the snow.

As the old woman returned to the girl, Nit pointed to a wooden box and said the things she'd set aside for the birthing were in it. Hennie fetched the box, which contained a baby blanket, a diaper, a basin, string, scissors, an old quilt, and a turkey-tail fan. Hennie didn't know why the last item was there, but she laid it out on the table with the other things, then turned to the girl. By the time Zepha returned with Monalisa Pinto, Hennie had dressed Nit in her nightgown and Nit was lying on the birthing quilt that Hennie had spread on top of the bed.

"You've got it pretty good here," Monalisa said, looking

quickly around the room. "I'll take a closer look when I've got the time." She put her coat on a chair and glanced at the stove, where the teakettle simmered. "Mrs. Massie, please fill the kettle to the top, and when the water's hot, pour some in the basin, for I don't care to birth a baby with dirty hands."

Before going to Nit, Monalisa checked the items that Hennie had laid out on the table, which she'd pushed close to the bed. Monalisa nodded her approval. "You've got everything just right. Thank you, Hennie. I don't know what we'll do in Middle Swan after you leave."

Hennie didn't reply but instead gaped at Monalisa, whose attitude was new to her. Monalisa was such a sour woman that Hennie had expected her to act put-upon at being called out in the storm and to make the girl feel bad, too. In fact, if she had thought of anyone else to help with the baby, Hennie wouldn't have sent for Monalisa at all. But here the woman was, acting as if she were glad she'd gone out into a blizzard to help birth a baby. Hennie guessed there was nothing that brought women together like quilting and childbirth.

Monalisa paid Hennie no attention. After she was satisfied that everything was in readiness, she went to the bed and put her hand on Nit's forehead, smoothing back her hair. "Is this your first?" she asked.

Before Nit could reply, the girl's face twisted in a pain. So Hennie answered for her. "She had a baby last year, but the poor thing never took a breath."

"We'll try to do a better job this time. I've delivered many a baby, so don't you worry."

"I'm obliged, Mrs. Pinto," Nit said after the pain sub-
sided.

"You call me Monalisa. We'll all be first names now. Don't
hold back with the pains. Scream your eyes out, if you're of
a mind to. There's nobody but us to hear you in this storm,
and sometimes it helps. It surely did with mine." Monalisa
smiled at the girl.

She started to say more, but Zepha came alongside her, a
butcher knife in her hand, and stooped down. "This cuts the
pain. I've seen it done before," she said fiercely, as if she
would have to argue down Monalisa.

"I can't say it does, but it surely does not do harm. You go
ahead and put the knife under the bed."

Hennie shook her head, wondering if this was the same
Monalisa Pinto who once told her that superstition was one
of the failings of Christianity. The old woman pulled herself
out of her reverie and hurried to the stove, adding wood to
the firebox to keep the blaze going. The water was boiling
now, and Hennie and Zepha filled the basin, carrying it to
the table. Monalisa let it cool a minute before the three
women washed their hands. Monalisa told Zepha to throw
the water outside and fill the basin again, this time dropping
in the string to sterilize it.

Before she could say more, the girl screamed, and Monalisa examined her. "I think this baby's ready to be born." She
exchanged a glance with Hennie, and the two women posi-
tioned themselves on either side of the bed, Hennie rubbing
the girl's back, while Monalisa coached, "When the pain
comes on, pant like a dog."

Nit did as she was told, and when the pain let up, she

said, "This is the god-awfulest hurt. I don't remember it being so bad before."

"You can have a dozen, and you never do remember. That's the Lord's gift. The Reverend Shadd says the Almighty's with you in your pain. And if things aren't meant to be, you'll wake up in the arms of God," Monalisa told her. Hennie frowned, because she knew that Monalisa wasn't a believer. She wondered where the woman had heard the minister's words, certainly not in church.

"I won't!" Nit cried. "I'm not going anywhere."

"I expect you're not at that."

Hennie almost chuckled then, for Monalisa had merely intended to rile the girl. Nit would need the fight before the borning was over.

Monalisa rubbed her sleeve over her sweating forehead, and Zepha picked up the feather fan and swished cool air back and forth over the woman's face, then fanned Nit. The women worked together for better than an hour, until the girl gave a scream that Hennie swore carried as far as her own house and Monalisa announced that the baby's head was coming out. The girl's face contorted as she pushed. There was another push, and another, and the baby slid out into Monalisa's arms.

"Is it alive? Is it?" Nit cried, sweat running down her face into her nightdress. "It has to be alive."

Hennie and Zepha held their breath while Monalisa steadied the child on one arm, the top of its coconut head sticking above her elbow, and put a finger into the infant's mouth. The baby made no sound, and Nit stared at it, her eyes wide with fear. She didn't seem to breathe, nor did Hennie and Zepha. Hennie put her arm around the girl and held her tight as she prayed for air to reach the tiny lungs. At last, there was a mewling and then a cry, and the women grinned at one another.

"You did it, Nit. I never heard such a healthy cry," Hennie told the girl, who leaned back with a look of rapture on her face.

"Just let me tie the cord," Monalisa said. "Then you can see it."

Nit suddenly sat up and laughed. "I forgot to ask, boy or girl?"

"Boy."

"Oh." Nit sighed, sliding back down.

"Prettiest boy that ever I saw, with hair the color of Mr. Spindle's. And his eyes sparkle just like a diamond ring," Hennie said.

"Your husband will be proud to see him," Zepha added.

Monalisa told the two women to look after Nit while she cared for the infant. Hennie and Zepha began to clean up the girl, but after a minute, they looked at each other, confused. Then Nit gave a gasp.

"Monalisa," Hennie said.

The sound of the old woman's voice made Monalisa stop what she was doing and turn around.

"There's something…"

Monalisa frowned. "What is it?"

"I think there's one more."

"What?" Monalisa handed the baby to Zepha and turned back to Nit.

"She got another little feller ready to come out," Zepha

said. "No wonder this one's all swiveled up. He's been sharing space with his brother."

Monalisa examined the girl and exclaimed, "Nit Spindle, I don't want to dishearten you, but I believe you're having you a second baby." She chuckled. "Now I know you didn't expect to do this so soon again, but you got to give birth one more time."

"Two babies?" Nit asked, confused. She started to say more, but a pain stopped her, and she began to push. The second child came out quicker, and before a few minutes had passed, Monalisa held up a squalling baby girl.

"You got any more in there?" Zepha asked.

"That's the last one," Monalisa answered. She handed the boy to Nit, and after she checked over the girl, she gave that baby to Nit, too, so that the mother held one in each arm.

"They're both breathing," Nit said happily. She turned her head to look at first one baby and then the other. "I sure am proud, but how am I going to take care of two babies?" she asked.

"I'll help," Zepha told her. "There's nothing I like better than babies. I'll come every day."

"Hennie and me will throw a pitch-in, seeing as how you likely don't have enough for two little ones. Why, there's baby stuff all over Middle Swan that women haven't gotten around to tossing in the dump. They'd be obliged to you for taking it," Monalisa added.

The women tended to the new mother and put away the birthing things, then helped Nit off the bed so that they could remove the soiled quilt and straighten the covers.

Zepha reached for the babies, but Nit wouldn't let them go. "I've got to make sure they keep on breathing," she said.

After Nit was settled and Monalisa and Zepha had gone, the one promising to bring the Spindles' supper, the other to take the news of the twins' birth to their father, Hennie stayed on, fixing tea from an herbal concoction that the girl had prepared. Hennie convinced Nit to let her lay the babies end to end in the cradle, while the girl drank the tea to restore her strength and bring on her milk. Hennie took down the good china for her.

Bone-tired herself, Hennie sat down in the blue chair next to the bed to wait for Dick, and with her foot, she rocked the cradle back and forth. "I plain forgot to ask you, Mrs.... Nit, that is. I forgot to ask what are these babies' given names? Do you know how you call their names yet?"

"I do," Nit said importantly. "I've been thinking on it for a long time. The boy, he's Dick Spindle—'Dickie.' That's what we'll call him." She finished the tea and handed the empty cup and saucer to Hennie. "And the girl, her name is Columbine Spindle—Collie, for short."

Hennie smiled as she set the cup on the table and closed her eyes for a minute, rocking back and forth in the chair in time with the cradle. She'd have to make a second baby quilt before she went below, and then she'd go through her belongings to see what she had that the girl could use. Hennie wished she could offer something special. Nit might want the big rocker from Hennie's living room, or she could make the young couple a quilt after she went to Iowa. Maybe she'd buy Nit that feather-edged platter the girl had spotted in Ye

Olde Shop. But was there something else she could do for them?

Suddenly, Hennie stopped in mid-rock and opened her eyes. Why, of course there was, you old fool with mud for a mind! Why didn't you think of it sooner? You've got you a present that nobody else can give the girl—a fine log house! Hennie chuckled a little. The Spindles could move into her house while she was away. They would take care of it, and Hennie wouldn't have to worry about somebody breaking in and robbing her or the pipes freezing up and bursting. The old woman wouldn't mind at all having the Spindles live there, and Mae would be more likely to let her return summers if she wasn't in the house by herself.

The old woman smiled with satisfaction. There would be little ones in her home, just like she and Jake had planned when they built it. Hennie closed her eyes and began to rock again, while she softly said a word of thanks. The Lord had just replied to another of her prayers. The only one left unanswered was about that secret that had pricked her for so many years. Maybe the Lord was going to keep his answer to Himself and make Hennie come to terms with it on her own.

Chapter 10

Tom Earley brought along a loaf of bread that he had baked that morning, and they sat in front of the fire eating their bread and soup, wiping out the bowls with bits of crust. Tom smacked his lips like any man in Middle Swan would do to show his pleasure with the supper. It was a simple meal, made of leftovers from the Christmas dinner the two of them had shared with Nit and Dick.

"There's no hereafter. I was going to make a custard, but I got so busy rearranging the house for the Spindles that I disremembered," Hennie said. The Spindles were moving in the next day, because Hennie wanted them settled in before she left. They ought to get to know the place while she was there to answer questions, because like most houses in Middle Swan, the Comfort home was temperamental.

Hennie leaned back in the rocker, thinking how satisfying it was to be with a man who liked her cooking.

"I never ate a bite of custard in my life. I'm satisfied without dessert," Tom replied.

"Well, I'd like a bit of sweetness for myself. Wouldn't a dish of ice cream taste good?" Hennie mused.

"Let's go get it. The drugstore's still open. Would that suit you?"

Hennie grinned. "It would!" She stood and helped her friend to his feet. They put on their jackets, and Tom with his cane and Hennie with her walking stick left the house.

At the drugstore, they sat at the counter eating fudge sundaes, scraping the dishes and licking the spoons, greedy as schoolchildren, remembering back to the early days when Hennie had made snow ice cream from fresh-fallen snow, milk, and a drop of vanilla. "I can't say this is any better," Tom said, pointing with his spoon at his dish.

"The company is every bit as good," Hennie replied.

After they had finished and wiped their mouths with paper napkins from the tin dispenser, the two swiveled around on the stools and helped each other down. They buttoned their coats and went out into the night, which was cold but clear. Snow was on the ground now and would be until spring, but there was no sign of a fresh storm brewing. The sky was blue-black in the moonlight, and the stars twinkled like pieces of broken quartz.

"The frost line's gone deep in the ground," Hennie said. She'd have to tell the Spindles to keep a drip of water going through the winter so the pipes wouldn't freeze. There were so many things they needed to know that she'd made a list—

who to call for coal, how to spread the stove ashes on the
walk in winter, where the roof shingles were kept and the
ladder and the garden tools.

Dick and Nit had been overwhelmed when Hennie invited them to live in her house. She'd waited until a few days
after the twins were born, until the Spindle cabin was so
crammed with baby things that the couple barely had room
to turn around. Then she'd said that it would be a kindness to
her if they would look after her house while she was away,
staying there so that nobody broke in. They protested, telling
her the offer was too generous. So to keep them from feeling
beholden, Hennie said she'd take seven dollars a month for
the house, less than what they were paying for the Tappan
place, and the couple could pay the electric, too. They all
knew the house was worth twenty-five dollars anyway, maybe
more, but paying her a little something was a way the boy
could feel he wasn't taking charity. And he wasn't, Hennie told
herself, because the place was better off with someone in it.

"You're thinking about your house," Tom said, and Hennie almost replied how odd it was that the two of them always seemed to know what the other was thinking, just like
an old married couple. But that was too familiar a thing to
remark on.

"I am."

"Don't worry. The Spindles will take good care of it, just
like he does the Yellowcat." After he took over managing the
Yellowcat Mine, Dick made the muckers clean up the adit,
and low and behold, he found a nice little pocket of ore
back behind a pile of waste. He named it the "pay chute."
"That was good advice you gave me to hire him," Tom said.

"I disremember it was me that thought it up. It was you."

"*We* did." Tom took her arm, and they slowed beside the cribbing of an old mine. "I believe I'd like to sit awhile," he said.

"Are you tired, Tommy?"

"No, not a bit, but I've got something to say, and now seems a good time." He eased himself onto a rock, and Hennie sat beside him, looking up toward the heavens.

She pointed out a falling star with her walking stick. "I wonder if I'll ever be this close to the sky again."

"You'll never be happy going to Iowa, will you?"

Hennie shook her head. "I don't know why I dread it so. Fort Madison is as nice a place as you could ask for. But I just don't love it, not like Middle Swan. I just don't. I guess I'm lucky to have a daughter that wants me, even though I wish she wouldn't keep saying I can't live alone anymore."

"And what do you say?"

The old woman shrugged. "If I had my way, I'd never say 'deep enough' to the Swan. But the time's coming when I might not be able to do for myself. I hate to admit it, but Mae's right about that. So what else is there for me? I'm resigned to it."

Tom squeezed her hand but didn't let go of it. "You could go to China."

Hennie gave him a curious look. "I could go to the moon, too."

"You said once you wanted to visit China."

"I'd like to see the King of England, too, but you have to have a pocketful of money to get anywheres."

"I can arrange that."

The dredge groaned and roared, and Hennie waited until it had settled down to a clatter before she spoke. "You're going to send me around the world?" Tom was talking foolishment, and she was puzzled.

"No, I won't send you," Tom said, then turned and looked Hennie full in the face. "But I'll take you."

Hennie said nothing, just stared at her friend, the blood rising in her face, as an idea of what he meant crept into her mind.

"I should have asked you to marry me all those years ago, after Jake died. But I was too busy making money. Besides, I was scared you'd turn me down, and if you had, we might not have been able to put it behind us and remained friends. And having you as a friend means the world to me. So I let the time pass, and then it seemed like it was too late. I contented myself with seeing you in the summers. I never thought you'd leave the high country. But now..."

He smiled, a little embarrassed himself, and let go of her hand. "Now, maybe I have a chance. I wouldn't like to wait any longer. I've been lonesome most of my life. There was somebody I cared about a long time ago, before I came to the Swan, but it wasn't right for us. She was married. You're the only other woman I've ever cared about. Now, I'd like a little companionship before I cross over. I believe maybe you would, too. So I'd like it fine, Hennie, if you'd be my wife and move in with me instead of your daughter." He paused and added, "You and your quilt frame and your prayer sign. I'd get down on my knees to ask you, but I might not be able to get up again."

Hennie laughed, and something inside her let go, as if

the stitching on a too-tight garment had suddenly broken. The cords that had bound her since Mae first asked her to move to Fort Madison were asunder. "You're asking me to marry you? At our age? Why, I'm eighty and six. I can't get married."

"And you'll be eighty and seven next year whether you're married or not." He thought a minute. "You told me once you thought 'can't' was the awfulest word you ever heard, so I don't believe it when you say it."

"I did tell you that, didn't I." Hennie laughed, then grew silent. "Oh, Tom, we'd be a pair of old fools."

"I feel young right now and not so much of a fool. In fact, I believe this is a pretty smart idea I've come up with." He rested both of his hands on his cane and looked out at the black humps of the Tenmile Range, barely visible in the moonlight. "What do you say, Hennie?"

Hennie herself studied on the mountains for a time, then looked up at the sky. She didn't believe she'd ever seen so many stars. "I left Tennessee to come to Colorado in a covered wagon to marry a man I'd never met," she said slowly. "I guess it won't be any trouble to go to Chicago and marry a man I've known for seventy years and loved for a good number of them. We let a long lonesome time go by, didn't we? I believe we ought to make up for it."

"We will at that." Tom leaned over and kissed Hennie then, harder and longer than she would have thought. It wasn't a kiss of friendship, either, and Hennie surprised herself by wondering if a marriage to Tom Earley might be every bit as complete as her marriages to Billy and Jake had been. The idea made her blush, and she was glad the sky was too dark for Tom to notice.

Hennie smiled at Tom and kissed him back. Then she pulled away and cocked her head and asked, "Could I really meet the King of England?"

"Any king you want," he said, taking her hand again and raising it to his lips. "We'll spend the year going wherever you please—China, Persia, even the North Pole, which they tell me isn't quite as bad as Middle Swan in January. And in the summer, we'll come back to the Swan, take a private railroad car to Denver and hire a car and driver to bring us up here."

Hennie chuckled and then began to laugh. "Why, I'm not looking at the end of my life anymore but a beginning. I believe we could have some good years."

"That we could. Will you do it, Hennie?"

"I'll do it, Tommy. I'll say yes to you." He clasped both of her hands, pulling her to him and kissing her again. Then the two of them stood up, making their way back to Hennie's house, Tom using his cane only a little now.

"Imagine," Hennie murmured, as she slipped her hand through his arm, "the King of England."

⟡

She told the Tenmile Quilters a few mornings later, after the Spindles were settled into the house, when the women had stopped by to present Hennie with a Friendship quilt that they had made for her in secret as a going-away present. This one was every bit as finely quilted as the old quilt that Hennie had brought with her from Tennessee seventy years before. Made in Chimney Sweep blocks and embroidered with the names of Hennie's friends in Middle Swan, the quilt contained more than one block that had been pieced from the peacock blue that Hennie had given the quilters. The old woman ran her hand over the names, then said slyly, for only the Spindles knew of her plans, "I don't know if you're giving this to me because I'm leaving or because I'm getting married." She looked down in hopes her friends wouldn't see her face turning red.

"At your age?" Monalisa asked, shocked.

"You think she should wait till she's older?" Zepha asked.

"I think it's wonderful!" Carla said quickly.

"I bet Charlie Peace finally made you say yes!" Bonnie exclaimed.

"Not Charlie. I'll wager it's Noah Justis," Carla interrupted, and the other women frowned, because Noah Justis was an old batch, and most people thought his head was not done.

"You're both wrong," Nit jumped in, too excited to let Hennie give out the name. "It's Tom Earley. Tell them, Mrs.... that is, Hennie?" Nit still found it awkward calling Hennie by her first name. "Tell them."

"It is," Hennie told them. "Tom and I are getting married."

"That's a wonderful thing. I only wish the Reverend Shadd wasn't too sick to officiate. He's nearly crossed over," Bonnie said.

"They're going to be married in Chicago. Mr. Earley went back yesterday to get the house ready for her," Nit explained. "If she's married there, we won't fight over who gets to stand up with her."

"Well, that's fine," Edna said, and the others nodded. "Tom Earley. Imagine."

The women crowded around Hennie then and told her what a lucky man Tom was. They asked about the wedding, whether it would be in a church or Tom's house, which, after all, was a mansion as big as a cathedral. Edna said she had a piece of lace that Hennie might like to have as a veil, and not to be outdone, Monalisa told the old woman that she could have the borrow of her own wedding dress if she could remember who she'd loaned it to last. Hennie thought it unlikely that Monalisa ever had a wedding dress, since Monalisa and Roy Pinto had never had the words said over them, but it was a thoughtful gesture anyway. She shook her head. "Thanks to you, but I'm going to stop at Daniels and Fisher in Denver and buy me a whole new wardrobe. I never got married in a new dress before."

"If you ask me, you ought to buy you a silk nightgown with lace on it, lots of lace," Bonnie said.

"Bonnie!" Monalisa frowned. "At Hennie's age!"

"Well, I do," Bonnie insisted.

"I intend to," Hennie said, looking Monalisa in the eye and not blushing.

Nit scurried around, fixing coffee and cutting a cake that one of the women had brought, because, as Edna Gum had told the girl, "You're the woman of the house, now."

Nit had nodded at that. "I've got it pretty good here," she'd replied, as proud as if she owned the place. She took down Hennie's fine china, and the women chattered about Hennie's good fortune as they ate the cake.

As soon as they were finished, Bonnie and Carla got up,

because they had the duty of looking after the Reverend Shadd. They explained that they'd left him in bed with a terrible hurting in his head and had promised not to be gone long.

"He does not expect to get better," Bonnie said. "He's living in the end of time."

"I shouldn't wonder. He's older than Abraham," Zepha remarked.

"I'm making him some beef tea. That'll keep his strength up," Carla said.

"If he wants it up," Bonnie replied. "If he's ready to die, I don't know that the Lord allows us to interfere with His will. It might be blasphemy."

"It might be starvation if you don't," Monalisa told her.

"He's been asking for you, Hennie," Bonnie said. "I don't know why. Maybe he still wants to save your soul. The man surely is at heaven's gate."

"We didn't tell you before, because we thought you wouldn't want to see him," her sister added. "But now that you know he's ready to cross over, you ought to go. He wants to see you bad."

"Well, I don't want to see him," Hennie told them.

"Quit that. You're not a hard-minded woman. I don't understand you," Bonnie said harshly, then calmed down as the other women stared at her display of rudeness. "You with all the good luck you have now, you ought not to begrudge him a moment of your time."

Hennie didn't reply but stared out the window, rousing herself only to say good-bye as the Tenmilers filed out of the

house, leaving Nit and Zepha and Hennie. Zepha went upstairs to rock the twins in their cradle, saying she couldn't
get enough of Dickie and Collie, but Hennie wondered if
Zepha had a presentiment that the old woman wanted to be
alone with Nit.

Hennie sat down in Jake's chair then, her hands clasped
between her knees, her head bowed, feeling the prickers that
lurked inside clutch at her heart again, while Nit sat on a pillow on the floor beside her. "Is there a story you'd like to tell
me?" Nit asked, for it was clear that the old woman was troubled. Hennie didn't reply and sat there so long that Nit got
up and folded the Friendship quilt and started to clear the
plates and cups.

At last, Hennie sighed and said, "I've got something that
needs doing. The Lord's answered all my prayers, and I believe He expects me to do my part, although I'd rather take
a whipping than do what it is He wants." She sighed deeply
and went to the hook beside the door and took down her
coat. "I believe He's told me what He wants me to do, and
it's a hard task."

"It's the Reverend Shadd, isn't it?" Nit asked. "Do you
want me to go with you?"

Hennie shook her head, then stopped and pondered a
moment before she decided that she did want the girl with
her. Without someone to accompany her, the old woman
might turn around before she reached the minister's cabin.
"I'd like that. Yes, I believe I would."

"I'll get the makings for a horseradish poultice for his
head," Nit said, going to her medicine chest and taking out

some dried bits, folding a piece of newspaper around them. She called upstairs to ask Zepha to stay awhile longer, then put on her own coat, and the two walked out into the cold.

The sky was the color of lead, and the wind swept down off the Tenmile, bringing the dampness that heralded snow. They walked with their heads down, facing into the wind, which was so strong that it seemed for every three steps they took forward, they were blown back one.

The Reverend's shack was far across town from Hennie's house, and the two women were near frozen by the time they reached it. Still, Hennie wished the man lived even farther away, for she had turned over in her mind what she would say to him and had come up only with confusion. Hennie paused as they reached the cabin, not sure whether she could go ahead, but Nit knocked boldly at the door, which Bonnie opened.

"Why, here's Hennie Comfort come to see you, Reverend," Bonnie said with gladness in her voice. "Remember, you asked for her." She smiled as she moved to a side wall to make room for the two women to enter. The place was that small.

Hennie didn't return the smile. "What I've got to say is of a personal nature. I'd like you to leave us," she told Bonnie. "Please."

Bonnie glanced over at the bed, but there was no reaction. "All right. You take your time, Hennie. I'll be back," she said. Bonnie slipped on her coat and tied her scarf under her chin and went out into the cold, closing the door behind her.

Alone in the cabin now with just Nit and the reverend, Hennie glanced around the room, unwilling yet to look at the man in the bed. The place was sparse. A fireplace instead of a cookstove provided the heat, and a spider and a heavy iron Dutch oven sat on the hearth. Besides the iron bed, which was so bent that it must have come from the dump, the only furniture was an old bureau, a table, and two wooden chairs that didn't match. A Bible lay open on the dresser next to a shaving glass and a tin basin. A crude wooden cross aged the color of burnt toast, its bottom broken off, hung on the wall; it might have been salvaged from a graveyard.

Hennie let her eyes go as far as the bed quilt, and after a moment, for the quilt was so washed and worn that it was hard to see the design, she recognized the Seven Sisters pattern, and she put her hand on the wall to steady herself. The wall was made of peeled logs, the wood as smooth as glass.

Nit followed the old woman's gaze and said, "There's an awful lot of living in that quilt."

"And an awful lot of suffering, I expect," Hennie added. She still had not looked at the man who lay under the quilt, and he seemed not to want to speak until she did.

After a minute or two, Hennie went to the door and opened it wide. The sickroom was close, but that was not the reason that Hennie fussed with the door. She couldn't find words to say to the man and wanted a reason to delay the moment of facing him. She stared out at the yard, where stinging bits of snow were starting to come down. Smoke scattered as soon as it left the chimneys, and the wind blew an old bushel basket down the street and into a bare aspen tree, where it lodged. Hennie pushed the door almost shut, until only a crack of light showed through the opening. Then she turned and walked purposefully to the bed, standing where the man could see her, and looked into his face, which was worn and wrinkled from too many years of living close to the sun. "Well, I'm here," she said at last, for the man still had not spoken to her. "I brought Mrs. Spindle with me."

The reverend did not turn his head to look at Nit but kept his eyes riveted on Hennie's face. He swallowed twice before he said, "I need to buy a prayer of you, Ila Mae."

Nit started to say something, perhaps to note that the reverend had gotten Hennie mixed up with someone else. And then she stopped, and Hennie wondered if the girl remembered the story Hennie had told her the first time she'd called at the Spindle cabin. She'd explained that her name long ago was not Hennie but Ila Mae.

Hennie herself could barely breathe as her old name hit her. She took a moment to calm herself before she replied, "I don't sell prayers. It's just a sign nailed to the fence. I give them away to those that need them—rightly need them, Abram." Hennie stumbled over the name, for she had never expected to say it to him again, and it left a bitter taste in her mouth.

"I thought a thousand times of stopping by your house and paying you whatever you would take for a prayer, but I didn't, because I knew you wouldn't sell me one."

"She doesn't sell them to anybody," Nit put in. The girl picked up a chair and set it beside the bed for Hennie, then seated herself on the far side of the room. Hennie eased herself onto the chair, her eyes still on the minister's face.

"Since I first saw that sign, I've woken up every morning wishing I could buy your prayers. But I knew nothing I offered would be enough. I believe I'd sell my soul for your forgiveness." He paused, and when Hennie failed to reply, he added, "I've lived my life trying to do good, to make it up to you."

The man's words brought such a hurting to Hennie that she began to shake, and tears fell silently. She felt as if there were a hole in her heart and that the winter wind was blowing through it. The minister did not speak again, waiting for Hennie to reply. "Is that why you came to Middle Swan?" she asked at last, not wiping the tears but letting them streak her face.

"No. There's a story to it, not one as good as the stories they say you tell and maybe not one you care enough to hear, but I'll tell it anyway." The voice was stronger than the man's frail body, and Hennie knew that he had saved his strength in hopes she'd come. She didn't say anything, and the minister continued.

"Many long years I lived a life of dissipation, for I couldn't face what I'd done. I said it was your fault for choosing Billy. And I blamed the men with me that day at your place, because it was in me not to want them to think me soft toward you. I had it in mind to come back to unloose your bonds, and I did, but I was too late. I never intended for your baby to get hurt."

"To die." Hennie squeezed her eyes shut to stop the tears, but they fell anyway.

"Yes, to die." The minister's words were interrupted by a fit of coughing. When he finished with it, he breathed deeply, let the air out of his lungs, and continued, "One morning, I woke up with the stench of drinking and whoring on me, and I believe the Lord took pity on me. He told me He loved even the vilest sinner and that my life would be re-stored to me if I gave myself over to good works. So that day, I forsook my evil ways. I changed my name, for Abram Fletcher was a name of wickedness. I studied on the Bible and became a preacher."

Abram stopped and swallowed down another cough. "I knew you'd gone to Colorado, so I came here, too, although I didn't expect we'd ever meet. I worked with sinners in the gold camps, and finally, I came to Middle Swan, where I stayed."

"And you found me," Hennie said, twisting her hands in her lap. Her quilt square might have calmed them, but this was not a time for stitching.

"Not at first. So many years had passed, and you didn't call yourself Ila Mae anymore. You wouldn't go to church after I arrived, and whenever we passed on the street, you turned away. It was when I heard your voice."

"I knew you the minute I walked into church the first day you preached. Caroline Pinto was playing "God Moves in Mysterious Ways" on the pump organ—I remember that—and then you lifted your head. You were older, and your hair was white, but your face was the same. I couldn't ever forget your face. It was etched with acid in my heart. After that, I couldn't step foot inside the church again. But then, maybe I was expecting you. I always knew we'd meet," Hennie said.

"You gave no sign you'd recognized me, but after a while, I came to think you had."

"Why did you stay?"

The old man thought that over. "To see you every day and be reminded of my sin. It was my purgatory."

And mine, Hennie thought, for the blue devils seemed to visit her the most after she'd seen the minister.

Nit rose from her chair, closed the door, and added a log to the fire, for the shack was old and poorly built, and the cold came in through the cracks in the boards as well as the doorway. Abram looked over at her, and Nit said, "I brought you horseradish for a poultice, but I think you don't need it." Then she added, "I don't pass along other folks' business."

"She knows the story. I told it to her," Hennie said. "But I never told her you were Abram."

"It's not my story to keep," Abram replied.

When the log caught, Nit added another, and the flames in the old stone fireplace leaped up, spreading warmth through the small room. "You want you some water?" Nit asked, and without waiting for the man to answer, she took him a dipperful of water from the bucket on the table. The sick man drank it down, and the girl returned to her chair, her hands between her knees.

The minister was silent for a few minutes, and his eyelids fluttered and closed. The old man's skin was as thin and mottled as old paper. Hennie sat quietly while Abram gathered his strength, and in a moment, he opened his eyes and said quickly, as if he might die before the words were out. "I ask your forgiveness, Ila Mae. My soul won't rest easy without it." He seemed to hold his breath while he waited for Hennie's reply.

The old woman took a long time answering. She looked down at her shaking hands, and with an effort, she stilled them. Then she sighed deeply and said in a trembling voice, for his words had burned her as surely as if they'd been writ with fire, "You have it." And he did, she realized. After all those years, she was able to forgive. At that moment, she felt the tiny wild licorice prickers on her heart crumble and fall away as if the burrs were only feathers.

The minister tried to raise himself up in the bed, but he couldn't. So Hennie leaned over him. "I don't deny I wanted to kill you, would have done it with these hands if I'd had the chance." She lifted her hands and looked at them. "I thought the fires of hell were too good for you. But after a time, I stopped hating you. One day when I was asking the Lord why He'd let Sarah die, the Lord said back to me that I was asking the wrong question. He told me to wonder why Sarah had lived, and I knew it wasn't so that I could carry around enough hate to fill an ore cart. So I let the hate go, but until now, I never forgave, and that hard-heartedness ate away at me all these years, just like an assayer's acid. I saw the good you did, but I still held that long-ago time against you. In all these years, I never knew that forgiveness would heal my soul as well as yours."

Abram started to reply, but Hennie held up her hand. "I should have forgiven you a long time ago, Abram, but I couldn't do it, couldn't bring you that ease. All those times I was praying for everybody else, I ought to have sent up a prayer for you. I believe if I had, it would have eased me." She thought that over and added, "I can't rightly ask the Lord to answer prayers when I have bitterness in my heart."

Abram smiled and held out his hand, and Hennie leaned close, and in a minute, she grasped the hand. "You can call it 'deep enough' knowing I forgive you, Abram."

A look of calm came over the man's face, and he was silent.

Then he remembered something and whispered, "Your ear-bobs. I kept them all this time. They're in the dresser drawer."

Hennie smiled back, and the two old people looked at each other for a long time, no longer talking. There was no reason for further words. They'd said what they had to, and they needed no more spoken between them. In a little while, Nit went to the bucket and filled the dipper, carrying it to the bed, and Abram drank again. The girl stood beside Hennie then, watching as the old man closed his eyes and slept. She moved her chair next to Hennie's, and the two women stayed at the bedside for a long time, not stirring when schoolchildren rushed by, running a stick across the old boards of the cabin. Somewhere, a woman called, "Come and get your dinner or I'll throw it out," and Nit smiled, but Hennie didn't seem to hear. After a time, Bonnie came into the shack, then Carla with the beef tea, and Nit stood up.

"Is he . . . all right?" Carla asked

"He's sleeping," Hennie replied, rising from the chair. "I can't say how he is, but it won't be long. He'll be gone before morning."

"We're planning for the worst. The coffin's made," Bonnie said. She added kindly, "It looks like you've blubbered up, Hennie, but I won't pry into it. Whatever's between you and the reverend isn't my business."

Hennie didn't reply, and in a minute, the two sisters sat down in the chairs beside the bed.

"I'll bring something to line the coffin with. I'll bring it in the morning," Hennie told them. The old woman stared down at the minister for a long time, then put her hand on his forehead. "Tap 'er light, Abram."

As Hennie and Nit started for the door, Bonnie said softly to her sister, "I guess Hennie doesn't know it, but the reverend's given name is Paul, not Abram."

After she and Nit returned home, Hennie removed the second of the burro quilts from the frame in the big room and put it aside. Then she went to her trunk and took out the half-finished Murder quilt, the one Abram had slashed so many years before. It was age-spotted now and one of the corners was mouse-nibbled, but the colors were bright, and for a moment, Hennie remembered that she had dyed the fabric herself; the crimson came from poppy petals, the green from hickory bark, the yellow from black-eyed susans. She mended the slash that Abram had made in the quilt, then put it into the frame, thinking that seventy years before, the quilt had been set in that very same frame, outside, in front of the house Billy had built. Then she began to quilt. If she worked all night, she would finish it by morning.

Hennie quilted for hours, stopping only to nibble at the supper Nit fixed. She continued her stitching after the babies went to sleep and Dick and Nit closed the bedroom door. It was past midnight when Nit crept down the stairs. "I couldn't sleep. I thought you might want other hands. With two of us at the frame, we can finish this quilt afore you can scat a cat. But if you feel the need to quilt it by yourself, I understand," she told the old woman.

Hennie pushed back her chair, rising slowly, for she had sat so long at the frame that her muscles were knotted. She had indeed thought to finish the quilt by herself, but now, she was grateful for the young girl to share the duty. "I'd be obliged. Just you sit," she said, not altogether surprised that Nit was sensible of what Hennie was doing. Sometimes the young girl and the old woman seemed like slices from the same loaf of bread.

"You want tea?"

"Coffee," Hennie said. She stretched to soften the hurting that was in her back. After Nit brought their coffee, her own doctored and Hennie's plain, the two women sat down across the quilt from each other.

Before she threaded her needle, Nit removed two earbobs from her basket and held them out to Hennie. "I took these out of the reverend's drawer for you before Bonnie and Carla came back."

Hennie stared at the earrings, two thin gold hoops, and smiled. "Billy gave them to me for a wedding present. You keep them," she said.

The girl was startled and said they were Hennie's, but the old woman waved her hand. "What will I do with them? I can't wear them now. My ears closed up a long time ago. Besides, all that's gone and past. I'm thinking about tomorrow."

Nit returned the earrings to the basket. She started to thank Hennie but stopped herself and instead, she said, "I've got to be real careful with the stitches, for we're sewing for eternity."

Hennie laughed for the first time since she'd left her house to go to Abram. It was nice, she thought, that quilting with a friend, even in the darkest times, made her feel better.

Nit poured them more coffee, and later, she went to the stove to make a second pot. Hennie paused once to run a hand over the smooth rails of the frame, stopping with her little finger over one of the holes that had been made with a hot poker. Suddenly she said, "I believe I'll leave this frame for you to use. It wouldn't be right, a person walking into this room and not seeing the quilt frame set up." Nit protested, but Hennie, holding her needle, waved her hand. "I'll be too busy to quilt."

Nit swallowed hard, sensible to what the frame had meant to Hennie all those years, and said, "I'll treat it like a precious thing." Then the girl giggled. "Are you leaving the PRAYERS FOR SALE sign, too?"

Hennie thought about that and nodded. "I expect your prayers are as good as mine. We both of us are blessed enough to have prayers left over."

They took the Murder quilt from the frame as the dark was leaving the sky, and tacked the binding in place. Nit took her final stitch, then returned the needle and thimble to her sewing basket.

Hennie, too, was done with her sewing. She ran her hand over the quilt and decided that only the sharpest eye would see that it had ever been slashed. She and the girl folded the quilt, and Nit set it on a chair by the window. Then she turned to Hennie, pondering something. "The time when I first came to Middle Swan, after you told me that story about Abram Fletcher, you said it didn't have an ending. Now it does."

Hennie fixed her needle to a bit of flannel that was tied to the frame before she nodded at Nit. "It does," she repeated, "and I believe it's a good one."

"And now, you've started on another story."

Hennie looked past Nit to the sky, where the gray of dawn was giving way to red streaks that were rounded like the ridges on a washboard. A storm that was brewing over the Tenmile made her twitchy. She hoped it wouldn't be a heavy snow that delayed her departure from Middle Swan. "Yes, I have." The old woman smiled and cocked her head. "I'm hopefuller than can be that it'll be a while yet before I know how that story comes out."

PRAYERS FOR SALE

by Sandra Dallas

About the Author

- Biography
- A Conversation with Sandra Dallas

Behind the Novel

- Quilting and the Women of *Prayers for Sale*

Keep on Reading

- Reading Group Questions

For more reading group suggestions,
visit www.readinggroupgold.com.

 ST. MARTIN'S GRIFFIN

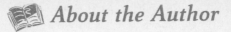# About the Author

Award-winning author Sandra Dallas was dubbed "a quintessential American voice" by Jane Smiley in *Vogue* magazine. Her novels, with their themes of loyalty, friendship, and human dignity, have been translated into nearly a dozen foreign languages and optioned for films.

A journalism graduate from the University of Denver, Sandra began her writing career as a reporter with *Business Week*. A staff member for twenty-five years (and the magazine's first female bureau chief), she covered the Rocky Mountain region, writing about everything from penny stock scandals to hard-rock mining to contemporary polygamy. Many of her experiences have been incorporated into her novels. At the same time, she wrote nine nonfiction books, including *Sacred Paint*, which won the National Cowboy Hall of Fame Western Heritage Wrangler Award.

"I wanted to write a novel ... combining the brutality of gold dredging with the comfort of quilting."

Turning to fiction in 1990, Sandra has since published eight novels including *Prayers for Sale*. She received the Western Writers of America Spur Award for *The Chili Queen* and *Tallgrass*, and the Women Writing the West Willa Award for *New Mercies*. She was also a finalist for the Colorado Book Award, the Mountain and Plains Booksellers Association Award, and a four-time finalist for the Women Writing the West Willa Award.

The mother of two daughters—Dana is an attorney in New Orleans, and Povy is a photographer in Golden, Colorado—Sandra lives in Denver with her husband, Bob. Visit her on the Web at www.sandradallas.com.

A Conversation with Sandra Dallas

What sparked the idea for *Prayers for Sale*?

I'd been intrigued with gold dredging since I lived in Breckenridge, Colorado, in the early 1960s. (Middle Swan, the book's setting, is based on Breckenridge, which was a gold mining town long before it became a ski area.) Since then I'd toyed with the idea of writing about those treacherous gold boats on the streams near Breckenridge and the people who had a love-hate relationship with them. I'd also wanted to write a collection of stories about Colorado, told by a quilter, similar to the classic *Aunt Jane of Kentucky*, written by Eliza Calvert Hall a hundred years ago. But I'd never considered combining the two ideas until I read a Civil War story about a baby who died while his mother was detained by soldiers. I was so moved by the story that I began thinking about how I could incorporate it into a novel. That was when I realized I could make it the departure point of a novel combining the brutality of gold dredging with the comfort of quilting.

When you write a novel, do you begin with the plot or the characters? Or the setting?

I almost always start with the setting. The characters come next. Then the characters and I go looking for a plot.

What sort of research did you do for *Prayers for Sale*?

I'd already done some of the research when I wrote my ten nonfiction books, most of them on Colorado history. When I lived in Breckenridge, I talked to the old men who had worked on the dredges and heard their stories. But *Prayers for Sale* took additional research, of course. I researched gold dredging and read 1930s accounts of life in the mountains. And I studied the books and notes of two old women, novelist Helen Rich and poet Belle Turnbull, who had taken me under their wing when I lived in the mountains. In fact, in my Breckenridge file, I have a letter from Helen in which she told me she was glad I was going to write about Breckenridge. She wrote, "You've really got the bug about doing Breckenridge. I feel quite sure about you and you have the grace to grow. . . . As you have found out the stuff out of which such books are made has to steep into a person." She wrote the letter in 1967.

"For women in isolated areas, forming a quilting bee . . . was a joyous social occasion."

Quilting plays an important role in many of your novels, including this one. Why?

Quilting defines a woman—the type of stitches she makes, the colors she picks for her quilt tops, the pattern she chooses. And quilting, especially in an isolated town such as Middle Swan, brings women together. Sharing their secrets, they bond over the quilt frame.

Why did you choose to have such an age difference between the two heroines in this novel, Hennie and Nit?

Hennie had to be a Civil War survivor for her story to work. I wanted to incorporate characters from my other books into the story—Zepha Massie from *The Persian Pickle Club*, Tom Earley from *The Diary of Mattie Spenser*, Ned and Emma from *The Chili Queen*. The only way this worked was to set the story in 1936 when Hennie was a very old woman. Because she was so vulnerable, Nit had to be young, barely more than a girl.

What do you feel are some of the most important themes in this novel?

Friendship, human dignity, survival, forgiveness, redemption.

Would you name some other books you've enjoyed recently?

I'd like to say I've just curled up with *War and Peace*, but in fact the books I've read recently include: *Going Together* by Arnold Grossman, *This Republic of Suffering* by Drew Gilpin Faust, *Traveling Mercies* by Anne Lamott, *The March* by E. L. Doctorow, *Spoon* by Robert Greer, and various short stories by Truman Capote.

About the Author

Behind the Novel

Quilting and the Women of *Prayers for Sale*

Sandra Dallas was on the Rocky Mountain Quilt
Museum's board of directors when she wrote *The Quilt
That Walked to Golden* (Breckling Press), a history of
women and quilts in the Mountain West. The book
became a major quilt publication, winning the Benjamin
Franklin Award and underscoring the importance of a
western quilt museum. To learn more about the author's
passion for quilting—and to subscribe to her *Piecework*
newsletter—please visit www.sandradallas.com.

•

*A woman who takes small, even stitches is different from
one whose stitches are big and sloppy, just as a quilter who
uses primary colors differs from one who chooses black and
white. Patterns define a woman, too. Hennie, who is eighty-
six, likes the traditional old patterns—Lone Star or Bear
Claw, for instance, patterns that date back to her girlhood.
But Nit, seventeen, is more modern and picks popular
1930s patterns such as Dutch Tulips and Coffee Cup.
She even considers making up her own design using aspen
leaves. Both are frugal women, however, and they make
string quilts, which are tiny strips of leftover fabric put
together in a hit-or-miss pattern.*

—Sandra Dallas

Quilting Bees

Historically, women were not encouraged to pursue art seri-
ously. So they incorporated their artistry in everyday works,

A quilting party.

such as quilting. For women in isolated areas, forming a quilting bee—in which a group of women stitched the quilt in sections—was a joyous social occasion, a time to catch up on news and gossip, and to share joys and sorrows.

Twinkling Stars

Stars are probably the most beloved of all quilt designs. Hennie would have likely made an old-fashioned Lone Star whereas Nit might have preferred the more modern Twinkling Stars pattern.

Courtesy of the Rocky Mountain Quilt Museum. Photo by Povy Kendal Atchison.

Dutch Tulips

In the 1930s, women appliquéd their quilts using patterns printed in newspapers and womens' magazines, or on wrappers of store-bought cotton batting. Tulips and roses, cut from pastel fabrics, were popular and would have appealed to Nit, who liked realistic designs.

Courtesy of the Rocky Mountain Quilt Museum. Photo by Povy Kendal Atchison.

Behind the Novel

Reading Group Questions

1. Hennie Comfort's sign outside her house says PRAYERS FOR SALE and yet she doesn't sell prayers. Why does Hennie keep the sign?

2. As Hennie begins her story for Nit, she says, "Back then, I wasn't Hennie Comfort. In those days, I was called by the name of Ila Mae Stubbs." What else has changed about Hennie from her teenaged self to her eighty-six-year-old self? More importantly, what has stayed the same?

3. One of the themes of this book is surviving the "unsurvivable." What would you consider "unsurvivable?"

4. Another theme is forgiveness. Is there ever a time when forgiveness isn't possible? Can you relate to the way Hennie forgives at the end of the book— and whom she forgives? In Hennie's shoes, would you have forgiven? Would Hennie's life have been different if she had forgiven earlier?

5. What are some of the qualities you see in the women of Middle Swan that help them survive life there? What is the most important quality?

6. Maudie Sarsfield says, "Quilting keeps me from going queer," meaning "insane." Why would this be so? What is the significance of Maudie adding her initials to her quilts? And what role do quilts and quilting play in the lives of the characters?

7. What is the most tragic aspect of Maudie's life?

8. What is the most important lesson Hennie teaches Nit?

9. Is it ever too late to find true love? How do you define true love?

10. Discuss the phrase "deep enough." What does it mean in the story? What would it mean to you in your own life?

11. Middle Swan is a cold, harsh town. What makes Hennie love it, and why has she stayed all these years? What draws people together in such an environment?

Turn the page for a sneak peek at
Sandra Dallas's new novel

Whiter Than Snow

Available March 2010

CHAPTER ONE

No one knew what triggered the Swandyke avalanche that began at exactly 4:10 p.m. on April 20, 1920. It might have been the dynamite charge that was set off at the end of shift on the upper level of the Fourth of July Mine. The miners claimed the blast was too far inside the mountain to be felt on the surface, and besides, they had set off dynamite hundreds, maybe thousands, of times before, and nothing bad had happened. Except for that one time when a charge failed to go off and Howard Dolan hit it with his pick when he was mucking out the stope and blew himself and his partner to kingdom come.

Still, who knew how the old mountain took retribution for having its insides clawed out.

Certainly there was nothing to suggest that the day was

different from any other. It started chill and clear. The men, their coat collars turned up against the dawn cold, left for their shifts at the Fourth of July or on the dredge up the Swan River, dinner pails clutched in their mittened hands. A little later, the children went off to school, the older brothers and sisters pulling little ones on sleds. Groups of boys threw snowballs at one another. One grabbed onto the back of a wagon and slid along over the icy road behind it. The Connor girl slipped on the ice and fell over a stone embankment, hitting her head. It hurt so much that she turned around and went home crying. The others called her a crybaby, but after what happened later that day, her parents said the blessed God had taken her hand.

After the children were gone, the women washed the breakfast dishes and started the beans for dinner. Then because the sun came out bright enough to burn your skin in the thin air, came out after one of the worst blizzards they had ever encountered, they got out the washtubs and scrubbed the overalls and shirts, the boys' knickers and the girls' dresses. When the wash was rinsed and wrung, they climbed onto the platforms that held the clotheslines far above the snow and hung up the clothes, where they would dry stiff as boards in the wind. Then because it was such a fine day, as fine a day as ever was, they called to one another to come and visit. There was a bit of coffee to reheat, and won't you have a cup? Cookies, left over from the lunch pails, were set on plates on the oilcloth of the kitchen tables, and the women sat, feeling lazy and gossipy.

"You know, the Richards girl had her baby last week," announced a woman in one of the kitchens, taking down the good china cups for coffee.

"Was her husband the father?" asked her neighbor.

"I didn't have the nerve to ask."

In another house, a woman confided, "The doctor says Albert has the cancer, but he won't have his lungs cut on."

"Then he'll die," her friend replied, muttering to herself, "at last."

It was that kind of a day, one for confidences or lazy talk. The women blessed the bright sun after so many winter days of gloom. Nobody thought about an avalanche. What could cause trouble on a day the Lord had given them?

Maybe the cause was an animal—a deer or an elk or even a mountain sheep—making its way along the ridge of Jubilee Mountain. The weight of the beast would have been enough to loosen the snow. That happened often enough. Nobody saw an animal, but then, who was looking?

Or worthless Dave Buck might have set off the avalanche. He'd put on snowshoes and taken his gun and gone high up to hunt for a deer—a fawn, really, for Dave was too lazy to cut up the bigger carcass and haul it home. The company forbade hunting around the mine, but Dave didn't care. He snowshoed up near timberline, where he'd seen the footprints of deer. He didn't find any, and he stopped to drink from a pint he'd put into his pocket. One drink, and another, and he sat down beside a stunted pine and picked off the cones and slid them down the white slope. Then he tossed the bottle into that cornice of snow that dipped out over a ridge.

But perhaps it was nothing more than the spring melt. That storm a few days before had dumped five feet of snowfall on top of a dry, heavy base of winter-worn snow. The wind had driven the snow off ridges, leaving them barren, and piled it into large cornices high up. But now the day was cloudless, the sun shining down as harsh as if it had been midsummer. It was so bright that it hurt your eyes to see the glare on the white, and some of the miners rubbed charcoal under their eyes to cut the sharpness.

But who cared what the cause was? *Something* started the slide that roared down Jubilee Mountain in Swandyke, Colorado, and that was all that mattered.

There was a sharp crack like the sound of distant thunder, and then the cornice of snow where Dave Buck had thrown his bottle, a crusted strip two hundred feet long that flared out over the mountain ridge, fractured and fell. It landed on layers of snow that covered the mountain slope to a depth of more than six feet—a heavy, wet, melting mass of new snow on top, falling on frozen layers of snowpack that lay on a bed of crumbled ice. That bottommost layer, a mass of loose ice crystals formed by freezing and thawing, lubricated the acres of snow lying on top of it just as much as if the bed had been made of marbles, and sent the snow careening down the mountain.

The miners called such a phenomenon a "slab avalanche" because a curtain of snow slid down the slope, picking up speed at a terrible rate, until it reached one hundred miles an hour. Nothing stood in the way of the terrifying slide, because the mountainside was bare of trees. They had been torn out forty years earlier in the second wave of mining that came after the prospectors abandoned gold pans and sluice boxes. Men had trained giant hoses on the mountain, washing dirt down the slope to be processed for precious minerals. Hydraulic mining, as it was called, also rid the mountainside of rocks and trees and underbrush that would have interfered with an avalanche—not that anything could have held back the tons of white that slid down Jubilee Mountain that afternoon. The slide would have taken anything in its path.

This was not the first slide on Jubilee Mountain. The hillside, in fact, was known for avalanches. But it was the worst, and it spilled over into the forest at the edge of the open slope, tearing out small trees by their roots and hurling them into the rushing snow, which turned them into battering rams. A cabin that perched under the pines was wrenched from its foundation, its log walls torn asunder and broken into jackstraws.

The slide rushed onward, churning up chunks of ice the

size of boxcars, gathering up abandoned hoses and machinery and the other detritus of mining that lay in its path. It hurtled on, thrashing its deadly cargo about, not slowing when it reached the bottom of the mountain, but instead rushing across the road, filling the gully with snow as heavy as wet cement and flattening the willows. The avalanche hurtled on until it started up Turnbull Mountain. Then, at last, its momentum came to an end and the slide was exhausted, the front stopping first, the back end slipping down the mountain and filling the gulch with snow higher than a two-story house.

Snow hovered in the air like a deadly mist. The debris caught up in the avalanche rolled a little and was still. A jack pine, graceful as a sled, glided to a stop in the snow covering the road. Clumps of snow fell from the trees still standing at the edge of the deadly white mass, making plopping sounds as they landed. Snowballs broke loose and rolled down the hill, leaving little trails in their wake.

For an instant, all was quiet, as silent as if the slide had occurred in a primeval forest. Then a high-pitched scream came from somewhere in the mass of snow, a child's scream. The slide thundered down Jubilee Mountain just after the grade school let out, and it grabbed up nine of thirty-two schoolchildren in its icy grip. Five of the victims were related, the children of the Patch sisters—Dolly's three, who were Jack, Carrie, and Lucia, along with Lucy's two, Rosemary and Charlie. The slide was no respecter of class, because it took Schuyler Foote, son of the manager of the Fourth of July Mine, and little Jane Cobb, the Negro girl, whose father labored in the mill, and Sophie Schnable, the daughter of a prostitute. And then there was Emmett Carter, that near-orphan boy who lived with his grandfather. All of them were swept up and carried along in that immense swirl of white.

Four of the children survived.

CHAPTER TWO

Lucy Patch was the smart one. People had always said that about her, ever since she was a toddling child. They still did on occasion, although she was a grown woman now, grown and married, with two children of her own. "Lucy's the smart one," they'd remark when Lucy was coming up. It really was not meant as a compliment, because that was only the half of what they told. "Dolly Patch is the pretty one," they'd say at the beginning, and then add, "Lucy's the smart one," as if being smart was honorable mention.

Dolly, whose real name was Helen, wore her hair in yellow-white curls as long as the spiral of a drill and kept her skin as white as quartz. She was plump, with a happy disposition, and her eyes were still the bright blue of a china doll's, just as when she was a baby and her father had called her "Doll Baby," and, when she was older, "Dolly." The name had stuck, even after a packet of doll-size Patch children came along following Dolly. Everyone had called her by those names, even Lucy, who thought they were perfectly dreadful. People still did even now when Dolly was thirty-two, because she was still sunny as a summer's day and lively in step, although she was portly in build. She still wore her hair in corkscrews, the color coming from a bottle, because with her pregnancies, her hair had darkened to the color of a mountain stream during spring runoff.

Only a year younger than Dolly, Lucy had been pretty in her way, if you were partial to dark hair and skin and girls who were too tall and angular, which most folks weren't. Nobody remarked then or now on Lucy's looks, although they were generous in their praise of her intelligence. She believed it herself and had always been a bit of a show-off about it. Whatever she did in school could not be done better. Lucy couldn't help herself. If being smart was her only attribute, why pretend to be stupid? There was this thing about Lucy: She'd been told so often that she was intelligent, she thought she was smarter than anybody else. It got a little tiresome.

And incidentally, Lucy did not care for her own name, either. She wished she had been named Lucia, after the saint the Swedes in Swandyke honored with a parade each Christmas, although the Patch family was not Swedish. Lucia was romantic and exotic, and it would have been silly on someone as plain and straightforward as Lucy. Only Dolly knew Lucy preferred that name, and Dolly sometimes called her sister Lucia when the two were alone.

Although the distinctions might have pitted the girls against each other, the fact was that during their coming-up time, the two were inseparable, as close as any two sisters could be. Lucy helped Dolly with her schoolwork, because Dolly was not much taken with learning. And Dolly, who collected beaux the way an old woman collects blue columbine on a June day, was sensitive when it came to Lucy's feelings. She told a boy on a hayride once that he ought to sit next to Lucy. "At conversation, she beats it all hollow," Dolly said.

"Lucy's okay if you want to hear the Gettysburg Address. Come to think of it, she *is* the spit of Abraham Lincoln," he replied.

"And you're the spit of Theodore Roosevelt," Dolly replied, pushing him off the wagon.

Dolly was smart enough to know that her looks would fade in time—in the bright, harsh mountain sun that turned a woman's skin into a wrinkled brown paper bag, there wasn't a woman over thirty-five who didn't look as if she'd worn out four or five bodies with the same face—but Lucy would always be smart.

By the time she was fifteen, Lucy had skipped two grades

and was in her last year of high school, something for which she was sorry after she realized she would be just sixteen when she graduated. Life didn't hold much for her after that. She would get a job in the office at the Fourth of July Mine—her father had already discussed it with the mine manager—and that would mean long hours performing boring tasks. Her only option was to marry, and she shuddered at the idea of being the wife of somebody who mucked out a mine.

"I wish I could go to college," Lucy confided to Dolly that spring, only a month before graduation.

"What in the world for?" her sister asked. For Dolly, who was made after the timid kind and never contemplated a life that went beyond marrying and raising three or four dandy-looking boys and girls, the idea was shocking. She'd never known of a Swandyke girl who had gone to college, although a few boys had done so. They'd never come back.

"There's got to be something more than working at the mine office."

"It'll only be till you're married."

"But I don't want to be married. I want to go to college, someplace that's green, where I don't have to see a brown mine tipple or a yellow mine dump every time I look up."

"You'll be terrible lonesome away from Swandyke," Dolly said, then frowned. "You'd come back, wouldn't you? I couldn't bear it if you didn't. You wouldn't leave forever, would you?"

"It doesn't matter, because I'm not going anywhere."

"Why not, if that's what you want? We both want something better, and we have to get it the best way we can."

"Unless I can order a college diploma from the Sears, Roebuck catalog, there's no way I'll ever have one. We haven't got a dime for school, what with all the little kids Mama and Papa have to take care of."

"You must ask Papa to send you," said Dolly, who had not the slightest idea what a college education cost.

Lucy scoffed. "How would he do that? He's no good with money. Papa's already spent his wages from now to Christmas. Mama would like for me to go. She told me so, but she won't stand up to Papa."

"No, he wouldn't allow that," Dolly agreed.

"Besides, Papa expects me to go to work to help him carry the family."

While their father, Gus Patch, worked suitable, he made little, and his wages slipped through his fingers. He was a sucker for a hard-luck story, and many a time, he was skinned out of his pay envelope. So the family lived from hand to mouth, and in the few days before payday, there wasn't much to put into all those mouths. In the past year, they had heard their father say often enough to this or that debtor, "When my girl Lucy goes to work at the mine office, I'll pay that bill right off."

The afternoon of their discussion, the sisters were sitting on a rock in the willows that filled the gully at the bottom of Jubilee Mountain. Lucy leaned back so that she could look up the mountainside, up past the barren slope that had been washed clean of rocks and topsoil by hydraulic mining, to the Fourth of July Mine. That was where their father was employed. "I told Papa I wouldn't work there until I finished high school. Graduation's on a Friday night. So he's fixed it up that I start on Saturday morning."

"You must talk to Papa anyway," Dolly insisted. "If you explain it to him, he's sure to go along with you. That's what I've found."

Lucy didn't reply that as the favorite daughter, Dolly usually got her way with their father. "I did talk to him, Dolly. He said I have a responsibility to him. His exact words were, 'I don't care for nothing about college. I got no more use for it than one of those airplanes.' He told me while I was in high school that he'd let me do as I pleased, but now that I'm done with it, I'll have to do as I can."

Dolly flung back her yellow curls and stood up. "I'll talk to him."

Not more than a week later, Gus Patch announced at the supper table that if Lucy could get a job in Denver to pay her way through college and would live with her aunt Alice, a sour old woman whom no one in the family cared for much, he thought he could spare her for a few years. "I expect with a college degree, you could make two or three times what you'd get typewriting letters in the mine office," he said, stirring his potatoes and green beans together, then leaning over his plate and using a spoon to shovel the mess into his mouth.

Later, when the girls were alone, Lucy asked, "It was you who gave him the idea I could be a bookkeeper, wasn't it, Dolly? What did it cost you?"

"I don't know what you mean." Dolly looked down at a ribbon she was ironing between her fingers. "Besides, it was Mama's idea."

"I know Papa as well as you do. It was you, not Mama, who had to promise him something. He's not for giving away a thing for nothing." Lucy grabbed Dolly's hand so hard that her sister dropped the ribbon. "You're not quitting high school, are you?"

"It cost less than it was worth. Besides, I don't care so much for school."

"I won't let you quit."

"Well, there's nothing you can do about it. They keep asking me at the Prospector if I won't come and be a waitress. I've made up my mind."

"So have I, and I won't go to college if you quit school."

The next morning, Lucy picked up Gus's lunch bucket and told him she would walk him to the mine. That was what the children did when they wanted to talk to their father or ask for a favor, since the old man was usually hungover in the early mornings, and his mind was a clutter. "Dolly's not quitting high school," Lucy said.

"Oh, she don't mind."

"Well, I do, and I say she's not."

"I guess when you're head of this family, you'll have a say."

"Papa, I won't go to college if she has to wait tables at the Prospector."

"Suit yourself."

The two walked along in silence until Gus said, "Doll thinks you might not come back if you go below to school."

Lucy didn't reply.

"I don't reckon we could let you do that."

"I don't reckon you could stop me."

"Oh, I guess I could."

Lucy slowed down a little as she mulled over her father's words. She knew then what he was after.

"Wages aren't going up at the mine. I need you to help carry us in these scarce times."

"I could send you money. I'd do it every month."

Gus stopped and put his foot up on a rock to tie his shoe. The leather was scuffed and worn, the toe capped with metal. Lucy stared down at the top of his head, where the hair was thin and the scalp scaly from the mountain dryness. He was asking her to help support the family, maybe carry it all herself if he lost his job. He'd barter that for college. She thought it over before she replied. If she didn't go to college, she'd work at the mine and hand over her paycheck to her father. If she got an education, she'd do the same thing, but at least she'd have been away for four years,

WHITER THAN SNOW

and she would be getting a better job. "What if I promise to
come back? Will you let Doll finish high school?"

Her father pretended to think it over, but his head hurt
too much for him to put much effort into it. "Well, I expect
so. If you'll promise, promise no matter what, you'll come
back."

"Oh, I will," Lucy said.

Gus sighed. "Then I reckon I could spare you."

It was only later that Lucy thought she had been bought
too cheaply. Both Gus and Dolly had gotten what they
wanted. Lucy would be bonded to Swandyke, where she'd
supplement her father's salary and be a companion to Dolly
for the rest of her life. Still, she told herself, she'd have those
four years.

"A quintessential American voice."

—Jane Smiley, author of *Ten Days in the Hills*

SANDRA DALLAS

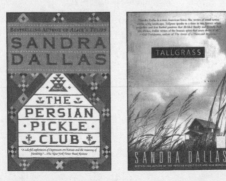

 St. Martin's Griffin

www.sandradallas.com   www.stmartins.com